Praise for Elizabeth Gill

'Elizabeth Gill writes with a masterful grasp of
conflicts and passions hidden among men and
women of the wild North Country'
Leah Fleming

'Original and evocative – a born storyteller'
Trisha Ashley

'Wonderful . . . full of passion, pain, sweetness, twists and turns'
Sheila Newberry

'Enthralling and satisfying'
Catherine King

'An enchanting read for all true romantics'
Lancashire Evening Post

'Drama and intrigue worthy of *Call the Midwife*'
Big Issue

Also by Elizabeth Gill

Available in paperback and ebook

Miss Appleby's Academy
The Fall and Rise of Lucy Charlton
Far From My Father's House
Doctor of the High Fells
Nobody's Child
Snow Angels
The Guardian Angel

Available in ebook only

Shelter from the Storm
The Pit Girl
Under a Cloud-Soft Sky
Paradise Lane
The Foxglove Tree
The Hat Shop Girl
The Landlord's Daughter

. . . and many more!

Orphan Boy

Elizabeth Gill

Quercus

First published as *The Homecoming* in Great Britain in 2003
by Severn House Publishers Ltd.
This edition published in 2019 by

Quercus Editions Ltd
Carmelite House
50 Victoria Embankment
London EC4Y 0DZ

An Hachette UK company

A CIP catalogue record for this book is available
from the British Library

PB ISBN 978-1-78747-464-2
EB ISBN 978-1-78429-246-1

10 9 8 7 6 5 4 3 2 1

Typeset by CC Book Production

Printed and bound in Great Britain by Clays Ltd, Elcograf S.p.A.

For Marjorie
Thank you for looking after me

Prologue

County Durham, 1897

Luisa McAndrew stared up into the shadows of her bedroom. It was the room she had been born in. When she was a little girl she lay and listened to the River Wear, which flowed beyond her window, across the path and through the field at the bottom of the dale. She had loved it here then. The sound of the river and the secure feeling that was home lulled her to sleep each night.

She was afraid to sleep now. She thought that if she closed her eyes she would never wake up again and she was afraid of the darkness too. She did not want to die and she had the feeling that night took you off like an ebbing tide. You went out never to come back in and the day would break without you. She could not bear that the day should break and find her gone forever.

The doctor and the nurse fussed and the child which they had taken from her cried. The pain was over. They moved around the room and she could see her husband, George, holding the baby. She felt the hatred of him running through her weakness. She wished she was strong enough to protest. She wished she could leap out of bed and grab the child from him. It was not his and he knew it so why did he look down and smile on the baby like that?

George was incapable of loving a woman in any respect. He had married her because she was beautiful and twenty years younger than him. He liked to look at her naked, he liked to dress her up and parade her before other men's envious eyes but it had taken a boy of twenty with nothing to recommend him but the world's most honest green eyes to make her understand love.

She had wanted to leave here. How stupid it seemed, how naïve she had been. She had thought the Durham moors boring and the people parochial. It had seemed to her that they led small lives. She had wanted a grand house, an influential, prosperous husband, rich and clever friends, diamonds, furs, travel. She had had all those and would have given them away to spend a single week with the man she loved and the child she had borne, in his shabby old house upon the fell where the wind was bitter in early spring, the snow lay deep in February and the heather laid its purple cloak all around in August. Joe's house, the home she had never had, though in some ways now it would always be hers, albeit she had visited fewer times than she had fingers on one hand. She had not liked it. Now she would have gone if she could have crawled there. She was not going to be crawling anywhere. Indeed, she could hardly see the room.

She thought of all the hotel rooms where Joe had made love to her. There was one in Berwick which looked out over the sea and one in Alnwick on the main street so that you could hear the people talking down below outside and best of all the one in Newcastle where they were almost certain to be discovered and yet had not been.

Joe wasn't like somebody twenty, he had always seemed to her much older than she was but his body was twenty and that was very nice. It made her smile, thinking about it, how kind he was, how caring, how careful, how sweet and smooth and unused. She had felt very used by the time she reached Joe. He had not been her first lover but he had been her last and the best in every way. She just wished that she didn't regret having cared for things which didn't matter. It was too late. She could feel the energy leaving her and with it the will. She knew that he was somewhere close. Earlier that day he had kissed her all over her face and told her that he loved her. Where was he?

She could no longer say the words. She could see George at the side of the bed with the baby in his arms. She wanted to say to him that the child belonged to Joe now. Her husband was looking down at her and Luisa thought suddenly that she should tell him if he did not give the boy to Joe then no good would come of it. If he could not be honest he would not prosper though she knew that was not the way of the world. Evil men always prospered. Good, honest men like Joe had to fight for everything. Was it a battle worth taking on, she wondered? Did it matter in the hereafter? She had a terrible feeling that it didn't.

What if Joe was not aware that he had a son? Would he find out? Would he care? She had betrayed him in so many ways, had told him that she didn't want him when they could have been married, had seduced him out of idleness and boredom, destroyed his peace of mind, inflicted all the hurts of love upon him. She smiled to herself. It was a lot to do to a man. And he had loved her. She thought it was the only pure love of her life. You needed just one to make everything worthwhile and there was a child from it. It was as much as a woman could ask, she thought.

She wished that George would not hold the child, she did not trust him even though the nurse hovered behind him and he looked gleeful. She didn't like it when he looked like that, it spelled triumph, unholy joy. He thought that he had won. He had wanted a son. Strange how badly he had wanted that when Joe had never discussed children with her, was too young to care for such things.

Her mother, Alice Morgan, came to the bed and Luisa did not mistake the look in her eyes. It was grief. Her mother had always told her that she must marry well, that she should have nothing to do with the pit owner's son because they were nobody. If she married George McAndrew she could have everything that her mother had not had. Her mother had been right, she had had everything and had lost the house upon the fell and the boy who loved her. She could have made so much of it, been happy, and yet . . . it was her own fault she had not had such things. Perhaps she would have always been restless and wanted things which Joe could not have given her and she would have spoiled their love and he would have despised her. Perhaps it was better this way with the bloom of illusion still upon it, stolen, illicit, every delicious moment in Joe's arms, aware that he was not her husband. Husbands and lovers could never be the same thing. How many women had made that mistake and regretted it?

She would have hated being poor, the lack of society, dowdy dresses and dull dinners. She was too beautiful to be hidden in such a backwater with nobody to admire her but him. He had no friends, no education, no ambition. He had never been anywhere or done anything and yet the times when she had gone to him there she had somehow been able to see the sense of it all, with the darkness falling upon the fell top, the sky coming down to kiss the heather, the wind in a never-ending sweep across the grey stone walls and the road which beckoned to all those stupid people who thought there was more to be gained elsewhere. She had not known it then but that was the road home, it was the way back to Joe and even she had found it in the end. It was not quite too late then, it was not quite over. She had put herself into his arms in the shadows of his shabby house and, outside, the wind had chased the rain all the way across the fell to throw itself at the windows and whip round and round. Joe's house was a testament to the way that men lived here. They endured the hardest life of all. He wouldn't leave. He wouldn't leave his pit and the people and the two days a year when the sun might almost shine. She liked that idea. It was nearly true. People joked and said there had been snow here in July. She believed that. They were proud of it, called city people soft, lived up there under an endless sky, broke their backs and their wills in the search for coal. That was what she had loved most about him, that he wouldn't give in. He wouldn't be bettered nor turned from his task. She loved his stubborn endurance. She would always love it.

Where was he? Why didn't he come to her? She could hear her mother's voice in the distance, tried to say his name so that they would understand she had to see him. She couldn't manage it and it didn't seem to matter somehow. The room was growing dim but it was not a room she cared for, it was Joe's house that she wanted with its champagne air and rain-soaked garden. They would be there together, Joe and herself and the baby.

Daylight came. George held the screaming child in his arms. Babies were horrible little things. They did not look as if they would grow into people. It had a gurned-up face, red and wrinkly, and a shock of dark hair. Where was that from? Luisa and her bloody lover were both fair. Perhaps it was his child after all. He laughed. The last time he had bedded Luisa had been a long time ago and he could not stop, did not want to stop remembering it. She had turned her face from him in disgust. He had never forgiven her for it. She had married a rich clever middle-aged man and given her affections to some lad off a hill top. She had wanted everything. The trouble was that because she was so disgusted he found that he could not make love to her though he wanted to. She had gone to other men. He knew all about them. He knew that she was a slut. All women were sluts but there was some satisfaction in watching the progress of her affair with that boy. Joe Forster would never amount to anything. His father had been a wastrel and he could barely keep the pit going. He had nothing that would have brought a woman to him except that he was young and handsome. Well, if that was to be the way of it, George decided, then it was. He had known for a very long time that he could not give a woman a child, if so Glasgow would have been filled with his bastards by now because in his young day he had had a different woman every day and none of them would ever have dared look at him the way that Luisa had.

He had plans. He would sell the shipyards and everything that he owned in Glasgow and move permanently to his house in Edinburgh and bring up the child as a gentleman. Joe Forster had no rights to this boy and George would have his revenge on both of them by taking the baby away.

He could hear Joe Forster. He had been trying to get into the house all night and now it was almost day. George didn't intend to stay here any longer. Luisa was dead. Her parents could bury her here, there was nothing for him to stay for. He had ordered the carriage. He wrapped the child carefully and without a backward glance he walked out of the room.

One

Edinburgh, 1904

There was a very big table in the blue and crimson dining room. His father would stand Niall on a chair at the end so that he could see the laughing faces, the men sitting on both sides. The table would be covered with discarded food and the white table-cloth was dark where wine had spilled and there was the smell of food growing cold and cigar smoke. Their voices were very loud and their laughter made your ears hurt. They wore black suits and white shirts and threw questions down the table which he was supposed to answer and never could. Sometimes they gave him wine. He didn't like the taste of it, he didn't like the noise and wanted to get down and run outside into the wide grey Edinburgh streets and squares where he was not allowed to go alone. He loved his home, the house near Charlotte Square, just off Princes Street, the garden in the middle of the square, with the iron railings all round and the houses where people were always busily coming in and out, the castle all big and dark and mighty on the hill, the gardens below, the rain and the wind and the bleak summers and every stone that made up his home town, the firth and the fishing boats and the hills, the places where he played and the grass and the first spring flowers, the coffee shops and tea rooms where Jean took him and Princes Street where the ladies shopped and he was always bought a new toy and toffees. Jenner's at Christmas all glitter, and spring with daffodils, and winter afternoons covered in snow; horses and carriages and tramway cars, markets and trains and shops and offices, and the Mile stretching from Holyrood to the castle.

Sometimes women in pretty dresses came to the house and there was music and dancing and they sat him on their laps and kissed him and told him how handsome he was, that he looked just like his mother. They wore sparkling jewellery and had painted faces and their eyes were bold. He would much rather stay upstairs with Nanny and Jean. He felt safe there. Jean would read to him when he was in bed or Nanny and he would sit over the nursery fire and eat cake. Jean and Nanny were both from Fife and his father said of them that they were staunch Presbyterians, whatever that was.

The parties at the house became more frequent and he thought as he peered through the banisters, picking out his father's short round figure with the bald head, that he was very often dancing with the same lady. She was small, dark and pretty. She came to the house at other times, though not to the nursery, and once when she arrived in the early evening he was ushered from the room. It angered Niall that he was so unimportant, that he was not wanted, that once Alison was there his father ceased to notice him. Alison noticed him but he thought that she did not like him. If she had done, she would have looked at him, talked to him, allowed him to stay in the room for a little longer.

Niall had no friends, his father did not seem to want him to mix with other children. The servants were kind. He particularly liked Mrs McLaughlan, the cook, and spent many hours in the kitchen, sitting at the table or by the fire, eating biscuits and watching as she and the maids prepared the dinner. Sometimes Niall watched the rest of the square from his window. Other children played games and in the early evenings when Jean had read him his story and left him he would hear their shouting and laughter as the summer evening shadows lengthened on the walls.

When he was small he and his father and Jean and Nanny would go to St Andrews for holidays and he remembered with great joy the long beaches, the ruin of the cathedral, the sea, the links, the men playing golf, the ladies walking in the town and shopping and the sky in St Andrews which went on forever, the Forth with its fishing boats and the train which took them to holidays. In the summer there was the big market with fairground rides and stalls selling bright pink sugar hearts, sweeties and gingerbreads. The fair people's caravans parked in North Street. There were picnics on the beach every day and wonderful food from enormous baskets which the women carried and the lime trees which graced the streets. They stayed at the Grand Hotel and he would go to sleep listening to the sounds of the waves making their way over the beach.

Other times they went to Lewis and Harris and Skye. He could remember the smell of mushrooms which they gathered from the fields and in the evenings Jean would read the works of Sir Walter Scott and the sun would set and the night sky would come down to meet the day and Jean would carry him to bed and he would be drowsy in her arms. The silver sands of Morar where he played and Loch Fyne where he and his father hired a boat and fished for mackerel in the late afternoon were precious memories and soon they were all he had.

He well remembered the day that he was taken downstairs all dressed up amidst much fuss. It had to be something important because Nanny and Jean had talked in low voices so that he could not hear and when he got all the way downstairs he was taken into the drawing room and there was his father with Alison. She smiled at him. Niall didn't like the smile, it held triumph. It made him want to run back upstairs.

'Niall,' his father said. 'Alison is to be your new mother.'

Niall didn't see how she could be a new mother since he hadn't had an old one or any kind before but he thought you could only really have one kind of mother and she was apparently dead. Would he have to come downstairs more often? He hoped not. Every evening before he went to bed he was called into the drawing room and spent a little time there with his father. The drawing room had gold and white walls, dark pink sofas and two huge fires. It was the only time he saw him other than the parties where his father and friends were very merry.

After that he saw his father less rather than more and Nanny said that they had gone travelling and would be back. Niall was relieved that he didn't have to spend any time with them. Life went on just as before except that Jean very often took him on to her knee and said that she knew where it would all end and then what would happen and there were lots of conversations in the house among the servants but not in front of him.

By the time they came back from wherever they had been, and it seemed to him like a very long time, Niall was seven. He was called downstairs and into the library and there they both were, smiling, and he looked up into his father's face and was told, 'We're going to send you to school.'

That made him feel excited. There would be other boys at school and he could learn things and they could come home to tea. He said that he thought it would be very nice. He couldn't understand why Jean was crying or why Nanny's face was tight when he went back upstairs.

A great big trunk appeared and was open on the bedroom floor for many days. Niall liked the look of it, you could have stored exciting things in it, and he liked his uniform. Nanny and Christine filled up the trunk with his belongings and one September day he was bundled into the carriage, taken to the train and set off on a long journey to school. It had not occurred to him that it would be the kind of place where you could not come home at tea time and he wondered how he would manage and how Jean and Nanny would get on without him.

After a long time a man in uniform came to him in the carriage and said, 'This is Carlisle, where you get off,' so he did and they put his luggage down with him and a pale thin man came across to him.

'Niall McAndrew?'

'Yes.'

'I've come to collect you.'

He didn't tell Niall who he was, which Niall thought particularly ill mannered. His luggage was loaded and he got into the carriage and then he stared out of the window. The road was narrow and there were great big hills all around and a river which eventually turned into a lake. It was very pretty indeed but it went on and on, more hills and more water, and more road, which twisted and turned for so long that he thought they must never get there until they came to a small village where they must surely stop but they didn't. There was mile after mile until Niall was exhausted and rather frightened and the autumn day drew in and became dark and he thought it would never end. Eventually the carriage turned in at a long narrow drive. Niall could see the huge building at the end of it. His stomach went round and round. He wished that he could run home. They got out and he was ushered in through the front door and it opened into a great big space that went all the way up to the roof. Niall wished he could cling to the man who had collected him but he had disappeared, after pushing Niall in the direction of a big oak door. Niall opened it.

The headmaster introduced himself as Mr Duff.

'You call me "Mr Duff". You call the other masters "sir".'

Niall wasn't listening. He wanted to go home, back up the stairs to where Nanny and Jean were waiting. It was so big and so confusing and the rooms were all grey. He went to bed almost immediately and that too was a shock. He had never slept in a room with anyone else, but the room that they gave him to sleep in was huge, with windows so high that you couldn't see anything out of them. The walls were grey there too and the noise was something he thought he would not get used to and there were so many boys in the room that he couldn't count them. They didn't speak to him and when he spoke to them they laughed at his accent and imitated it.

There was never silence and there was never peace or being alone and he had not the courage to make friends as he had thought he would and he missed everything about his home. The food was served in a great big dining room and it was inedible. The potatoes were hard, the gravy was sludge, the meat was chewy. Everything was cold. There were big water jugs on the tables and the noise again was tremendous. He couldn't find his way to anywhere and the older boys were so big. The one thing that he became pleased about was the fact that he could do his lessons, which was just as well because the boys that couldn't find the right answers were beaten daily. Niall was terrified but not so afraid that he could not remember what was asked of him and he was so grateful not to be beaten. The bad food and the freezing dormitory were unimportant beside that.

All he could think about was Christmas. He would go home for Christmas. Everybody went home for Christmas. He worked hard, he kept quiet, he learned to sleep amidst the noise and he thought of home and what it would be like when he went back. That term was the longest time of Niall's life, learning to find the right places for the lessons, not meeting the masters' eyes, not saying anything when the boys laughed at him, not crying, because there was no privacy in which to do it. He did his lessons, he ate the awful food and he dreamed of home.

He did not think the day would ever come when his trunk would be packed and the carriage would come and he would go back on the train, but it did and he was overjoyed. Every minute was an hour, every hour was an age. When he finally reached home he ran in, without thinking, up the stairs, up the next flight to the top storey where Nanny and Jean would be waiting and then he stopped. He ran into the nursery and into the night nursery and into the room where Nanny and Jean slept. Nobody was there. The rooms were strangely empty, and then he heard a noise and turned around. It was his new mother.

'Niall. What are you doing up here?'

'I . . . I came to see Nanny and Jean.'

She laughed.

'They aren't here any more. You're a big boy now, you don't need people like that.' She came over and got down and pushed back his hair or something like that, she got her fingers into it anyway. He wanted to move away but he made himself not do it. He could not imagine a world which did not have Nanny and Jean in it.

'You have a big boy's room now. Don't you want to see it?'

'I want Nanny and Jean. Where are they?'

He saw his father that evening but only briefly. They were going to some kind of party and were all dressed up. His new mother looked very beautiful and when he told her she laughed and said that he would be a charmer. Niall went to bed in his new room. He had waited for so long to come home and now it was all spoiled. The following morning when he went downstairs he thought things had changed. The servants were not the people he remembered so well and there was very little furniture and there were big spaces on the walls where pictures had hung. There was nothing to do and nobody to talk to. It was mid-afternoon before his father and his new mother came downstairs and they had nothing to say to him. His father went to sleep on the sofa in the drawing room. Niall went upstairs and read a book. When he came back down again in the early evening, hungry, his father said to him, 'We're going away for a few days after Christmas.'

'Where are we going?'

'Not you, Alison and myself. We've been invited to the kind of place where small boys don't go, but you'll be all right here until you go back to school.'

It had not occurred to Niall that he would ever be glad to go back to school, because school was so awful, but it was as though he had no home any more. The servants drank and did not heed him. There was a good deal of laughter coming from the kitchen but he dared not venture there. Several days afterwards he made the journey once more to school in the train and this time he did not look out of the window, because he knew what there was to see.

After that the cold became the important thing. He was always cold because it was impossible to get near a fire, the big boys hugged it. He thought spring would never come but then he had thought Christmas would never come and then he had wished it hadn't. But spring didn't. The cold weather went on and on. The icicles were a foot long from the buildings. The ice beneath your feet was hard when you went out running, which they did twice a week. You washed in cold water. You ate cold food. Niall began to feel angry. Surely he deserved better than this. Everybody did. His only pleasure was lessons. And that was ridiculous. But he found that he could please the masters. He could watch their faces lighten, he was so good. Nothing defeated him, not mathematics or English or Latin or Greek or anything that they chose to teach him. It became his sole ambition to bring a smile to a master's face. It never happened but he held on to the idea. He had no friends. If you tried hard at lessons you couldn't have any friends and he hated sports and that was the only way you could make friends.

January went past. February was worse, it was colder. March was just as bad but he knew that Easter would arrive. He would go home. This time it was different. His new mother was not there and a great many of the servants had gone. The house was empty of furnishings and echoed, and his father, who had always been jolly and gone to lots of parties, did not go out any more and, whereas there had been fires in every room, now there were not. The one consolation Niall had was that he spent a lot of time with his father. Although there was no pleasure in it. His father had nothing to say, seemed to get through a great deal of wine and slept, rosy-faced, before the drawing-room fire. He did not tell Niall where his new mother had gone, so that after the first few days Niall enquired for Alison.

His father laughed but it was not the kind of laughter which Niall enjoyed.

'She ran off. Can you imagine? Ran off with somebody. Left the country. Took everything though. Took everything she could and went. There's nothing left. I shall have to sell the house, move to somewhere smaller.'

Niall couldn't think why that mattered. To him only one thing mattered.

'Will I be going back to school?' he said.

His father assured him that he wouldn't and the relief was so big that it made Niall happy. He didn't care if they lived in a tiny house just so long as he did not have to go away to school and Alison was not there. He would be happy to live in a little house with his father. He lay in his cold room at night while his father sang songs down below and he thought how pleasant it would be, only the two of them. He would be able to sit by the fire and read while the weather was wet and in the summer . . . Would there be a garden, just a little garden? And maybe there would be other boys so that he could play games with them and his father would teach him to play golf and they would be happy together? He made plans every night when he went to bed.

He grew tired of sitting in the house with his father. Day after day it went on and the house became even emptier until all the furniture had gone except for their beds and the two chairs by the fire. The house echoed even more after that. Each day he expected that they would move and each day they did not and men came banging on the front door and shouting and there were a good many letters and notices put through the letterbox, which his father ignored. Niall would have brought them to him except that his father was rarely awake. The pile of letters and papers grew and grew in the hall and there was nothing to eat.

The house was dank and chilly without fires and the shadows seemed to him to get longer and longer so that in the evenings he was afraid to leave the drawing room, where his father snored.

Niall rifled through the kitchen cupboards. At first there had been things in boxes and cans and some of them were nice to eat, everything was good to eat when you were hungry, but after a while the only food left was the kind which needed heat and water and there was none of that. Luckily his father said to him that they were going to leave, that they were going to travel and there was no need for them to stay there where there was nothing good to eat.

They were going to Durham. Niall did not understand why they had to leave Edinburgh but he suspected it was something to do with the way that the men came banging on the doors and shouting and how his father kept everything locked and how they kept the curtains closed in the drawing room all day in case the men should take to the garden and come banging on the windows too.

When it was dark and late one early summer night his father urged him out of the house. They moved carefully, his father watching around him all the time for the men who came to the door but there was nobody about. It was very late. Niall had not been out that late and thought that perhaps it was an adventure such as boys had in books. The lights were burning in the houses. His father grasped him by the arm.

Niall had assumed that they were going by train. When he had gone to school he had travelled by train and with his father there it might be exciting. It would certainly be more exciting than sitting in the house day after day with the curtains closed, bored because there was nothing to do, nobody to talk to and nothing interesting to eat. He had run out of biscuits long before they left even though there had been boxes and boxes of them to begin with.

They walked. At first it was easy because the day broke and it was fine. They rested during the day and walked at night and he knew why, because his father did not want them to be seen though how the men could have followed them this far Niall did not understand. His father drank as they went. He had a hip flask, a silver vessel which he kept in his pocket but it soon ran out and he cursed it. As the days went on they began to walk during the day and stop at shops for something to eat and that was all right except that it began to rain. Walking when you were very wet and tired was, Niall decided, almost as bad as being back at school and his father would not stop even when he cried. He was too big to be carried, his father said, and would drag him until Niall lay down on the road and that was when they stopped.

Sometimes they stayed in boarding houses. They all smelled different. They were never clean and the food offered was always the kind of thing that you had to be really hungry to eat but since he was always hungry he always ate it. They were noisy too and he had to sleep with people he didn't know and he and his father had to creep out before daylight so that they didn't have to pay. Niall grew fed up with walking. His shoes gave out and his father got him some others which were a bad fit and made his feet blister so that sometimes after that his father was obliged to carry him because otherwise they couldn't go anywhere. Niall longed for home. He thought of what his life had been like before his father married Alison, when Nanny and Jean were there and there were good things to eat and the rooms were warm and he had nothing to worry about.

It was full summer by the time they reached Newcastle. His father said he had not the strength to go on any further so they found a room for the night. It was just like all the others except that Niall found he had to listen hard to understand the woman's accent.

The Newcastle streets smelled of rotting fish and the house smelled of it too. The woman offered them fish for dinner and it looked disgusting. Niall couldn't eat it. His father never ate. He drank. He always had whisky on him, Niall had grown used to the smell of it on his breath. He went to sleep with the smell of warm whisky and woke up to it, his father snoring on none too clean pillows beside him. He quite liked his father's snoring. At least when his father was snoring you knew you weren't going to wake up by yourself or with dozens of other boys. It was reassuring.

The morning after they got to Newcastle he ventured to ask his father what they were doing here.

'That's a good question,' his father said as the light reached through the thin curtains and made a pattern on the ceiling.

They were still in beds that smelled of other people so Niall was not inclined to linger, he thought he might like to venture out into the streets but, when he asked, his father said, 'Not today.'

Not today became the next day and the following one until Niall was desperate to get out and sat for hours beside the window noticing small things like a cat crossing the backstreet. He heard the church bells that Sunday and saw every coming and going. On the Monday there were strings of washing in the street, flying like flags in the warm breeze.

'Please can we go out today?'

'No.'

Niall left the window and went over to the grubby bed and looked at his father, who didn't look much like his father any more, he hadn't shaved for months and had a tangled beard, his hair was never brushed or combed and the clothes he was wearing he had been wearing for as long as Niall could remember. He could not think that this man was the one who had married Alison, laughed with his friends.

'Why are we staying in Newcastle?'

'We aren't. We're going to Durham.'

'Why?'

'Because I think I should take you home.'

'Can we go home?'

'Not that home,' his father said.

Niall didn't understand but his father turned away as though he was going back to sleep.

That day his father drank all day until the smell of whisky sickened Niall and he was hungry and his father would not go down to supper so that Niall longed even for the dreadful fish which they had had the night before.

'Please let us go downstairs,' he begged. 'I'm hungry. Please, Father.'

'I'm not your father. My name's George.'

Niall knew it was only the drink. He was more worried however when George sat up. He had a gun in his hand. They had had guns at home but they were shotguns, the kind of thing men used for shooting grouse and ptarmigan and deer. This little gun which sat in George's hand like a toy did not look dangerous.

'Have you ever thought of what it would be like to be dead?' George said.

That made Niall afraid. Was his father going to shoot him? George pointed the gun at him.

'We could both die and that would solve everything. There would be nothing left. I should have thought of it before we set off. This is a godforsaken place and Durham's worse, the people and the dirty little villages and . . .'

Niall wasn't listening, he was staring at the gun, wondering if he was about to be blown into the next world by a drunken father.

'Do you want to live, Niall? Do you?'

Niall had backed into the door.

'There's nothing left.'

George got up from the bed and Niall pushed further into the door as though it would give. He couldn't watch any more. He closed his eyes and put his hands over his face and waited for George to shoot him. He waited and waited. It felt like a very long time but he did not think it was, just a few seconds, nothing at all. He couldn't move. He thought that if he moved even an inch George would shoot him and his life would be over when it had barely begun. Then he heard the shot and waited to be dead. He didn't move. He thought it was taking a long time. He stood and wondered if this stillness was eternity and then he thought he heard footsteps on the stairs and Mrs Riley, the woman who owned the place, rapped on the door.

'Are you there?'

She banged harder. Niall took his hands down from his eyes and then he wished he hadn't. George was lying on the floor, Niall could see him and half his face was shot away and there were bits of it all over and he was still. Niall put his hands back over his eyes again and slid down the door, crying. He didn't know whether it was relief that he was still alive or horror that George was not. George was the only person he had in the whole world.

Mrs Riley banged on the door and then she tried to open it but it was locked. She began shouting and then screaming and her husband's loud voice could be heard too. They tried to open the door. Niall could feel Mr Riley's weight behind it and so he made himself crawl away to the side and when he had done that he reached up and turned the key in the lock and Mr Riley almost fell into the room, staggering.

'Oh Jesus!' he said and stood still.

Mrs Riley followed him in.

'Holy Mary, Mother of God,' she said.

Niall sat against the wall and stared and the room filled with the smell of George's death, sweet and warm.

Mrs Riley got him up and walked him out of the room and down the stairs into the kitchen. It was a greasy place and Niall thought of the house in Edinburgh and Mrs McLaughlan singing in the huge spotless kitchen with copper pans bright and clean sinks, the whitest ever, and of her singing the Skye Boat Song, which always made her cry but she kept on singing it. She made lemon biscuits and gave them to him warm. Mrs Riley sat Niall on a chair and told him to keep still and that wasn't difficult. He thought he might never move again.

A policeman came. It had not occurred to Niall that he might lie but he thought back to the way that they had left Edinburgh and when the policeman began to ask him questions lying seemed important somehow.

'They're called "Mc" something or other,' he could hear Mrs Riley say as the policeman came into the room. 'Scotch people. They're all alike. He didn't pay me nothing neither.'

The policeman was very big. He got down to Niall who was sitting on a hard chair beside the long narrow table.

'What's your name, lad?'

'McLaughlan,' Niall said.

'Where are you from?'

'Glasgow.' The policeman didn't look like the kind of man who could tell different accents.

'And what is your address there?'

'I don't know,' Niall said.

He kept on saying that he didn't know. Some of it was true, he had no idea why George had brought him here, he only knew that they could not have stayed where they were and it seemed to him that if George had brought a gun with him, perhaps for protection on the road, he had gradually decided that he would kill himself, if not both of them. Niall did not see that giving information to the police would make any difference.

He became drowsy and eventually fell asleep to the sound of Mrs Riley saying, 'We can't keep him here you know. He's nothing to do with us.'

And then it was morning and Niall's only hope as he awoke and realized he wasn't dead was that it would be the morning before and that George would not be dead. It was a false hope. A cart came with a coffin on it and he was shut into the kitchen as the two men went upstairs to bring George's body down and then he heard the cart amble away up the street and the shouts from outside.

There were several visitors, word had spread and people were curious and Niall heard Mrs Riley say again and again that she thought it was just awful people could do such things in her house and she didn't understand it and she wasn't being left with that bairn, she didn't understand a word he was saying and he looked sullen to her.

Niall understood her perfectly, he was good at different languages, hadn't he learned Latin and Greek? He could hear exactly how she sounded and even speak like her, he thought. She came back into the kitchen after seeing her visitors out of the parlour and Niall said to her, 'Where have they taken my father?'

'To be buried, of course. Mind you, they won't be burying him among respectable people. There are places for those who think God's earth isn't good enough for them,' and she crossed herself as he had seen her do several times already.

Niall didn't know what to do. He wondered whether he should leave. He had no money and nowhere to go and nobody had said anything to him. He didn't know what he was waiting for, for George to come back?

Before long, however, Mrs Riley went to the door and came back with a man.

'Mr Wilson's here from the children's home. You're to go with him.'

Mr Wilson was a big man, the biggest Niall had ever seen and obviously did not like small boys. He looked out from narrowed close-set eyes which had no colour. He was not tall, his bigness was in how wide he was. He wore shiny, greasy clothes and his hands seemed to Niall as big as dinner plates.

'Any belongings?' he said.

'No.'

'No, sir,' Mr Wilson corrected him.

'No, sir.'

'Foreign then, are you?'

Niall had never been foreign before.

'I'm from Glasgow.'

'You don't sound like you come from Glasgow. Are you a liar then, lad?'

'No, sir.'

But he was, Niall realized. He had been lying ever since George had died. He didn't understand why, just that he needed some form of protection. What difference could it make now? Nobody would come for him. His father had no friends and neither had he. Mr Wilson grasped hold of him by the shoulder as though he might try to run out of the door. Niall could not think where to.

They walked through the middle of Newcastle. Niall realized that he didn't like it, he was afraid of it and he was afraid of Mr Wilson and the grip that Mr Wilson had on his arm. The streets were thronging with people and horses and carts and trams and the buildings seemed so high and dark. The markets where the farmers sold dairy produce and rabbits and other dead things upon the stalls were on, but Niall didn't watch. There were other things too, which reminded him that he had hardly eaten in weeks, sweets and fruit. They went past the tea rooms and the coffee shop and the tailors and the boot shop on Grainger Street, the Empire Theatre further on and the jewellers and a dozen public houses. Off Percy Street were smaller dingier streets, Liverpool Street and Percy Court, and here the houses were poor and men sat about on the corners and children in rags played in the road and had dirty faces. Part of the way along, Mr Wilson opened a door and ushered Niall inside.

He had been in a good many places which he disliked in the last few months but none like this. There was an air of defeat, it was like something out of another age. The afternoon sunshine did not venture here, the windows were high and barred. It smelled of bodies long unwashed and food kept too long. A woman came into the hall, she was big too, very wide with greasy hair that fell to way below her shoulders like she was a young girl. She smiled and her cheeks dimpled.

'Well, what a little picture,' she said. It reminded Niall of the women at his father's parties. They had been skinny by comparison but they had put their fingers into his dark hair and admired his clear skin and bright blue eyes. He didn't think there was much to admire any more. He was very thin. His clothes were old and worn and going into holes in places and he had grown out of them so that his trousers flapped above his ankles and his jacket was too short in the sleeve and too tight across the chest. He said nothing.

'What's your name, sweetheart?' she said and she said it in a nice voice and he thought of Jean and Nanny and how if he had been able to get to them they would not have let any of this happen to him. Had Nanny gone back to Fife and did she not think of him any more?

'Niall McLaughlan.'

'It's a long name for a small person,' she said. 'My name's Mrs Mackenzie. Are you Irish?'

'He claims he's from Glasgow. Don't you think he sounds like a southerner?'

'Maybe,' she said. 'You're just in time for tea.'

Things were improving, Niall thought, suddenly hungry. She put a hand into the middle of his back and propelled him along the hall and into a big room. It was just like school, Niall thought, heart sinking, but in fact it was worse. The children did not wear neat uniforms and they stared back at him through unkempt hair from dirty faces. Mr Wilson sat him down on the end of the wooden bench and they put a plate in front of him. It had on it a piece of bread and butter and to the side of it a mug of water.

Niall didn't know where the anger came from but it did. He had to fight it down so that he wouldn't say anything, so that he wouldn't get up and protest at his treatment and shout at the woman who had been nothing but kind to him up to now. He ate the bread and drank the water and said nothing and didn't look up. There would be supper later, no doubt. There was not. There were long prayers after the meal and then there was bed and it was a dormitory, much bigger than the one at school and more than one child in every bed. In some beds there were two at the top and two at the bottom. High above him the summer sun set late, just as it had done when he was little and the world was contained and organized. There was silence. Nobody moved.

Niall couldn't sleep, he relived George's death over and over and when he finally did doze he relived it again in all its detail.

At six they got up and there were prayers again and breakfast. It was porridge. Mrs McLaughlan would have wept if she could have seen it, it was so thick and grey, but Niall ate every scrap.

'I like to see a clean plate,' the woman said.

She was in the right place then, Niall thought, every plate was clean. Some children, when the woman wasn't looking, licked their plates.

There were lessons that morning and that was the first time Niall had ever thought about education and its having different levels. He was very far in advance of these children, many of them didn't even know their letters and when Mr Wilson wrote on the board Niall could have pointed out his spelling mistakes. He was obliged to pretend that he could not read and write and knew nothing of mathematics when in fact he knew all about multiplication and division and such like. He knew Greek and Latin, not a lot, he had not been at school for long enough to learn much, but it was a great deal more than any of these children would ever understand.

Next to him sat the most exquisite girl in the whole world. Niall did not dare to look at her. She was older than him, two or three years, and just as uncared-for as the rest, but she was small, dainty, fine-boned and fair-haired, with very dark eyes surrounded by long lashes, ears like shells on a beach and slender fingers. She couldn't do her sums. Niall tried not to tell her how to but when he drew a little closer as Mr Wilson's back was turned and said softly, 'The answer's twenty-four,' she didn't move or look up but she said, almost without moving her lips and certainly without anybody else hearing, 'You'll get leathered if you don't shut up,' so Niall did.

The answer was twenty-four.

At midday there was soup. Niall had no idea what had gone into it and he didn't much care any more. He couldn't see her. He wished he could have sat with her but it would have been no real advantage because you were not allowed to talk. In the afternoon the girls did sewing and the boys did woodwork. It was the first time that Niall had been stupid at anything. He had not realized that he could not use his hands. Nobody complained, perhaps Mr Wilson was used to boys who were stupid at such things, but Niall was unhappy. Tea time was the slice of bread and butter again, so thinly spread you could hardly see it, and prayers and then bed.

He hadn't spoken all day. He wondered whether the children were ever allowed to talk. It didn't seem so. There were so many children, he thought, you could lose yourself in them and that, he decided, was his best bet for now. He couldn't think beyond it. He didn't want to be noticed, to be special or to stand out in any way and he would if he said much or if he knew too many answers. From that day on Niall kept quiet, ate what he was given, tried to keep out of trouble, did not ask for anything and in his mind he tried to come to terms with the idea that George was dead. During the long hours of the night he thought about it so that when he went to sleep it would not come at him again and again.

The summer days did not last and the autumn came in cool and dark so that when he got up it was dark and when he went to bed it was dark and Niall began to think that his life at the home had gone on forever. At first he clung to some kind of idea that Nanny or Jean or some person who cared would come and find him. He imagined himself standing in the hall and holding somebody's hand and somebody saying to Mr Wilson that it had all been a mistake and it was time for Niall to go home. He dreamed of home, sometimes it was home as it had been and sometimes home as it had never been and his father was not always there. Sometimes it was a cruelty to wake up, because he would dream of the meals he had had there and wonder if he would ever taste good food again. He dreamt of cake and jelly and chocolate.

The only day he got to go out was Sunday and that was to church. They walked in twos and didn't speak. They could sing the hymns when they were in church. Niall came to enjoy the singing, it was the only time he was encouraged to speak. He thought he would forget what his voice sounded like. The church seemed rich and sumptuous compared to the children's home. It had blue and red stained-glass windows. That autumn the cold pale sun sent shafts of red and blue light down upon the floor of the church. There were gold candlesticks and embroidered altar cloths. One Sunday in November when it was so cold that Niall could barely move and the sermon had gone on for so long that he was numb and in danger of falling asleep he began to wonder what things like that were worth. He knew that it was a very bad sin to steal from a church but churches were very often open and if they left valuable things about surely people stole them. In his brief walks between Percy Street and here he had seen people living on the streets with nothing but a blanket, mothers with children who cried from the cold. Why was the church so rich and the people so poor?

Christmas came. He could have laughed now to think of how badly off he had thought he was the year before when George and Alison went away after Christmas and left him with the new servants who sat in the kitchen and got drunk and didn't bother with him. He had still had a comfortable bed, a great big room to himself, gardens, all of Edinburgh around him, warm clothes, books. There were books at the home. Niall had discovered them, hidden away in cupboards, and he stole them frequently. Mr Wilson didn't notice. He had no idea that anybody could read well enough to want the books and some of them were in Greek and Latin so Mr Wilson wouldn't have understood them. Niall didn't understand much himself but he was so bored with the lessons that he had to do something. Pretending to be stupid was becoming impossible. He got everything right because if you didn't you were punished but he never volunteered any information or added anything to his answers in case Mr Wilson should notice him.

Christmas Day was just like any other except that they went to church and saw the nativity scene and sang carols. The food was just the same. It was just like Sunday, they didn't have lessons but they had to read the Bible in the afternoon and there were prayers more often and longer than any other day. That evening after prayers Mrs Mackenzie called Niall into her little room. It held a bed and an easy chair, a fire and a table and looked very comfortable. It certainly was a lot better than any of the rooms he had seen before.

She smiled at him and beckoned and in her hand there was a biscuit tin. The biscuits in it were cream and broken and nothing like the kind of thing which Niall had been used to.

'Take one,' she said.

Niall stayed back.

'Come and take one.'

Niall looked for a complete biscuit but there wasn't one, they were all broken. He took the biggest piece he could find, less than a half. Mrs Mackenzie reached up and touched his cheek with her hand.

'Are you happy, Niall?'

He gave her the required answer.

'Yes, Mrs Mackenzie.'

'Good.' She cradled his cheek with her hand and put her fingers into his hair. Women had done it before but they had not looked at him like she did, at least he didn't think so. He thought she might offer him another biscuit but to his surprise she undid the buttons at the top of her dress and she took the hand that didn't have the biscuit in it and guided it inside on to her bosom. Niall was astonished, horrified, fascinated. Her breasts were enormous. It made him want to giggle and then it didn't. She held his hand over the tip of her breast until Niall wanted to run away.

'Move it.'

'What?'

'Move your hand around.'

Niall tried to extract his hand instead and she caught at his wrist.

'Try it again,' she said, 'and you can have another biscuit.'

'No. No.' Niall wrenched free and ran.

That night, in bed, his heart thumped so hard he thought it would come through his skin and he imagined that Mrs Mackenzie would tell Mr Wilson that he had not done what she wanted but nothing happened.

*

The child he had sat next to and told the sum answer to was called Bridget. He didn't know what her second name was but he watched her a lot as the days after Christmas went by and he waited to be asked back into Mrs Mackenzie's office to be offered biscuits and told to touch her. As much as there was any privacy, Niall took books from the top of the linen cupboard outside the bathroom and read them when he could.

One day in March Mr Wilson found a book on Niall. It was a Latin primer and Mr Wilson noticed the shape of it under Niall's rapidly wearing clothes.

'What is that, McLaughlan?' he said.

'It's a book, sir.'

'Really? Give it to me.'

Niall handed the book over. Mr Wilson stared at it.

'You read Latin?'

'No, sir.'

'So what are you doing with a book on Latin?'

'I wanted to read it.'

'Where did you get it?'

'It was in the linen cupboard.'

'You stole it?'

'No, sir. I was going to read it and put it back.'

Mr Wilson got hold of him by the hair, pulled him up and out of his seat and over the desk at the front of the gloomy classroom and beat him. Niall had always thought he would cry when somebody did that but he didn't. He just stored it up along with the gold candlesticks in the church and the biscuits in Mrs Mackenzie's room and the way that George had died. He thought it was a very hard beating, it hurt for such a long time afterwards. When Mr Wilson shoved him back in the direction of his desk nobody looked up. The one good thing was that there was no such thing as triumph here. Nobody wished you to be beaten and nobody was glad because everybody was the same. Niall was allowed no food that day or the next. During meals he was made to stand in the corner. Towards the end of the second day he passed out. It was a weird feeling, like he imagined dying might be. All of a sudden you just weren't there any more and in a way he was grateful. The floor enveloped him like a blanket. When he woke up he was disappointed. Mr Wilson was standing over him, telling him to get up and when he did shoved him in the direction of his bed with the comment, 'You shouldn't thieve.'

Prayers were going on below, Niall could hear them but at least he was alone in the bed, for the first time. As he lay there Bridget slid into the room. She was not allowed in the boys' dormitory. She closed the door softly and came to his bed like a wraith.

'Do you really read Latin?' she said.

'A bit.'

'You've got to stop stealing,' she said.

'I wasn't stealing.'

'Is there another name for taking things which aren't yours?'

'I didn't take it, I only borrowed it.'

'Was that how you felt when Old Wilson hit you?'

'I didn't do anything wrong,' Niall said.

'You don't have to be wrong, you just have to be found out,' she said.

'You'll get found out being here.'

She went without another word but Niall felt happier. That night he went into the girls' dormitory and in the cold quiet he moved past the beds until he saw her unmistakable, almost white hair. She had a bed to herself. How lucky. He sat down and touched her on the shoulder. She jumped and opened her eyes.

'What are you doing?' she whispered.

'Can I get in? I'm frozen.'

'No. Yes. They will kill you.'

'I have to tell somebody.'

'Get in then. Only don't touch me. Nobody touches me.'

'I don't want to touch you,' Niall said.

He got into the bed. He could feel the warmth of her on the bedclothes.

'Bridget.' He said it just to say her name, just to say somebody's name. He had talked more today than he had for weeks, months. 'Mrs Mackenzie got me into her room and gave me a bit of biscuit and got me to touch her.'

'She does that to everybody. What makes you think you're so special? It's just her tits, isn't it? Boys like tits. Besides, what does it matter? Take the whole frigging biscuit tin while you're doing it.'

'I don't want to do it.'

'Think about something nice. Something nice must have happened to you some time.'

'I don't think it's right,' Niall said. 'Nobody asked me to do that before.'

'Don't kid yourself,' Bridget said. 'It's not going to be the last time some woman does, not the way you bloody look.'

Niall didn't understand.

'I don't know what you mean.'

Bridget laughed into the pillow.

'Jesus, Niall, you look like you fell out of heaven.'

The funny part about it was that was exactly how he felt, as though he had been in heaven, bypassed earth and gone straight to hell.

*

She was right, it was not the last time. Within another month he had been called back into the room and given biscuits three times and on the third occasion Mrs Mackenzie made him sleep with her. He didn't have to do anything after the breast bit, just sleep, and she didn't touch him so it wasn't that bad but she made him take all his clothes off. He felt sick. Why Niall felt so awful about it he didn't know. It seemed to spoil the memories of Jean and Nanny though they would never have done such a thing to him in a million years. His mind got all mixed up and he didn't want to go near anybody. He didn't go into the girls' dormitory again to see Bridget and he didn't talk to anybody. He didn't steal any more books, he just went through the day-to-day of boring lessons and being hungry all the time and other people's elbows and legs in the way when he wanted to sleep. He had stopped thinking about things like being clean and having clothes which fitted.

Niall could no longer disappear among the other children. In class Mr Wilson did not forget the Latin grammar and he gave Niall work which he could not do and then beat him when he got it wrong. The misery grew on him like a hard shell. He no longer expected to be happy or for there to be relief of any kind. The days and the weeks and the months went on and on.

In time a new boy came to the home, much bigger than Niall, a tall, thin, dark-haired boy called Rozzer with an accent so thick Niall could hardly decipher his language. He was pushed on to the long wooden bench beside Niall that first afternoon and tried to take the slice of bread from Niall's plate. Niall went for him and within seconds they were rolling on the floor and Niall had his fists all over the other boy's body. Mr Wilson beat Niall and threw him down the cellar steps.

He hadn't been locked in anywhere cold and dark before and

there were rats, big rats. They didn't exactly frighten him, he had hurt himself as he fell so he couldn't concentrate too hard on the rats. They ran into the corners, he could hear them, but when he eventually fell asleep he could feel them scurrying over him. He lay there in the darkness and wondered what it would be like if Mr Wilson forgot about him. He dismissed the idea at first but it came back because the door at the top of the steps did not open and the time went on and on. He was hungry but it was thirst which became his biggest thought, it filled his whole mind, the idea of water, taps, waterfalls, even half a glassful. It had become unbearable when the door finally opened and Mr Wilson trod down the steps.

'Get up,' he said.

It took Niall quite a long time to get back up the cellar steps and when he did so he was pushed into Mrs Mackenzie's room. The door closed. She had a glass of water in her hand.

'You're getting too big for those clothes, Niall,' she said. 'Why don't you take them off? I've got you some others and you can have a drink. You're getting to be a big boy now, aren't you?'

Niall hadn't realized that it was night-time. She held on to the glass until he undressed and then she made him get into bed and she gave him the water. Niall was concentrating so hard on the water that he hadn't realized she had taken off all her clothes and got into bed with him.

There was a yard behind the home. Sometimes on fine days they were allowed out there. The gates were padlocked and the walls were high so you couldn't see anything and there wasn't any way out. The boys played games when they were out there and the girls stood about as girls did. Niall stood by the wall. Nobody asked him to play and nobody spoke to him. One afternoon in the autumn after Niall was fourteen, Bridget came across. He hadn't looked at her in so long he had almost forgotten what she looked like.

'New clothes, eh? Grown out of the others?'

Niall glanced past her so that he wouldn't have to look at her and for the first time realized that he was bigger than she was. He pushed his hands into his pockets and walked away. He stood against the opposite wall where there were no girls. He had only been there a few seconds when Rozzer appeared. Niall ignored him. Rozzer stood there for a little while and then he looked down at his boots and said, 'I didn't mean to get you into all that bother.'

It was the closest anybody had come to an apology for a very long time. Niall looked at him.

'You haven't done much fighting, have you?' Rozzer said. 'I could show you. I could show you a lot of things.'

Niall wasn't very keen on the idea but there was nothing else to do or think about other than things he couldn't bear. All that winter whenever they got the chance Rozzer taught Niall how to fight. Niall didn't ask him how he had learned all these things, they hardly ever spoke except for instruction, and because Niall wanted to occupy his mind he let the new learning run over him like water. Rozzer showed him how to use a knife even though they didn't have one and how to pick a lock.

'If you can pick a lock what are you doing in here?' was the only question Niall asked him.

'It's better than the street.'

'I'd take my chance.'

'You would die out there.'

Rozzer was right, Niall thought. It was cold in here but the winter outside was the worst he had known. When it was cold it snowed and when it got colder it didn't and there was ice everywhere for weeks. It was so cold in the dormitory that Niall couldn't sleep and the food which was supposed to be hot was less than tepid. The alternative of course was Mrs Mackenzie's bed. It was warm enough in there.

Rozzer developed a bad cough and it got worse and worse. He couldn't get the food down and some days could barely stand. He couldn't do the work he was set in class and one day in February when he had got everything wrong Mr Wilson pulled him out of his seat by the hair, which was the usual way, and began to hit him. Niall couldn't bear it. He got up and tried to stop him.

'He's ill. Can't you see he's ill?'

It was a foolish thing to do, he thought afterwards, and he remembered the class looking on in horror as Mr Wilson turned from Rozzer. Niall got a couple of good punches in. Rozzer would be proud of him, he thought, but Mr Wilson was too big. Niall fought all the way out of the classroom and down the hall because he knew what was going to happen now and sure enough Mr Wilson yelled for Mrs Mackenzie. She came waddling along the hall and opened the door and together, while Niall fought, they pushed him inside and threw him down the steps and after that there was nothing.

When he came to, it was dark. From time to time as he lay there on the floor he could hear footsteps above and hoped that there would be the noise of bolts going back and they would open the door but they didn't. He lost track of time and knew from before that what seemed like a long time could be just a matter of hours down there but it was endless. He got past hope, beyond despair. At first he tried to imagine better things, holidays and Christmases and the joy of security. He brought the images of his early childhood to the front of his head like pictures but after a while he seemed to lose it all. Day and night had ceased. He began to understand for the first time why George had taken his life. It was all so pointless. Consciousness went. He was grateful. There was warmth and light and . . . and somebody was putting water to his lips and making him cough. His nose told him it was Mrs Mackenzie, the smell of old biscuits and cheap perfume and sweat.

'Leave him, Amelia, he doesn't deserve your help.'

Mr Wilson too then. She was called Amelia? It was too pretty a name for that mountain of flesh.

'We don't want him dying,' she said. 'Here, bonny boy, you drink that and everything will be all right.'

Just when Niall was getting the idea of drinking she took the water away and seconds later they had trooped back up the cellar steps and the door slammed again.

After a little while the images in Niall's head didn't need any help. They came to the front of his mind without any summoning on his part. He was a very small boy again and he was on the beach at St Andrews with Jean, at the Scores. There was spiky sand and the waves were small and warm because the water came up for a long way over shallow ground, that was what made it safe for small boys, Jean said. She was so pretty. Some of her hair had come away from the neat way she always kept it held up and it wafted around her face like ringlets and she was kneeling down and making a sandcastle for him. It was such a relief. He was not in the cellar any more. None of this had happened. He knew it couldn't have. She had finished making the sandcastle and gone to the top of the beach to search for yellow flowers in among the sand dunes and he was going the short distance with a pail for water to put into the moat. Each time he filled it the water disappeared but he was happy trotting backwards and forwards to the water. There were little bubbles as the waves spread and the sky was blue and there were gulls and all the boarding houses and hotels had big stone fronts and little turreted roofs and great big windows and when he went to bed at night Jean opened the window of the hotel where they were staying. He was staying in a room way up high and she would stand him on the window ledge and he could see ships on the horizon and he would go to sleep listening to the sea making its constant and never-ending way up and down the beach.

Jean came back and she placed the flowers at intervals in the sandcastle and she fashioned a drawbridge because she said there might be visitors coming to tea that afternoon. When the shadows began to lengthen she took him by the hand and she put the bucket and spade in her other hand and they began to walk slowly back up the beach, past the links towards the hotel. Nanny would have the tea ready, she said.

When Niall came round he was lying in Mrs Mackenzie's bed. He was naked and so was she and she was moving her hands over him. He gave himself a few moments and then he got hold of her wrists and moved her from him. She smiled brightly at him.

'Better than we thought you were, eh?' she said. Niall put her on to her back. She seemed to like it. Her eyes gleamed. 'Oh yes,' she said.

'Close your eyes,' Niall said.

'Have you got something nice for me?' she said.

'Something very nice.'

She shut her eyes and he let go of her and then he took a

pillow from his side of the bed and put it over her face and then he put the whole weight of his body on top of it. She struggled. Niall did not pretend to himself that he was strong but he was big enough to lie on her face in spite of everything she did and after that all he had to do was wait because however much her arms and legs flailed, however much she tried to breathe, there was no room and no air and he pressed down as hard as he could because he knew that everything depended upon it. She made a good mattress. After a while her arms and legs were not moving as much and her body ceased to shudder and she gradually went limp. Niall didn't move. He wanted to make sure that she was not deceiving him, she might be, she might be waiting until he took the pillow and his body away and then she would leap up and strike, but when he finally decided to look it was obvious to him that she was dead.

He slid down off the bed and since there were no clothes he searched in the big wardrobe nearby where he knew she kept a good many things and found some that more or less fitted him and then he looked for her keys. He thought she might have left them in a pocket. He didn't like touching them, they were soiled and sticky and grey with dirt and the pockets were empty. After that he searched the room, the drawers and the wardrobe and finally found them at the back of the dressing-table drawer. He also found a great deal of money, so he took that too.

It was late, night. He let himself quietly out of the room and walked along the hall and tiptoed down the stairs. A cold white winter moon tried to shine its light into the house but the high windows blotted out all but the beams which reached the ceiling. Every room was locked. It was one of the rules and, in order to get into the kitchen, Niall had to try half a dozen heavy keys but eventually he got to the right one and it turned. It was very dark in there. He moved carefully. If he fell over anything or made much noise somebody would hear him. Mr Wilson slept above. He found the old dresser which took up one wall. The middle drawer of it was locked. Niall unlocked that too and his fingers closed around a knife, a good sharp knife. He tested it and then he closed the drawer and went silently back across the room.

He thought about going to the dormitory and finding Rozzer but, if anybody awoke, the noise would alert Mr Wilson so he decided to go into Mr Wilson's room first. A sleeping man surely could soon be disposed of but the trouble was that Mr Wilson was not sleeping. There were sounds coming from the room. Somebody was crying. Niall hesitated. If Mr Wilson saw him come into the room the element of surprise would be lost and with it the possibility of doing serious damage before a man much bigger than him could retaliate. Once Mr Wilson retaliated the advantage was gone.

There was light coming from under the door. Niall didn't understand the light or the crying. It was late, it was the middle of the night. He stood, unsure, and began to sweat, worried in case his fingers should slip on the doorknob but they didn't. He opened it soundlessly.

It was almost the perfect opportunity, Niall thought. Mr Wilson had a girl in his bed and was on top of her so he had his back to the door. The only trouble was that if she saw him she would give him away and Mr Wilson would turn around before Niall had time to reach him.

There were signs of a struggle, the bed was a mess, but it was over. Mr Wilson had won. His balding head and lard-white back were visible and he would not easily be distracted, Niall decided, because he was having the girl. She had her eyes closed and she was crying but her white blonde hair was unmistakable. It was

Bridget. He crept to the bed. After that it happened very fast. He got his arm around Mr Wilson's body and then he brought the knife as hard as he could across the middle of Mr Wilson's throat just as Rozzer had shown him. He wasn't convinced that a single stroke would do it though Rozzer had said it would and, as Mr Wilson realized what was happening and tried to stop him, Niall put the knife into him anywhere he could, any place would do. He got into a rhythm with it and couldn't stop and didn't ever want to stop, he wanted to go on and on knifing Mr Wilson until the world should come to an end.

He did not notice Bridget until she was standing bare and pale beside him, saying, 'For God's sake, Niall, he's dead.'

Niall stopped, moved back. He was covered in blood up to the elbows. It was all over his clothes and all over the bed and all over the body which had been Mr Wilson. There was blood everywhere.

Bridget poured water into a bowl and began to unearth clothes from the wardrobe and when Niall had washed his hands and arms and the knife they dressed in whatever they could find. He remembered the money, which he transferred to his new clothes and he also searched the drawers here and found more money and then he bundled the old clothes into his arms and they left the room.

'Where are you going?' she asked as he turned towards the boys' dormitory.

'For Rozzer.'

'Rozzer died on Saturday.'

Moments later they were standing in the street. Niall smashed at the lock on the front door.

'What are you doing?'

'Making it look like somebody broke in.'

'They'll know it was us.'

'They'll only know that we're gone,' he said.

'You should get rid of that knife,' she said.

'We might need it,' Niall said.

He got rid of the clothes, he stuffed them down into a back alley along with a whole load of other rubbish. The streets were silent. It was bitterly cold. Suddenly he didn't know where to go. It was not a good idea to stay outside, he was weak from a long time without food and Bridget soon began to drag behind, like somebody tired.

They walked down to the quayside. It was the one place where he thought they wouldn't be noticed, because there were all kinds of buildings and hostelries and people and there were places that were open all night. They could get lost there. There were also a number of places that might take them in, that took in all manner of people off the ships and asked nothing. Bridget was half asleep when Niall dragged her into one of them. The man taking the money asked nothing, just gave him a key.

'You do food?' Niall said.

'What would you like?'

'Anything that's edible. A lot of it.'

They trod up the stairs and along the dimly lit hall and at the far end he unlocked the door and was surprised at how comfortable it was. But then people coming off the ships had money to spend. There was a big bed with a quilt on it and there was a rug which covered most of the floor. Bridget sat down on the bed. Niall lit the lamp, pulled the curtains across the window and put a match to the fire. Bridget hadn't spoken for the last hour.

'I can sleep on the floor if you like,' he said.

'Oh Niall, you are funny. Do you think I mind you after Mr

Wilson?' She threw her boots on to the floor and stretched out. 'It's a wonderful bed,' she said.

Niall took off his boots too and lay down beside her and stared at the ceiling. He kept seeing Mr Wilson and all the blood and the frenzied way he had wanted to kill him and Mrs Mackenzie struggling like a necked chicken. There was a knock on the door. He got up and opened it and there stood a girl of about Bridget's age with a tray. He thanked her and took it from her and put it down on the bed. On the tray with knives and forks and plates were a cold cooked chicken and bread and butter and cheese and some kind of chutney. It was the best meal of his life. Afterwards he moved the tray to the far side of the room and they took off most of their clothes and lay in bed, watching the firelight.

'Do you think they'll find us?' she said.

'Who's going to tell them? I don't suppose there were any records. What's a child more or less? Did anybody mind Rozzer dying?'

'No.'

'Well then.'

'If they find us they'll hang us.'

'You didn't do anything. I don't care anyway.'

'What do you think we should do?'

'I think we should stay in bed and eat a lot for a few days.'

'It sounds fine to me. Niall . . . ?'

'What?' He didn't even look at her, he was mesmerized by the fire, but she didn't say anything until he looked round. She looked so tired. 'I don't mind being in bed with you but I don't want you to touch me.'

'I'm not going to.'

'I think I might go to sleep now.'

She was soon fast asleep. He thought he wouldn't sleep because of what he had done but the food and the warmth and the soft feather bed were too much for him. He listened to Bridget breathing for a little while and gradually he joined her.

Two

When he awoke he thought for several terrifying moments that he was down the cellar at the home and then he opened his eyes. Behind the curtains there was light. The fire was dead in the grate, shadows filled the room and Bridget lay in his arms, almost across him she was so close, her face buried against his chest. He was comfortable, didn't want to move and went back to sleep. The next time he awoke, Bridget awoke too.

The girl from the night before brought hot water. Bridget took all her clothes off. Niall made an excuse and retreated out of the room but he didn't go far. He gave her what he thought was ample time and then went upstairs. Bridget was dressed to her petticoat. She dried her hair by the fire, combing it through with her fingers so that it was no longer a tangled mess but a mass of pale curls, and she offered to wash his hair for him. When Niall was clean and dry and had some clothes on, the girl brought breakfast. It was a proper breakfast, bacon and eggs, bread and jam, a great big pot of tea. They ate it all and, after she had collected the dirty dishes, she cleaned out the fire, laid it, lit it and left them alone.

They went back to bed. Bridget lay luxuriously against the pillows.

'You aren't worried about killing Mr Wilson, are you?' she

said. 'He did that to me lots of times. He did it to some of the other girls too.'

Niall looked at her.

'I killed Mrs Mackenzie as well.'

'Jesus, Niall!' she said, staring. 'Why the hell did you do that?'

'For the same reason I killed him.'

'What did you do to her?'

'I suffocated her with a pillow.'

'I'm glad you did,' she said. 'That way there's nobody to say anything and besides I hated them both.'

'Do you have any family anywhere?'

'No. Do you?'

'No.'

'We could leave and go somewhere else.'

'I don't see why we should unless there's a fuss.'

'One of us could slip out and get a *Chron* later.'

In the middle of the afternoon, when the *Evening Chronicle* was published and the vendors shouted from the street corners, Niall went out and bought a newspaper and took it back. The death of the two people who ran the children's home had made headlines. It was a 'mystery surrounds' story. Niall was pleased about that. He hoped it would always go on being a mystery. They called it 'a particularly vicious killing'. The following day the death no longer made the front page because there was nothing more to add. The day after, it wasn't mentioned at all and although it kept surfacing from time to time there was never any fresh evidence so it became a 'mystery still surrounds' story and after that it died. He was not surprised. They did not find the clothes with blood on them in the dirty streets and he had the murder weapon on him, at least when he went out at night, which wasn't often.

It was strange. Having gained their freedom all they wanted to do was hole up in the little tavern where nobody asked questions and the food was good and plentiful. When they ran out of money, Niall said he would get some more and went to put on his boots and his coat. Bridget was sitting on the side of the bed.

'Where are you going to get it from?'

'I'm going to steal it of course.'

'If they catch you you'll go to gaol or worse. There is another way.'

'What's that?'

'I can go and lift my skirts.'

'No.'

Bridget slid off the bed.

'You're younger than me.'

'What's that got to do with it?'

'I did it for Mr Wilson a lot and I did it for two of the older lads. It's nothing.'

The way that she tossed her head made Niall decide.

'No,' he said, making for the door. Her hand came out to stop him from going but he was quite a lot bigger than her now so she couldn't really do anything.

'You're just a boy,' she said.

'I won't be long. Lock the door after me.'

He didn't feel like a boy, he didn't even feel young any more. He felt as though he had lived for a hundred years and yet he felt empowered as though, because he didn't care about anything, it didn't matter what he did. He tried to think back to what Rozzer had told him about breaking into houses and really it was as obvious as everything else. For the past few nights he had gone out when she was asleep and walked around the city and noted in the evenings when houses were unlit. When they were unlit for three or four nights running it was a fair assumption that the people who lived there were not at home. After that, all he had to do was make sure he got the right house in the middle of the night. He chose rich houses, big places, and he ignored the things that most people would have taken. All he took was jewellery and money that first time, but he remembered that Rozzer had laughed when he told Niall that his dad had said there was nothing like finding a safe in a house. The makers went to such trouble with heavy doors and locks at the front but the way to break in was through the back and all you needed was something heavy and enough strength to do it. The other thing to remember was time. You shouldn't mess about. You must be in and out in as few minutes as you could manage. You got in through the back, it was best if there was a garden because it would hide you and the neighbours would hopefully not notice. The other important thing was that no matter what they did to keep you out – and they did very little – there was always a way in if you went about it in an intelligent manner. Niall thought that Rozzer was an idiot to go into the home when he knew so much and then he realized that what Rozzer wanted, what everybody wanted, was a family.

The house he chose was terraced but large, with bay windows. It had a back garden that would have hidden ten of him and all he had to do was slide the window open where somebody had neglected to fasten the catch across it. How very careless, Niall thought. There was no moon, so it was very dark inside but he gave his eyes a second or two to get used to that. He ignored the downstairs, he went up to the bedrooms and there on the dressing table of the first was a jewellery box. He emptied it into his pockets. He had no idea whether any of it was valuable so he went through the top drawers on either side and there were small velvet boxes. He left the boxes and put the contents into his pockets. He went into two more bedrooms without result and then he left. He had been about five minutes and it was long enough.

Pleased with what he had done he went to the next house that he had chosen and this time he had to break a small window to get in but he was able to put his hand inside and undo the catch and slide the window open. Upstairs in the biggest bedroom there was money on the mantelpiece, quite a lot of it, as though somebody had emptied their pockets before leaving, but most of it was paper money. There were no jewellery boxes but he found money in the drawers too. He was less than five minutes again.

He walked slowly back to the tavern. Bridget was sitting over the fire in the bedroom but she jumped up when he got in.

'You've been a long time. I was worried.'

Niall emptied his pockets on to the bed and the jewellery shone in the lamplight and the paper money was in little wads crumpled from being stuffed deep among the jewellery.

'There's a fortune here,' she said when she had tried on the diamond earrings and a ruby and gold brooch.

'I won't have to do it that often.'

'You won't have to do it at all for me,' she said, turning from the mirror. 'I can keep myself.'

'On your back?'

'How else do you suggest I do it?'

'You like that?'

'Do you like stealing?'

'Yes, I do actually.'

'I do actually,' she mimicked him. 'You are so polite.'

Niall took in the severe way she was looking at him so close up like a predator.

'You don't have to worry. I'm not going to put you on to your back, I'm only a boy.'

Bridget laughed bitterly.

'I'll remind you of that the first time you do it to me,' she said and her mouth trembled.

'I will never hurt you, Bridget. I swear it to you.'

She shook her head and her eyes were brilliant with tears.

'Don't make promises to me,' she said.

'You think I'd kill for just anybody?'

She laughed and a tear ran down her face. Niall put his arms around her and drew her in against him.

'Never,' he said.

Before a fortnight had gone past the killing of the two people at the children's home had been forgotten by most people and the police appeared to make no headway. As for the burglaries there was little mention of them in the newspapers, it was such a common crime and there were so many people poor and out of work that it was almost taken for granted there would be a lot of thieving. The city was rife with it.

Bridget suggested they should rent a house, not a big house but they could not go on living in the tavern forever. She added, 'We could open a brothel.'

'What?'

'Why not? We could make money. I know lots of girls who turn tricks, some of them used to be at the home. If we could give them somewhere to do it comfortably we could take a percentage and if we could make enough money you wouldn't have to steal and I could run it.'

'We could do something respectable.'

She laughed. They were sitting on the bed, at least he was, she was lying down looking up at the ceiling and concentrating on her idea. Niall didn't want to leave the tavern, he didn't want things to alter again and, though he wasn't about to tell her, what he liked best about it was the way that when she slept, though she didn't seem to be aware of it, she snuggled in close against him. It was bliss. He didn't want to give that up and he had the feeling that when they moved she would object to having him in her bed, no matter what the circumstances.

'You mean work in a shop or a factory or something? Do you know what it pays? I've been poor long enough. Now I want the best.'

They went looking for a likely building to rent and Bridget went on to the streets for several nights. He insisted on going with her but she made him stay at a distance. She said he would frighten people, hanging about like that. There were lots of girls on the streets and women too. Bridget chose carefully. They were all agreeable. The winter weather was colder than ever. Niall knew nothing about prostitutes. He had thought they were without intelligence, without ideas. Some of them were young and some of them were beautiful, always they were poor.

'We don't want anybody with children—'

'Don't they need lodging more?'

'We're not running a frigging charity, Niall. We don't want anybody who's had trouble with the law and nobody old and nobody plain and nobody desperate.'

Niall thought that you would have to be desperate to be a prostitute but he didn't say so. She was enthusiastic, organized. She found the house. It was not that far from the home, which Niall thought rather funny in a way except that he didn't much care for going back into the centre of the city.

'The centre is best,' she insisted. 'We'll get more punters there.'

It was a big house. The thing Niall liked about it most was not that it was big and wide and had three storeys but that it had a garden, a courtyard if you wanted to call it that, a place all to itself which caught the sun in the afternoons. He could imagine he and Bridget sitting there together, drinking tea and talking things over. Bridget said she wouldn't have any time for sitting about and swept a hand around every time she went into a room, because she had gone on her own the first time and was now showing him round like a proprietor would. He had seen the very big kitchen and the reception rooms downstairs, there were three of those and lots of room for people to come in and wait, she said, and then there were the bedrooms, the lower storey had five of these and the third storey had another five but smaller.

'So we'll use the big rooms for the customers and then these for us. You could have this one if you like.'

Niall glanced around him. It was big enough and had a nice view across the garden and the roofs of other houses and it had a half-moon fireplace, black and with green and white tiles.

'And I could have the one next door,' she said.

He said nothing. She rounded on him. She was doing that a lot. He thought that the hatred she had felt for Mr Wilson was not dissipated by his death. If anything she felt worse because while it was going on she could not think of anything better but, now that she had better, she realized what he had done to her.

'Of course, some of the girls can go home and they won't mind sharing, I daresay, at least at first until we get something bigger, when we can afford it. You were going to say something.'

'No.'

'You were.'

'It's a nice room, I like it.'

'But you would rather sleep with me. I will never ever sleep with anyone again. Do you understand me?'

'Yes.'

Her eyes dared him to say something. Niall thought she was going to hit him.

'I hate you,' she said. 'If I didn't need your money I would put you out.'

'That's all right, I'll leave and you can have the money to set you up. There's plenty more where that came from.'

He left the money on the window sill of the bedroom and walked out. She let him get into the street and then she ran after him and when she reached him she put herself into his arms, crying.

'You daft idiot!' she said. 'Don't you know you're the only person I love in the whole world? Don't you ever do that again.'

'You told me to go.'

'Sometimes you're such a child!' she said, thumping him. 'I wanted you to say that we were going to sleep together. You think I can get through the night without you?' She turned wet eyes up to him. 'I can't. I can't sleep when you're not there. Is that enough? Will you come back? Did you ever kiss Ma Mackenzie?'

'No. I never kissed anybody. I don't know how to.'

'I want you to kiss me. Right now and forever and always afterwards. Always, always.'

Niall did. He didn't think he was very good at it but it was nice and he thought he would enjoy however many kisses she chose to bestow upon him. They didn't go back into the house, they went back to the tavern and went to bed and spent all night kissing each other. Niall hadn't realized it was such a wonderful thing and this time she went to sleep in his arms. He didn't think he could be any happier.

They moved within the month and were open for business within another week. Niall didn't understand how men would find out they were there but somehow word got round. The girls who came to live there were all beautiful. There was Gypsy, who was tall and dark-skinned, with eyes like coal and hair like night. She had very white teeth. Then there was Ella, who was very curvy and had wavy brown hair and big brown eyes like velvet curtains and bought him sweets, for some reason, but Niall didn't complain about that. There was also Minna, who was very small and came from Newbiggin on the coast, where her father had been a pitman and had drunk himself to death, so she sent money home to her mother and the four younger children. Other girls lived in the town but came in and did shifts. Niall had thought it would all be night work but it wasn't necessarily, men seemed to have needs of all kinds at all times. He had also thought that the men who came there would be like Mr Wilson, with mean eyes, but they weren't. He watched covertly everything that happened over the first couple of weeks. They were mostly monosyllabic, eyes cast down, and they were all sorts, from men who were poor and probably spent the money they should have taken home to their wives on prostitutes, to professional people in nice suits, like doctors and solicitors, a good many sailors and, because it became known as a high-class establishment, they brought in the very cream of Newcastle from the big houses in Jesmond and the villages beyond, where the coal owners and the shipyard owners and the businessmen of the area lived. Some of these would stay all night even though it cost a great deal of money.

They were not all old either. There were a good many rich young men in evening dress who came to the brothel when they had been out. Sometimes they were drunk but Bridget employed a very big man called Carl to stand around near the door and if there was any trouble he threw them out two at a time.

Bridget was younger than the others and smaller too and looked as though a bad wind would knock her over but she kept control of everything. Niall had no idea that her friendship with him was the source of gossip to the other girls until one night about six months later in high summer. He usually kept to the bedroom or at least the garden during the night hours from ten onwards, when most of the men came to the house, but one night he was in the kitchen when Gypsy came in. She looked hard at him. He wasn't doing anything, just sitting there drinking tea and thinking that he would go out into the garden with his tea and enjoy the night sounds and the warm air.

Gypsy paused when she saw him. The girls gathered in the kitchen when business was slow, which it rarely was any more, and sat about, grumbling at the customers and smoking.

'Should you be in here?' she said.

Niall was stretched out with his feet up on a chair, smoking a cigarette and considering the evening.

'Why?'

'Somebody might see you and think we run a nursery.'

Niall pulled a face at her.

'We don't all sleep with boys, you know,' she said.

Niall was surprised and rather hurt.

'Bridget doesn't sleep with me,' he said. 'At least, not like that.'

'I should think she doesn't. What good would you be to any-body in bed, at your age?'

'I could make your eyes water,' he said.

She looked at him for a moment or two and then she started to laugh. Niall didn't. It made him think of Mrs Mackenzie. Gypsy didn't laugh for long. She said, 'You're going to be good and dangerous shortly.'

'I'll make you a cup of tea if you like,' he said.

She went back to normal after that and called him her sweetheart like she usually did but Niall didn't forget it. He thought it was probably very sinful to sleep with Bridget like he did and kiss her but then what was one sin more? He had killed two people and would burn in hell for eternity.

They made a lot of money. They ate well and had new clothes. Bridget had beautiful suits made for him and then complained because he almost instantly grew out of them. She was very busy organizing and looking after everything so it was the following winter before she actually said to him, 'Are you going to do anything?'

They were lying in bed. It was Monday evening and Mondays were always slow. The fire was burning in the bedroom, they had eaten and gone back to bed and he was surprised at the question.

'What do you mean?'

'I mean what are you going to do? You don't do anything.'

'You want me to help?'

'No, I don't want you to help.'

'You want me to go back to thieving? I thought we didn't need it.'

'We don't. You used to read. You don't seem to do that any more.'

The truth was that Niall found reading difficult, he couldn't concentrate for long enough. If he gave his mind things to do, the awfulness of his life at the home and the killing of the two people who ran it dominated his thoughts.

'You want me to go out and get a job?'

'No, I want you to do something with your life. I think, though you're so damned close you never tell anybody anything, that you come from intelligent respectable people. You can't sit around a whorehouse for the rest of your life.'

'I don't see why not. It's what a lot of men seem to do.'

'And how long do you think you're going to be happy here?'

Niall looked at her.

'Happy? I didn't realize we were as far as happy.'

'You're being obtuse,' Bridget said. 'Go away.'

'Last time you threw me out you ran after me, crying. I'm not going anywhere, unless you want Carl to put me out, of course.'

Bridget said nothing else, she put on a robe and stormed out of the room. Niall lay there for a long time and then he got up and bathed and dressed and then he looked for her. She wasn't in the kitchen. He found her in the sitting room, drinking tea and looking very annoyed.

'If you want me to leave, Bridget, just get up and tell me that you do, only, you'll look me in the eyes when you do it and after I go out that door I won't come back no matter how much you want me to.'

She didn't answer. She didn't look at him.

'Are you bored with me?' he said. 'I'm not old enough for you. You've got somebody else?'

She fidgeted.

'I'm not bored and I won't ever have anybody else but this isn't right for you.'

She spoke in a very low voice as though each word was difficult.

'Brid, look . . .' He went and got down in front of her but she wouldn't look at him. 'I have no education, no background, no family. Who would ever take me on except in some lowly position which I don't have the temper for any more?'

'Then get a bloody book and read it,' she said and slammed out of the room.

Niall had kept his own room. He had never slept in it but that evening he went and stayed there until it was late. He had half an idea that she would come in and say that she was sorry and she didn't want him to sleep by himself and that she hadn't meant it but she didn't. The sensible part of Niall knew that she was busy and she probably hadn't had time to realize that he wasn't in her room but he had so little control over himself any more that he couldn't bear it and all he could think of was that it would serve her bloody right when she did realize that he wasn't there, so he went out.

He wasn't afraid of the night, he knew the town well and he knew the various night people but even so he carried a knife on him always just in case somebody got the wrong idea. It wasn't the knife he had brought from the home, it was a flick knife and went into his pocket easily. He hadn't ever used it but he could, so that was comforting. He walked for a long way because he didn't know what to do, he didn't take any direction in particular but he eventually reached Jesmond, the most prosperous part, where all the big houses were. The sun was coming up and, as he stood and watched, the houses came alive. First of all the maids drew back the curtains and he caught glimpses of them bustling about inside and then the man of the house left for work and the children left for school and various people came to the door and the ladies of the house stepped out to shop for the latest fashions or to go out for coffee. Families. That was what Bridget meant. It wasn't something he thought he could ever have again but the trouble was that he lingered, watching, and the hunger in him to have a home to go to was so huge that he couldn't move. He wanted more than anything in the world to be able to go up to the front door and be admitted by people who knew his name. He didn't belong in such places any more, time and brutality had taken care of it.

He walked towards the town. He didn't want to go back to Bridget, he was still too angry. He wandered about. It was mid-afternoon when he was walking along Collingwood Street, where the business people had offices. There were banks, colliery offices, insurance companies and engineers there and as he passed a certain building an old man got carefully out of a motor car while a man in uniform held open the door. Niall paused to let the man go in front of him into the building and as Niall stopped beside the door the man looked hard at him, said, 'Are you Nicholson's grandson? You're late,' and walked in.

Niall was about to walk on and then changed his mind and followed the old man into the gloom of the building. There was a lift. Niall got in it with him and was taken to the top of the building and when he got out he thought it all very fine. The walls had wood panelling and everything was ultra-clean and smelled of polish. The old gentleman, assisted by a gold-topped cane, walked slowly down the corridor and opened the door of the biggest office that Niall had ever seen. It had a great big desk in it and as the man entered, a plump woman wearing a white blouse and dark skirt, very neat-looking, came in and said, 'Mr Nicholson sends his regrets, sir, his grandson is poorly.'

She went back out again. The man regarded Niall.

'So they thought you would do. What's your name?'

'Niall McLaughlan.'

'What are you, fifteen? You're far too young. Sit down. Sit

down.' He waved Niall into a leather chair across the desk. 'What can you do?'

'Just about anything, sir.'

The old man regarded him narrowly.

'Nice suit,' he said. 'Isaac Walton's?'

'Yes, sir.'

'Waste of time buying good suits for lads your age. Your mother must have money to burn.'

That made Niall smile.

'You should be at school. Whatever is your father thinking of?'

'He's dead,' Niall said.

'I see.'

'And I wasn't much good at school.'

'You look sharp enough to me,' the old man said.

'It's not the same thing though, is it?'

'You're presentable and it'll do for this job. You can go. You come back here for eight o'clock in the morning. If you're late you're finished. I'll give you a week and then we'll see.'

Niall went back to the house. Bridget must have heard him come in because she flew into the hall.

'Wherever have you been?'

'I've been out getting a job.'

'What sort of job?'

'I don't know yet.'

He was the old man's legs. He was also the old man's hearing at meetings of all kinds. The old man was a builder. He needed somebody to carry papers and his briefcase and to go with him to sites to look at houses which needed knocking down, and to sites where people had to be moved out so that the buildings could be knocked down and new ones built, and to sites where people had to be moved out to make way for commercial buildings. It was strange but, although the old man was slow with his movements and with his speech, it seemed to Niall that he ran about all day after him, relaying messages and carrying them and telling people that Mr Lauderdale wanted this and wanted that and measuring everything. Mr Lauderdale liked to know the size of the buildings and each room within and how big the site was and there were lots of drawings of new properties which Niall would spread out on the desk.

For several months things went well until the day when Mr Lauderdale turned around and asked him where he lived. Niall didn't know what to say. The old man looked shrewdly at him and Niall thought he had deliberately waited until they were alone in his office with the door closed.

'I know now that Mr Nicholson didn't send you, Niall. I have known for quite a long time.'

It sounded very much like dismissal. Niall was sorry.

'I didn't actually say that he did.'

'You didn't say that he didn't either.'

'You wouldn't have taken me on if you hadn't thought you knew who I was.'

'And would I have taken you on if I had known who you were?'

'Never in a million years.'

Mr Lauderdale smiled. 'Is there anything else I should know?'

'I don't have a mother and I don't really have a home either.'

Mr Lauderdale fingered the lapel of Niall's jacket.

'But somebody pays for your suits. You don't buy cloth like this on the kind of wages you earn.'

Niall looked him in the eyes.

'I get kept,' he said.

Mr Lauderdale didn't say anything for so long that Niall prompted him with, 'Do you want me to leave?'

'No, but it might be an idea if you had an address.'

It was as though Bridget defined what was happening. You had to hand it to her, Niall thought, she was always several steps ahead, because that same week she suggested to him that he should move out and this time he thought she meant it.

'I will still look after you,' she said.

'I don't need you to look after me.'

'And you can come back here any time you like . . .'

'How the hell can you do this to me?' Niall said, glaring at her across the kitchen table. 'You know I have nowhere to go and nobody to go to.' When she didn't respond he got up and went upstairs and packed and then he left without seeing her.

He walked to the nearest hotel, the Crown, and booked in there, pleased that it was somewhere he couldn't afford, and lay there on the bed all night, fuming. The truth was, he thought to himself a week later, living at the brothel wasn't any good anyway because he was out all day and Bridget worked all night so that when he was in bed she was not. He blamed her for making him go out and get a job and he missed her like a grief.

Mr Lauderdale put up his wages considerably without being told that Niall was staying in a hotel, so that in fact he could afford the hotel and new suits. It was lonely and there was nothing to do in the evenings, so he began to read and when the autumn came he went to night classes, Greek, Latin, Mathematics.

That winter Bridget came to see him. It had been several months since they'd met. Dozens of times he had almost gone back but pride prevented it and she did not come to him even though she must have been aware that he was only a few streets away. She looked stunning. They met in the foyer of the hotel and she was wearing furs and her hair was golden wisps and her eyes were so blue and so calm.

'Hello, Niall,' she said.

Niall thought of all the nights sleeping alone and couldn't think of anything to say to her.

'Is there something you want?' he said.

'I just wanted to see how you were.'

'I'm fine.'

'You've grown again.'

'Are you somebody's bloody mother?'

She glanced around her in case anybody was listening.

'Do you want to come upstairs?' he said.

'Are you allowed?'

'I live here.'

He regretted asking her the moment they got there. Her eyes missed nothing. She went straight across to the books on the desk by the window.

'You are studying,' she said.

'I can swear in several languages. Would you like to hear it?'

'I know you think it was wrong of me—'

'Don't worry. Give me a little time and I'll come over on a Saturday night all dressed up like all those other bloody idiots and screw the arse off you.'

She went for him but Niall was expecting it and caught her.

'You can't reach any more,' he said.

She stopped fighting with him and he let go of her but she

said in a low voice, 'I never sleep with the customers. I never have and I never will.'

'That's all right then,' Niall said and he got hold of her and drew her into his arms and against his shoulder where she sighed and relaxed.

'I love you, Niall. I've always loved you. Please come and see me.'

'All right then,' Niall said and he kissed her.

When he let her go she looked around and she smiled on everything and said, 'I like the idea of you in business.'

She came back to him. Niall loved the feel of the fur, all soft and warm around her, and the stupid little hat that she wore, framing her face like an angel. She had leather gloves on her fingers and lipstick on her mouth. He kissed all the lipstick away.

'Come back and sleep with me,' she said.

'Are you sure you can afford the time? After all, it's not Monday . . .'

'Oh, shut up,' she said. 'You're so clever.'

'You want me clever.'

'I do, yes.'

They walked back downstairs. Niall was aware of the manager, Jonty Stevens, watching him. He was young too and that was unusual. He had the feeling that Jonty knew exactly how long he had had Bridget in his room, but Jonty didn't say anything. Niall didn't even acknowledge his presence. He put an arm around Bridget and walked her out of the hotel.

Three

Very often after that Niall spent the night with Bridget. Always on Mondays and Tuesdays and sometimes on Thursdays. The rest of the time he worked and studied. Mr Lauderdale had friends in all kinds of different businesses and he took Niall everywhere with him. Niall thought Mr Lauderdale became so used to him that he almost forgot Niall was there, he was like another limb. He never spoke out of turn, which meant that he never spoke unless spoken to, but very often Mr Lauderdale didn't have to say anything, because he was a man of habit and Niall knew what he wanted before he said it most of the time. The old man liked him, smiled on him, and Niall had to remind himself that he was nothing to Mr Lauderdale but an employee, because he found that he wanted to please the old man, to matter to him. He wanted someone to look up to. He had daydreams of Mr Lauderdale taking him home for tea but he never did, or asking him to a party at his great big house but he never did that either. He did not talk about his family but Niall knew from local gossip that he had a wife and grown-up children and grandchildren. He had people to go home to at the end of each day.

Niall made sure he went back to a hot bath, a good dinner and a bottle of wine, or part of a bottle of wine, he didn't want to end up like George. When he went to stay with Bridget she gave him champagne. He liked that best. He had no friends outside the girls and Bridget. He wanted none. People asked questions and his past did not bear other people's scrutiny. He had nothing in common with other young men. Those who came to the house were rich and careless, older than him, but they seemed younger, and he had nothing in common with boys his own age. It was as though he had not had a childhood after the age of seven but had leaped straight into adulthood.

Niall tried not to care about anybody and, because Mr Lauderdale continued to treat him as an employee, so Niall made sure he did not think too much about families. He lived for the times when he could be with Bridget. There was nothing else. But he learned a good deal. Mr Lauderdale went into shipyards, coalmining offices, steel foundries, anywhere that needed a building pulling down or putting up, he was involved in, and all Niall had to do on these occasions was to ask a question or two when Mr Lauderdale couldn't hear, and his enthusiasm got him down mines and into shipyards and iron and steel foundries where castings were made for ships. Sometimes he went back and talked to the people on Mr Lauderdale's behalf but only occasionally, because Mr Lauderdale was considered by his board too old to work and for him to delegate responsibility to anybody as young as Niall was considered reprehensible.

Niall had been working for Mr Lauderdale for more than two years when the Great War began and he was introduced to the most powerful man in the area. He was a Scotsman but had lived in Newcastle for most of his life. He was called Aulay Redpath. Mr Lauderdale asked Niall to go and see him. He had his offices in Cathedral Buildings, Dean Street, where most of the colliery offices were. He had met Aulay Redpath once before in Mr Lauderdale's office but he did not understand what he was doing here.

He thought somebody as important as Aulay Redpath would keep him waiting but he didn't. Mr Redpath was tall and slender and like his name his hair was red. Niall didn't think he was particularly scary but he had enough experience of people to know that you could never tell at first. Aulay Redpath was a self-made man and you did not get to own businesses and become rich by being stupid.

'Come in, Mr McLaughlan,' he said genially. 'Would you like some tea?'

'Thank you, sir, I would.'

Mr Redpath asked him to sit down. Niall sat and tried not to look around him. There were lots of books and a view across the buildings in the centre of the town.

'Mr Lauderdale tells me that he is about to retire and that when he does so he does not think there will be a job for you with his company. Would you like to come and work for me?'

Niall had thought that it would not be long before Mr Lauderdale decided not to work any more and he had already made up his mind what he was going to do but he was surprised and pleased to be offered a job by so eminent a man, even if it meant doing what he had done for Mr Lauderdale. It was just this side of being a lackey and Niall didn't want to do that again.

'That's very kind of you, Mr Redpath, but I'm going to go into business for myself.'

'Indeed?'

'Yes.'

'Doing what, if you don't mind me asking?'

'Doing the same thing as Lauderdale and company, only better.'

Mr Redpath laughed and then he studied the desk in front of him for a short while and then he said, 'There are a great many men in this city who are prepared to do whatever is necessary to reach the goals they choose. Buying and selling, especially buildings and land, is sometimes very dubious legally.'

'And you don't think I'm up to it.'

'I think you're very young and . . . I don't think you have any money.'

'As a matter of fact I have a regular income other than from Lauderdale.'

'So I understand.'

Niall was surprised.

'You knew?'

'This is my town, Niall. I know everything. I know that you, young as you are, have a mistress who is the most beautiful woman in Newcastle. I know that she makes a lot of money and that a good deal of it goes into your pocket. What I meant was that you don't actually have any capital. You live in Newcastle's most exclusive hotel.'

'I have to live somewhere,' Niall said.

'Other than the house which Miss Black keeps.'

'That's right.'

Aulay Redpath studied him. Niall was beginning to wish he hadn't come here.

'She likes boys?' Mr Redpath said.

Niall was starting to lose his temper.

'She doesn't like anybody very much and I should think especially not boys.'

'Then what are you to her?'

'I'm her family. Look, Mr Redpath, I don't need a job and I resent your curiosity.' Niall got up.

'It isn't curiosity. I half thought you might want to start up in business. I just wanted to make sure that I knew what you were like before I offered to loan you some capital.'

'Why should you do that?'

'You intrigue me.'

'That's very kind.'

'War creates business. It's sad but true, and people like you and I make money out of it. When it's over there's usually a slump, so be careful, and if you need help let me know.'

'Thank you.'

Mr Redpath got up and shook him by the hand and said, 'I'll put some work your way if I can. I have no loyalty to Lauderdale's now the old man's leaving. I don't like them and, let's face it, if they'd had any sense at all they would have kept you on.'

'I wouldn't have stayed.'

'They may be sorry about that in time.'

When the war ended there were a lot of people out of work but men always needed sex and they always needed buildings. Niall went into business and because he began in a very small way the money which Bridget gave him paid for what he needed as he went along. He didn't want to borrow from Mr Redpath or from anybody else, but Aulay Redpath gave him information on various buildings within the city which were coming up for sale and which either needed pulling down or selling on and that was when Niall realized he couldn't go on any further without capital. Aulay Redpath loaned him what he needed. There was interest on it but Niall found within a few months that he could buy and sell at a profit and pay Aulay Redpath what he owed and still make a good living.

Aulay had one of the big houses in Jesmond that Niall had looked so enviously upon the day that he had gone to work for Mr Lauderdale. He was married and had a daughter. He didn't talk about home to Niall when they met, which was fairly frequently for some reason. Aulay developed a habit of turning up at the small office Niall inhabited in Collingwood Street. Aulay would arrive in the middle of the day when Niall was busy and insist on going to a hotel or a pub for something to eat. They talked about work. Niall was very careful what he said and after his experiences with Mr Lauderdale did not think of Aulay as a person, just as a businessman. He was unprepared therefore when November came and Aulay said casually to him as they sat over beer in the pub nearest to Niall's office, 'I'm having a party next month. Would you like to come?'

'Thank you, that's kind but—'

'I shall be very offended if you don't come.'

'I don't go to parties, Mr Redpath.'

'I know you don't, which is all the more reason you should come to mine.'

'I don't think I'm going to fit in among your friends and I don't have any evening wear.'

'Get some and bugger my friends,' Aulay said, finishing his beer.

When Niall told Bridget she hurried him off to buy him appropriate clothing and although he tried to tell her that he was not going, that it would be dreadful, that nobody would speak to him, that he couldn't dance, that he wouldn't go, she got him into evening dress and then gazed at him through the mirror.

'My God, you look a picture,' she said.

They did look like family, Niall thought, looking at their reflections, so dark. The real reason he didn't want to go was because he couldn't take her but she wanted him to go. He wondered what it would be like dancing in a ballroom with her and was sad because it would never happen. He thought of her in a beautiful gown, so much lovelier than anyone else, and all the things she would never have. Niall turned around.

'Let's get married,' he said.

Bridget looked disconcerted.

'What on earth makes you think I want to marry you? You're far too young.'

'I'm twenty.'

'You bloody liar,' Bridget said. 'I think you make it up as you go along. The suit's perfect.'

'You're always telling me you love me.'

'That does not mean I want to marry you. Put your clothes on and I'll pay for it.' She left the room.

'I can pay for it!' Niall shouted after her.

She insisted on teaching him to dance and he had not realized that it was so complicated. They spent a week, on and off, while Gypsy played the piano, doing the polka and the waltz and all manner of other difficult dances until the day before the party, when she declared that he wouldn't disgrace himself. It was Friday. They would be busy later. He followed her up the stairs and into her bedroom.

'I was serious about getting married,' he said as he closed the door.

Bridget didn't reply.

'Brid?'

She turned from the dressing table where she had been putting on make-up.

'You're going to make me say this, aren't you? Men expect their wives to go to bed with them and I will never ever do that with anyone again and that includes you. Do you understand?'

'You run a brothel.'

'I do it for money and the girls here, they do it for money too.'

'You could have done something respectable.'

She came to him and she looked quite threatening for somebody small.

'I don't choose to be respectable.'

'But you want me to be.'

'You are.'

'No, I'm not.'

'You could be.'

'I don't see why I should be for you and I don't see why you won't marry me. I don't want to have you—'

'Niall . . .'

'I went through the same thing as you went through and I don't care about things like that any more. I don't want anybody that near but if I have to go on living on my own without you then I haven't got anything worth having. I want to be with you.'

'I think you should go back to the hotel and get changed now or you'll be late,' she said and she turned and went back to the mirror.

Niall left. He walked slowly through the cold clear night to the hotel. There were a thousand stars above and a great big full moon and everything seemed so pointless. She was all he had and he was terrified that she didn't appear to need or want him. Holding her was like holding water in your hands. If it wasn't for her he would be completely alone and he didn't think he could bear that.

There was nothing else to do but get ready and go. It was a busy night at the house on a Friday. She wouldn't even think about him. When he got to Aulay Redpath's Jesmond house he wished he hadn't gone. He didn't know anybody and everybody else seemed to know everybody and they were standing about in groups and talking and laughing and there was nobody his age. He didn't like to draw attention to himself so he stood about, feeling stupid. Aulay Redpath's house was huge and had its own ballroom. Niall didn't realize people did or had he forgotten? Had their house in Edinburgh had a ballroom? After a while a young man rather older than him came to him and said, 'Have we met? I'm Simon Anstruther. My father owns pits. What are you called?'

'Niall McLaughlan.'

'Do you know Caitlin?'

'Who?'

'The daughter. I want an introduction.' He nodded towards a young woman who was standing well back as other people danced. 'I think she's divine.'

She didn't look divine to Niall, she looked bored and out of temper and he wouldn't have approached her in a thousand years. She looked as though she would bite. She had her father's red hair and was very fashionably dressed. Bridget would have approved. Her dress was silver and white and low-waisted and her hair was short. Niall thought it was a shame to have hair that colour and wear it short. She was watching the dancers and when the music stopped half a dozen young men went to her with the idea of asking her to dance but they all went away again.

'Isn't she beautiful?' Simon Anstruther said.

'She's all right,' Niall said. He was used to beautiful women and he didn't think she was a patch on Bridget or Gypsy or any of the others. It was her sour expression.

'Her fiancé died in the war,' Simon told him. 'She had her wedding dress, the date, the church, everything. I'm going to go over and ask her to dance. Do you want to come with me?'

'What for?'

He reluctantly followed Simon but he could have told him it was a waste of time. She had the expression on her face which Gypsy had when some customer had tried to get clever and failed. The best Simon could hope for was that he and Niall would go and get a drink and call her names at a distance. However, Simon didn't seem to want his company when she had said her piece. Niall didn't hear what she said and he didn't care to. When Simon had gone she looked at him.

'Well?' she said.

Niall thought she was talking to somebody else and glanced behind him.

'Who, me?' he said.

'Yes, you. I don't dance.'

'I didn't ask you.'

'You were going to.'

'No fear. I only learned yesterday. I'm not dancing with all this lot, I'll fall over somebody.'

There was a little pause and when he looked at her she was almost smiling.

'Who are you?' she said.

'I'm Niall McLaughlan.'

'Well, Mr McLaughlan. You just earned yourself a dance.'

'Oh no,' Niall said.

She didn't mean in the ballroom, she meant in the room next door, and not the room where all the food and drink was – Niall had been looking in that direction and thinking it would be a good place to go next but she dragged him off to the room at the other side and made him do the polka in there.

'You aren't very good at it,' she said.

'I told you and at least I didn't stand on you. Now I'm going to go and get something to eat.'

'Just a minute.' She stopped him. She put her hand on his arm. Niall looked at her slender fingers. 'You're supposed to take me with you.'

'Why?'

'Because it's good manners. You offer to get me a drink and a plate of something nice.'

'Play your cards right and I'll let you come with me,' Niall said, beginning to enjoy himself. She was just like the girls at the house. He thought he might like her.

It wasn't until he had walked her through the hall and into the dining room that he noticed a hundred pairs of eyes on him. He concentrated on getting drinks – champagne, very nice – and the food, which looked quite strange to him, little bits of nothing on tiny pieces of bread and he didn't recognize any of it. And she was a bugger. She hung on to his arm and made eyes at him like it was some daft game and other people watched. He badly wanted to down the champagne in one but he didn't because they were looking. He didn't understand what Simon had been talking about. She was a nice lass, she just didn't want people slobbering all over her. You couldn't blame her for that.

They got out of the way, as far as they could. Niall examined the food on his plate.

'What in hell's name is it?' he said.

'It's caviar,' she said.

'It looks disgusting.'

'It is. Come outside.'

'Won't people think . . .'

She had already begun moving away so he followed her. The night in the garden of her house was just as clear as it had been in the centre of town. She walked well away from the house. It was bitter. Niall thought about Bridget and his heart did awful things. She really didn't want him. This girl didn't want him either or anybody else by the look of things but he was with her and the night was freezing so he did the gentlemanly thing and gave her his jacket. He glanced back. The music was wafting out of the house and in the creamy light people were dancing and talking and the women's dresses were so pretty, all different colours. It reminded him of being at home when he was little and Jean letting him go halfway down the stairs and peer through the banisters when his father had parties. That hurt even more than the fact that Bridget didn't want him. It hurt so badly he could hardly breathe. All he wanted was to go back.

'People will think I'm doing things to you out here,' he said.

'So why aren't you?' she said.

'What?' Niall looked down into Miss Redpath's green eyes, at least he thought they were green, it was so bloody dark out there he wasn't sure. He thought she was smiling.

She ran down the garden. Niall went after her. There was a tennis court to one side and there was a great big conservatory and there were lots of trees all over the place and . . . It was a home, a proper home. He had seen her mother when he came in and she looked really nice. She was called Fiona. He thought that it was a lovely name for somebody's mother. It was so soft and nice and warm. Did she read with her daughter and tell her to put on her gloves before she left the house and did she preside over meals and fuss about what people ate? If she cared very much then at any moment she would come into the garden and protest, only she didn't.

'Shouldn't we go back inside?' he said as they reached the far end of the garden and the stone wall.

'Why, are you cold? Do you want your jacket?'

'Won't your mother be concerned?'

'My mother is already concerned. All she wants is for me to marry.'

'She doesn't want you to marry me though.'

'Why not?' She was looking intently at him.

Niall didn't answer. Didn't she know what he was or didn't she care?

She said, 'I'm sure you know that the man I wanted to marry was killed at the Somme.'

'Simon told me.'

'Have you ever lost anybody?'

'Yes.'

'Then you know that I don't want anybody else but my parents are determined I shall marry.'

'They don't want you to be an old maid.'

'I suppose not.' Her eyes filled with tears. 'He was called Rob. Sometimes in the night I say his name out loud because I have nothing left and in the meanwhile my mother has stupid parties like this and expects me to dance with vapid young men.'

'Vapid ones? Oh, that's awful,' he said and she laughed through the tears.

'You're very bad,' she said. 'I'm so glad you came to the party. Do me a favour?'

'What?'

'Come inside and dance with me. It'll confuse everybody and my mother will be so pleased.'

They walked slowly back inside and there she gave him his jacket. He slipped it on.

'They're playing a waltz,' she said. 'Do you waltz?'

'Of course,' Niall said recklessly and followed her into the ballroom.

Four

That Monday morning Niall scarcely had time to settle down in his office before the door opened and Aulay Redpath strode in. He slammed the door behind him. Niall looked carefully at him. Aulay's gaze was not friendly.

'I want to talk to you,' he said. 'You abused my hospitality. You took advantage. You created a scandal.'

'I did?'

'You spent most of the evening dancing with my daughter and twice during the evening you took her out of the ballroom, once I am reliably informed into a side room and after that outside. If this was twenty years ago she'd have to bloody marry you. She never dances with anybody. She never goes outside with anybody. If you did anything to her I'll kill you.'

Niall was beginning to feel sick. It was true that he had enjoyed the party and that he had liked Caitlin Redpath but to him it was just like talking to Minna in the kitchen or Gypsy in the garden when it was a nice day. They often sat there and smoked cigarettes together and Gypsy told him funny stories about the customers. The last time she had done that, though, he felt suddenly uncomfortable, it hadn't seemed funny any more, he didn't know why – and then he did because she was wearing a thin robe and nothing else and he could see the outline of her body underneath it and he had wanted her. It was as simple as that, only it changed everything and when he thought back honestly, Bridget was right, he no longer wanted to sleep with her and not touch her, he wanted to feel her body close and to have her. But he had not wanted Caitlin. In the first place he didn't know her and in the second place she was in love with a dead man and that was very unattractive. She was bored, that was the only reason she played up to him and he was used to that. The girls at the house got bored all the time and in the old days when he was still living there he would play cards with them to pass the time and they would talk about the men.

When Gypsy had told him the stupid things men had done that last time he tried not to listen because he felt more like one of them, realizing how awful they must feel to come here and pay for what should be free and how they must know that the girls didn't really want them. He ventured to say so but she only laughed and said men were so conceited they thought the girls actually wanted them. Men were ridiculous, pathetic, vain.

Niall was hurt and offended that Aulay might think he would compromise his daughter but the truth was that he knew nothing of the rules of society because he had never been in any and didn't understand.

'When I think that I allowed you to come to my house, you of all people,' Aulay said.

Niall knew that this wasn't going to be complimentary and he made another mistake.

'Aulay—'

'Don't call me by my first name. God damn you!'

It was very quiet in the room somehow even though Aulay was shouting at him. There seemed to Niall to be great big spaces around him, the way that Aulay was shouting, and his words went into the spaces like echoes. He would have explained himself, apologized, if Aulay had given him time but he didn't. He went on being insulting and the pleasure Niall had from remembering the evening evaporated like morning mist in the valley.

'You're a guttersnipe, an adventurer. Don't come near my daughter again. If you do I'll have you bloody well dealt with.'

He slammed the door when he went out. After he had gone Niall wondered whether it meant he wanted his money back and whether he would send somebody round to demand it and whether the work which he sent so frequently would dry up and that mattered, but what mattered most of all was that he withdrew his friendship. He sent other people to deal with the work between them and Niall didn't mind that really but he regretted the loss of the friendship. When he went to see Bridget now, which he did only on Mondays these days, she very often told him that she was too busy to see him and the only other social contact Niall had were the young men at his evening classes and they seemed like children to him so he began to stay at work longer and longer hours. The hotel got used to him coming in late and would leave something for him and he found that the more he worked the more he wanted to work because there was nothing else.

The spring came and even though Niall went to the house less, Bridget refused to spend the night with him. He didn't blame her, he would have refused too on the basis that he wanted her close. One night in May, it was the first time he had seen her in six weeks, and she brushed him off with how busy she was. He decided he wouldn't go back any more. On his way out he met Gypsy in the hall.

'Niall. I haven't seen you in ages. How are you? Come and have some tea.'

He went into the kitchen. It was deserted. Even Monday nights were busy around here.

'Don't you have customers?'

'No, I'm having the night off.' She made some tea, urged him to sit down and then peered into his eyes, pulled a funny face and said, 'What's the matter?'

'Nothing.'

'Oh, how very like a man.'

'I am a man.'

'I had noticed. If I didn't know you better I'd say you were quite nice.'

'But you do know me and other men.'

'I do unfortunately.' She stretched out her legs to the nearest chair and put her feet up on it. 'You never come here any more.'

'I'm not welcome.'

'You must be the only man in Newcastle that isn't. Besides, we all love you.'

Niall stared down into his tea.

'She wanted better for you,' Gypsy said.

Very carefully he put the cup and saucer back on to the table. Gypsy looked at him. Niall couldn't look at her. The thin robe she wore concealed nothing. She looked harder at him and then she put down her own cup and saucer and said, 'Come here.'

Niall didn't move.

She got up and got hold of his arm.

'Come on,' she said.

He didn't understand where she was taking him, along the corridor past the rooms where they entertained men and up the stairs. She opened the door of her bedroom, where he had never been before. He hesitated.

'Don't stand there. Come in.'

It was as unlike the rooms downstairs as it could be. No colours, no fuss, no trimmings, just white covers and plain furnishings, all very expensive and clean-lined, and there was a little writing table and some books on the bedside table and candlesticks and a fireplace. He remembered the fireplace from when he and Bridget had looked round. What a long time ago that had been.

'You're the first man who's ever been in here and you'll probably be the last.' She came over and started to undo his tie and the buttons on his shirt.

Niall caught hold of her hands.

'What are you doing?' he said.

'What does it look as if I'm doing?'

'No,' Niall said.

She looked patiently at him.

'You think Brid's going to do this for you?'

'No, I don't.'

'You're going to go into a monastery, are you?'

'I don't want to.'

'Oh yes you do. Last time you came here you couldn't take your eyes off me.'

'No.' He wanted to tell her that he cared too much about their friendship, that he didn't want to lose her, that if she did to him what she did to other men it would be lost forever and she was far too valuable to him to lose for such a reason, but she didn't take any notice of him. She started putting her mouth and hands on him until Niall's body began to fight against his mind. She went into his nightmare. Niall closed his eyes against the misery of Mrs Mackenzie's hands and wobbly body and Mr Wilson's slimy grasp. 'No. No.' The door wouldn't hold him up and when he opened his eyes he was sitting on the floor with both hands up to his face to shut it all out. The smells of the home came back to him, the warm boiled cabbage and the three-day-old gravy and the cellar with the strong odour of rats.

Gypsy was sitting on the floor with her arms around him, crooning over him. The robe that she wore had come loose at the top and gave Niall a spectacular view of her breasts but all he could think of was Mrs Mackenzie urging his hands on to her. He had his face in against Gypsy's neck somehow and she smelled wonderful, like flowers in the rain and all sorts of other stupid things that he had almost forgotten women smelled like, all the good things like bread on their hands when they were baking and mint out of the garden when Mrs McLaughlan brought it in for when they had lamb on Sundays. There was always rain on it and she would shake it to get rid of the rain and the smell coming off it was lighter nights and brighter days and garden paths. She would gather lavender and bring it inside and the sheets smelled of it all summer and there was rosemary which she bashed with a rolling pin until the scent went oily and then into the pot with vegetables for dinner.

Somehow his lips found Gypsy's neck. She had a long neck and it tasted just as good as it smelt and then he drew back, remembering where he was and who she was.

'I can't do this.'

'Really? What are you going to do then, go home and help yourself? Waste it?'

'Shut up.'

Niall got to his feet. She got up too and as she did so the robe slipped to the ground and her body was exquisite.

'Still can't do it?' she said and her eyes and her voice were full of scorn.

'I'm not a customer. You can't play me like that.'

'Oh no? You think I'm doing this for nothing? This is five pounds worth, mister. You don't think I'm cheap, do you?'

'Five pounds? Who in the hell pays five pounds?'

'You damned well do!'

'I wouldn't pay five pounds for you if it was the last thing I was ever going to do!'

She closed the distance between them and smacked him hard round the face and Niall got hold of her, cursing. After that it wasn't a contest and he knew later that she had never intended it to be, she was so good at what she did, she was like a fly fisherman, standing in the river knowing exactly how the fish were thinking, luring them towards her and reeling them in at exactly the right time, slowly and carefully, playing them so very well. She played him beautifully. He was so angry and wanted her so much. Somehow she had let down her hair, it reached to her waist and her eyes were like black fire. He couldn't remember wanting to have anything as much as this and even though his clear reasonable mind told him what she had done it didn't stop him from continuing. Nothing could have stopped him.

Her eyes were like smiles and her hair was like a cloak between them and the rest of the world and he was so glad that she had brought him here. She had known that she would not get him into one of the other bedrooms that were bedecked with ruched velvet and tassels. How many times had they laughed at the furnishings and at the men who went there to be pleasured? She would never have got him to do this in one of those rooms but she had done it here. He didn't understand the personal triumph in it. Was he just somebody else to be laughed over?

Would she tell all the other girls when he had gone that she had 'done him'? That was what they called it, 'doing' the customer, the sex and the money somehow together. He had thought he would never want anybody, whereas in fact he was just like all the rest and she would have a good laugh over it. She would tell Bridget and Bridget would be disgusted, but then Bridget was already disgusted with him so it didn't matter. He didn't belong here, he had just proved it. He could come here like anybody else. He was not one of them any longer. Nobody would ever sit down in the kitchen with him over tea and talk carelessly and include him ever again.

'Niall?'

'You bitch. How could you do that to me?'

To his dismay tears fell down his face and worst of all he couldn't stop glaring at her through them. He flinched away from her hands and then he got up and began to put on his clothes.

'I thought we were friends.'

She shrugged. 'You're a man,' she said.

Niall tried to knock the tears away with his fingers.

'You can stay if you like.'

'What in the name of hell makes you think I want to stay with you?'

It was late, dark, but he found his clothes and she got up and lit the lamp and watched and put on a robe, a bigger one than she had had on before. It covered everything. Why the bloody hell couldn't she have worn that to begin with, he wondered? He reached into his pocket and then he handed her the money. She stared at it.

'Take it. After all, I might want to come back.'

Gypsy stared uncertainly at him.

'I didn't mean it, it was just—'

'I know what it was just. Take it. After all, I'm just another man. I'm nobody to you.'

'No. It's ridiculous.' She put her hands behind her back when he urged the money on her so he dropped it on the bed. 'Niall, please . . .'

He went. She called his name after him. He clattered down the stairs, moving past Bridget without even acknowledging her.

He walked slowly back to the hotel but it wasn't far enough away so he walked on until it was very late and even the drunks had gone home. It began to rain. He was sopping wet by the time he reached the hotel doorway for the second time and it was locked. He banged on the glass of the door and after a while Jonty Stevens came and opened it.

'Want a drink?' he offered.

Niall did. They went into the bar and he sat down and Jonty went behind the bar and found the brandy and two glasses.

He poured generously.

After the first, Jonty came out from behind the bar and they sat in big leather chairs. Niall realized that he was not used to drinking a lot but by that time it was too late and he just wanted to go on and finish the bottle. The brandy was almost as good as the sex and after a long while it was even better. He tried to imagine what both together would be like and couldn't. There were a few moments when he wanted to go back to the house and knock hell out of Gypsy and after that he decided that he wasn't going to go to bed because it was such a long way and besides there was some brandy left and as long as there was he would drink it. The world was a much better brighter place now. He could quite understand why George had taken to drink in a big way. It put everything in perspective. It took away all those awful hurts. It stopped him thinking that Bridget and Gypsy were sitting in the kitchen and Gypsy was telling Bridget how awful he was at it and how he didn't know how to do it and how stupid he was and men were in general and how pathetic they were because they couldn't think about anything but sex. They couldn't help themselves, they actually paid for it. They were ridiculous. They were idiots. They did not deserve that anybody should care about them.

Five

After that Niall worked. He didn't get drunk again and he didn't go back to the brothel and Bridget did not come to see him so he knew that Gypsy had told her. It was as though he had broken some bond which could not be repaired and he could see that he had been holding on to that bond because it was all he and Bridget had between them any more. He understood why she had talked to him so much about his age and how tall he was getting, how much older. She didn't want him to get older and have a man's needs and requirements, she wanted him forever thirteen so that he would be content to lie beside her and protect her against the dreadful things which had happened. He had been her shield, and then he had turned into the enemy. Between them she and Gypsy had turned him into the aggressor.

The trouble was that having slept with Gypsy his body tried to take over his life and the more he didn't go to women the more he wanted to, so it was only a short time later that he went to Charlton's, which was, much to Bridget's chagrin, the classiest brothel in town. He knew that the code was the same everywhere and if you wanted to be anonymous you could but his presence there was obviously too much for Mrs Charlton's equilibrium. Seeing him standing in her hall she stared. She was the opposite of Bridget, a middle-aged dark-haired woman, well built, wearing black. Niall had no doubt that a lot of men went there in the hope of sleeping against those large round breasts but he knew that like Bridget she didn't sleep with the customers.

'Mr McLaughlan,' she said.

'You know me?' Niall had been hoping to get away with it.

'Everybody knows you, bonny lad,' she said, grinning.

'I was afraid of that.'

'You don't need to be afraid. I can be discreet. I just wasn't expecting you, but it seems to me that even you would know that at Charlton's we have the most beautiful girls in the north. It's early yet and Nora is free.'

Nora Cowan was, after Gypsy, the most beautiful whore in the area. Niall had been hoping to spend the night with some girl he wouldn't remember in the morning. If he slept with Nora, Bridget and Gypsy would be bound to find out. On the other hand why shouldn't he? He wanted to wipe out the awful way that Gypsy had treated him. What better than to go to a woman she considered to be her biggest rival? Mrs Charlton led him up the stairs and along the hall and into a very big sparsely furnished room.

Although it was cold and dark the curtains were open to the night and from the window there was a wonderful view of the river. It shimmered like ribbons under a full moon and the lights from various buildings threw cream squares across the night.

It wasn't a typical whore's room, Bridget would have been surprised. There was no velvet, no gold, no red, as though Nora Cowan despised and didn't need such trappings. He heard her come in and turned around and was glad for the first time that he had come here. She was smiling. She was older than him, blonde, but not nearly as fair as Bridget. Her hair was like buttercups and she had deep blue eyes and a very curvy figure.

'Bored at Black's?' she said.

'Something like that.'

She chose carefully, or Mrs Charlton did that for her. Some nights, Bridget had told him, Nora Cowan didn't work at all because she considered the clientele beneath her. Mrs Charlton had paid him a compliment.

'I've always wondered what you were like,' she said.

'I'm just like everybody else.'

'I don't think you are. If you were you wouldn't be here with me,' she said and she went over and reached up and kissed him.

Spending the night with Nora, and it was the first of many, freed Niall. Each time he saw her he was less hurt. It was not like going with Gypsy. Nora didn't care about him, Niall didn't think she cared about anybody, but she made it easy. He saw her when he wanted to if she was available. If she wasn't available Mrs Charlton gave him another girl. Niall didn't care. Sometimes he woke up in the mornings and couldn't remember who he was with or where he was at first but it didn't matter. Sometimes he went back to the hotel. It was a simple business arrangement. He had no idea whether she even liked him. He was sure she treated everyone the same. The most comforting thing was that as far as he could judge she did not hate anyone as Bridget did, there were no prejudices, no problems. He had her and he paid her. There were no complaints, no demands and very little conversation. Nora's body was as lovely as her face. She was perfect and he could have as much of her as he wanted. He never regretted leaving her. He didn't think about her when he wasn't with her. To him this was just another appetite to be slaked. He no longer thought about Mrs Mackenzie and the dreadful nights in her bed. Nora Cowan had rid him of that by letting him control what he would do and when he would do it. There were no ghosts in the bedroom where Nora undressed for him. He paid her generously, sometimes three nights a week. It got to the point where it didn't matter which night he went, she was available for him. Niall deliberately varied the times and the nights but Nora was always free. She was always there but never waiting for him.

One night – the nights were getting lighter by then, it was almost summer and he liked to go early and spend time in Nora's bed while the sun sank and the light faded across the river – she was lying in his arms and he said to her, 'What do you do when I'm not here?'

'Nothing. I don't need to on what you pay me.'

'I'm keeping you?'

Nora moved back to look at him and it was a very straight look.

'Don't let it bother you,' she said. 'There were other men before you, sweetheart of mine, and there'll be others after you. Just enjoy it.'

Jonty was his only friend. Jonty's father had died and Jonty had to run the hotel by himself but Niall thought he made a good job of it. Sometimes they sat up late and drank and sometimes in the afternoons they played billiards but not often. Niall was always going to work and Jonty had the hotel to see to every day.

Niall did have business difficulties but he overcame them as they arrived. He gave all his energy to it and thrived. He didn't see Aulay any more. He paid back the rest of the money which he owed him and then thought Aulay might withdraw his business but he didn't. Neither did he come to Niall's office. Niall was determined not to miss him. He got on with the day-to-day running of things. He could have bought a house for himself.

He did buy houses and then sell them on, sometimes as offices, sometimes he knocked them down and built something else. He made a lot of money but he didn't spend it. Beyond Nora, his hotel bills, his tailoring and a car, there was nothing to spend it on. He worked more and more until he was so tired that he couldn't sleep or eat and the days went by and he barely knew what month it was. So it was a long time later that Aulay turned up in Niall's office.

It was August, that much he did know, the appointment had been made a week but he didn't think about it because Aulay usually sent someone else. They were not friends and Aulay did not consider him important enough for individual attention. Niall didn't care any more. He had other business acquaintances who invited him to their homes. He very rarely went and somehow the less he went the more he was invited but they expected him to dance with their daughters. That was strange, Niall thought at first, until he realized that it was because he had money. They would forgive him having no background because he had money. It made him want to go back to the hotel and talk to Jonty about things that didn't matter. He felt threatened as Newcastle society tried to gather him in. He didn't want to be a part of it so he kept out of the way.

The appointment was for ten o'clock. Niall stood up when his secretary opened the door and to his surprise Aulay Redpath stepped into the office. He was forcedly jovial, as though embarrassed, shook Niall's hand and said, 'How are you, Niall?'

'I'm very well, thank you. How are you?'

'Fine.'

'Do sit down.'

'I thought you might have moved,' Aulay said, glancing around him at Niall's modest surroundings.

'Why?'

'Well . . .' Aulay eyed him. 'You're a rich man, so they tell me.'

'I would have had to do a great deal to be rich in so short a time, don't you think?'

'It isn't that short a time,' Aulay said and then the silence fell between them. Niall didn't help him out, he sat back and waited.

Aulay sat back too.

'I have a steel foundry up on the Durham moors. There is a rival foundry, very close. The owner, Thaddeus Morgan, is old and not very well. I want you to buy it and shut it down. They know who I am, I can't do it myself. Thaddeus Morgan wouldn't sell it to me but you could do it. I'm sure you would have no difficulty in charming Mrs Morgan.'

'I didn't know you owned a steel foundry!'

'I wish I didn't. It's an encumbrance. It was a mistake, I should never have bought it.'

It was hardly a good investment, Niall guessed, especially in these lean times. Steel foundries existed mostly to feed ship-building, they made castings of various kinds for the ships, and since the war was over shipping had slumped, which meant that the foundries that supplied shipping parts had also slumped and everything related had slumped in its turn. Business was like cards supporting one another, once one went they all fell. It was a bloody stupid system. He remembered George saying that bankruptcy was a good thing in business because rather like the runt in a litter it got rid of weaklings. He had nothing against this as long as it was nothing to do with him directly. It was one of George's gems, the things he remembered his father saying. No wonder Aulay wanted the Morgan foundry closing. There was not enough work to go round.

'I'll go and have a look,' he said.

'Thank you. I'll hear from you next week? Why don't you come to the house? We're having a party next weekend.'

'No, thank you,' Niall said. 'I'll contact you at the office.'

Aulay got up, made as if to go and then hesitated.

'Are you going to make me apologize to you?'

'You have nothing to apologize for, Mr Redpath. You were very kind to me. You loaned me money when nobody else would have and you went on giving me work when you personally didn't approve of me. I'm very grateful to you.'

'You are shite!' Aulay said. 'You think I'm only bothering with you now because you're so bloody successful.'

'I didn't say anything of the kind.'

'No, you just looked down your nose at me. You're so tall, you can.'

His tone made Niall want to smile but he remembered what had happened last time and didn't.

'I'm quite happy to take on the work, Mr Redpath.'

'All right,' Aulay held up both hands. 'I give in. Don't come to the party. Make me sorry. I'm bored. I wasn't bored when you were around.'

Niall thought it had taken him a very long time to decide that, but he didn't say so. He smiled very politely and saw Aulay to the door, shook his hand and watched him leave. Then he went into the office and sat down and threw a paperweight at the door.

After this Niall was busy for several days but eventually he motored out in his Daimler. For all he had lived in Newcastle so long, he knew nothing of the Durham dales. If you had been the kind of person who cared for views and trees and neat stonewalled fields and long grey houses and lots of sheep – he had never seen so many sheep – you would have admired it, but Niall was too busy looking out for the house. He went through numerous little mining villages – they were horrible, like boils amidst the lovely countryside, worse somehow on this bright morning. Little children without shoes ran about the shabby straggly streets. The children wore ragged clothes and were dirty. There were few signs of prosperity. Down two steep hills into Weardale and along a winding track. It was indeed the very centre of nowhere, Niall thought.

Following his directions he got out of the car at the end of the long rhododendron-covered drive – why did people plant rhododendrons in such vast quantities when they only flowered for a short time in June? The rest of the year they hung there like dependents.

He left the car and made short work of the steps up to the house. He supposed it was a nice house, all honeyed stone and twiddly bits, sprawling across a lot of land just above the river. To his surprise the door opened and an old lady stood there, skinny, short, expensively dressed and smiling.

'Mr McLaughlan, I'm Alice Morgan, it was good of you to come. Thaddeus is so poorly and we need your help.'

'Not at all, Mrs Morgan,' he said.

He followed her into the house. All around there were portraits of a beautiful woman with the kind of colouring he had, blue eyes, blonde hair, pale skin.

'That was our daughter, Luisa,' Mrs Morgan said. 'She died a very long time ago.'

Families, people who belonged. He didn't care now. There was no gap, no waking in the night, wondering what he was doing. He went in to see Thaddeus Morgan. The man was not so ill that he could not get up and greet Niall enthusiastically. Niall always worried about enthusiasm. He did not run his own business ventures on it but he had no objection to watching other people closely and observing their weaknesses. Thaddeus Morgan's weakness was his love for his foundry. It was almost like a person to him, Niall thought, listening as Thaddeus talked about it. It was his whole life.

They sat down together in the drawing room with the sunlight on the river and the flowers beyond the window and Thaddeus said, 'Do you think you might want to buy the foundry?'

'I can't say until I've seen it.'

'I would be so glad to sell it to somebody who would look after it. I have a lot of men working for me. I have to think of them and their families.'

'I'm sure you do,' Niall said.

'Are you an engineer, Mr McLaughlan?'

'No, I'm just a businessman.'

'You must stay and in the morning . . .'

Niall had no intention of staying. He didn't listen. He had heard it all before. He had already booked into a good hotel in Durham by the river. He was not interested in spending the evening with old people and in there being no champagne and the food automatically dreadful. He made polite noises and left. He could have gone back to Newcastle but he didn't choose to. He wanted to think about this away from the office and all the other responsibilities. He would come back in the morning and accompany Mr Morgan to the foundry which was his life's work and which shortly Niall would demolish. He went to his hotel and it was as he had thought. His room looked out over the river, which was low because it was summer. People were boating, walking in the long evening. His room had a balcony. Niall sat outside and drank his champagne. They had good food and a big comfortable bed for him. It was all you really needed, he thought, sinking into a bath after an evening spent working on the balcony.

He slept well. Mr Morgan was to take him to the foundry that morning and he was looking forward to it. He knew the basics about such places but he had not taken an interest in any of them because he had never bought one before. He drove Mr Morgan through the little dales town, with its neat stone houses and little shops, to the far side of the river where the business lay in Sweethope, which was part of Wolsingham. Mr Morgan had owned another small foundry three miles away in the little pit village of Deerness Law but it had closed some time ago, he told Niall.

The Morgan steelworks was on a good site just above the river and Mr Morgan proudly showed him around the various shops where the different processes went on and into the buildings and across the ground. The ore came from Spain, it was brought in by railway, the coke came from the Black Prince pit three miles away up the hills over the valley at Deerness Law.

'I don't like the men that run the pit but you have to say it's the best coking coal there is,' Mr Morgan said. 'The sharp sand which we use comes from just the top of the hill from the Cleugh Sand Company. It's just a small place but they send everything on time.'

They made goods for mines, ships and railways, so there should have been plenty of work but Niall knew that there was not. It had not been modernized with new melting shops and rolling mills to develop manufacture of plate, as other steel foundries had been during the war. Nothing had been updated in the way that Niall had seen in other steelworks and it would require a great deal of money to do anything useful here now. He had never before felt so interested in anything, he couldn't work out why. He had seen the lovely red ores, the pig iron, the melting troughs, the open-hearth processes, he knew how steel was produced, but it fascinated him. He liked the way it was tapped out into ladles and into ingot moulds and how it was left to cool and solidify. The men took great care because everything had to be exactly right. One mistake could cost a man a bad injury with liquid so hot, but the temperature and the timing was crucial. The steel ran white-hot from the furnaces, glowing so fiercely that the men had to wear goggles so that they would not damage their eyes. The noise in the foundry was loud. As they walked around they had to shout. Cranes moved overhead and the dirt and dust were thick and there was sand on the floor.

The place wasn't at all like Niall had thought it would be. Mr Morgan must have been ill for a very long time and he did not notice things which were obvious to any trained observer. The manager, Ian Souter, seemed ill at ease and Niall didn't like the atmosphere. He didn't like the way the men didn't lift their heads from their tasks to see who was there and, as he walked about the pattern shop, an old man stumbled into the way and, since Mr Morgan was distracted, Mr Souter scowled and spoke roughly to him and Niall itched to knock Ian Souter down. He saw himself in the old man, if he had not had the ability to get himself out of poverty he could have been here or worse. He could have been dead. There had been a great many times in his life when loneliness and poverty had almost suffocated him. He had not realized that he cared about that happening to people he didn't know. If he bought this place and shut it down, the old man with the watery blue eyes would lose his job. They would all lose their jobs. Suddenly he wished he had not promised Aulay he would take on this task. The nasty taste in his mouth was real and had nothing to do with the excellent breakfast the hotel had provided.

Mr Souter showed Niall around and answered his questions,

not showing even by a slight smile that he thought Niall naïve. It was, Niall thought, a stupid man indeed who assumed other men knew little, but very often you could learn a great deal by seeming ignorant.

On the way here he had invented for himself a polite background just in case the Morgans asked. His parents had both died when he was small. He had an aunt. He liked this idea so much that he was sorry to think she had to leave the scene too. She had lived in Jesmond in Newcastle and had looked after him when his parents died. She had died too some time back.

Carefully now Niall let Ian Souter inform his ignorance and he watched all around him. This business would not last, it was in a bad way already. The machinery was old, the men were dispirited and Ian Souter was that worst of men, one who despised the weak, the helpless and the poor. Niall did not doubt that the standard of castings made here was bad and that the reputation of the place had already gone. Mr Morgan was too ill to see what was happening. He saw the place as it had been and he loved it. It was like watching a man stumble around in a graveyard, pausing here and there to point out dead relatives.

It was hot and dusty in the foundry and the men worked and sweated and moved about the sandy floors. They seemed incongruous to Niall in their big boots and dirty clothes, with pink perspiring faces, and he could understand how owners thought of their workers as less than real. Had it not been for the old man knocking into Ian Souter they would have seemed alien to him, for the most part silent.

They went into the offices. Niall could see by the cowed appearance of the office staff that everything was done exactly as Mr Souter wanted it, without question, without intelligence, without any other man's mind to help things along. Mr Morgan was exhausted by the tour of the works. Mr Souter ordered tea. Niall declined. It would either be so watery that it would be disgusting or so black that it nearly took the enamel off your teeth.

Niall perused the order books after Mr Souter had attempted not to show him, and there was very little work coming in. He looked at the other books, the work going out, the castings coming back because they were badly made, the numbers were wrong, they were too few or too many or the wrong kind. The books were a mess, everything was in disorder. Niall didn't like disorder. He asked whether the accountants could come in for the rest of that week to look through the books properly and Ian Souter said in a large manner, 'Certainly, Mr McLaughlan. We have nothing to hide.'

They had, Niall thought, a great deal to hide, but if they wanted to sell the place they couldn't afford to go on hiding it. A good accountant would have it all in hand within hours.

As they sat, there was some kind of fuss going on in the outer office. The inner wall was glass from waist-high and Niall could see a woman, small, badly dressed, trying all she could to get beyond the man who was trying his best and doing better than she was to keep her out. She wore a headscarf, so it was difficult to determine what age she was.

'Who is it?' Niall asked softly.

'Paddy Harper's wife,' Ian Souter said and shook his head. 'He stole. We got rid of him.'

Niall listened to Ian Souter's flat, dismissive tone and decided that he really didn't like him. Mr Morgan didn't even look at the woman.

'Why can't she come in?' Niall said.

Ian Souter gazed at him as though he was an idiot.

'She's a whore, McLaughlan,' he said. 'I assume you know what whores are.'

It was such a rude thing to say that Niall had to stop himself from smiling. He thought that Mr Souter didn't want the place sold because he was afraid for his job and it was not surprising therefore that he was unhelpful. He wanted to go on misman-aging it for as long as Mr Morgan was prepared to foot the bills. If Mr Morgan had to go on like this for the next couple of years he would end up losing everything, Niall thought.

Even Mr Morgan noticed the rudeness. 'Mr Souter—'

'No, no, I'm interested,' Niall said. 'What can she want?'

'She wants nothing. We have nothing to do with her or for her. She has six children. God knows who their fathers were.'

Niall could imagine the children, like he had been, like all the children in the home were, the feeling of constant hunger, the cold rooms . . .

'I'd like to meet her,' he said.

'Nothing can be gained by it,' Ian Souter said.

Niall held his eyes.

'Nevertheless . . .' he said and he let the word hover in the air.

Mr Morgan said nothing. He had a foundry to sell. Ian Souter gestured that the woman should be allowed to come into the office. Niall regretted his impulse almost immediately. The wom-an's gaze was so frank, so unflinching, that he had difficulty in meeting her eyes. He wanted to distance himself from the other two men so that she should not think he was like them. She had disillusioned eyes.

'Mrs Harper,' Mr Souter said. 'What can we do for you?'

'You can give my Paddy his job back and you can give me my house.'

'Your husband stole.'

'It was seven shillings,' she said.

'He broke into the offices . . .'

'We have no money and we have no house. I want my house back.'

'Houses are for the men who work here.'

'My furniture is all in that house, at least what was left of it after you had your bully boys break up our home. They put us on the street,' she told Niall. 'They haven't put anybody new in it and we have nowhere to go.'

'It's summer,' Mr Souter said helpfully.

'What are we supposed to do, eat grass? My Paddy can't get work because you told people he thieved. He doesn't thieve, not really, he didn't think it was thieving.'

Ian Souter had obviously had enough. He got up.

'You'll have to go,' he said.

'Mr Morgan, please . . .' she appealed. The old man didn't look at her.

She allowed herself to be ushered to the door and there was something hopeless about her defeat. Niall reached into his pocket and brought out the wad of notes he had stuffed into it when he left Newcastle. He had no idea how much there was but it was a lot of money. He always carried a lot of cash around with him. You never knew what you might want to buy. He had another stash in the hotel safe. He went over and took her wrist and put the whole wad into her grimy palm. She looked at it and then she stared at him. Ian Souter began protesting. Her face changed. She grinned at Niall. He smiled back at her.

'My, you're kind,' she said.

Ian Souter didn't say a word until she had gone and then he turned on Niall.

'What the hell did you think you were doing? It'll be all round the village by tea time that you gave Jemma Harper money. You don't know anything about these people. You shouldn't interfere.'

'Mr Souter . . .' Mr Morgan said tiredly.

'Seven shillings?' Niall said.

'That wasn't the point!' Mr Souter was shouting now. 'We have to set an example. They don't understand anything. They are unworldly and uneducated. We had to get rid of him. We can't condone theft.'

Niall was very angry by now but it didn't cause him to say anything or even to change his expression. He had learned to school his anger of late and employ emotions which were more useful. He hated petty moralities like this one. He got up to leave and Mr Morgan went with him.

'I'll have the accountants call tomorrow, bright and early,' Niall assured him.

When they had left the office Mr Morgan said, 'I hope that if you do decide to buy the business you will consider keeping Mr Souter on. He has been a good manager these past months while I could do nothing. Growing old is hard.'

Not as hard as dying, Niall thought, not as hard as feeling so awful that you blew your brains out, not as hard as being brought up in a children's home and mistreated. Mr Morgan had had a long life, he had lived it in a beautiful house with his wife. He had had a business that he loved and a child. Niall couldn't see what was hard about any of that.

'Having no one of your own family to take over the business . . .' Mr Morgan shook his head. 'When will you let me have your decision?'

'I'll need to have access to the offices for several days. Say next week?'

He took Mr Morgan home, sent his thanks to Mrs Morgan and drove away. He went back to his office to think.

*

On the night of Aulay Redpath's party Niall was bored. He couldn't settle. He didn't want to go to the party but he did want to talk to Aulay about the foundry. He told himself that he should wait until Monday and then he bathed and changed into evening dress and went to the party. They didn't know how lucky they were, he thought, smiling grimly at himself.

He thought as he drove that his mythical aunt had probably lived quite close to Aulay. She had been his mother's sister and called Armstrong, a good local name. Sarah Armstrong. He liked it. As he went he made up stories for himself concerning her. She was kind. She tried to teach him to play the piano. She had tucked him up in bed when he was little and read him stories. She never flogged him or threw him down the cellar steps or made him take off his clothes and get into bed with her.

His aunt had been a wonderful cook. She had been warm and kind and he had had friends to tea and there were fires in every room and he had gone to a school not far away. As he drove he looked for the school and for the places where he had played in his mythical childhood and he looked out for older women who went by and wondered if any of them looked like her. She must have been a lovely woman.

Last time he had been to Aulay's house he had admired it. This time it was the kind of place which he abhorred, very over-furnished and with every comfort, chandeliers glittering, pale green ceilings with white intricate mouldings, dark blue and green wallpapers and great big chairs with gold arms and legs. It was a monstrosity, Niall thought, striped walls and great hanging curtains everywhere and enormous mirrors with ornate gold edgings.

Music was playing in the ballroom. People were standing about in the big entrance hall, peeping over one another's shoulders and gossiping. Fiona Redpath had obviously been coached by her husband because she came straight to him, smiling and trying not to look surprised.

'Mr McLaughlan,' she said. 'How kind of you to come.'

'Mrs Redpath. Good evening. I just wanted to have a word with Aulay.'

'I shall find him for you and Caitlin will look after you. Do come into the sitting room.'

Niall, left alone with lots more golden chairs with yellow satin cushions, was not happy. He did not want to be accused of being alone with Caitlin Redpath – or had his elevation in society improved so much that her mother didn't mind now? Shortly afterwards she came in and she was smiling. Her eyes were lit.

'Niall!' she said. 'How lovely to see you. I haven't seen you in so long and I wanted to talk to you. My father behaved appallingly. He seemed to think it was a romance. I was so upset. I didn't mean to cause you trouble.'

'No trouble,' Niall said.

He thought she looked much better, much happier. She wore black, very dramatic, with silver bangles, and the black somehow brought out the creaminess of her skin, the red of her hair and the green of her eyes. A manservant came in with a tray on which were a bottle of champagne and two glasses. He poured it out and then left them.

'You look perfect. You've become somebody important. Every girl in the place knows you're here.'

'I'm not staying,' Niall said.

'Scared?'

'Very. How are you?'

She hesitated, looked down into her champagne and then back into his face and she said, 'I'm in love.'

'Who is it?'

'I can't tell you. Nobody knows. I wanted to come and see you but I knew it wasn't the right thing to do and I didn't like to, I thought after what happened that you wouldn't want to see me. I'm desperate to tell somebody about it.'

'You can come and see me any time.'

'You live in a hotel,' she said. 'People would notice.'

'Come anyway. I never get visitors.'

'What's the best time?'

'Any time. Send me a note to my office or if you prefer we could meet in the town, then nobody would know.'

'I would like to do that.'

She glanced at the door and a moment later her father came in. He looked frostily at them, said, 'Thank you, Caitlin, that will do,' and dismissed her. 'She likes you,' he said to Niall.

'She's been in here five minutes. It wasn't quite time enough for me to seduce her.'

'With your reputation, Niall, you can't afford to spend time alone with anybody's daughter.'

'My what?'

'Do you think people don't know about your association with Bridget Black? I only have one daughter. I'm not about to sacrifice her to a man like you who associates with whores and God knows what else.'

Niall put down his champagne glass on a table that was leather-topped and had golden feet.

'I'm not interested in her,' he said.

'She's interested in you. Do you know how hard we have tried to persuade her to marry someone respectable? The war has been over for four years. In that time she has gone nowhere. We have these parties because it is the only way we can move her into society. She won't go anywhere, yet when she sees you she lights up like a bloody Christmas star!'

'That's because I don't want her,' Niall said. 'And she knows it. She feels safe.'

'That's very funny,' Aulay said.

'It's true. Do you want to hear about this foundry or not?'

'I'm surprised you came here at all, which was what made me think that Caitlin was the goal.'

Niall looked hard at him.

'All right,' Aulay said. 'So how was Durham? It didn't take you long.'

'It wouldn't have taken you long either if you'd been there.'

'You mean I could have saved myself the expense of sending you?' Aulay said.

'I think you could save a great deal of money. There's no need for us to buy it. It's falling to pieces. The old man's dying, the old lady knows nothing of business and the manager is a first-rate arsehole.'

'Do they have any family?'

'Nobody, apparently. They had a daughter, they have pictures of her all over the place, but she's dead.'

Aulay poured him some more champagne and then he said, 'The trouble is, I can't afford to wait. My business is on the way down.'

'It'll be gone in a couple of years. You can take my word for it. Just be patient.'

'That's too long. I want you to buy it.'

Niall suddenly realized that he didn't want to have anything to do with Aulay's plans. He had bought and sold a great many things in the last four years but he didn't want to buy this place and shut it down. He thought he would never forget the old man's eyes or the woman who had braved the manager's office.

'It employs a hundred men,' he said. 'That's a lot in a village. Would you be able to expand your foundry and take some of them on?'

'Expand it?' Aulay stared at him. 'I want to keep it going until things pick up, if I can. It may cost me money. You know that. You've done these things before. What makes this different?'

'I don't know.'

'Developed a sentimental side all of a sudden, have you?'

'The accountant says the books are a disaster. He wouldn't touch it.'

'Would you like some more champagne?'

'No, thank you. I have to go.'

'You will buy it for me then?'

'That's my job.'

In the middle of the following week Niall was sitting in his office waiting for his ten o'clock appointment. His secretary opened the door.

'Mr Forster is here to see you, Mr McLaughlan,' she said.

Niall got up. The man she ushered inside was someone he didn't know and Niall was always keen on mysteries. He spoke politely and extended his hand and the man, who was tall and lean and fair and about forty, looked back at him from clear emerald-green eyes. Niall was slightly disconcerted. They were the most honest eyes that he had ever seen.

'Do take a seat,' he said. 'How can I help?'

Joe Forster sat down.

'I heard a rumour that you are going to buy up the Morgan steelworks and close it down.'

'Really?' Niall said.

There was something about the man which was familiar. Had they met before? He usually remembered people or their names and their business, but he didn't remember Joe Forster and it worried him slightly.

'I own the Black Prince pit at Deerness Law, three miles from Sweethope, where the steelworks are situated. I produce coking coal and I sell it to the Morgan steelworks.'

So that was where Niall had heard of him. Mr Morgan had said he didn't like the owners. Niall didn't see anything to dislike about Mr Forster but there was time yet.

'I see,' he said.

'So, are you going to buy it?'

'I don't know yet.'

'And sell it on? I know something about your business practices, Mr McLaughlan. I presume that is what you are going to do.'

Joe Forster made him sound like something that had crawled out of a hole, Niall thought.

'You can presume anything you like, Mr Forster,' he said.

Joe Forster looked down for a few moments and, when he looked up, his eyes were much more friendly.

'I didn't mean to be offensive,' he said, 'but I'm worried. The Morgan steelworks takes a lot of coke and I need the custom, you see. A great many people will be put out of work if you close it. I don't just mean the men at the works but the shop-keepers and the businesses both at Sweethope and in Deerness Law. It's a very small place. Do you know it?'

'I've been through it,' Niall said.

He had, and quickly. It was not the sort of place you would want to go through slowly. It had one very long straggly main street which went along and then down a hill and then up the other side and then along a bit more and then branched off at the top of the next hill in two directions. It had nothing whatsoever to recommend it and here was Joe Forster talking about it like enthusiasts talked about New York or Paris. It was a grubby little pit village up on the Durham moors in the middle of nowhere with nothing around it except fell as far as anybody could see. Why should anyone care?

'If you close the steelworks it will affect everything in the town and so it's important to us all, you see. I've lived there all my life and the people matter to me and so does my pit, obviously.'

'I have a buyer.'

'You would hardly be in there if you hadn't.'

'We're going into a recession, Mr Forster. There are two steel foundries in the area and very little work. If things are left as they are I predict that within three years there won't be any.'

'How do you know that?'

'Because it's my job to know it.'

Mr Forster looked down at his hands. They were working man's hands, Niall thought, and he liked him the better for it, somehow.

'Why did you call it the Black Prince?' Niall asked.

'I didn't. It was already called that.'

'And did your father have it?'

'Yes, and his father before him. We have lived upon the land there for a very long time, so long that we don't know when we lived anywhere else. Where do you come from?'

'Newcastle.' Niall wanted to smile because he had almost fallen into that.

'Don't you have any family?'

'No.'

Mr Forster nodded. 'We do hear about you,' he said. 'There aren't many people of your age with your ability and influence . . .'

Niall didn't think he wanted to know what came after that. Mr Forster was so polite, he wasn't going to tell Niall what he thought about him. The stupid thing about it was that Niall wanted to be whatever would impress Joe Forster. How ridiculous. Country ways were nothing to do with him.

'How much do you want for it?'

'What?' Niall tried to concentrate. Mr Forster was not even particularly well dressed, as though he did not concern himself with such things, as though he had more important matters on his mind. He looked distracted, and those green eyes could see everything, Niall thought.

'The Morgan steelworks. How much do you want for it?'

'You want to buy it?' Niall couldn't believe it. What would a man like this want with the steelworks? He didn't look as though he could afford to buy anything.

'Yes.'

'To keep it open?'

'Why else?'

'It's not a viable proposition.'

'I think I can decide that for myself.'

Niall was intrigued and rather pleased, excited. What kind of man bought a business that was on the way down, especially when he knew it was?

'You'd lose your shirt,' he said.

'I have another at home,' Mr Forster said, and his green eyes were suddenly warm on Niall like emeralds lying on a woman's soft neck. Niall liked him so much that he wanted to smile.

'I haven't bought the steelworks yet,' he said. 'If you want it why not go and talk to Mr Morgan about it. I'm sure that if he thought you were going to run it he'd sell it to you.'

'I can't.'

'Why not?'

Mr Forster looked regretful. Niall wondered what his life was like, whether he had a wife and a family. He looked happy. Most of the men Niall dealt with in business did not look like that. It was more than happiness, Joe Forster looked fulfilled. Whatever life had thrown at him he had dealt with, Niall thought. He had done what he should have. There was a completeness about him which many men would have envied, yet he was not rich, he lived in an awful little place and by the look of him he got his hands dirty every day down his nasty little pit.

'Because many years ago Thaddeus Morgan and I quarrelled very seriously. We were in partnership, he owned half of the pit and I owned half of the steelworks. I want to keep it open. I want things to go on.'

Niall couldn't remember when he had felt more uncomfortable. Joe Forster didn't care about personal gain, what he cared about was the village and the people and his blasted pit with the romantic name.

'Tell him I'm going to shut it down,' Niall said.

Joe Forster didn't say anything after that. He considered his work-worn hands. His mouth was tight as though he didn't want to give in but knew he didn't have a chance.

'You're working for Redpath, aren't you?' he said.

'I can't say. Why don't you go and see Mr Morgan? He's very ill. I'm sure that—'

'I did. I went several times and I sent my pit manager, Dryden Cameron, and between us we did everything we could. I told him what I thought you were going to do.'

'And he still wouldn't sell it to you?' How odd for a man to put himself first to that extent. 'I don't see what I can do.'

'Then I think that concludes this meeting,' Mr Forster said and got up. He had been sitting with his hat in his hands all this while and now he clutched it like it was vital. Niall had the strangest desire not to let him go. He didn't want Mr Forster to leave the office and it was partly because he didn't understand how somebody so well meaning and naïve could have got so far, even if his grandfather and his father had been in business before him. Niall thought he might trip over a paving stone and hurt himself. Mr Forster held his hat in his hands and his suit was so neat on him and he was so tall and lean and just nice like biscuits were nice with tea, and strawberries with cream, and cheese with wine. Niall wanted to barricade the door and not let him out. He was reminded of George dying and of nobody being there and it seemed to him somehow that after Mr Forster left the office it would be more empty than it had been before he came in.

'I'm sorry I can't help. I would have liked to be able to sell the steelworks to you. Would you like some tea before you go?'

'No, thank you.'

'I can't sell it to you.'

'You must honour your obligations.' Joe Forster's eyes shone. Why did they do that? Was he not disappointed, hurt, lost? Mr Forster, hat in hand, turned and that was the first time it struck Niall that he was fifty. He had been through a lot and lost other battles and knew that he would live to see another day. And then he turned back and looked hard at Niall and he said, 'Would you like to come to Sunday lunch?'

Niall stared. He didn't know this man and Mr Forster had nothing to gain by asking him.

'You're very kind,' he said, 'but I couldn't.'

'Oh please. I would like to see you there at my table.'

It was such an intimate thing to say and Niall couldn't bear that Mr Forster should have an empty seat at his table the following Sunday.

'Very well then. Thank you,' he said.

It was rare to get a good day up on the moors but when one came along, Joe thought with some prejudice, it beat the hell out of everything else for being wonderful. As he drove back from Newcastle he enjoyed the day, especially when he got nearer home and there was nothing to be seen but sky, land and the cleanest, purest air anyone could imagine. It was like champagne, so people said. It made you feel good just to breathe it in. He pulled the car into the yard of the Black Prince pit, which his family had owned since 1840, and gazed about him with some concern. They said it took one generation to build it, one to sit on it and one to lose it. He didn't want to lose it, it meant more to him than anything except his wife, and if he should lose it he would have nothing. He parked the car and walked into the office. Dryden Cameron, his manager, was seated at the desk in his small office with the door open and looked up as Joe came in.

'Any luck?' he said.

Joe went inside and closed the door. There were few secrets in a small business like this one but he tried his best. He sat down in the only other chair in Dryden's office. It was a rickety dining-room chair, they didn't have many visitors.

'Nothing,' he said.

'The little shit,' Dryden said. 'The jumped-up little bastard.'

'He's cleverer than you or me,' Joe said.

'I'd like ten minutes with him. I'd wring his bloody neck. If he sells the steelworks on to Redpath we'll be lucky if we last two years. Things are bad enough now.'

It wasn't just the work they did for the foundry, Joe thought. Losing that in itself couldn't bankrupt them but things were sliding fast, though he had the strange idea that if he could combine the foundry and the pit he could make it work. He had no reasonable grounds for thinking so, he just knew instinctively that he could. He must, because if he didn't, if the pit and the steelworks both closed, the area would go into a bad decline and there was no knowing where it would end.

'I asked him for a meal on Sunday.'

Dryden stared.

'You think we can talk him round?'

'No, he just looked as though he never gets a decent dinner.'

'You asked McLaughlan to spend time with us? Why?'

'I don't know. I don't think he has anybody . . .'

'Oh, for God's sake!' Dryden said, getting up. 'He lives with some bitch who sells herself . . .'

'That's not the same thing, is it?'

'Vinia will love you,' Dryden said.

He was right, Joe reflected later, when he went home. It was the middle of the evening and his wife was there before him. That was rare. She owned and ran half a dozen clothes shops, she designed the clothes herself. He was very proud of her, very proud of her achievements. They had no children and he was glad that she had found something else in her life which mattered besides him, because he knew how much she had wanted children. So had he. Dryden had had a child but he was dead. How important Tommy had been to them. He had run away to war and died. It was the greatest grief of their lives. Both he and Dryden had made plans for Tommy to run the pit. He had been a big tall dark lad, just like Dryden, and Vinia had adored him. He was the son she never had.

She came into the hall when she heard him, she was still dressed in a dark suit that she had worn for work. Her face was worried.

'How did it go?' she said.

'Very badly.'

Her shoulders went down.

'He's not much more than a boy,' she said. 'How could he do this?'

'It's what he does.'

'We know. Forcing people out of their houses so he can put up office blocks. Closing down companies where people have worked for years. Putting people on the street is what he does. What sort of person is he?'

'He's actually very nice,' Joe said. 'He does his best to hide it, of course, and be a hard man.'

Vinia looked at him.

'What?' she said.

'I asked him to come and eat with us on Sunday.'

'You didn't! Joe, why? He's not one of your usual waifs and strays. For goodness sake. He's rich and horrible and . . .'

'He's just a lad. The age Tommy would be now,' Joe faltered. He couldn't mention Tommy's name without his voice disappearing somewhere around his throat and eyes. 'He sat there all defensive and clever. Surely you wouldn't begrudge anybody a meal?'

'He's going to ruin us.'

'He's not doing it on purpose, it's not because he doesn't like us, it's just what he does for a living.'

'He's not respectable, Joe.'

'Oh well, that's all right then,' Joe said, angered. 'If he isn't respectable . . . How respectable was Dryden when he was that age?'

'If it hadn't been for you, Dryden would never have got anywhere.'

'Precisely,' Joe said.

It was August and the fell beyond Deerness Law was like a vast sea. There was something about it so pure and so clean that Niall stopped the car in the middle of it, drew over to one side and gazed away down the valley at the full sweep of land, the odd grey stone house like a doll's house in the distance and the sky without a single cloud to spoil it. Birds flew low. Beside the road, sheep, shorn and skinny, ignored his car except when their offspring had ventured too close. Niall slowed down when this occurred. It was a hot day and he was already regretting having said he would come here.

Mr Forster had given him directions and Niall did not miss Stanley House. It was not difficult to find. It stood alone upon the fell, a wide shabby stone building. It was big and square and had around it walls which were falling down and must have done very little to keep out the kind of weather which masqueraded as seasons up here. He liked it the minute he saw it. Nobody had tried to update it since however many years ago some idiot had put a Palladian house up here where there was nothing but farms. It had a kind of laughable dignity, all fussy and ornate, with a garden of sorts and nothing else to stop the wind and the rain and the hail and the snow. On the fell no tree stood, no bush existed. There was nothing but gorse, low, dense and crouching. There was not another building in sight, nothing but the horizon and the sky and Niall thought that it would have taken a far more sophisticated man than he was not to be awed by such resolution, stubbornness and sheer bloody-mindedness. Nothing but those qualities would have made any man stay here.

You would not have mistaken it for a rich man's house. Was Mr Forster modest then? Niall liked that somehow. He liked also the way that Mr Forster came to the door himself and showed him in and introduced him to his wife and his pit manager. His wife was a pretty woman, dark and with the kind of figure which men like – generous breasts, a small waist, neat hips. She was, like him, open and smiling. Mr Cameron, the pit manager, was dark like a gypsy.

They had dinner in a room where the French windows opened to the garden and allowed in what breeze there was. It was a good dinner, one of the best Niall had ever had – beef and raw onions and pints of gravy and at least half a dozen vegetables slick with butter and Yorkshire puddings like golden clouds and good red wine and then a cold trifle with thick cream, then cheese, four different kinds with yellow butter and brown biscuits and lots of coffee.

The house was full of books. He imagined it in the winter with the wind howling around it, lamps glowing. There were thick carpets and doors in sturdy oak to keep out intruders and beyond the windows and the garden the fell went on for miles and miles, uninterrupted.

Mrs Forster asked him whether he had any family and Niall was inclined to tell her a new story which he had just thought up about how his Auntie Sarah used to come and watch him play cricket at the ground in Jesmond. He actually hated games but he couldn't tell her that either. All she said was did he have any family and all Niall said was no, he didn't, and she said,

'Nobody at all?' so that Niall was almost prompted to say, 'Well, as a matter of fact the woman I love runs a brothel and she's the nearest thing to family I have,' but of course he couldn't and other than saying that he remembered his father and not his mother and inviting further curious questions he couldn't think of anything so he didn't say anything and Mrs Forster took the hint and let it pass. She was probably wondering what the hell her husband had invited him here for.

After they had eaten, Niall went out into the garden. Mrs Forster followed him there, saying, 'I try to keep it right but nothing much grows up here. It's too wild and there's nothing to stop the wind. You've chosen a good day to visit. It's rarely as calm as this.'

'You don't have any children, Mrs Forster?'

There was a pause before she said, 'No. No, we don't.' She looked away as though the fell would give her answers and a little bit of hair escaped from where it was drawn back from her face, each strand perfect. The escaping curl nodded about her pretty face. 'Do you really live in Newcastle's best hotel?' she said.

'Is it the best? Jonty will be so pleased when I tell him.'

'Who's that?'

'Jonty Stevens. He manages it himself.'

'How long have you lived there?'

'Years.'

'Do you remember your parents?'

'Not my mother.'

'But your father? He was Scottish?'

Niall was surprised at her perception, or was his accent slipping?

'What makes you say that?'

'I can hear the slight intonation in your speech. We hear stories about you.'

She was looking straight at him.

'How you came out of the gutter and made a fortune by the time you were twenty.'

'It wasn't a fortune,' Niall said.

'But it must be. You live in a top hotel, you drive a gorgeous car and your suit was made by an expert. I should know, being a dressmaker myself.'

Niall wondered what else she knew about him and how soon he could get out of here.

'Are you going to close Mr Morgan's steelworks?'

Her eyes were so frank, so direct, that Niall didn't know where to look.

'I don't know yet.'

'But you wouldn't sell it to Joe? He would keep it open.'

'That would be foolish,' Niall said before he could stop himself.

Vinia Forster drew back slightly and Niall wondered what it was like to have parents. Did they always think they knew better than you did just because they were older? She answered him softly however.

'Why?'

'Because there is a recession coming and there won't be the work to keep it open.'

'And the Redpath steelworks?'

'That's not my problem.'

There was a short silence during which Vinia took to looking out at the garden again. Niall considered what she would be like as a mother. He liked her house, he thought she was very organized and the atmosphere she created was safe, secure, comfortable, almost luxurious, everything a man could want. Then she said abruptly, 'If the Morgan steelworks closes we may lose everything,' and Niall was so incensed that without thinking he said, 'Mrs Forster, you have no idea what it's like to lose everything.'

She didn't answer but she looked at him so he went on and tried to disperse the excess of feeling in business sense.

'It's only a question of time before one of the steelworks goes, and Aulay Redpath is a clever, prosperous man. He can afford to pour money and resources into his works if he chooses. Closing one may save the other and the pit.'

'Aulay Redpath is a bad master,' she said.

'So is Morgan.'

'Joe wouldn't be. He's a good man.'

Her dark earnest eyes once again made Niall say something that normally he wouldn't have said.

'He's lucky then. Most men have to compromise their principles in order to go forward.'

'You've certainly compromised yours,' she said.

'I didn't have any,' Niall said.

Vinia Forster held his gaze.

'So I believe,' she said.

And then, just when Niall was about to make polite noises and leave, she faltered and said, 'Oh, Niall, now you're insulted and I made chocolate cake for you.'

Niall's temper melted like snow in sunshine. Her and her blasted cake. The last time anybody had made cake for him he had been seven. His mind gave him up to the house on the fell and parents and what it was like to have Sunday dinner every week with a woman like this who loved you.

'I ought to go,' was all he could manage.

'Joe would be so hurt. Stay here while I make the tea, or better still come inside and help me.'

Niall followed her in, drank the tea, ate the cake, and all the way home he thought about the agreement he had made with Aulay and wished it was different. He also wished he hadn't gone to Joe Forster's house. It was unlike him to become involved personally and it was not a good idea.

The following day he received a note from Caitlin Redpath to ask if he would spare her an hour on the Tuesday. She would meet him at Pumphreys Coffee Shop in the Cloth Market. So much for discretion, Niall thought, but he went because he liked her so much, taking the stairs up past the roasting department to the coffee rooms above. It was full of ladies who had nothing better to do. She was already there, sitting smiling at him, and since neither of them was inconspicuous he thought it would be all over Newcastle by the next day.

'I thought this was supposed to be a secret,' he said as he sat down amidst the wonderful smell and the hum of gossip.

'I decided that since we had nothing to hide this was a better idea. People will hardly think anything is going on if we meet here.'

'It's one view,' Niall allowed. 'Why are you smiling like an idiot?'

'I'm in love,' she said. 'I told you.'

'Really? Who with?'

'Nobody you know.'

They ordered coffee.

'I'm bursting to tell somebody all about it. I've nobody to confide in. You have nothing better to do on a Tuesday morning, have you?' It was almost an apology. Niall smiled at her.

'I work enough,' he said. 'Tell me all about it.'

She did. He wished she hadn't, though somehow he had known that it was disaster in waiting. She was not the kind of biddable girl who would fall in love with somebody suitable, she had already proved that. She was awkward, difficult. Aulay as much as said so, that he despaired of finding her a husband, somebody she would agree to marry. He drank his coffee and listened to her and tried to think of something positive to say.

'He's called Arthur Peterson. He's a librarian at the local branch.'

Her father would not let her marry a librarian in a million years, Niall thought. Was that why she had chosen him?

'He's good and kind and he loves me and we spend hours talking about books.'

'Has he asked you to marry him?'

'I wouldn't be telling you otherwise, would I?'

To Niall's dismay she fished around her neck and brought out a ring on a chain. It was not an expensive ring, a pearl, but she was so proud of it that he told her it was lovely.

'We're unofficially engaged.'

'And when are you going to tell your father?'

Her face changed, closed up.

'I can't tell him.'

'You can't get married until you do.'

'Yes, I can. I can run away with Arthur.'

'You can't run very far if he's the librarian at the local branch. Your father would break his neck.'

'He could leave his job . . .'

'And what are you going to live on?'

'Must you be so practical?' she whispered furiously and Niall could see the tears start into her eyes.

'Caitlin,' he said. 'You're not used to living badly. You're used to everything of the best . . .'

'I don't have to have the best.'

'Being poor is very uncomfortable. Your father is the most powerful man in Newcastle. Do you really think he would let you marry a man who has no prospects?'

'He's the first person I've cared about since Rob. What am I going to do?'

Niall finished his coffee and thought that he knew now why he didn't normally have a social life. It got in the way. He had got himself into two messes this week already and it was only Tuesday.

'I have nobody to talk to, nobody to help.'

'Don't cry here. Everybody will look.'

He paid for the coffee and they left. They walked slowly down Grainger Street. Caitlin put her hand through his arm.

'Have you talked to Arthur about it?' Niall said.

'He wants to keep it a secret for now but I don't see what's to be gained by it.'

'Quite a bit, I would think. Your father would go completely berserk for one thing.'

'You think he would?'

'You know he would, that's why you're not telling him.'

'I want to be Arthur's wife. He seems happy to go on like this with little secret meetings and kisses but I want to be married and have a house of my own and a child.'

'Then you're going to have to be honest, aren't you, and take the consequences.'

She stopped.

'I think he wants me to marry Simon Anstruther. He keeps mentioning him and the Anstruthers come to our parties and he tries to persuade me to go to theirs. I had to pretend to be ill last time. Come to the house at the weekend, Niall, will you?'

'You want me there when you tell him? Wonderful!' Niall said.

'Oh, please.'

'He thinks I have an ulterior motive.'

'He won't after I tell him.'

'I'm busy all week.'

'Try.'

'I will see what I can do,' Niall promised. He was only glad when she went off to get her tram. How on earth had she got herself into such a mess and why should he get involved? He thought in a way she did it to get back at her father because Aulay would have her marry respectably and Arthur Peterson hardly fell into that category.

Niall had more pressing matters to attend to. The following day he motored back out to the Durham moors and made Thaddeus Morgan what Mr Morgan would think was a generous offer for the foundry, which would in fact make Niall a healthy profit when he sold the business on to Aulay. Thaddeus Morgan accepted. He did not ask whether Niall would keep the works open, he assumed it, he talked about how pleased he was that somebody young would be taking over and what a good thing it would be for the town and for the little villages around it. Perhaps he was so ill that he no longer cared to probe deeply into other men's motives. Niall had the papers with him and Thaddeus Morgan signed them.

The steelworks had cost Niall a lot of the money he had, so he was surprised at himself when, instead of going directly back to Newcastle to see Aulay as he had planned, he motored across the river and brought his car to a halt outside the steelworks itself. He sat there for a few minutes. He had thought that the effect the steelworks had on him the first time he saw it was just an illusion but he could see now that it wasn't so. It mattered to him. He didn't understand how and why there was a great longing inside him to have it for his own. He had never wanted anything in his life so much as he wanted this.

It looked to him like a living thing, not just for the men but for itself. Somehow within it there was a heart, sound and movement, hot and cold, the wind whistling through the open doors in winter, snow trodden in on the men's feet to melt on the floor, and now the warm breezes of summer no doubt thankfully received by the men as they went about their sweaty tasks.

Niall left his car just beyond the big gates and walked the dusty road through the untidy entrance and up the path which led to the offices. Nobody moved when he got there, none of the clerks said anything, but he was quite certain that it was all around the town by now that he was the man who was going to put them out of a job. Then one young man got up, came over and said, 'Can I help you, sir?'

'I'm Niall McLaughlan. I'd like to see Mr Souter.'

The clerk led the way.

'What's your name?' Niall asked him.

The young man stopped and looked at him. They were about the same age.

'Silverton, sir, Angus.'

'Don't go far, Mr Silverton. I'm going to be needing you.'

Angus Silverton opened the door of Mr Souter's office and Ian Souter got to his feet.

'Don't you knock?'

'Not any more,' Niall said. 'I'm taking over.'

'I resent your intrusion.'

'You're going to resent me a bloody sight more soon,' Niall said. 'You're sacked. Get out.'

'You can't do that.'

'I just did. I'll send you six months wages.'

'You can't run this place without me. You don't know anything. Even the short time before you shut it—'

'Get out!' Niall said.

After he had gone Niall looked around the office. It was neat in the way that offices shouldn't be, he thought, the neatness of an idle mind, as though nothing was ever done which was not very necessary. It was a good site for any office, it looked out over the entrances to the various shops where the work was done and you had a clear view of the men going in and out and the general running of the place. He opened the door and shouted Silverton's name down the corridor and moments later the young man scuttled in.

'There's no need to hurry.'

'No, sir.'

'And don't call me sir. Do you know Paddy Harper?'

'Yes, sir. I mean . . . yes, I do.'

'Is he any good?'

Angus Silverton looked startled at the questions.

'He was one of the best moulders we had.'

'Have him found and ask him if he would come here and see me. I want some tea, Mr Silverton, not so that the spoon stands up in it like your mother probably makes, nor so that the milk turns it pale. With just a touch of milk. I want a list of the names of the best men in the various shops. I'm going to look round. I'll be half an hour.'

Niall left the office. Everywhere he went the men stared and muttered. He didn't blame them. He wanted to stare and mutter himself. By now he should have been back in Newcastle. He had an appointment at Aulay Redpath's Newcastle office in about ten minutes. He knew that he was imagining it but he felt as though the place was lighter already for Mr Souter's departure. He knew that the news would be all round the works soon.

When he went back to the office his tea appeared and soon afterwards Mr Silverton ushered Paddy Harper into the office.

'Would you like some tea, Mr Harper?'

'No, thank you.'

'Sit down, do.'

The man, thin, small, stubble-faced, poorly dressed, sat down.

'Mr Souter is no longer with us, as I'm sure you're aware. Would you like your job back?'

Mr Harper stared from blank eyes.

'I understand you're about to shut the place,' he said. 'What's the point of giving a man his job when you're closing it down?'

'When I'm closing it down, Mr Harper, you'll be the first to hear about it. Do you want a job?'

Mr Harper's face changed. It didn't exactly lighten but almost.

'Yes, I do,' he said.

'And your house, which I understand is empty.'

'Thank you,' Mr Harper said, getting up.

'You can start next week. You can have your house back now. Mr Silverton will give you the keys. And, Mr Harper . . .' Niall waited until they were looking straight at each other. 'You take a grain of sand out of here that isn't yours and I'll cut your balls off.'

It was late evening by the time Niall got back to Newcastle. He was not very surprised to discover Aulay Redpath seated in the foyer of the Crown Hotel.

'Aulay, my apologies,' he said. 'I couldn't get away. Have you eaten?'

'It's ten o'clock, Niall, everybody's eaten.'

'I haven't,' Niall said, leading the way into the bar. 'Whisky?'

'Where is my contract?'

'Two large whiskies, Mr Kenton,' Niall said to the man behind the bar. He liked this bar, it was shining brass and there were clean glasses through which the lights in the bar gleamed and it was quiet, thickly carpeted and well staffed. 'And will you get somebody to make me a sandwich? Beef would be nice if you could manage it. Aulay, did you want a sandwich?'

'What the hell is going on?' Aulay said as Mr Kenton disappeared round the back of the bar.

Niall could hardly move for tiredness but he thought he had never spent a day as enjoyably. He had gathered all the men and told them that he was not going to close the works and then he went back to the offices and called in Mr Silverton and asked him to explain who they dealt with and all about the orders coming in and going out and a good many other things, most of which he had now forgotten. It was hard pretending that you knew what you were doing when most of it was incomprehensible.

They sat down by the window. All Niall wanted to do was drink his whisky and eat his sandwich and stare out at the evening sky and think about what he had done without interruption, but that wasn't going to happen, he could see. When Aulay sat down Niall said, 'I'm not going to sell it to you.'

Aulay let go of his breath.

'I knew when you didn't turn up to the meeting that something was the matter. You've never done that before. I don't understand what you're doing. What's going on?'

'I know. I'm sorry. I did intend coming back a lot sooner than this.' It had been such a long time since that morning. When had he made the decision not to sell the works to Aulay? He didn't remember making it, yet subconsciously he must have, because he had not come back, he had stayed and tried to move things on. Somehow the steelworks had become vitally important, something he could not do without. 'There were a couple of things I had to do first.'

'Like what?'

'Oh, I don't know.' Niall sat back in his chair.

Aulay was watching him carefully, like a man playing poker who has no idea what his opponent is doing.

'You'd had a better offer? That sanctimonious bastard, Joe Forster?'

'How do you know about Mr Forster wanting the works?'

'He's been sniffing around for months. What the hell does he want with a steelworks? He doesn't know his arse from his bloody elbow. You can't sell it to him.'

'I'm not going to,' Niall said, swallowing the whisky, and that was when he realized that he was not going to sell the steelworks to anybody, he was going to make it a viable proposition, no matter what it took.

'How much has he offered you?'

Niall shook his head.

'I'll better whatever it is,' Aulay said.

'It's not for sale.'

Aulay stared at him.

'Not for sale? Then what are you going to do?'

'I'm going to run it.'

Aulay started to laugh and then stopped.

'You've lost your mind. What the hell do you know about making steel?'

'Not much, though I do know more than I did this morning. It's a product. There's a demand. If it's good enough and the price is right people buy it.'

'But the demand is going down.'

'Yes, I know.'

Aulay sighed. Mr Kenton came with Niall's sandwich, very big, thick with beef and lots of horseradish, just the way Niall liked it. He attacked the sandwich, asked Mr Kenton for more drinks. Aulay sat for a long time and said nothing and Niall was aware of having upset him. He knew very well that taking on the other steelworks would be making a rival and possibly an enemy out of Aulay Redpath and he didn't want to do that. If he could have, he would have explained what that day had felt like, how drawn he had been to the place, how much he had wanted to put the light back into Paddy Harper's face. He had seen the look on the other men's faces when he had gathered them together and told them that he would do his best to keep the place open. He would not forget quickly the way that they had looked at him and at one another and how the old man in the pattern shop with the watery blue eyes had smiled. Niall only wished he could have been there when Paddy Harper went and told his wife that he had been given back both his job and his house.

Aulay finished his first drink and began on his second the moment Mr Kenton brought it and Niall considered what it would be like without Aulay, like it had been before, and he wondered whether it was going to be too late and he was going to be too tired to go to the house and sleep with Bridget. He needed her arms around him. He needed her kisses. He didn't want a whore, he wanted somebody who cared about him to take him into her arms and tell him that everything would be all right in the morning, even though it wouldn't.

'You've lost your mind,' Aulay said. 'You're completely bloody mad. You'll go down and take that place with you.'

'It was going anyway and, as for the money, I can't say I care.'

Aulay shook his head and they sat in silence for a long time, so that Niall could hear the hotel staff talking in the room behind the bar, not what they were saying but the sounds of their voices.

'There's something else I have to say to you before I go,' Aulay said. 'Stay away from my daughter. You create a scandal every time you breathe out and you had no more sense than to take her to one of the best coffee shops in the town so that everybody knew. She is not for the likes of you. I want her married to a gentleman.'

'I don't want to marry her.'

'She has this thing about you. Why is that? Why does she not like any of the other men she is introduced to? I mean, I can see that women like all that . . . that golden hair and blue eyes bit but really, what are you?'

'You hate what I am, don't you?'

Aulay didn't answer that and Niall could hardly breathe. He didn't want to lose Aulay's friendship a second time but he could see that he and the circumstances had made it impossible. Aulay turned cold eyes on him.

'You're just like I was,' he said. 'I dragged myself up out of nothing and pretended to the world that I was somebody until I became somebody, but I don't want Caitlin involved anywhere in your sordid little life.'

'You invited me to your house.'

'Don't think I'm not sorry. I didn't realize my daughter was going to defrost before my eyes for you.'

'She hasn't. Really, she doesn't like me that way.'

'Do you know, Niall, you are so charming it's quite disgusting,' Aulay said and he put down his glass and got up and walked away.

Six

Every day that week Niall was there by six and worked until midnight, so by early Saturday afternoon he was exhausted. He drove back to Newcastle, went back to the hotel and to bed early and slept very late into the next day. It was mid-afternoon by the time he came downstairs to a meal that was both breakfast and lunch and he was just thinking that he ought to do some paperwork when Jonty came into the lounge.

'There's a lady to see you. Miss Redpath?'

Niall groaned. He had forgotten about Caitlin and when Jonty saw her into the room he got up, glad that it was empty, and said, 'I'm sorry. It went from my mind completely but your father and I had a disagreement in the middle of the week so—'

'I know,' she said. 'I shouldn't have asked you. It wasn't fair.'

She was pale. Niall sat her down and ordered some tea and did not point out to her that she should not have come to his hotel when her father was so angry about their friendship. There were people around who knew them both and he had already told Aulay that there was nothing in it. How could Aulay believe he meant only friendship when they were meeting all the time? He tried to think what to do as she drank her tea and he decided that things couldn't be any worse between himself and Aulay, so what had they to lose by Niall going back to the house with her and talking to him. It was too much to suppose that Aulay would be glad she was seeing a librarian rather than himself but at least it would clear up that part of their disagreement. He didn't want to be involved but she seemed to have no friends, nobody who could help her with this, and he had the feeling that if somebody didn't help her she would run away.

'Your father doesn't like me,' he said to her.

'You're wrong, he admires you very much. He's just upset that you've gone against him and you can't blame him for that, can you?'

'I don't think it's going to help your cause much but I'm willing to try if you want me to.'

They drove to the house. Niall could not help wishing it had been a lot further away. He didn't want to see Aulay again, he felt as though he had let him down in a dozen different ways after Aulay had helped him so much in the beginning and he regretted the loss of Aulay's affection because he did think that Aulay had cared about him or he would not have gone so far as to help so much or been so offended when Niall crossed him.

Aulay and Fiona were sitting under the trees in the garden. The fruit was almost ripe, small hard apples swayed in the slight breeze and there were plums in their hundreds through the branches. It reminded Niall of Mrs McLaughlan's jam, the rows of clean warm jam jars which had been washed and then left in the bottom oven to dry completely, the big preserving pans on the stove, the sweet smell of the sugar as it boiled with the fruit and the way that she cut out rounds of pretty material to put over the tops of the jars. Niall had helped her to write out the labels, sitting at the big pine kitchen table, watching her pour the thick red jam into the jars and when they cooled he would stick the labels on. He was sure that Fiona did something similar.

Didn't every good housewife? She got up and kissed him but she looked ruefully at him.

'We didn't expect you. Do come and sit down.'

'Don't ask him to sit down, Fi, he's not stopping,' Aulay said. His wife looked at him.

'Please try to be polite.'

'How can I be polite when he's trying to seduce my daughter?'

'Aulay!' she said.

Aulay eyed Caitlin.

'That's where you've been all afternoon, isn't it, with him? My God, people must be loving it. If you've come to ask for her hand, no, you cannot have it,' he said, glowering at Niall.

'I haven't.'

'Then what do you want?'

'He doesn't want anything,' Caitlin said. 'It's just that I've got something to tell you and I wanted somebody there who'd be on my side.'

It was late afternoon. The shadows were lengthening and the cook was baking biscuits or cake in the kitchen, Niall could smell the sweet warmth. He wondered what kind of cake it was, not rich fruitcake, because you ate that in the winter. Maybe it was a sponge cake filled with jam. The kitchen windows were open to the heat and filled the air with afternoon tea. He wished they were friends and Fiona would ask him to stay and she would bring out the cake with icing sugar all over it and cut into it with a deep knife and there would be cups and saucers and plates and a matching teapot and they would talk about things that didn't matter.

Caitlin started up about Arthur and he watched their faces. Aulay's was already closed and it became dark and his eyes were angry, while her mother's face went quite pink with embarrassment and shame. What had they wanted for her that was so important and not her happiness? Or did they think, as parents, that the kind of happiness she had found would not last, would bring disgrace on them or . . . To their credit they didn't interrupt. He had imagined Aulay's ready temper erupting and that he would get up and shout and accuse her of deceiving them and that Fiona might weep, but it was as though they had no illusions and he should not have been surprised, because they had done everything they could to establish her in a creditable marriage and she would have none of it.

As the tale unfolded Aulay gazed across the garden as though he had half expected his daughter was about to present him with a fait accompli. Had he thought she was already married or that she was pregnant? Perhaps he had. Perhaps he no longer expected anything of her or hoped that she would marry to please him. Perhaps he had never thought it. Whatever, if Caitlin had been expecting a satisfying show of parental power she was denied it. Instead, as the shadows began to lengthen across the lawn, her father said to her, 'A librarian. How wonderful. I suppose it was all we could hope for. After all, a man like that is bound to be more attractive than a clever, successful, prosperous man such as the ones we know. And this is what you want, to live in a tiny house in a street with a lot of ignorant unambitious people and never meet anyone interesting again? How very boring.'

In a way, Niall thought, that was worse than somebody shouting at you.

'And did you know?' Aulay had turned his attention to Niall.

'No, he didn't,' she said.

'I think Niall can answer for himself. Oh, I understand. This was the nature of the meeting in the coffee shop and here was me thinking you had no time except for business. Affairs of the heart, Niall, how very amusing.' He got up and looked at Caitlin. 'If you must, then bring the librarian to see us, but I will tell you this now. I have no intention of giving a single penny of my fortune to a man like that. I will not pay for the wedding, I will not buy you a house. I will take great care to ensure that you live the lifestyle you have chosen and, however many grubby brats you bring into this world, not one of them will see anything of what is mine,' and Aulay walked away across the lawn and beyond the fruit trees towards the house and went inside.

Her mother's face was scarlet. She smiled awkwardly at Niall.

'His being poor doesn't stop him from being a nice man,' Niall said, feeling he had to contribute something positive.

'No, of course not,' she said and she laid a hand on Niall's arm for a second before she went off into the house after her husband.

Caitlin gazed after them.

'I should think the thing to do is to bring Arthur here to meet them. Once they see him they might change their minds.'

'I'm sure they would,' she said. 'I didn't want to upset them. I did try to fall in love with Simon Anstruther but he's so . . . tedious. He can't talk about books.'

Niall didn't like to tell her that most men couldn't, that he couldn't unless she happened to like classical works which nobody knew anything about. Arthur definitely had the edge on other men. Niall imagined him talking to old ladies at the library. They probably adored him.

'He doesn't want to come here,' she said. 'I'll have to go and see him, except that my mother will watch my every move.'

'I can go and see him if you like.'

'Would you? I think he would like that.'

Niall couldn't imagine why but he promised that he would and then thought he should get back to his paperwork. It was much easier than dealing with people. He left without going near the house but when he turned the corner he could see Aulay leaning against the car.

'My apologies, Niall,' he said. 'You weren't the worst thing that could happen to my daughter.'

'There's no reason why he shouldn't turn out to be very nice.'

Aulay looked sharply at him.

'You're not one of these people who think people are better because they're poor, are you? What did you say to her?'

'I said I would go and see him and then you might meet and like him.'

Aulay laughed.

'I hope you're this naïve at your foundry,' he said.

Inside the library it was gloomy and quiet. Niall didn't understand why libraries were like that. It must discourage most people from going there. You were not supposed to talk, like in church, so when did Arthur get the chance to talk to the old ladies or anybody else about books? Not here. The silence was as thick as ice and the high windows did not give light where it was needed most, and women who you would not want to lay in a month of Sundays, with their sour expressions and tight lips, presided behind the desk as though it was the only power they had. Why on earth would anybody want to work in such a place?

Surely when Arthur Peterson knew that a man like Aulay Redpath was willing to help he would be persuaded into a better place and have the talent to deserve it. Niall went to the desk and enquired of the young lady if Mr Peterson was there, only to be told that he had just missed him. If he hurried he might catch him. She described the man. Niall couldn't hurry much but he thought he caught sight of Mr Peterson's bowler hat as he turned the corner opposite the library. Niall kept him in view but couldn't manage to reach him. The streets were crowded. Mr Peterson caught a tram not far away and Niall got on it but it was packed and he couldn't get near him. When Mr Peterson got off he got off too but when he had a chance to catch up with him and speak to him he didn't.

He followed down the increasingly narrow streets. When Mr Peterson halted outside the door of a small terraced house, Niall saw the door open immediately as though someone had been listening for him and, instead of a sister or a mother, there stood in the doorway a young woman with a small child in her arms. She hugged him as though she had waited a long time. When he had spoken to her and gone inside, Niall stood against the wall at the end of the street unable to believe what he had seen. He knocked on the door of the house two doors away and enquired for Mr Peterson and the smiling woman who came to the door told him that Mr and Mrs Peterson lived two doors away at number twelve and Niall said he was sorry he had bothered her and she said that they had recently had a baby and that Mr Peterson often came home early to be with his family and wasn't it nice?

Niall made his way back to Jesmond as slowly as he could. It was early evening. The maid answered the door and when Fiona heard his voice she came into the hall and when she saw him she faltered.

'Aulay isn't at home,' she said.

'It's Caitlin I've come to see.'

She ushered him into the drawing room. The dark blue and

green curtains had been pulled across the big wide windows until the sunlight was almost closed out. No doubt she needed to protect her furniture but it gave a gloomy look to everything. They had so little sunshine, Niall thought savagely, why close it out for the sake of the bloody furniture? Fiona did not summon her daughter, she came in and closed the door and looked at him and it was not a warm look.

'I'm beginning to think you've made it up about this librarian and you have other motives.'

'I wish I had,' he said.

'What do you mean?'

'He's married. I followed him home. Caitlin asked me to go and talk to him, to persuade him to meet you. He has a wife and child. I saw them and I asked at the neighbours' just to make sure.'

Fiona stared, not at anything, just with shock, and then she put her hands up to her face.

'You can't tell Caitlin that,' she said.

'What else can I tell her? If you don't let her marry him I'm sure she'll run away and if she runs to him and he won't protect her where will she go?'

'Dear God!' Fiona said and sat down. 'The only other time she fell in love he was killed. Rob was such a nice young man. We wanted the marriage, we were happy, he was . . . How could anybody do such a thing and why?'

When he didn't answer, Fiona didn't press him, she just sat there and said, 'What on earth are we to tell her?'

'The truth. What else can we tell her?'

Fiona shook her head and she had that look about her such as women had when they were about to cry.

'She's not a child,' Niall said.

'I know, but she's been hurt so much. Rob was coming home and they were going to be married. Everything was arranged. She still has her wedding dress. I keep meaning to get rid of it.' Fiona got up. 'I'll go and call her. Would you like me to tell her?'

'No, I'll do it.'

'Would you like me here?'

'No.'

She went out into the hall and he heard her talking to the maid. Caitlin came in shortly afterwards. She really was quite beautiful, Niall thought, and there was an eager enquiring look in her eyes.

'It was good of you to come,' she said. 'Did you see Arthur?'

'I saw him, yes. I didn't speak to him. I went to the library but he'd just left. It was his day for going home early apparently so I followed him. You were right, he's not rich, he . . .' Niall didn't want to tell her exactly where Arthur lived or she might go there after what he was about to tell her.

Her eyes were so clear, so receptive. Niall wished he could hold the moment, give her even a few minutes grace before he destroyed Arthur Peterson forever, but when he hesitated her expression began to change so there was no point in putting it off. She had heard worse things of a man she loved.

'He's married, Cat.'

He didn't go on. He wanted to let that sink in. She gazed at him and, beyond the closed door, Niall heard Aulay's bluff tones in the hall. For once in his life he had come home early. What timing. Niall looked towards the French windows and then he took her by the wrist and hurried her out of the doors and into the garden and away from the house. She marched there with him until a big tree obscured the view from the drawing room and then she said, 'You've made a mistake.'

'I wish I had.'

'You're wrong.' Her eyes held desperation. 'You've got to be wrong.'

'I stood back and watched him . . .'

'Why didn't you just talk to him?'

'I don't know but I was right to do it. His wife came to the door and she had a child in her arms.'

'You're making this up.'

'Why would I make it up?'

'Because . . . because you're in league with my father. You don't want me to be happy.'

'Why would I do that?'

She searched his face for clues.

'She could have been his sister. He lives . . . yes, he told me, he lives with his family. She could have been married to his brother or his brother in law or . . .'

Niall shook his head.

'I asked.'

'I don't believe you, Niall. Arthur wouldn't do such a thing to me. He loves me. I'm going to him.'

'No, you're not.' He grabbed her as she tried to run back into the house.

'Let go of me.'

'Your father is home and your mother knows and if you leave the house now it's my belief your father will lose whatever is left of his temper in this matter. Then what will you do?'

'I don't care. I love Arthur. He wouldn't do such a thing to me.'

She tried to wrench free but Niall held her.

'People do things like that all the time.'

'People like you perhaps, not people like Arthur. You think everybody's like you,' she said and burst into tears.

Niall let go of her. He let her cry for a while and he glanced around him in case Fiona had told Aulay and Aulay was about to come storming into the garden. He was right. Seconds later the glass of the French windows shuddered and Aulay came striding across the lawn. Niall turned around so that he stood between them, while behind him she had heard her father too because she was trying to control the tears. Aulay stood back slightly and looked hard into Niall's eyes.

'So, he was a deceiver and a blackguard. It doesn't surprise me. Any man of honour would have come to the house formally and asked.'

'You wouldn't know a man of honour if you saw one,' she muttered behind Niall.

'Perhaps you have learned from this that you should let your parents be wise about these matters. God knows we've lived long enough. We can choose somebody for you with a great deal more success than you appear to be able to do yourself.'

'I would rather die!' she declared.

'I'm sure you would just at present. Go inside and make yourself presentable. The dinner is almost ready.'

'I am not going to marry Simon Anstruther,' she said.

'And what do you think you *are* going to do? We've put up with enough of your tantrums and your whims. I've kept you lavishly for twenty-five years. Do you seriously imagine that I'm prepared to keep you for the rest of my life?'

'You won't have to. I'm leaving,' she said and ran.

Niall watched her. He waited for Aulay to go after her but the door closed, shuddering again, and after that there was silence in the garden but for a few birds. Aulay turned to Niall.

'I'm in your debt,' he said. 'You quashed that very nicely.'

'You can't let her go.'

'She won't go. She has nowhere to go to.'

'The streets aren't safe.'

'I'm so impressed I would ask you to stay to dinner except that I think it will be a sorry affair,' Aulay said and he smiled stiffly and went back into the house.

Seven

Niall was amazed at his own ignorance. He had not known how little he knew or he would not have taken on the Morgan foundry. The men, even those who were good at their jobs, were of no help in the areas which a foundry manager specialized in. He did not know how to go about finding work, he did not understand the special language which the steel world employed, he had no contacts and it seemed to him that Ian Souter had damaged the business almost beyond repair. Amongst the paperwork were a great many unpaid bills, complaints about bad castings and all kinds of papers. The filing system was a mess. He had nobody to talk to, he dared not ask anybody about more than the basics because he knew it would undermine the confidence of the men.

He strode about, glad that these people, like Vinia Forster, undoubtedly knew the stories about him. Only in his office with the door shut did Niall despair. Thaddeus and Alice asked him to dinner and then to stay. Niall was reluctant but the journey back and forth to Newcastle each day was much too far for the long hours he was working and he sold almost everything he had to pay the men and the bills and buy new machinery and raw materials, so he was glad of the comfort of not having to trail back there each day.

He didn't want Thaddeus to be aware of how little he knew

about the steel industry but he was desperate to ask questions of somebody who knew something about it. He could no longer talk to Aulay. He struggled along at the beginning and then stopped telling himself that it would be all right. He drove up to Deerness Law, to the Black Prince pit, and asked if he might see Mr Forster.

The pit was situated on the very edge of the village, just before the fell and not that far from Mr Forster's house. It was not a large pit, along the coast the pits that Niall had seen were much bigger. Some of them employed thousands of men. He doubted that Joe Forster employed more than a hundred but it was, as he had told Niall, one of the main sources of employment in the area. It was neat, if you could call a pit neat, and Niall was impressed. Mr Forster might look poor but he had obviously put his resources back into his work. There was nothing out of order, nobody standing around, and it had a much better atmosphere than the foundry had had the first time he went there. The men weren't jumping around and laughing – he saw them because he got there when the shift was changing – but they didn't look unhappy. They were pleased to have their work over, but they were talking and joking with one another as they came away.

Niall was ushered into Joe Forster's office. It wasn't a big place, not the kind of thing which would have impressed Aulay. From it you could see nothing but the pit yard. Joe Forster got up from behind the small scarred wooden desk and came towards him, smiling and holding out his hand.

'Niall,' he said. 'How nice to see you. I'm so glad. I meant to come and tell you how pleased I am that you've taken over the foundry and to invite you to visit us, but I heard you were staying with the Morgans and I didn't want them to think I might get in the way.'

'I've come to ask you something particular.'

'Of course, yes,' Joe said and Niall was pleased at his openness. He didn't know any other businessmen who operated like Joe Forster. He wished he could be like that.

'I remember you telling me that for a short while you ran the foundry and the pit with Mr Morgan.'

Niall stopped there. He had never asked anyone for help and it was not easy. He got up and wandered around the office, finally stopping by the fireplace. It was too warm for a fire, the grate was empty and the shadow of the big pit wheel outside cast itself huge across the view from the window. Mr Forster didn't interrupt, so Niall took all the courage he had and turned around and said, 'I know you didn't get on with Mr Morgan but I do remember that you were interested in buying the works. I want to run it and I want to get it right but I don't know enough about it. Would you help me?'

'Certainly,' Joe said.

'You will?' Niall couldn't believe it.

'I'm free most of tomorrow.'

Niall felt the responsibility of the foundry ease from him. It was a strange feeling. Thaddeus Morgan wouldn't like it but he had to get help from somewhere and Mr Morgan needn't know. They arranged that Mr Forster would come to the works first thing in the morning and Niall went back to the Morgan household glad of the arrangement.

Joe spent most of the next fortnight at the foundry, saying that Dryden would be glad to be rid of him and, besides, with the foundry staying open, he was indirectly working for himself.

'Why did they buy your coal when Mr Morgan didn't like you?' he asked.

'Because it's the best coal in the area for his purpose.'

Niall soon came to realize that Joe Forster was a clever man. He had not worked with anybody like him before and Niall's enthusiasm got him to the office very early every morning and kept him there long after everyone had gone home. He began to go back to the house for something to eat and then drive to the works again for the pleasure of sitting in his office, listening to the sound of the river beyond his window. Sometimes he went out in the cool of the autumn evenings just to take a look at the buildings and remind himself that it belonged to him.

He offered to move out of the Morgans' house, since he was no longer the polite guest, but Thaddeus and Alice seemed determined to keep him there.

'I'm hardly ever here,' Niall said. 'I don't want to take advantage of you.'

'Since our daughter Luisa died so many years ago, we have had no young company,' Alice said. 'It's very pleasant just having you about. Please don't leave.'

'If it hadn't been for you there would be no steelworks still running,' Thaddeus said. 'That imbecile Joe Forster told me you would close it. I said to him, "I trust that young man. He's not like they say. He's as honest as the day's long."'

Which, Niall thought, considering it was autumn and the days were shortening rapidly, was about right.

Alice Morgan always went to church on Sundays. One Sunday morning she looked too tired to walk and Niall offered to drive her there. Thaddeus was increasingly unwell. Sometimes he got up only in the afternoons, his appetite was gone, he was continually tired and that morning they had had a row about Joe Forster. Niall didn't want to fight with a sick old man and he had no idea who had told Thaddeus about Joe's presence at the works but Thaddeus attacked him over breakfast.

'What was Joe Forster doing at my steel foundry?' he said.

Niall didn't like to point out that it was no longer his works.

'He had some useful information.'

'What kind of information?'

'Just . . . things,' Niall said. 'What does it matter? You bought his coal for long enough.'

'That was not my doing, I would never have bought anything from him. The manager always dealt with that sort of thing. You aren't to have anything more to do with him.'

Niall began to think his board and lodging was dearly bought here.

'Mr Morgan—'

'We're not discussing this any further, young man,' he said and got up.

Alice put her thin fingers on Niall's arm.

'Don't mind him,' she said.

She looked so tired that Niall tried to dissuade her from going to church but she insisted so he went with her. The church was at the end of a long muddy lane so he was glad that he had not let her go alone. It was a pretty building if you liked things like that, old but unimproved by the Victorians, he thought, gazing at the tower, which had different stone from less than halfway up. The graveyard was old too and beyond it there were fields full of sheep and the hills which rose up from the valley bottom in the distance, little grey farms dotted here and there.

He didn't like churches. Religion was a crutch for people who had no independence of mind, he thought, but he put up with it for her sake and then he realized that the reason he didn't like it was because he had no place there. He had gone to church readily enough as a small child with his father. It was as though he had been cast out of everything. He didn't even know how to follow the service any more and he associated that with the years at the home and never listening when he had gone to church every Sunday. He hadn't been in a church since, except for the odd wedding and funeral, so he just followed what Alice did and was only glad when after an hour they were let out.

Once outside, Alice wanted to go to her daughter's grave.

'I always go and say hello to her. You don't mind waiting?'

'Shall I come with you?' Niall took her arm because he was worried she would slip over the wet grass in the churchyard.

She smiled and accepted his help and he let her guide him along the side of the church and around to the back and there, not far from the wall which separated church and rectory, was her daughter's grave, and it was the biggest shock of Niall's life. It was written large on the gravestone – *Luisa McAndrew, beloved wife of George* – and her dates. She had died on the day Niall was born. He stared at it. This woman had been his mother. Alice seemed not to notice his preoccupation. She went forward alone and stood there, putting down the few flowers which she had gathered from the conservatory at the house.

He couldn't take his gaze from the stone. All the way back in the car Alice chatted and he didn't listen and they had Sunday dinner and Thaddeus started up again about Joe Forster but he didn't hear it. That afternoon Thaddeus went to bed, Alice dozed by the fire and Niall spent his time going around looking at the different portraits of Luisa and then at himself in the mirror.

When it was dark and they sat in front of the fire with the tea tray, Niall watched the portrait above the fireplace. She was beautiful and he looked exactly like her. Why hadn't they seen the resemblance? Perhaps if you didn't look for it you didn't see it. He had just spent a great deal of money on a business which was his grandfather's and which would have come to him by rights.

He thought of all those years when he had had no home and no father and no family, and he thought George had brought him south to be with these people.

How different his life might have been had George succeeded in reaching the Durham moors. He would have had family, friends, education, prosperity. He would have lived in this house and been cared for. He wondered whether he ought to tell them, but as he had no proof of who he was they might just think he was trying to take money from them. There was nothing to show that he was their grandchild. That night Niall lay in bed and listened to the clock on the landing strike the quarter hour, the half, the three quarters and then each hour of the night until it was time to get up and go to work.

For once Joe was there before him, asked if he had had a nice weekend. It was such a relief to forget the problem by working.

Thaddeus Morgan, old and ill, was still alert. Niall admired that in him. He didn't admire that Thaddeus knew Joe Forster came to the foundry almost every day. Finally he confronted Niall and told him that he wanted him out of the house.

'You don't seem to understand. That man is my enemy. If you are going to have business dealings with him then you must have them elsewhere. He has no right to be in my foundry.'

'Why, what did he do?'

'I'm not willing to discuss it with you. It's none of your business. You can leave. Pack your bags and go.'

'Mr Morgan—'

'I don't want to hear it,' Thaddeus said. 'You've betrayed my trust, lied to me, gave me to think that you wanted the foundry and could run it yourself.'

'I'm just a businessman, I don't know anything about foundries.'

'You could have asked me.'

'I didn't like to. I knew you weren't well. I paid you good money for the foundry. I consider that what I do is my own affair . . .'

'Get out!' Thaddeus said.

Niall went upstairs and packed his things. He debated whether to tell Thaddeus who he was and then decided that it wasn't the right time. It didn't ever seem to be the right time. Alice came up as he was finishing his packing.

'I'm sorry,' she said. 'I don't want you to go.' She began to cry. Niall didn't understand how she could cry over somebody she knew so little. He tried to say all the right things. He almost told her who he was but he knew that Thaddeus would not believe him, did not trust him, so he didn't.

Eight

It seemed to Caitlin that she would never have anybody, that she was one of those women fated not to marry. All around her other women had the same problem. Were they as afraid as she was? Some of her friends who had been married were now widowed with young children and she thought them lucky. It was awful to lose a husband, how much worse never to have one, never to go to bed night after night with a man you loved, never to hold a child in your arms. Millions of men were dead. Millions of women would be spinsters. What would they do? She was lucky then in some respects. She had a home and parents and money. She would not have to teach or look after horrible children all day or work in a shop or any of the mindless things which women had to do in order to earn their keep now that their marriageable prospects were no more.

Rob was dead. Arthur was a liar. Simon Anstruther was . . . What was he? Rather silly. He came to the house regularly with flowers. If she had not known what it was like to love someone she might have enjoyed his visits. He was rich. Her father liked him. Her mother would have liked anybody who might be persuaded to marry her, that was, anybody in their social bracket, of course.

For all her brave talk of leaving she had not done so. She had no illusions about life without money and security. There was nothing to be done but try not to worry her parents and try not to think of what life would have been like if she had married Arthur. No, not Arthur, the man she had imagined Arthur to be. That was quite different. Arthur had been an illusion. The real Arthur Peterson wished her nothing but ill. She could face that now. She was so grateful to Niall but resented him too for discovering the truth. If she could have lived here and had Arthur as she had thought he was, she could have stayed in love. As it was there was nothing to do but be pleasant and not make things worse by letting her daydreams go back to what things would have been like had Rob lived. She had no doubt that thousands of women sat over the fire in the afternoons and thought what it would have been like had their men returned from the front. How much easier it would have been, how much happier, what it would have been like to taste their mouths and bodies again. There would have been a future.

That autumn Simon Anstruther came to the house two or three times a week. She would rather he had not. She wanted to see Niall but he was busy and Simon's company was better than no male company at all. She knew that her father and mother liked him, that he was eligible, so she put up with him, smiled, made conversation, came to the conclusion that she liked him well enough, lacking anybody better. Sometimes she even thought she saw in him glimpses of the man she had thought Arthur to be, shades of Rob's smile.

One cold afternoon when she and her mother had been shopping she came back to find her father at home rather earlier than usual and he called her into the library. She was irritated, she wanted tea. No matter how often she stopped for coffee or tea when she was shopping, she found that the first thing she needed when she got home was another cup of tea. Her father obviously did not share this idea. He called her inside and she was grateful enough to get in out of the cold. The fire burned all day in the library, even though he was rarely in it except at weekends, but the room was warm and she liked it. She liked the books and the papers, she would have liked to be involved in business, she thought, but she remembered being younger and asking questions and being brushed off. He rarely invited her into his study. It was where work was done and therefore nothing to do with her.

'I've had Simon to see me today. He wants to marry you.'

Her father could not lead into anything. He was always straight to the point. He did not give her time to get used to the idea. He said, 'Well?'

She didn't know what to say. What was there to say, after all? He must know that she didn't care for Simon. Her affections had been engaged twice in twenty-five years and both times she had come to disaster. How often did he think women fell in love? Did he think it was like playing billiards and almost any partner would do? She stood, speechless, and her father shrugged into the gap the silence had left and then he said, 'I know that you don't care for him very particularly but what are the alternatives?'

That was the point, cruel and true. The only alternative she could see was that she should stay single, be an old maid, never hold a child in her arms, never manage her own household, have nothing that was hers, always be a daughter. Simon had money and prospects and she had come to realize that he did care for her, or he thought he did. He was her last chance of a respectable alliance. The other men who had seemed to like her, who had tried to get her to dance and talk with them in the past, had fallen away. They had married other women, been snapped up no matter what their looks or fortune, because men were in such very short supply. Simon was nobody's dream.

'Would you consider it?' Her father looked hopefully at her, or was it desperation that she saw? 'He's coming back tomorrow. Will you at least talk to him?'

Her father was being so reasonable that she could hardly say no. She could not tell him how she had felt about Rob and, looking back, the liaison with Arthur Peterson had been her trying to get back to something so precious that she thought she could not live without it. But she had. Arthur had been nothing but lies. Only Rob stood in her memory as right and true and she could not spend the rest of her life burying her face in her wedding dress and trying to remember how it felt when he made love to her. She was young even now and she wanted him. Only in her dreams did she remember Rob's face. When she awoke, the years in front stretched out in night after night of loneliness. Would Simon be enough to help? Would having children and a pretty house with a garden be better than what she had now?

She lay awake most of the night, deciding in the dawn that it would be, that she could fill her life. First there would be the wedding to plan and it would be a big wedding because her parents were rich and well known and so were his family and there would be houses to look at unless he wanted her to live with his parents. They had an estate in Northumberland and various houses in various parts of the country. She would meet his family and he would no doubt buy her a beautiful ring and he would take her away to somewhere exciting after the wedding and she would be part of something important. It had to be better than the day-to-day living here, where going shopping with her mother and changing her library books was all she had to look forward to. She did not have to love Simon, if she could just like him would not that do?

She glanced in the mirror while her maid did her hair and thought, with eyes that heavy, it would be a miracle if Simon proposed, but later in the morning Simon arrived complete with a huge armful of hothouse flowers and he was smiling. She tried to look at him and wonder what he would be like to live with and it didn't seem so bad. There was nothing objectionable about him. He was just as good-looking as Arthur had been and younger too, and he was who he seemed to be, which was a bonus. The thing that she didn't like about him was his self-assurance and that was strange, as though he had assumed, though he didn't imply it, that she would agree to marry him eventually because he was who he was, he was so important. He was neat, precise, and keen to secure her.

'I talked to your father yesterday. I have a vast fortune, as you know, mostly from mining in this area, but we have been an important family here for a very long time, you must know that too. I didn't speak to your father lightly. It isn't every day I ask a woman to marry me. My parents are agreeable, my father especially, because probably like your own father he would like to be assured that he will have grandchildren. They have wanted me to marry ever since I attained my majority. I think they're relieved I've found the woman I want. So what is it to be? Will you have me?'

She said that she would.

'We'll have the biggest wedding that Newcastle has ever seen. I'll take you to Paris, you'll like that, and then we'll come back and find a piece of land and build the best house in the north. I won't spare expense, not where you're concerned. You'll have everything you want.'

Everything she wanted. Everything she wanted was buried in France in a soldier's grave along with thousands of others. At least Rob was not alone. She wondered whether he missed her in heaven? Would she always miss him with an ache which nothing alleviated? She had been so hopeful with Arthur. She did not feel hopeful about this. She felt a slight happiness because of the way her parents looked when she agreed. They were so relieved, she thought. She felt excitement that he would take her to Paris. She would like to travel and there would be enough money for that. She would be her own mistress. She would leave home. She could have the house she wanted and she would never have to worry about money again.

Niall began to go regularly to his mother's grave. He knew it was stupid but he couldn't help it. The very idea of having somebody, even somebody dead, who belonged to him became important. He liked seeing his name on the gravestone and imagining what she had been like. He wished he could go back to Thaddeus's house and take one of the portraits off the wall and hang it in his room at the small hotel he used during the week. The road past the hotel led out of the village and up the banks towards Deerness Law and the fell.

Things were going badly. Joe was busy at the pit, mostly trying to find new work. The foundrymen were put on four days a week and to Niall's surprise Aulay actually came to the office.

It was November. Aulay hadn't made an appointment, he hovered in the doorway, knocking gently until Niall looked up from the paperwork on his desk. Niall had no idea how he had got past the clerks in the outer office.

'Hello, Niall,' he said. 'I was in the area, at the only real steelworks around here, so I thought I would come to see you.'

'Do come in,' Niall offered. He came in, shut the door, sat

down across the desk and Niall thought of his own sumptuous office in Newcastle and how bad this must look to Aulay.

'This doesn't suit you,' Aulay said. 'Why don't you let me buy it?'

'You have a dozen business interests. Does it matter to you?'

'As a matter of fact it does. Everything I have matters to me and I don't like being bettered.'

Niall sat back in his chair, threw down his pen.

'I'm not bettering you though. I thought I had a contract with Dundee's at Walker and then they rang me yesterday and told me they were getting the same thing more cheaply from you and it isn't the first thing you've taken from under me. I've had two orders cancelled within the past week because you're undercutting me, one of them I was halfway through completion.'

'What did you expect me to do, lie down and let you walk over me? You're making this hard.' Aulay looked out of the window at the view of the river. 'You're the closest I have to a son.'

'Don't,' Niall said and he got up and waited for Aulay to leave but he didn't.

'I'm going to have a son-in-law, though, so that will fill the gap, I expect. Simon Anstruther has asked Caitlin to marry him and for once in her life she's agreed to do something sensible.'

Niall stared at him.

'You're invited to the engagement party. It will be a week on Saturday.'

'You're forcing her to marry Simon Anstruther?'

Aulay frowned.

'That's a nasty word. I'm not forcing her to marry anybody.'

'I can imagine,' Niall said.

'His father owns half of Northumberland, just the kind of young man I want in my family.'

'What did you do to her?'

'I beat her and locked her in her room. Don't be ridiculous, Niall, I didn't do anything.'

Niall couldn't think of a thing to say. He shook his head and Aulay said softly, 'Like most women she wants to be a wife. She wants her own house and a child or two and ... that's what women do. You can't blame her for that. I'm aware that the women you ... consort with don't do such things but believe me it's usual. Simon will be able to buy her a beautiful house and give her all the comforts she needs. How are your men enjoying short time?'

Niall didn't answer that either.

'You're going to lose it all and if you aren't careful you'll take Joe Forster with you. Do you want him to go down, considering how pally you are with him? He's got a lot to lose. Give it up, Niall, you don't stand a chance. I can afford to run at a loss to get rid of you and I know everybody in this game. Nothing will stop me from winning.'

Aulay went. Joe came in just in time to see him go.

'What did he want?'

'Nothing.' Niall brushed past him.

'Niall!' Joe called. Niall escaped into the works.

He went to his mother's grave every week and stood there, trying to imagine what her voice had been like and why she had married George McAndrew. He must have been very much older. Was it for money or had she loved him? Had George hated that Niall had caused his mother's death? Which room had she died in at the Morgan house? There was so very much of Luisa left there somehow, amongst her father and mother, and he felt there was something of himself too in his grandparents and yet he couldn't go.

The weather before Christmas was cold, wet and foggy. Every Saturday afternoon Niall went to the churchyard and then, one day, just as he was about to leave, he saw Alice Morgan behind him. The look she gave him was not kind and not understanding. Niall couldn't think what to say.

'The rector told me you come a lot. What are you doing by my daughter's grave?'

Niall silently cursed the rector's busybodying ways. He glanced around him at the stone to Mary Elizabeth Wardell and the other nearby, Sirus Weir.

'This . . . this man is a distant relative.'

Her face darkened.

'You are a very poor liar, Niall,' she said.

Was he? He had always thought lying one of his talents, but then he had never tried to lie to somebody he loved like he loved her. He couldn't tell her the truth, she wouldn't believe him.

'Do you know something which matters?'

'No.'

'You aren't from round here, how could any of this have to do with you?'

'It doesn't.'

Better to have this old lady as a friend than not to have her at all. Niall couldn't bear her suspicious look any longer. He wasn't going to have her as a friend, she wouldn't trust him so he said it.

'My name isn't McLaughlan, it's McAndrew. She was my mother and you and Thaddeus are my grandparents.' He didn't stop there, he didn't watch her, he rushed on. 'I hid under another name after George died because I didn't know anybody. He was trying to get me to you only he died in Newcastle. He had lost everything. We had a big house in Edinburgh, we moved there when I was small. He told me my mother was buried in Glasgow. I wondered why we never went to her grave.'

There was a long pause and then Alice said, 'You're making this up.'

Niall shook his head.

'No,' he said. And then he smiled at her. 'All you have to do is look at me. I'm exactly like her, aren't I?' He looked straight into his grandmother's eyes and she put a hand over her mouth and her own blue eyes filled with tears.

'It can't be true. You can't possibly be my grandson. He's . . . he's rich and respected and lives with George on the Clyde. I . . .'

'Have you ever heard from him?'

'George and Luisa . . . quarrelled and after she died he took the child away. We used to send letters, presents. We never heard anything. We never saw him again.'

'George sold everything and lived in Edinburgh as a gentleman,' Niall said and it made him want to laugh bitterly. George, a gentleman? What kind of a man loses everything and then leaves his child to go through life alone? What kind of father would do such a thing?

'If you're telling me this because you hope to gain something, you're mistaken,' she said. 'Thaddeus would never believe it. It's all lies. You've been listening to what people say about us. I'm not taken in by this and neither would my husband be. Don't come here any more, insulting the dead like this and hurting us.'

She did her best to make a dignified exit, considering how old and feeble she was. Niall watched her totter down the path and out into the lane.

That evening when he was sitting in his office he heard the sound of a car and, after it stopped, footsteps, slow and hesitating. A short while went by and then his grandmother appeared in the doorway. She regarded him severely.

'I cannot afford to take the risk of believing that you are lying to me and, after all, you bought the steelworks from us. You could have come up with this story first and tried to take the works in other ways. If you had thought to gain anything you would have said it sooner, I believe, but Thaddeus will never have it, so there can be no financial gain from this, you must understand. I have . . . no one but my husband, and I would like to believe that you are my grandson, whether it is true or not.'

'I am,' Niall said.

'You do look like my daughter but then I'm old and confused. I want you to tell me everything that you remember,' she said and she came inside and closed the door.

The following Saturday afternoon he went back to Newcastle. He didn't want to go to the engagement party but he felt guilty about Caitlin. He had not seen her for weeks and although in that time he had assured himself that things would get better in the Redpath household he now saw that it wasn't so.

The house was filled with people and because it was only a few weeks from Christmas the place had in it a huge tree, great vases of holly, decorations, big fires and there were candles everywhere. Caitlin was the first person Niall saw when he walked in. She wore a beautiful dress. It was grey and pale mauve in shiny material that looked like satin, with another part over it in silver, low-cut at the neck, sleeveless to show off her pretty arms, with a silver sash at the hips and high-heeled kid shoes. The dress must have been new, because she had lost a lot of weight and it fitted her perfectly. Her face was devoid of colour and her eyes were dull.

'Niall,' she said and put out her hand. 'How kind of you to come.'

'I'm sorry I've neglected you,' Niall said.

'You were busy. I heard all about it. My father is taking great pains to bankrupt you. I didn't think you'd come anywhere near us, I thought you had your hands full.'

'So you're going to marry Simon?'

She smiled.

'Yes.'

They didn't have time for more conversation, she had to meet her other guests and she met them all in the same way, hand out-stretched, smile, and Simon Anstruther joined her, put his arm about her waist. There was music and dancing. Before supper Aulay made a little speech, none of which Niall remembered, and Simon put on her finger a diamond so big that it was ugly. Niall thought she was going to faint. Fiona went about brightly, introducing people, and Niall wished that he had not come to the house, that he had gone with his first instinct which was to go to Bridget and hide, but it was Saturday and she would be busy and she would not have time to listen to his stupid business worries.

When it was late, when he could decently take his leave, he would have done so except that he went past the door of a small room off the main rooms and heard some kind of disagreement going on inside and Caitlin's voice was distinctive.

'No, Simon, don't.'

Whatever Simon was doing or saying, Niall thought, it had absolutely nothing to do with him. They were engaged to be married and . . . He stopped. Simon was laughing.

'No, don't,' she said and then there were muffled sounds. Something fell to the floor, something else. Niall very softly opened the door.

It was the library. The walls were lined with books and in the middle of the room towards the window, which was now thickly curtained to keep out the cold, Simon had his fiancée backed against the desk. Niall hesitated. Maybe she liked being backed up to a desk, maybe she was protesting in that way in which women sometimes did when they wanted to disclaim responsibility for what was about to happen. Perhaps it was a game. Some women liked to play games.

He knew also that he had a nasty habit of overreacting. He had once been in bed with Nora at Charlton's, heard a fracas next door and burst in only to find that the girl shouted at him for interrupting. To him women were always Bridget being forced again and again by Mr Wilson and he could feel the temper blind him, so he had to be careful. This was not his business. She was not Bridget. She was a rich young woman who was engaged to be married to a rich young man and, if he was not the by now idealized figure of the young man who had died, Niall knew that there was nothing very objectionable, as far as he could see, about Simon Anstruther. If they wanted to have sex then that was entirely up to them and he must not interfere.

She wasn't even vocally protesting, because Simon had covered her mouth with his mouth in a way that reminded Niall rather of somebody eating a peach who hadn't eaten a peach in years and was bloody well sucking it dry. It was quite nauseating he thought, but then again he had to be careful because his memory always associated physical closeness with nausea and violence and there were an awful lot of people, the majority of people, who would never think of such a thing. She wasn't trying to push him away either, and her hands, white and clenched, could have meant anything.

He had one hand inside the top of her dress, the other was

holding her still. Niall remembered with awful clearness Mrs Mackenzie's body, smelling of damp biscuits and old sweat and the feel of her flabby thighs against his smooth skin and her hands on him, her hands . . . Simon's fingers were busy on Caitlin's breast and he took the other hand and slid it up her thigh. She was wearing long diamond earrings which had fallen back across her ears, at least the one Niall could see from where he was standing, and as he stood there a single tear ran sideways, across her cheekbone and into her hair.

As Niall went across, Simon heard him and stood up. Niall didn't give him time to turn around. He kicked him behind the knees and as Simon fell backwards Niall caught hold of him around the neck.

Caitlin screamed.

'Niall, no!'

It was only then that he realized the knife which he always carried in his trouser pocket was in his hand, the blade flicked open, and while one arm held Simon there the other was just about to slit his throat. He stopped. As he did so there was a very nasty smell. Simon Anstruther had shit his pants. Niall let go of him distastefully while Caitlin leaned against the desk, staring. Simon got so far across the room, moving awkwardly, as he would, Niall thought, and then he turned, and he was crying.

'You are bloody well mad!' he said. 'You are a murderer, you crazy sodding bastard!' and then he walked, as best he could, from the room, leaving the door open.

Caitlin watched as Niall returned the blade to the knife with his thumb and slipped it back into his pocket. Other tears had followed the first and she was carefully wiping them away with her thin fingers. The big diamond glittered on her hand.

The tears were turning her eyelashes to dark spikes. Aulay came in.

'What is going on?' he demanded behind Niall. 'Simon says you went mad and pulled a knife. Is that how you settle everything?'

Niall didn't answer him.

'I think you had better leave,' Aulay said.

Caitlin didn't say anything. She didn't move away from the desk, as though it was the only thing holding her up. She certainly looked as if it was, she was almost transparent she was so pale.

'Get out of my house,' Aulay said and his voice shook.

Niall watched Caitlin, waited for some of the colour to come back into her face. He couldn't think what he had been doing. After all, if she hadn't wanted Simon to treat her like that, all she had to do was shout. He wished he could have said to all the people who were crowding into the room that it wasn't what he had seen that made him try to stop it, it was what had happened all those years before, but then that was not altogether true either. It was as though somehow he and Caitlin had got mixed up together and he knew that she didn't want Simon to touch her like that. Nobody should ever do such a thing to another person.

As he stood there Amelia Mackenzie rose before Niall's eyes and swept away his childhood with her thick white arms, probing fingers and huge slippery thighs and he wanted to kill her all over again.

Fiona was there, putting an arm around Caitlin and making comforting noises but Caitlin didn't say a word. Niall walked out of the house.

It was late and in the middle of the city, as he drove back to the hotel, it was heaving with men who were making the best of the biggest night of the week. A drunk staggered into the road. Niall swerved to avoid him. He was only glad to get back to the hotel. He went into the bar and ordered brandy and for some time his hands shook so much that he couldn't pick up the glass. The room around him was full, groups of men talking and drinking. He knew some of them by sight but he didn't acknowledge them. They ignored him. They would all know that he had thrown his money away on a venture that was bound to fail and that Aulay Redpath was bettering him there, as he had bettered so many men in so many ways.

Time went by. Niall clutched hold of the glass, sipped at the brandy and got it down, even though he felt sick. The brandy put up some kind of barrier against the sickness. Mr Kenton poured him another. Niall sat, watching the brown liquid in the glass on the bar and wishing he was somebody other than the person who had almost slit Simon Anstruther's throat for what seemed now very little reason. He had lost his mind.

The talk and laughter went on. He didn't mind. It provided a background without which he could not have borne himself. And then suddenly there was silence. It took a while for him to realize that the noise had ceased and an even longer time to notice that it had not started up again but the whole of it must have happened in seconds, because when he turned around and looked towards the door, which was where every man in the room was looking, he was in plenty of time to take in the figure of Caitlin Redpath. She was dressed exactly as she had been at her engagement party. She had not even paused to put a wrap over her bare arms and in the glow from the lights she looked like something out of a fairy tale, her dress all silver and grey, her hair burnished like a fire, while her slender arms were cream and she wore high heels.

She stood in the doorway, looking into the room, and as he watched she crucified her reputation by walking all the way across the room to where he was sitting at the bar. The only sound was her feet. Niall tried to get up but by the time he realized what she was doing it was too late and to make a fuss would somehow have made things worse.

She was as pale as she had been before. The only difference as far as he could judge when she put her slender hands on the bar was that she no longer wore the hideous ring which he had seen Simon place on her wedding finger earlier in the evening.

'What are you doing here?' he said.

'I have nowhere else to go. You're the only friend I have.'

Niall looked down into his brandy.

'I'm not safe, Cat,' he said.

She didn't speak for a few moments. Around them quiet conversation started up again though it did not reach the level it had been at before she entered the room. Dozens of pairs of eyes were still on them.

'You thought he was forcing me, didn't you?' Her voice was so soft that only he could hear her. 'You were going to kill him.'

Niall gazed into the brandy and then said roughly, 'He had his hands and mouth on you when you didn't want to be touched. That was all I could tell.'

'I should never have said I would marry him,' she said. She laughed but it sounded bitter to his ears. 'I was at my last prayers. I'm almost twenty-six, you know.'

She was beginning to cry, he could see by the way she turned her head from him. Oh no, not here, Niall thought. He pushed the brandy glass towards her and she took the glass in both hands and swallowed the brandy in one big gulp.

'You can't stay,' he said.

'Why not? It's a hotel.'

'Because you came to me. Everybody can see.'

'I didn't think of it like that. All I knew was that, if I stayed, my parents would talk me into marrying Simon, because they don't know what else to do with me. I don't see why I can't be an old maid. Thousands of women will be and it can't be any worse than what's happened to me so far. Simon has hot sweaty hands and a hot wet mouth. Being an old maid is nothing by comparison.'

'What if I took you home?' Niall said.

'No,' she said and other people heard her and every man in the room was looking at them again. She either didn't notice or didn't care, because she looked at him and said, 'My luggage is in the hall. I'm not going back and if you won't help me I'll go and order a room for myself.'

'If you stay here people will think we're having an affair.'

'I don't care what people think,' she said. 'Now are you going to help me, or not?'

Niall got down from his stool and followed her out of the bar and into the reception area. As they reached it Aulay Redpath stepped in out of the night.

'I thought I might find you here,' he said to his daughter. He didn't look at Niall, only at the suitcases which littered the area around the reception desk. 'Are these yours?'

Niall thought he had never seen Aulay more angry. He couldn't have met Aulay's eyes but it wasn't a problem because Aulay regarded him as thin air. The child in Niall wanted to explain and be forgiven, he longed to be inside the circle of Aulay Redpath's affection but the man in him was aware of Caitlin standing behind him. It was the second time in her life she had taken refuge there, the first time had been in the garden at her home when she had been in love with Arthur Peterson. This time was a much more serious business somehow. Then Niall had felt like an arbiter and it was not like this. He could feel her face in against his back as though she could not manage any more and had come to rest there. Her fingers had closed over a portion of his jacket and were mangling the material. Niall tried not to think how expensive the suit had been. Her other hand was edging its way around to the front of his waist. He dared to think that she had never before in her life relied on anyone else completely to shield her from her father. She might have done, of course, if any of them had been reliable, but Rob had died, Arthur had betrayed her and Simon Anstruther had thought a woman's body was a toy for his tongue and fingers and, very probably, Niall thought savagely, other parts of him, if he'd got that far. He was her last hope. If he didn't stand up for her, then any woman who went to any man for succour was somehow let down. If God had meant men to treat women as she had been treated so far he would never have made them bigger and stronger, have given them the ability to misuse such power. The choice was open. God was a bugger that way.

Niall thought that if he could have chosen any man to be his father he would have chosen the man in front of him. Aulay was basically decent. He was also brilliant and although he had mis-used his talents in certain ways he had also been kind, tolerant, even indulgent to Niall, but that was all over, Niall thought, as Caitlin sighed in against his back and Aulay's eyes focused on his face and then beyond him to the girl.

'I knew all along it would come to this,' Aulay said. 'I tried to marry you to a good man and now look. Caitlin, don't you know a bastard when you see one? Don't you know what he's like? God knows I have tried to shield you but even you must be aware. He is the lowest.'

Aulay was nearly smiling at Niall in some kind of abject apology and his voice was amused.

'He has done some awful things, Cat, some of them to women. He has no honour, no family. Do you know who waits for him on a Saturday night? Low women. Yes, they do, and not just one. He sleeps with prostitutes. He lives with them. I tried to befriend him and make him respectable but he has disgusting appetites. You saw how he reacted with Simon. He would have killed him.'

Caitlin's face was deep into his back now, as though by doing so she would not be able to hear what her father was saying, and her left hand had closed around the front of him. Niall could feel the pressure of her thin fingers like she was holding him up. Her other hand released the material of his coat and came around at the other side and her hands met and her fingers laced themselves so in a way she had him in her arms.

'He's a thief and a liar and he's capable of murder,' Aulay said. 'You can never come back if you stay here with him now. You'll drown in the muck of him. Please, Cat, come home. You'll regret it a thousand times if you don't.'

It seemed to Niall that the whole of the hotel was listening. There was nothing but the sound of Aulay's voice and he thought that at any moment Jonty Stevens, whom he could see in the shadows to one side, was going to come over and tell him to leave. Jonty had seen Bridget, knew what his life was like. The scandal of this in Newcastle's best hotel was not to be considered, but Jonty didn't move.

'You're all I have,' Aulay was saying to his daughter and after that there was silence. And then he looked at Niall, acknowledged him for the first time. 'This was what you wanted, wasn't it? Those little games you played. You think you can take my daughter?'

Niall made himself go on looking at Aulay but it was hard. He had wanted Aulay's respect more than anything in his life, would have been proud to be his friend.

'I will destroy you.'

The reception area was full of people somehow, even though the furthest most of them had got was the doorway of the rooms which led into the central hall. Caitlin was crying. Niall could hear her sobbing against him.

And the worst of it all was that fond though he was of her Niall did not love her. It was Aulay he loved. There was a great big chasm in his life where George should have been. He had wanted to fashion Aulay to fill that. He should have known that it was no good. George had left him alone and Mr Wilson had mistreated him and there was no reason for Aulay Redpath even to speak his name in friendship. When Aulay turned around and walked out of the Crown Hotel all Niall felt was relief. He didn't feel as if anything was lost or spoiled, he just watched the doors go on moving when Aulay had vented a little of his anger on them.

People moved away, moved back into the various rooms, no doubt to spend time discussing what had happened. Caitlin let go of him, Jonty came across with one of the porters to take Caitlin's luggage. Niall walked her slowly up the stairs behind the porter, Jonty in front with the keys of one of the best rooms, which he opened with a flourish.

The porter put down the luggage. Caitlin sat on the bed. Jonty said that he would send someone to help her. Niall followed him back downstairs. Jonty went into the office at the back of reception. Niall went in and closed the door and leaned against it.

'My apologies,' he said. 'Thank you for what you did. I will leave in the morning.'

Jonty stood against the side of his desk like a visitor and then he went over to the filing cabinet and from it extracted a bottle of brandy and two glasses, poured generously into them both, handed one to Niall and downed the other. Niall took the glass and swallowed the brandy and then he put down the glass on top of the desk and said goodnight.

Nine

The Weardale Hotel in Sweethope was not on the same level as the Crown. It stood in the middle of the small town not far from the market place, within walking distance of both the Morgan steelworks across the river and the Redpath steelworks, which was on the edge of the town leading out of the dale towards Deerness Law. It served two purposes. It was the local pub for many of the quarrymen and general workmen and it had rooms for rent, only four. It was owned by Fred and Olive Bentley and Niall had the impression that, in a village of five churches including Presbyterian, Primitive Methodist, Wesleyan, Catholic and Anglican, they would object to him bringing what people would no doubt think of as his fancy woman to stay.

Caitlin was very fancy, Niall thought, trying to look objectively at her. Her luggage matched, she wore expensive clothes, her hair was cut in the latest style, she was fashionably thin and she wore diamonds in her ears. However, when he asked for a room for her, Mrs Bentley did not question him. No doubt they needed the money.

Caitlin said nothing. When they had left the Crown with all their luggage she had not questioned him, nor during the hour-long drive from Newcastle. She had sat and stared out of the window.

Mr Bentley carried her luggage up to her room. She stared out of that window too, at the small square fields and the way that the hills rose up beyond to the moors. Mrs Bentley prepared a Sunday dinner, so they sat in the little brown dining room at the back of the hotel and neither of them ate anything. They were the only guests. A small fire burned in the grate but Niall could see his breath. It was a dark room with windows which overlooked the yard and on a winter's afternoon there was little light.

After dinner Caitlin sat by the fire in the residents' lounge, another cold little room at the back, and pretended to read. She fell asleep until Mrs Bentley came in with the tea tray. She drank her tea and then she said brightly, 'I could come to work with you tomorrow. I want to do something useful.'

Niall had no objection to that. He couldn't think what else she might do. He liked her, he was very fond of her but he didn't want her. His life was complicated enough. All he wanted was to go to Bridget and hide in her arms and he couldn't.

He took Caitlin to work with him and asked his secretary to look after her. That night after she had gone to bed he drove to Newcastle.

Bridget was sitting at her dressing table when he got there and looked back at him through the mirror. The expression in her eyes made him feel uncomfortable, so that he wanted to avoid them.

'I didn't think I'd see you,' she said.

'Why not?'

'Because it's all over town that you ran away with Caitlin Redpath.'

Niall lay down full length on the bed.

'I did not run away with anybody,' he said.

'I said you couldn't have.'

Niall closed his eyes and thought about that and then opened them again and said, 'Why not?'

Bridget turned, laughing.

'Oh, please. She's engaged to that slob, Simon Anstruther, and he's worth a fortune. It's likely she'll leave him for you!'

'She didn't leave him for me.'

'I said that.'

'She's staying at the hotel with me in Sweethope.'

Bridget put down the brush she had been using on her gleaming hair. It was loose and formed a curtain around her and was the prettiest on God's earth, he thought. She turned around and when he said nothing she got up and came over and sat on the bed and said, 'What?'

'She came to the Crown and so I . . . I had to help her.'

'Whatever did you do that for?' she said.

'Because he was pushing her down and . . .'

'What?' Bridget's eyes were almost navy, they were so dark, and was there a hint of jealousy there?

Bridget looked hard at him and then raised her eyes before she said, 'You interfered? You complete bloody idiot, Niall.'

'I shouldn't have?'

'She's marrying him. You think men don't use their wives like that? It doesn't count.'

'I don't believe you said that,' Niall said, sitting up. 'After all you've been through.'

'She agreed to marry him. It was her engagement party, for God's sake, she wasn't . . .'

'What? She wasn't a young girl in a greasy man's bed?'

'Precisely,' Bridget said. 'She has a tongue, she could have said she didn't want to marry him and you didn't have to get involved. What on earth are you going to do with her, apart from shagging her?'

'I am not shagging her.'

'Will it be cheaper than Charlton's or not?' Bridget said and she got up and went back to the dressing table and began to brush her hair fiercely.

Niall was so angry that he didn't move because he knew that he had to control his temper. It was not surprising that Bridget should be jealous. Nora Cowan was a whore and she knew all about that, but Caitlin Redpath was the beautiful daughter of a wealthy industrialist and that was an entirely different matter. Also he knew that she was right, he should not have become involved. It was none of his business, he had nothing to gain from it and he had made an enemy of Aulay Redpath. Before, they had been merely competitors, he thought it even amused Aulay to have Niall take him on. It was a challenge, it made life interesting, but this was something else. Niall wished that she had not said all the things that he had been thinking. He got up and went across and looked at her through the mirror.

'What the hell does it matter to you who I go to bed with?'

Bridget looked back at him.

'You go to bed with me.'

'I'm a man, Brid . . .'

'Oh please. Don't do me "a man has needs". Only a man could go through what you went through and still want to shag half the universe.'

'I don't want to shag half the universe . . .'

She got up, very fast indeed, and turned on him.

'No. Then what do you want?'

Niall had no idea how they had got there, only that it was a very difficult place to be. The last thing he wanted was to admit to the woman of his dreams that his love for her was not the pure, spiritual desire that she wished it to be. He had always had the feeling that if he ever did admit it to her she would put him out forever.

'I love you, Bridget.'

'Love has nothing to do with what people do to each other in bed. That isn't love, that is biology, it's nature's joke against us all. It controls men, they do dreadful things for it. I thought you were different.'

'I have never touched you.'

'You're the only person who does or ever will or . . .' She broke off there, breathing quickly.

Niall didn't argue. She was the last person he ever wanted to argue with, she was the only place of refuge in his life, if he destroyed that he would have nothing.

'I don't love Caitlin Redpath,' he said. 'Only you. There will only ever be you, I swear it.'

'You're only saying that so you can stay,' Bridget said but her tone was softer.

Niall did stay and he was so happy there that he didn't want to sleep, didn't want the time to pass too quickly as it always did when he was with her. He told her over and over again how much he loved her and he held her while she slept.

He intended to leave early but Bridget didn't want him to go so he got back to the hotel at the exact moment Caitlin came downstairs to breakfast. She didn't say anything to him but her look said it all. It was a strange feeling to be judged, like having parents or being married, having some commitment to somebody so that they noticed when you came in like that and drew conclusions. He told himself that he didn't care but it was strange to watch Caitlin seeing him differently. She looked very businesslike in a dark suit. Niall was relieved to go to work, at least he knew what he was doing there and they could talk without anything personal going on.

Ten

Every Saturday afternoon Niall met his grandmother at the churchyard. He was always there before her because he did not want to keep her waiting in the cold. Sometimes he wished she would not come because she was old and he was afraid to lose her now that they had found one another. He had learned to love her so much that he was afraid of it. He wished that there had been a lot of people so that he could have diluted the love but there was no one else. Thaddeus didn't know and he wasn't close enough to Joe and his family to tell them. Bridget didn't want to hear anything about other people and he was spending enough time with Caitlin without getting her involved any further.

He wanted to hide from Alice Morgan the amount he felt for her but she delighted in his company. Her face lit when she saw him. She adored his embraces and the kisses which he placed on her dry old face and the way that he took her into his arms. He tried to be discreet but the overwhelming feelings would not let him be. He hoped that the rector was not watching too closely but he suspected that other people knew of the meetings. It was the one thing beside his work which he cared for. He could not give it up and he knew that it would hurt Alice deeply if he did not keep their weekly appointments. He thought he was her only joy. Thaddeus was difficult in his illness, bad-tempered and forgetful, she said, though Niall did not know, because he did not go near the house.

On the second Saturday in December, a cold bright day, she didn't come to the churchyard. Niall waited and waited and became colder and colder. After an hour he walked up and down to keep warm but still she did not arrive. He walked around until the sun sank beyond the horizon in gold and grey and then until it was completely dark and the moon rose full and round and then, without making a decision, he got into the car and drove to the Morgan house.

He tried not to drive too fast but there was on him a sense of doom which no amount of rationalizing would disperse. If his grandmother had been ill or there had been some kind of problem surely she would have sent a message. He told himself that she had got the time wrong and turned up when he wasn't there and was disappointed and sorry that she had missed him.

He was beginning to feel better when he turned in at the drive, embarrassed at having panicked. There was nothing wrong, she had just mistaken the time, that was all. He drew up in front of the house. He got out and ran up the steps and the maid, Clare Atkins, opened the door.

'Is Mrs Morgan at home?'

Clare looked out into the darkness.

'Oh, it's you, Mr McLaughlan. You'd better come in.'

It seemed to Niall that this house had never been the home of anyone he knew. If his mother had been born and brought up here he should have known, he should have felt more than he did. It could have been anybody's house. Clare ushered him down the hall and into the drawing room and there Thaddeus sat alone by a huge fire. He looked old and ill. He had a big shawl around his shoulders. He glanced up at Niall from red-rimmed eyes.

'What do you want?' he said.

'Nothing.'

The fire threw huge shadows on to the walls and there was very little other light in the room. It made the portrait of his mother look different somehow, as though she had lost her way and was staring at an unknown place.

'I just came to see how you were.'

'Alice died yesterday,' Thaddeus said.

'Died?'

'Yes.'

'But . . .' She could not have died, he was due to meet her in the churchyard that day. She had not been ill, Thaddeus had been the one who was ill. 'What happened?'

Thaddeus didn't answer him immediately. Niall wanted to shake him into speech.

'I know what you've been doing,' he said. 'The rector told me.'

'What happened to her?'

'It's nothing to you.' If Thaddeus had been a well man his voice would have been savage but it was only hoarse and thin.

'Please . . .'

'Leave,' Thaddeus said.

'What did she die of?'

'She was old. She fell down and died. People do.'

'No.' No, no, not yet, not before he had become used to having someone that belonged to him. She could not have died while he still needed her to walk to the grave with him on Saturday afternoons with the autumn leaves massed around the grave-stones and people exercising their dogs through the fields. 'Tell me what happened.'

Thaddeus looked at him. The old man's eyes were hooded and weary.

'I know your game,' he said. 'To think I trusted you. I thought you were . . . I had heard all the stories about you but I thought it wasn't true, couldn't be, you took such an interest in everything, but you are deceitful and ill-intentioned and you tried to ingratiate yourself here.'

'No.'

'Yes, you did. Alice was a gullible old woman. You thought you could get to me through her, you thought to have everything that was mine. I've met your type before. You were very clever but you went too far. You thought you could charm a fortune out of her but the fortune is mine and I'm not a gullible old woman. You played on her.'

'No,' Niall said again.

'Yes, you did. You pretended to be the grandchild she wanted so much. You cannot imagine what the years have been like, knowing there was a child. I don't think there is. I think he probably died in childhood. I stopped believing in such things but Alice didn't. And you . . . How could you treat an old woman like that for the sake of money?'

'I didn't,' Niall said.

Thaddeus laughed.

'You think you're going to bamboozle me now. Well, better than you have tried. Go on, tell me you're my grandson. As though I would believe you.'

His instincts had been right. His grandmother had indeed missed her appointment with him and she would miss all the other appointments. Forever and forever somehow she would be late for their meetings and he would never speak to her again.

'The rector knew your game and he told me when it first

started what you were doing. At least it brought Alice some kind of comfort, your pretence. I don't know where you thought it was going to get you but understand this. You will never see a penny that belonged to her. Never. Now get out before I call the servants.'

Niall went. There was nothing to be said, nothing to be done. Alice was dead and his brief time of belonging to somebody was gone.

He walked down the steps of the house very slowly. He felt that he would never do it again and the house which might have become so important to him, where his mother had lived, where he had been born, was being snatched from him. The loss of his grandmother left a great big hollow inside him which filled with panic. Was he never to have anybody? Thaddeus didn't believe him and all the talk in the world wouldn't alter that.

He thought he was never going to reach the bottom of the steps and once he did he couldn't breathe. All he wanted was to run home to Bridget but the weather had turned dark, it was snowing hard and Newcastle would be such a long way across the fell in a blizzard. He went back to the hotel and into his room and sat down on the bed. It was cold in there. He had been at work all day and Mrs Bentley, after cleaning and laying the fires, left her guests to light them when they came home. That way she saved fuel and work.

He sat there in the quiet for a long time until he was too cold to move. Vague noises filtered up from the bar below but it was too early yet for the men to be in drinking. There was a soft knocking on the door. He didn't answer but Caitlin opened the door and came inside.

'I thought you weren't here,' she said.

Niall didn't say anything.

'It's freezing. Why haven't you put the fire on? Do you want me to light it for you?'

'No.'

'Are you going to Newcastle?' She put the question carefully, perhaps disapprovingly, he wasn't sure. Of course he was not, he never went to Newcastle on Saturdays. Didn't she know anything? Bridget would be too busy to bother with him, and besides, he couldn't leave Caitlin here alone at weekends. It was rowdy. The men very often got drunk and although he did not think any harm would come to her he was not sure that he trusted the Bentleys to take care of her.

Caitlin was watching him and she came over.

'Is there something the matter? Are you all right? Has something happened?'

Niall didn't trust his voice but he had to say it.

'Mrs . . . Mrs Morgan died.' His voice sounded as though it was at a distance.

'Did she?' Caitlin sat down on the bed beside him. 'How awful. When did this happen?'

'Yesterday.'

'What a shock, when Mr Morgan was the one who was ill. Who told you?'

'What?' Niall couldn't think.

'Who told you that Mrs Morgan had died?'

'I went to the house.'

'I thought Mr Morgan didn't like you.'

Restless, Niall got off the bed.

'He doesn't.'

'Then what made you go?'

Niall could smell faintly the perfume that she wore. Sometimes when he leaned over her the scent of it drifted towards him. It was the kind of thing you couldn't quite catch which made you want to lean closer. He put a match to the fire.

It didn't light at first, probably everything was damp. It always was. Mr Bentley followed the stupid practice of leaving his coal outside in the wet, so after a few feeble flickers the fire went out. Niall got down and twisted some paper and moved the sticks around and lit it again and watched the blue and orange flames make their way around the sticks until the crackling sound would assure him that the sticks had caught fire and then it died again.

Somehow Niall couldn't get up from the dead fire. The idea of travelling all the way to Newcastle through the snow, which was the only thing he wanted to do, to find Bridget brisk and busy, seemed impossible. He desperately wanted to cry but he couldn't possibly do it in front of a woman, if at all, and the effort of not doing so meant that he couldn't do anything else. The idea of lighting the fire for a third time seemed insuperable.

Caitlin got down beside him and fussed over it and she stayed there on her knees, saying softly, 'I wish you would tell me what's the matter.'

Niall shook his head and turned away because she was so close and then to his horror it was as though the dam burst and he began to cry. It was hardly noticeable, he thought. He didn't move and he didn't look at her. He didn't even sniff or let his face shift about like people did. The tears that escaped were few but his vision was gone and Caitlin was obviously an expert on such matters, as most women were, and was undeceived by the lack of evidence. She said, 'Oh God, Niall!' and tried to get hold of him.

Niall hadn't been in any woman's arms for the purposes of affection in fifteen years except Bridget's so he shook her off and got up. Caitlin got up too and watched him for a long while before asking, 'Why are you crying over Mrs Morgan?'

'I'm not,' Niall managed.

'Yes, you are. She's not another of your conquests, is she?'

Niall smiled at the attempted witticism and he thought that in a way Alice was. She had loved him and he had adored her, because there were so few places where his affection was acceptable. He thought of her bright bird-like eyes and how she would stride out, pretending that she wasn't old, and would touch his cheek with her thin hand. She knew the truth, at least part of it. Alice knew that he was her grandson and it was all lost after that brief acquaintance was gone. Thaddeus did not believe him, would not have him near or acknowledge him. It was like being put outside. It was forever looking in through the window at other people's houses.

Beyond, where the curtains were pulled back as far as they could be, snow fell, not gently as it sometimes did in the wide Newcastle streets but in small hard flakes with a wind that had seen the moors, blowing up and down and sideways and all over the place as though it didn't know which way to go.

The noise from downstairs was growing, he hadn't realized that the evening had moved on. Some drunken joker was singing 'Silent Night' above the row in a loud and untuneful tone and he thought of Joe and Vinia together in their house on the moors and of Thaddeus alone before the fire in that enormous house and he wondered what it was like to be old and bitter and lonely so that you would not take a chance on somebody who, if you only lifted your eyes to the portrait above the fireplace, was the very image of the woman there. How different it would have been if Thaddeus could have accepted him. He would have belonged and not just to Thaddeus but to the whole

Morgan family, however far back they were remembered, and to the house which he thought he could have loved and to the foundry which was his inheritance, and people would have stopped one another in the street and said, 'There's Thaddeus's grandson.'

He would have been the Morgan lad. He wondered whether to go downstairs and join the revellers awash with beer. He reached the window. The noise from below sounded like it was about to break the ceiling and outside there were lights on in various windows beyond the storm. Caitlin said, 'It's freezing in here. Why don't you come back to my room?'

Niall laughed.

'That's the best offer I've had all week,' he said.

'I didn't mean it like that.'

'I know you didn't. What the hell would you want with somebody a whore owns?'

Caitlin came nearer.

'Does she own you?'

'Yes,' he said.

Caitlin reached the window.

'Why?' she said.

'She's the only woman I've ever loved.'

'No, she isn't. You loved Mrs Morgan.'

'That was just . . .' Niall said and then didn't know how to explain himself without going into the kind of detail that he didn't want to reveal. He leaned back against the shutter. Caitlin gazed out of the window.

The snow was stopping. It had covered the street in white and beyond the rooftops it cleared now and a bright moon was emerging. The light made Caitlin's face even more beautiful than it already was. It made him think of Bridget and how he should have been in her bed. How he wanted to be there, in her arms with his mouth on hers. The trouble was that it was such an unsatisfactory arrangement because he was never content any more, he always wanted her so much.

'What are you looking at?' Caitlin said.

'Nothing.'

'Are you wishing you were in Newcastle in your whore's bed?'

'Cat . . .'

'Don't you mind sharing her with other men? Don't you find that disgusting?'

'It's . . .' He was going to say, *It's the only thing I've ever known*, but he didn't.

Caitlin didn't look at him.

'I've heard men talk about how beautiful she is. Is it like winning a prize?'

He was beginning to wish that she would just go, because he was starting to lose his temper and he was tired and the misery of Alice's death threatened to come between him and his sanity. To his surprise Caitlin sensed it.

'I'm sorry,' she said. 'I didn't mean to go on about something which is none of my business. You've always been very kind to me. It isn't every man who saves a woman so handsomely. Shall I light the fire for you before I go?'

He changed his mind then. He didn't want her to go. He didn't want her even to move away from the window and when she attempted to he got hold of her and it was not a casual gesture, both hands on her arms. He was surprised at himself. So was she. She looked up at him as he drew her to him and that was when Niall kissed her. He hadn't intended to but the emotions chasing one another through him were well ahead of what reasoning he could summon. Her mouth was sweet and he was quite sure that she was about to protest and tell him that she didn't want some whore's leavings but she didn't.

It wasn't at all like touching Bridget or Nora. To Nora you were just another poor bastard that had to pay for it, who either had some awful bloody bitch at home or, worse still, didn't. This was freedom of a different kind. She gave him her mouth and fastened her arms around his neck and he drew her closer.

Having recalled Bridget to his mind, suddenly Niall could not dismiss her. He didn't want to think about her, he wanted Caitlin badly. He had the feeling it would be wonderful to have somebody you weren't paying for, somebody who wanted to be there, but he couldn't do it. Sleeping with other whores was not a betrayal to Bridget but this would be. He thought that if it had not been for Bridget when he was younger he would either have died or gone completely to the bad and he could not go to bed with another woman who mattered to him and Caitlin did matter. Bridget would know if he did such a thing. Where he was concerned she had extra senses. She knew him so very well, she knew things about him which he never wanted anyone else on earth to know but because of them there was a bond which could not be broken and he had no intention of breaking it with stupidity.

He very gently disentangled himself from her and it took time because she didn't want to let him go, she didn't want him to stop kissing her, he could tell. She gave a little sigh of disappointment and then she pretended she hadn't really wanted him to touch her, that she had not intended taking part. Other men might have been deceived but Niall had lived around women for a long time and he wasn't. He hadn't thought she liked him that way. Maybe it was just that she confused kindness and desire or maybe she hadn't kissed anybody except Simon Anstruther in a long time or maybe she just wanted to kiss somebody. There was nothing wrong with that but she didn't like rejection, especially, he thought, since he had instigated the kiss in the first place.

Caitlin got herself out of the room before he had a chance to let go of her properly or say anything. She wrenched away, flung open the door and banged it shut. The revellers were making even more noise. Niall was rather glad of that. The last thing he could have stood just then was silence. He had to stop himself from going after her.

In the morning the weather had turned soft so he got up early and went into Newcastle. The house was locked and quiet but he had keys to let himself in. He crept to Bridget's room and got into bed with her and she turned over, smiling in her sleep, and drew him in against her.

When Caitlin got back to her room she cried hot angry tears. What the hell was she doing here with a man who didn't care about her, whom she didn't care about? Except that that wasn't quite true, she did care about him and he cared about her, differently than other men had but more, she thought, which was strange. He was the only man she knew who would have tried to kill somebody he thought was hurting her. He protected her from cold and hunger and loneliness and worst of all from having to go crawling back to her father. It was a strange protection, here in this awful little hotel. She hated it when he went to Newcastle to visit Bridget Black. She felt safe only when he was next door either at work or here. He was the only thing which stood between her and the rest of the world and while he was there she didn't need anybody or anything else. He could and would hold everything off, which was not to say that he had the right to touch her. She had thought she didn't want him to touch her, despite the fact that he was the most attractive man she had ever met. Now that was honest. He was. But they had been friends and she had wanted a friend more than she wanted a lover. The lovers in her life had left her, but Niall had never left her, not really. When she had wanted him or needed him he had always been there. She had not thought that she wanted him to kiss her. How very embarrassing.

It was just because he was upset, though why he was upset she had no idea. Why did he never tell her anything? If he had not been upset she would have pushed him away and Niall was the kind of man who would be pushed away, she knew that. In fact that was part of the reason she didn't, because he was not insistent like other men had been. He regarded relationships like other people regarded tennis matches, that it took two willing people and was much more fun with equals.

The trouble was that she had liked him kissing her and that was not how she had planned things. She liked the way things were. She didn't like the way that he went off to Newcastle to see his whore but she accepted it, was pleased to be his friend, to have him talk business to her when nobody was there. He did not hide who he was from her, at least not on some levels, and she knew that Niall was essentially a very secretive person, so it was a huge compliment to be that close to him. He would not give her up easily but she did not need the complications of his intimate life and she did not want it bound up with hers. She had told herself she did not care if she never kissed anybody again. It was not quite true but it had been ninety per cent there until just now. Besides, he loved Bridget Black. She knew he did. She knew nothing would dislodge that. She did not understand why he loved her but it was a powerful relationship, much more so than anything she had seen before and she had no intention of getting in the middle of it.

She dried her tears and went to bed. Having made her decision she slept well although she awoke from time to time and had to reassure herself that everything would be all right. She heard him leave. She hated him going. She always wanted to run out and stop him before he reached the stairs. He moved around in the room for a short while and then came out and shut the door with a quiet little click and her heart sank. She heard him go down the stairs and out of the door and then she heard the car engine as it started up.

It was the loneliest part of her life when he left like that. She wished he would never do it. She had nobody when he went. She told herself that he would be back that night or the following morning, he never stayed away long but he always looked different when he returned from seeing Bridget. She tortured herself then by thinking of them in bed. She tried not to. She tried to think about other things but somehow it always came back to the fact that Bridget Black was the most important person in his life and more than that the most important woman. Caitlin had the feeling that Bridget had always been the most important person in Niall's life and that likely she always would be.

Eleven

Niall did not go to his grandmother's funeral. He stayed in Newcastle. He should have been at the foundry, where things were going wrong, but he didn't want to go back. He wanted comfort. Bridget wasn't well, she had a bad cold and coughed a lot, but Niall didn't care. He wanted to be with her. She had dark shadows under her eyes, Gypsy said she had been working too hard for too long and kept bringing cups of hot milk and whisky into the bedroom where Bridget stayed. Niall slept there with her for three days, only getting out of bed occasionally and going to the kitchen to talk to the other girls. Here he could forget that Alice Morgan had died and that his business was failing and that the girl he wanted to bed was waiting for him there in a shabby hotel on the moors. He spent hours sitting by the kitchen fire, talking to Gypsy.

'You're looking at my legs.'

She was wearing a silk robe and it was forever falling away from her body. Niall didn't answer.

'You can have me, you know. It won't cost you five pounds.'

'No, thanks.'

'Or any of the others would—'

'No.'

She looked curiously at him. 'So who are you screwing?'

Niall got up and then for some reason felt compelled to say, 'I'm not.'

'It's not a crime, you know. Bridget would understand.'

'I don't need anybody to understand,' Niall said.

Gypsy took a spill from the long pot where they stood on the hearth and put it into the fire and lit a cigarette.

'You're right. She wouldn't. Oh, I don't think she minds you doing it, but if you were to fall in love . . .'

'I'm not in love.'

Gypsy considered the cigarette in her fingers.

'They tell me Caitlin Redpath is a beauty and that you are living in some awful little hotel with her.'

Niall got up. He felt safe here in Newcastle, he didn't want to be anywhere near the people who would put Alice Morgan's body into the ground, probably somewhere very close to her daughter's. It was his only good thought, that they might be together, if there was any heaven, if there was any justice, and he wanted to stay here in Bridget's bed and hide. The trouble was that he could not erase from his mind the sweetness of Caitlin Redpath's kisses.

'I am not sleeping with her,' he said.

'What a terrible disappointment for the poor girl,' Gypsy said.

After three days Niall felt compelled to go back. It was late afternoon when he reached the office. Nobody said anything to him. Caitlin must have heard him but she didn't leave the office where she helped Mrs Elmott, his secretary, and, when she did, it was only to come in with a pile of letters which needed signing, explain what had come through the post, that she had postponed the appointments he had failed to keep and to tell him that he had had a private letter which naturally she had not opened.

He slit the top of the envelope. It was from Alice Morgan's solicitors. Niall handed it to Caitlin. She read, frowned, looked at him.

'Why do Mrs Morgan's solicitors want to see you? Perhaps she's left you a keepsake. That would be nice. Isn't it?' She perused the letter again. 'Why do you have to make an appointment, isn't there usually just a reading of the will and, if she's left you something, doesn't it mean that you should be at the reading?'

'She thought I was her grandson.' There was not much point in trying to keep this quiet any longer. People would find out if Alice had left him anything significant and he would rather Caitlin found out from him than hear it through village gossip. She put down the letter and looked at him.

'Why should she think that?'

'Because I am.'

Caitlin stared for a little while longer and then she said, 'I don't understand.'

'I didn't know they were my grandparents until my grandmother took me to my mother's grave. Luisa McAndrew. She died on my birthday. I was born here, in Mr Morgan's house.'

'But nobody knows.'

'I didn't tell Thaddeus. I didn't think he would believe me.'

'Why not?'

'Why should he?'

Niall couldn't remember why he had not told Thaddeus who he was right at the beginning. He thought about it. If he had done, it could not have turned out worse. He had been afraid that Thaddeus and Alice would not believe him and he had wanted to keep the illusion of belonging for as long as possible. When Alice had been alive he had been able to carry it on. He could no longer do that.

'Oh, Niall, why didn't you tell me this before?'

'I couldn't.'

'Did you think I wouldn't believe you either?'

'Maybe.'

'But you bought the business from them.'

'I didn't know then and Thaddeus doesn't believe me now. He thinks I want their money. I changed my name because . . .'

'Because what?'

'It seemed like a good idea at the time.'

He had had visions of gaol, even of death. It seemed so foolish now, and then he remembered how small he had been and how very frightened. He had lied and that lie had taken over his life. It had followed him all the way to here and he had been paid out for it a hundredfold. What retribution would be required for all the really bad things that he had done, because he was beginning to believe that God let people get away with nothing. Only Bridget knew the truth. He hoped that no one else would ever know.

The solicitor's office was in Frosterley, a little town in the dale which was famous for its black marble. It was one long winding street with houses and farms behind it where the valley side rose up sharply from the narrow village. The solicitor, Mr Rayburn, had his office on the second floor of a Victorian building. The room was big and wide and had a decorated ceiling and there were books and papers everywhere. His view was of sheep and fields. Mr Rayburn was a small, neat man. He greeted Niall with a concerned look, asked him to sit down, and after he did so the solicitor said, 'We appear to have something of a problem, Mr McLaughlan. Mrs Morgan has left you some jewellery which she had given to her daughter and took back when her daughter died and which she says is to be given to your wife when you marry.' Mr Rayburn coughed and handed over the will.

Niall scanned it. His grandmother had owned very little. The money she had she had willed to the servants, her clothes also to be given to the maid, Clare, but she had left her emerald earrings and the pearl necklace to him. Mr Rayburn coughed again.

'The trouble is, Mr McLaughlan, as you can see, that she leaves you these items under the name of McAndrew. While I understand from various people that you claim to be this person, I have to ask you now, do you have any proof that you are Mrs Morgan's grandson, Mr McAndrew?'

'None.'

There was a short silence during which Mr Rayburn watched him.

'I also have to advise you that if you claim legally to be this person, Mr Morgan has told me that he would contest the will on the grounds that you cannot prove who you are.'

'I don't want anything,' Niall said. 'I never wanted anything.'

That was not true either, he had wanted his grandmother, her time and her affection, both in quantity. He liked to hear her say his name. He cared nothing for possessions, he never had, but he liked the warm glow of knowing that she had wanted him to have something of hers, that she had believed him, cared for him. That mattered to him very much.

Niall went straight back to work. It was Christmas and he was horribly aware of the men on short time. He thought he would sell his car and then at least he would be able to pay them more generously over the festive period. While in Newcastle he had cancelled the rent on his office in Collingwood Street. His other assets had almost all been disposed of.

He wished that he could go home for Christmas, that the old man would take him into the house willingly, joyfully, that Thaddeus would be pleased. He could feel the desperation on himself for somebody to love him because they shared the same blood and he could see that it was not going to happen. How wonderful it must be for people to love you for no reason, but just because.

He went back to work. Aulay had stolen two big orders during the three days he had not been there, orders which he had been counting on but he had failed to get them even with the price cut almost to leave him without any profit.

When he reached his office Caitlin came in.

'You were a long time,' she said.

'Mrs Morgan left me something in her will.'

'She did?' Caitlin's face lit. 'Was it a lot?'

'Just some jewellery and, since I can't prove who I am, I'm not entitled to it.'

'So when Mr Morgan dies he won't leave you anything?'

'I shouldn't think so.'

'But that's awful,' she said. 'They have that great big house and a lot of money and . . .'

'I'm going to go into Durham this afternoon and see if I can sell the car.'

'Sell it?'

'I have to have something to pay the men with over Christmas.'

Niall went into Durham and sold the Daimler and bought a small nondescript-looking vehicle which he told himself would do exactly the same job. Caitlin told him it was better than walking but only just, but at least it meant he could pay the men for Christmas and give them extra.

Joe came to the office and asked them to his house for Christmas Day. Caitlin looked relieved about that and he knew that she had had visions of a dreadful meal at the hotel and of drunken merrymakers. The only thing to have looked forward to would have been a walk along the river.

Joe and Vinia had made an effort. The house was decorated and the meal was as good as any Niall had eaten but there was an air of strain. While Joe and Dryden dozed over the fire and Vinia said she wouldn't move if somebody paid her, they went out in the afternoon and walked across the fell. It hadn't snowed but it was icy cold. Not that it mattered. Niall had bought Caitlin a fur coat for Christmas.

They had sat on her bed at the hotel while she opened it and then she blushed bright red and said, 'Oh, Niall, no.'

'Why not?'

'Well, because . . . because you can't afford it and because it's too much, people will get the wrong idea and . . .'

'Does it matter?'

'But the money . . .'

'I know. I may go back to stealing again,' Niall said, without thinking. Luckily she wasn't listening but, typically for a woman, had put on the coat and was looking at herself in the small mirror above the dressing table and bemoaning the fact that she couldn't see all of the coat at once. It was musquash and long and shiny and made her red hair look even redder.

Up on the moors, walking in a biting wind, Niall drew close and she stopped and turned and hugged him. It was lovely hugging somebody who was wearing a fur coat. What he wished more than anything on earth was that they could go back to a house that belonged to them and make love in front of a big fire. Why were things never like that?

They went back to the house and Caitlin went into the kitchen to help Vinia with the tea and Joe turned to Niall and said, 'How are you going to manage financially after Christmas?'

'I don't know.'

'I'm mortgaging the house. I'll lend you some.'

'No, you won't,' Niall said.

'If you go down you'll take us with you anyway,' Dryden said, sprawled in a big chair in front of the fire.

'I'm not your only customer . . .'

'No, but the others have deserted in their droves since you and Aulay Redpath started fighting.'

Niall stared at Joe.

'You didn't tell me.'

'Would it have helped?'

'Redpath is getting them coke much more cheaply,' Dryden said. 'He must be subsidizing it. Maybe you should give him his daughter back.'

'I haven't taken her,' Niall said and then realized what it sounded like. The silence in the room was as big as a sand quarry.

'You know around here living in a hotel with a woman you aren't married to is as good as living in sin, so even if you aren't, people think you are,' Dryden said.

Niall was beginning to wish he had refused tea and gone but the idea of the hotel was so depressing. Their rooms would be freezing. He had wished Joe had asked them to stay. Now he was changing his mind. The women came back in with tea and sandwiches and he tried to look objectively at Caitlin. Since she kept smiling at him and chatting and looked happy and sat on the rug at his feet he thought it did look bad but then he had bought her an expensive coat for Christmas and she had been pleased with it and they had had a day off and she had enjoyed it. Why shouldn't she look happy? He thought also that she was good at hiding her feelings. Was that experience? Did she spend her Christmases thinking of what her life would have been like had Rob Shannon not died? They would have had their own house by now and possibly a child. What did she have? On the other hand she could have been married to Simon Anstruther and have to put up with him every night, but at least she would have been rich, she would have had her own home and every imaginable luxury. All she had to look forward to was a lumpy bed in a cold room at a hotel and work the next day and she would not have that for very much longer by the looks of things. What would she do then? Was she worried about it? She knew the situation as well as he did, working with him every day.

After tea they left. He went into her room and lit the fire for her and she kept her coat on because the room was so cold you could see your breath. He glanced at her. She looked like a butterfly in a dirty cobweb.

'Did you think about Rob today?'

She looked surprised and then grateful.

'I always think about him.'

'What it would have been like?'

'Yes.'

'Regrets?'

'No, strangely. No regrets. I miss my mother, I thought she might have . . . They didn't understand about Simon, did they?'

'No, I don't think they did.'

'My mother thinks that when men have money they are automatically gentlemen, whereas in fact the reverse is very often the case. Most of the foundrymen are and you certainly are.'

'Me?' She was not the only one to be surprised.

'Yes, you. Thank you for lighting the fire and for my beautiful coat,' and she reached up and kissed him on the cheek and after that Niall went into his own room and lit the fire there and sat beside it, waiting for the room to warm up.

There was a knock on the door and when he opened it Caitlin put her arms around his neck and kissed him. Niall drew her inside and kicked shut the door so that he wouldn't have to let go of her. It was only then that Niall realized how much he had thought about her, how often he had wanted her. He could not imagine what it was like to touch somebody who really wanted you, not somebody you had paid who had allotted you a short time for so much money and wasn't interested in you. Neither was she like Bridget, where he was restricted to kisses. She lay in the middle of the bed and smiled at him and put her hands into his hair and he thought that whatever else Rob Shannon had managed he had not managed much love-making, she was guileless, the very opposite of the girls he knew. He had no doubt that Rob had taken her virginity but during the war when girls were still seriously chaperoned it was probably a few desperate fumblings behind a closed door, the work of moments.

She was eager but held back, her body craved and yearned but she was not used to being held. She didn't know how to touch him, she barely knew how to kiss him, and Niall estimated that men's clothing was a new world to her so he was very careful, very slow, especially remembering the way that Simon Anstruther had treated her. Niall had never tried to satisfy a woman before. The only time he had been with anybody he liked was the first time with Gypsy and he couldn't have told anybody what day it was but what was happening now was important. Rob Shannon was dead but Niall had no doubt that, however brief the love-making had been, she had gone over it so very often in her mind that it must by now be idealized to hell. Simon Anstruther had left the reverse impression, so Niall was meticulous but he began to realize that it didn't matter. She knew him, she liked him and she quite clearly wanted as much of him as she could get.

It wasn't at all the way that he had been led to believe ladies behaved. He had always thought that respectable women probably didn't like sex, that they put up with it because they must, but it wasn't like that. She put her hands all over him once he had got out of his clothes, mostly without the help of her inexperienced fingers, and she didn't put a limit on the kisses or where he touched her. Niall thought that in a way it was just as well that the noise from below was deafening, because the bed was old and creaked and she soon developed a very nice mixture of saying his name and giving a kind of pretty sighing that he really liked but he didn't want anybody else to hear it. The moon threw white light in at the window and turned Caitlin's hair to fire and her eyes to a green glow. Her voice went into a song.

This was what Rob was like, Caitlin thought, when Niall drew her into the room, into his arms. This was exactly what Rob was like. It was like having Rob back. How had she not known? This was what she had wanted Arthur to be like and he was not. Simon had never been in the least like this, which was why she had not wanted him near. She wanted Niall close now. All the resistance, all the years dropped away and she was very young and very much in love and she and Rob were standing on the station and the rain was dripping through the roof and the pigeons were doing their funny walk up the platform, only this time he was not going anywhere. She would not stand there as she had stood so many times and watch the train leave. She hated trains, she hated goodbyes, she hated how Rob had never come home, she hated all the days between then and now and all the men who had not died when Rob had, and all those women who had men to come home to them.

Niall was bad. She liked him bad. She wanted to be a part of it. Anything was better than being invisible and that was what she had been in the end, except to the kind of men she would never have given time to had Rob been alive. She wanted him to pull her clothes off her and put her down and take her and not care about anything beyond the fact that she wanted him to. She didn't want anybody who would hesitate, anybody who would be polite, anybody who would enquire whether she liked this or that, did she mind? Niall had always lived with women, from what she could understand, so perhaps he knew without her telling him what she wanted him to do. He certainly seemed to have the idea but then he had probably been to bed with dozens of people and that was good, experience was important here. Clumsiness and uncertainty would never do.

She liked where they were, that nobody who knew them well was anywhere near. This was a triumph over Bridget Black, who was miles away in Newcastle, and Arthur Peterson, whom she hoped was lying awake alone because his wife was exhausted and had fallen asleep after looking after their horrid little child all day. It was a triumph over her father, who had called Niall such names, most of which she suspected were true.

The noise from down below made a nice background and the big bed was at least clean though she knew the sheets, like those on her own bed, would be darned carefully. Nothing was new here and the feelings which she had thought would never surface again were slowly making their way across her body under Niall's deft hands.

He said all the right things too. He told her that he loved her and even if that was just bedroom talk it was comforting to hear and she liked being in his arms. She had never actually spent a night with Rob, it had always been stolen minutes, not like this, not the freedom of a bedroom and privacy. How many times had she wished that she and Rob had been somehow able to go away, even just for a weekend, and stay in bed and talk alone, to give her better memories to hold on to? It wasn't that it didn't matter now, just that it would no longer matter so much, now that Niall had crossed the boundary from friend to lover. The trouble was that she wanted his friendship too and she was not sure you could have both.

She didn't care. She thought she would give years of her life for a night like this. And it wasn't intense. It wasn't at all the way that Simon had behaved, all heavy and serious. Niall had lived too hard a life, she thought, to burden anybody, and he was not desperate like Simon had been either. No fumbling or hot hands, only the sureness of his mouth and it was not as though she could have been just anybody, because he gave her her name more than once. She had never before thought how good it sounded on a man's lips and he made silly remarks too and that made her laugh, as though this wasn't important in any once-before-dying way, so that was when it stopped being like Rob, because that had always been perhaps-never-again and she had learned that that was not how a relationship was meant to be. It was meant to be there-will-always-be-another-time. That was it. He gave the impression that there would be another day, another night, something lasting was happening here. He would not leave her. He was not Rob going away on a train, never to come back. She knew it was only illusion. He might leave her for good in the morning but for these hours he belonged to her and nobody else.

She told him that she loved him. It was true. It was not how she had loved Rob. It was not how she had loved Arthur. She could remember the very moment that she had fallen in love with him, there was no point now in denying it. It had been the night of the engagement when he had almost killed Simon and she had packed her bags and left home and she had gone to the Crown, worrying that when she got there he would deny her.

She remembered going in there, she remembered the confusion, how she did not know where the bar was and seeing him from the doorway and knowing that if she went in there she had crossed a line which she could not retreat from. He had looked up, he had turned on her those incredible blue eyes and he had not moved but he had watched her walk all the way from the door to him. He had not turned her away nor stopped her. In a way, he had taken her then, only she had not known it. He had taken her heart. It sounded stupid but it was true. Nobody else she knew would have kept her there. And it had cost him dearly in so many ways and that was why this was so precious now.

It had cost him her father's friendship and she knew how much he valued Aulay. Niall had wanted Aulay's friendship so badly. Aulay had been his adviser, had helped him in business since he was very young. Niall was the son he did not have. She knew it. And it had cost him her father's goodwill in business and that was something he could not afford. It was no game any more. Niall was going to fail, she thought. He was not the first man her father had been set against but he was young and inexperienced and had chosen something so difficult that even without Aulay's vindictiveness he would have had problems in succeeding. Without her father's good will it was almost impossible. It was something she loved in Niall, that as well as the rest. She doubted he had thought about it before he made the decision between them. As a lover she thought Niall was good but as a friend he was incomparable.

He had not thought that he could love her. He had not thought that he could love anybody in that way except Bridget but it was not the same. Having a woman made her yours in a way that he had not anticipated. She was asleep now. It was late morning, Sunday, the day after Christmas, and he could hear the church bells from down the road, where Alice and his mother were buried and, further across, Thaddeus was no doubt sitting over his breakfast by the fire.

Niall had woken up hundreds of times with Bridget but never ever when he had made love to her. He wanted to hold Caitlin close in his arms so that nothing would hurt her. He wanted to hear her tell him that she loved him. He wanted never to be parted from her again in the whole of his life. She opened her eyes and then she saw him and she said, 'Oh, it's you.'

'Who did you think it was going to be? Do you do this very often and don't know who you're going to wake up with?'

She closed her eyes again and smiled.

'You are so bad,' she said.

'Isn't that what you like best about me?'

'I like everything about you.'

She leaned over and kissed him and then she lay down on top of him and after that Niall didn't care about anything.

They stayed in bed together until they had to go to work the following morning and all that day Bridget was on Niall's mind. She would be expecting him. Would Caitlin expect him not to go or did she think that if she pushed him into making a choice at this stage he would not choose her? She didn't ask. They worked, they went back to the hotel and had something to eat and after that she announced loftily that she was tired, she was going to go to bed and read. She went.

Niall drove to Newcastle. There he found Bridget sitting over the fire, asleep. He had rarely seen her sleep except at night. As he closed the door and ventured across to her she opened her eyes.

'Niall. I was dreaming about you. Come here.'

He got down beside the chair and she touched his cheek with her fingers.

'I miss you. I know we didn't always see a lot of each other but I know that you're not in Newcastle and I miss you so much.'

'I can come back and see you any time you like.' Niall moved his face in against her fingers and kissed the palm of her hand.

'I knew you would come back tonight. Take me to bed.'

Niall carried her into the bedroom and she had indeed been expecting him. The room was warm from the generous fire, there was wine open and various things to eat on a tray and the bed was clean and fresh and smelled of lavender. Niall felt like the biggest traitor in the world.

'You look tired,' he said as he put her down. 'You have shadows under your eyes.'

'You aren't supposed to say that to whores. My face is my fortune. What have you been doing?'

'Working.'

'How's it going?'

Niall poured out some wine and took it over to the bed, where she was sitting against half a dozen pillows.

'It couldn't be much worse. Aulay Redpath is taking everything.'

Bridget looked down into her glass for a few seconds.

'You ran off with his daughter, do you blame him? As far as

he's concerned this isn't just a business problem, it's very personal. He had one child and you—'

'She has a mind and a will of her own. It had nothing to do with me.'

'Are you sure about that?'

Niall had never lied to her and even now it was difficult. He argued with himself later that he hadn't lied, except that each omission was a lie, and when he looked at her he thought of how much he had enjoyed being in bed with Caitlin, how he thought that he liked her so very much. Bridget's eyes were dark and troubled.

'I've never loved anybody like I love you. I never will again. You know that I would marry you tomorrow. All you have to do is say the word.'

He waited for her to laugh and refuse, just like she had done every time he had suggested it up to now, but she didn't. She sat in silence and avoided his eyes and in those seconds Niall realized that she suspected he was in love with Caitlin and chose to secure him.

'I think I would like to get married,' she said.

Twelve

It was mid-morning and snowing the day that Paddy Harper came to the office. Niall knew it must be something important. Paddy, like most good workmen, kept his head down, though Niall saw everybody every day. He knew each man by name. He thought such things were important and he was glad that he had kept the steelworks open this long, because he knew that without him it would not have happened and he was glad that he had been able to be generous to the men over Christmas but now he was ashamed to go into the works and wished to hide in his office because things were so bad. He didn't hide, he went in every day and watched over everything but he wished that he didn't have to. Angus knew that Niall would see any man who had a problem, so when Paddy arrived in Niall's office that morning, cap in hand, Niall knew that it was something serious. Paddy looked old, he looked awkward, upset. Niall urged him into the office, gave him a seat. Paddy tried to refuse the seat.

'How's Mrs Harper?' Niall asked.

Paddy shook his head.

'I got an earful before I left this morning and no wonder,' he said. 'She likes you, you know. She says if it hadn't been for you we wouldn't have lasted this long and that makes it worse.'

Niall tried to look into Paddy's face but the man was so down-cast that he wouldn't meet Niall's eyes.

'It can't be that bad.'

'Aye, it is,' Paddy said. 'I've been offered a job like, full-time with overtime, you see.'

'Well then, you have to take it.'

'Mr Redpath has offered jobs to all the best men. I don't like him, mind you, but I've got six bairns to feed. Jemma is mad as hell about it. She says I'm a rat leaving the sinking ship.'

'You have to be sensible,' Niall said and after that he made all the right noises. Why shouldn't Paddy go? Why shouldn't all the men go? He ought to have been pleased, at least if they left he didn't have to go on paying them. Paddy was a good man and if the management was not clever enough to provide work then there was no reason for him or anyone else to stay.

He was not having a good morning. He had come back from Newcastle very late and Caitlin had gone to bed. He was glad of that, the only thing was that he thought he should tell her what had happened in Newcastle but so far he hadn't had the opportunity, which was another good reason for hiding in his office. After Paddy left, Niall walked slowly around the foundry, trying to think what more he could do to find work. In the early evening, when everyone had gone home and the place was silent, Caitlin came through into his office. It was the first time he had seen her all day.

He couldn't meet her eyes.

'You went to her, didn't you?' Caitlin said. 'You slept with me and then you went to her. How could you do that?' It was what he had been waiting for her to say all day. Niall had no idea. He didn't know how anybody could do such a thing. Caitlin stood back against the wall as though relieved she had finally said it but distraught too because she was so upset.

'My father was right about you.' Her voice was low as though she wished to distance herself from it. 'You have done all those dreadful things and you sleep with women who take money. I kept telling myself that it wasn't true but I've heard you go and come back and seen you and . . . I tried to think of an explanation for it. I pretended to myself but in fact it's all true, isn't it?'

He didn't say anything.

She almost smiled.

'I'm sure you think I'm very naïve to imagine that a man might want to sleep with me and nobody else . . .'

'I don't think it's naïve,' he said.

'Unrealistic then?'

'No.'

Her eyes were like green knives. Niall could already see the outcome of this conversation and he didn't want to go through any of it. He didn't want her to stand there and call him names and accuse him of doing things he could not defend. He knew that none of what he had done was right but he couldn't alter it and he couldn't tell her and he couldn't explain any of it away. It was like being a boxer who had no corner to go back into, standing in the middle of the ring being continually punched without being able to hit back.

'You think men are entitled to more than one woman? You approve of those who marry and take mistresses? You think that whatever a man can hold he has a right to? Is that it?'

'No.'

'But that is·what you do, you sleep with different women.'

That was exactly what he did, there was no disputing it and he could no longer put off telling her what he had agreed to.

'I'm getting married,' he said.

'*Married?*' Caitlin said it as though she didn't recognize the word, had never heard it before. She started to laugh and it was so bitter that Niall wished himself anywhere but here because he knew that he would remember it and somehow, hard as other things had been, hurting the woman that he loved was a whole new feeling. 'You could blame me, I suppose. You could say that I came to you and that would be right, when you had already done the gentlemanly thing. That was what you did or was it something else, guilt or . . . perhaps I was just novelty.'

This was getting the better of him.

'Did you know then that you were getting married?' she said. 'You must have done, surely. People don't just suddenly decide to get married, or do they? I ought to know, I've been almost married so often. When did you decide?'

'Last night.'

'Last night? So you went to bed with me and then decided that you couldn't wait to marry someone else?'

'It wasn't like that.'

He hadn't meant to say anything, because anything he did say was somehow incriminating and, indeed, she held his gaze and moved nearer and said in interested tones, 'No? What was it like?'

'I promised Bridget that any time she wanted I would marry her.'

'Oh, right. So you were promised to Bridget all this time.' Her voice had been getting softer and softer all the way through the conversation until now it could not have been heard by anyone more than a couple of feet away. 'Did you tell her about me, was that what decided her?'

'No.'

'Then I wonder what it was? How very strange that she should want to get married now.'

She opened the door and ran. He shouted her name and would have run after her but she picked up her coat from the chair in the corridor outside her office and bolted from the building. As she did so a dark figure emerged in the doorway. It was Ian Souter.

Niall felt instinctively for the knife in his pocket but it wasn't there. He didn't carry it any more. He was so afraid that he might inadvertently kill or badly hurt somebody with his uncontrollable temper that he left it in his room every day, less afraid that Mr or Mrs Bentley might find it than that he would do damage with it. He had been inclined to throw it away. Now he wished it was there. He also wished that he had locked the doors but then, if he had, Caitlin would be there too and he knew that wasn't good. He never did lock the doors. He spent hours there in the evenings doing paperwork. The weather was bad and there was no reason for anybody to come to the works. Staying at the foundry was easier than sitting in the hotel worrying. At least while he was here he could do something about it and lately he had had the idea that he would travel further afield in search of work. There must be some way past Aulay Redpath. He would go abroad and find work, places Aulay had not thought of. This cheered him at least partly, though he had the feeling that any idea he might come up with, Aulay had already followed and made use of. He must be getting work from a long way off if he could take on more men, though Niall knew that Aulay would do it anyway, just to spite him. He hoped there was work for Paddy and the other men, he hoped Aulay would give them decent housing and good wages, but he knew that once Aulay secured them, when they had nowhere to go, then he would use them as badly as he chose. When the Morgan steelworks closed, Aulay could do whatever he wanted. Niall couldn't let him do that, whatever the cost.

'Mr McLaughlan. How are you?' Mr Souter said.

Niall could hear other people and he could see their forms in the shadows and he cursed himself for leaving the doors open. Ian Souter came around the desk and sat down on it and he pushed Niall's chair back with one foot. There was a kind of sweaty excitement in his eyes, a gleeful heat. Niall wasn't afraid of much any more but he was afraid of Ian Souter now.

'I've got a message for you from Mr Morgan,' Ian Souter said. 'He isn't well enough to deliver it personally so he sent us,' and he indicated to the men to come inside. 'He says you aren't to pretend to be his grandson for whatever motive you might have. It isn't going to get you any money or an entrance to the house again and you won't get anything that his wife left. He knows you think you can get your hands on it because you made up to her but you won't. Do you understand?'

Niall understood perfectly. He wished he didn't. Four of them was too many. He might have managed two.

Ian Souter got hold of the front of Niall's jacket and put him against the wall and they didn't give him time to try to hit them first. They hit him. He did the best he could but it wasn't a contest. If they wanted to kill him they could probably manage it just with their boots. The funny part about it was that the bit that hurt most was that Thaddeus Morgan hated him, he must have done. You didn't do things like this, things you had to pay other people to do, over a mild dislike. Was Thaddeus afraid of him? But if Thaddeus had thought even for a second that Niall might be his grandson he would not have done such a thing. Was Thaddeus afraid that Niall, as an imposter, could end up with the whole Morgan inheritance, however much it was, that he might try to prove he was a Morgan? Had Mr Rayburn not told him that Niall had relinquished all claim to the will or was Thaddeus afraid that he might change his mind, or was there some other reason Niall was not aware of? He was inclined towards the latter while he could still think. That didn't last long. Somebody knocked him back into the edge of the big cupboard, where he hit his head with such force that the pain made him dizzy and confused and shortly after that things became hazy. He couldn't hear what Ian Souter was saying to him, he was just vaguely aware that it was insulting and he could hear the papers drifting to the floor and the furniture being ill treated and his chair breaking and the photographs on the wall being smashed, glass everywhere. And they had knocked him about so much that he was down on the floor. The floor was so cold and his grasp on reality so slight.

It hurt an awful lot. He began to wonder how long it took four people to kick you to death and to hope that it wasn't going to be too long. He thought he was back in the cellar at the home, bleeding and cold and by himself again. He couldn't have his mother or George or Jean or even his grandmother on Saturday afternoons. It was dark and there was no entrance and no exit. Perhaps he was dead. Perhaps this was what coffins were like. He was in the churchyard, the lid nailed down and there was silence finally. He did remember where he was when they stopped. They must have thought he was dead. He felt dead. There was no movement in or around him. Nothing. It was almost like standing outside himself and watching them and he didn't think you could do that if you were still alive.

They talked as they went away. They spoke about normal things. How strange. As though they had spent the evening in a trivial way. They called one another by their names and mentioned food and somebody laughed but it was not the kind of laughter that was revenge well taken. It was not Ian Souter laughing. It was laughter which had nothing to do with him. He was just a job to them, something they had been paid to accomplish and now that it was over they could go home to their wives and children, who no doubt were fast asleep in their beds. He was fast asleep too, breathing very slowly, with the smell of blood everywhere, sticky where his hands lay. As the sound of their voices and their footsteps faded, everything else went with it until he was not there either.

It was very late when Caitlin arrived home and if she had had anywhere else to go she would have gone there instead. She knew that she did not have any right to go back there but she could not think of what else to do. At first she had not thought, just cried. She was jealous, she hated Bridget Black and she hated Niall for making her think he cared for her. She ran back to the hotel and packed and left so, after buses and trains, it took most of the evening before she finally arrived at the front door of her parents' house.

Luckily they did not go to bed early and the lights were on. She banged on the door. Her father answered the door himself and after initial hesitation let her inside. He carried her luggage in for her and then her mother came into the hall, saw her and stood still, putting her fingers to her mouth, trembling. They sat her down by the fire, gave her something to eat, did not ask questions, and when her mother took her upstairs her room was just as she had left it, the fire was lit by then and the bed was aired.

'You knew I would come back.' How dreadful that they had

known. What was it like to be middle-aged and know such things?

When she was finally in bed and exhausted Caitlin couldn't sleep. She had thought that Niall loved her. How could she have been so mistaken? Why had she thought so, when he was always sneaking back here? It had just been an impulse on his part. She missed him, she missed the dreadful hotel and her room and knowing that he was next door, she had liked hearing him move about. She had liked her work and the foundry but she could not stay there with him married to another woman. She could not bear it.

There were no sounds in this house and she was no longer used to the silence. She listened in vain for the noises of the bar down below, the men talking and laughing and sometimes singing and Mr Bentley's voice, darker and lower than all the rest.

She lay and thought that she heard in her mind the prison door swinging shut behind her. She had no future other than as a daughter, it would be all she ever was and she would spend the rest of her life being polite to people. She would be asked nowhere and she would have nothing to look forward to, and she realized what she had done to her parents. She should have married Simon Anstruther and they would have been proud of her and she would have been accepted by society and they would have had grandchildren. She wondered if they were lying in bed together now, talking of what a mess she had made of her life. They had done so much for her. All she had done was make them unhappy.

When Niall came round he was in bed at the hotel and Mrs Bentley was standing over him and so was a tall dark thin man, looking accusingly at him.

'Where's Cat?' he said and then wished he hadn't, not just that he hadn't spoken of her but that he hadn't come round at all, it hurt so much. He couldn't talk any more, he just wanted to go back to sleep but the pain kept getting in the way and he wanted to turn over but he couldn't because it hurt too much and he kept forgetting that it would hurt and tried to turn over and then the pain drove him back. It got very sweaty. The fire was blazing all over the place and the sweat ran in rivers and then the fire was out and he was coming in every evening and it was so cold that it made you want to sit down and cry because there wasn't somebody at home cooking a dinner and keeping the fire going but then there had not been anybody at home since Jean and Nanny and then Jean was there. How remarkable. Where had she been? She didn't look any different and he thought she should have done. Shouldn't she have been older than that? She drew him close just like she always did and he knew that everything was going to be all right. She was so kind. He was at home. He had always known that he would go back and they would be there, just as they had been when he was small and Edinburgh had been so wonderful, so cold and wet and grey and wonderful. Home. Sweetshops and kites and friends in the street, and little alleyways where people lived and the big houses where he could go because his friends lived there. It was cold in Edinburgh, the streets were white with snow and all the window ledges were so pretty and he was walking up Princes Street, holding Jean's hand and looking up at her and smiling and she was looking down at him and then they were on the beach at St Andrews and it was the best, it was the very best that life had ever been, the sea broke slow upon the sand and gulls called above and his father was waving from the dining room of the hotel which looked out over the eighteenth hole of the golf course. The little stone bridge and the green and his father waving and Jean taking him home for tea. They were waving back, they were on their way. The waves were breaking over the sandcastle and her fingers were warm and the sun was setting. They would soon be back in the hotel and there would be scones and butter and jam for tea and later Jean would read him a story. It was always the same story. He knew it off by heart. So why couldn't he remember it? Why couldn't he remember what the story was?

When Niall awoke the tall thin man was sitting asleep in a chair by the bed and Vinia was asleep in another chair by the window and a pale winter sun was making its way in through the window. It was early morning, at least he thought it was. Vinia opened her eyes and then she got up slowly, watching him all the while, and she came over to the bed.

'How do you feel?' she said and the man came over too. Niall recognized him vaguely. He was the local doctor.

'Strange.'

'Good morning, Mr McLaughlan,' Dr Jameson said. 'You look better.'

'I have to go to work,' Niall said.

'No, you don't. Joe is there, taking care of things,' Vinia said.

She wouldn't let him get up for any length of time and Niall was glad of that because standing up was inclined to make him dizzy and thinking about anything much was too difficult. He slept. Every time he woke up she was there, trying to spoon broth into him – it was disgusting – and giving him lots of advice which Niall ignored. She wouldn't let him have any visitors but Niall was rather pleased about that because conversation made him tired.

The local police came but Ian Souter had disappeared and Thaddeus Morgan, when questioned, denied any knowledge of what had happened. Mr Morgan was a well-respected man in the area and, since there was no evidence to link him to the incident and Niall could not identify the other men involved and they had vanished without leaving any clue, the police said there was nothing to be done.

'You can come to us and stay when you're well enough to be moved,' Vinia said.

'I'm fine,' Niall objected. 'Please don't give me any more of that stuff. I'll never eat soup again.'

He enquired after Caitlin but he didn't really need to be told that she had left, that she had got on the train and that they thought she had gone back to Newcastle. Vinia didn't seem to know any more.

After a fortnight he stopped sleeping so much, the pain had lessened considerably. He was beginning to get bored and he wasn't as tired. Joe or Dryden would call in every evening to keep him up to date with what was going on at the pit and at the foundry. They were hearty, enthusiastic, so that Niall suspected a lot of what they told him was untrue. One afternoon Vinia said she was going to pop out for a few minutes. Did he mind? Niall was desperate to get rid of her, to do without her fussing for a little while and when she had finally closed the door and left him in peace he lay down again and closed his eyes. He heard her footsteps die away on the stairs. He dozed. He enjoyed that almost-sleep when he could still hear everything but not actually have to do anything about it.

A short time later – at least he thought it was a short time – he kept slipping away into a half-dreaming state and his dreams

were wonderful, had been all the way through. He dreamed different aspects of his childhood and it made him happy.

'I don't know who all these women are you talk about in your
sleep,' Vinia had said, not quite joking. 'There do seem to be a
great many of them, Jean and Nan and Peggy.' Peggy was Mrs
McLaughlan and he didn't know why he talked of her by her
first name because she had always been Mrs McLaughlan to him.
Niall didn't explain himself. He told her he couldn't remember –
some time later footsteps came up the stairs and he was so used
to hearing the way that Vinia came up the stairs that he knew it
wasn't her and although his senses went into overdrive, thinking
somebody was there to harm him, he knew it was just panic. The
footsteps weren't heavy enough to be a man's. As he lay there
and waited somebody opened the door. Niall debated whether
to pretend to be asleep but the person, instead of coming inside,
hovered uncertainly in the doorway as though unsure of welcome and he thought it might be Caitlin so he opened his eyes.
It was Jemma Harper. She looked carefully across at him.

'I don't like to disturb you,' she said, 'but there's nobody
downstairs and . . . Paddy and me, we were bothered about you,
though after what he's done to you I don't know why you should
have anything to do with either of us.'

Niall smiled.

'Come in, Mrs Harper,' he said.

'Oh, you *have* been in the wars,' she said. 'How are you feeling?
I've brought you some cake.'

She indicated the basket on her arm and proceeded to take
out something covered in a cloth. It smelled like ginger. She put
it down on the little table which now lived near the window and
which held various medicines, the tray for his meals and other
things.

'I mustn't stay.'

Niall sat up. He found that he was glad of the company and Mrs Harper was one of his favourite people. It had been partly due to her that he had not sold the business to Aulay, so she was also part of his troubles, but he liked her. He thought she was what the girls in Newcastle would be in fifteen years or so, possibly sooner.

'Sit down,' he urged her.

'Paddy was going to come with me but he had to go to work. I'm sorry it's going so badly, Mr McLaughlan. We're all glad you tried to make it all right. Nobody else did. I told Paddy not to leave you, after everything you did for us when nobody else would. I've never forgotten that day when you stood up for me. It was the nicest thing that ever happened to me. We heard the news, well, everybody in Sweethope did, about you being Mrs Morgan's grandson and how the old man acted. I never liked him. He was never kind like you, never thought about anybody but himself. It broke his heart what his daughter died.'

'Did it?'

'Oh aye. He never wanted her to marry the Scotch man.'

'My father?'

Mrs Harper hesitated.

'Aye, your father. What was he called?'

'George.'

'George McAndrew. I remember him. Nowt was ever good enough for him.' Mrs Harper held Niall's eyes. 'You really are Mr Morgan's grandson?'

'Yes.'

'You look like his daughter.'

'Did you know her?'

'Everybody knew her. What a little miss. Bonny, just like you.

She thought she was too grand for round here so she would wed him and go off to Scotland and live like a princess.'

'And did she?'

'I suppose she did but she kept coming back. I don't think it was a very happy marriage.'

Mrs Harper didn't go on. Niall wished she would. He was enjoying her visit. He had never thought about the local people knowing his mother and about her marriage to George and her life, and it was lovely to hear somebody talk about all the things he didn't know anything about. George hadn't told him anything much about his mother other than that she was beautiful and beyond reproach, obviously nothing like she had been. Mrs Harper looked increasingly uncomfortable as though she ought to go.

'Tell me some more about her,' he urged.

'She was a star turn,' Mrs Harper said. 'Mr Morgan doesn't like you?'

'He doesn't think I'm his grandson. I don't use my name. I had . . . I had good reason.'

Mrs Harper nodded as though she understood and then she said, 'I must go.'

'Is there something the matter? There's not something wrong with Paddy, is there?'

She hesitated and then she said, 'No, it's nowt to do with Paddy.' Her eyes were grey and concerned. 'It's to do with you, my love. Paddy and me, we talked about it and about how kind you'd been to us and we didn't know whether to tell you or not. The truth isn't always the best thing and I think you've had a hard time, that's why you're so nice to us.'

'What is it?' Niall said.

'We talked about it a lot, night after night when he got home from work and you were having such a hard time and we nearly decided not to say anything but . . . the whole place knows that Mr Morgan is pretending you aren't his family or that he thinks that you aren't. Everyone knows that you've had to have dealings with those solicitors up at Frosterley and we thought it might help to prove who you are because, if you had all Mrs Morgan's money, you might be able to keep the steelworks open. And then it seems to us that given time you're going to find out anyroad and mebbe it would be better coming from somebody like us, rather than the way things have been for you lately. I mean, if you weren't his grandchild, it wouldn't matter but if you were . . . Paddy and me were wed a long time ago and we remember how Luisa Morgan kept coming back. She liked the good life but it wasn't enough for her, she had a reason to come back often.'

'What was it?' Niall said, sensing the worst.

'Mr McAndrew, he could give her everything and he was a gentleman . . . I mean, plenty of money, you know. The thing is that your mother . . . I don't know how to say this to you. Your father was old, at least old to your mother and . . . she had another man.'

Niall was wishing that he had pretended he was asleep when Mrs Harper came up the stairs, because he had the impression this was not something he was going to want to hear, but it was too late.

'Another man?'

The light had gone from the day and beyond the window it was snowing again. It was coming down harder than ever, almost sideways, as it did here, he had discovered.

'She had a lover?'

'People knew. Everybody knew, that's why I thought we should tell you in case somebody who didn't like you told you, and there aren't that many people that know . . . I mean, in the village there are but not up at Deerness Law, at least I don't think the gossip's got that far yet.'

What did she mean?

'Word gets round, you see. There was a bairn and she died. Now, your father and mother had been married for quite a long time and it may not be right to say it but the local gossip always had it that the bairn was not his, not Mr McAndrew's.'

Niall could hardly breathe. He felt dizzy even sitting down.

'There were people at the house when you were born, servants, and . . . the man came to the house and was there when she died, the day she died. After that Mr McAndrew took the bairn back to Scotland and nobody ever heard from them again. It was known that he had died and, naturally when there was no word, people thought the baby had maybe died before then.'

'Does the man live here? Is he still here?'

'Yes, he's still here,' Mrs Harper said and her grey eyes bored into Niall. 'It's Mr Forster that owns the pit.'

Niall's world fell. There wasn't a lot left holding it up and what there was broke right there. It crumbled, disintegrated. It was the finish. He had come through so much, but to discover that a man he liked and admired and respected more than anybody he had ever met was the father of an illegitimate son whom he had never acknowledged or done anything to look after swept away any good feelings that Niall still had.

'Joe Forster?'

'Yes.'

Niall's mind went all over the place, like a flock of pigeons newly released from the cree and one of them remained, would not be dispersed.

'He knew about me and he didn't do anything?'

'As far as I know.'

'Didn't he want me?'

'Mr McAndrew was a very powerful man.'

'But Joe Forster was quite well off. His family had the pit, didn't they, he was well respected, he had a . . . a nice house and enough money for a child, surely?'

'Yes, he had the pit. His father had died before then and he had run the pit even when he was a youngster. His father was a drunk,' Mrs Harper said.

She said other things and Niall was certain they were meant to be comforting but what he wanted was to be left alone in the gloom. When she had gone Niall wanted to die. All those years Joe Forster had been living there with his wife and no child, all that time when he was given up, treated badly, had no family, no friends, no education, when he was taken into the home and abused and then he had killed people and stolen and lived on the streets and done whatever he could, and all that time Joe and Vinia had been here living a proper normal family life and they didn't even have a son of their own.

The only thing Niall could think of now was flight. He had to get away. He got up and found clean clothes and washed and shaved and dressed and then he packed everything he could with the help of Mr and Mrs Bentley, who seemed concerned with nothing but that he should pay for Caitlin's room and his own, but they helped him carry his belongings into the car. Niall did not look back. He was tired, he ached, he felt dizzy, but his overwhelming need was to get back to Bridget. Other than that nothing mattered.

Thirteen

Niall remembered very little of his marriage to Bridget. He took George's way out and drowned himself in whisky. She seemed not to notice. The whole thing was laughable, he thought, the whore who wouldn't let a man near her marrying the gutter-snipe who was in love with someone else. Did she know it? He thought that she was like a mother who would suffocate her son with her love rather than let him lead a normal life with a woman who wanted him.

He tried to hate Bridget but he couldn't, she fussed like a wife and looked at him in the mirror when they were about to leave the house and told him he was a painting, which made him laugh. How long had she been having his suits made for him and admiring her own taste? The suit was silver-grey silk. Niall hated it, he looked like a kept man, like somebody who had never worked, the very opposite of Joe, the very opposite. His reflection told him of his father and yet, looking now, he could see Joe. He was like Joe without the honesty, without the security, without the love. It was an image of perfection. How ironical when he was in fact the very opposite.

Bridget wore a cream dress and she was so very beautiful that when they got to the church people stopped and stared at the vision who stepped out of the car – it was a new car, to replace the Daimler, and she had bought it. It reminded him of how very kept he was, but he told himself that she had wanted him, so there was no reason why she shouldn't keep him now. She had never done it like this before.

It was the church they had attended all those years ago as children and when he stepped inside its gloomy splendour the feelings which he had subdued for so long came back to him in a flood. He had wanted to steal the candlesticks upon the altar and the cups which were used for communion. He remembered being cold and wet and uncomforted and the darkness of his life all around.

It was not dark that day. Sunlight peered through the stained-glass windows and threw coloured sunbeams upon the floor like sweets. Gypsy was there and Carl and all the girls from the house, and the vicar, who surely should not have been associated with such people, conducted the ceremony so gravely, as though something real was happening. Bridget carried cream roses throughout the farce. Niall wanted to kill somebody.

Afterwards they went back to the house and drank champagne and ate cake. The dark winter day closed in, with lights through the fog that stole from the river, and Bridget took him into her arms by the fire and kissed him.

'Thank you,' she said. 'I know you didn't really want to do that.'

'I always wanted to. You were the one who held out.'

'I used to be able to tell when you lied to me. Now I'm not sure.'

'I never lie to you, Bridget,' he said and she laughed and he pulled her down on to his knee and it was almost as it should have been for married people, content in one another's company, in out of the cold night.

When she slept, when it was late and Niall lay awake, he thought about Caitlin. He had imagined before he slept with her that spending the night with her would be like spending the night with any woman. Perhaps if he had known what it was really going to be like he would never have done it. Nobody had ever loved him like Caitlin did. Nobody had ever kept him in bed for an entire Sunday. You could live a whole world, a whole lifetime, on a Sunday like that, how warm the bed had been and how cold the world had looked beyond it. How the light had come and gone and they had barely moved from the room. It was the day after Christmas. The noise of the merrymakers rose from below and the fire reflected blackly in the surround. That small shabby hotel room had become the most precious place on earth to him and as that day got further away from him so he clung to the memory of it like a lost toy. It had been the best day of his life.

Joe was surprised to get a note from Thaddeus Morgan. They had not communicated since the last time Joe had tried to buy the foundry from him. Thaddeus had refused to see him and Ian Souter had conducted the meeting and it had not gone well. He was reluctant to go this time but he went in the end, thinking that Thaddeus must have had a very good reason for asking. He was on time. It had been many years since Joe was at Thaddeus's house, he could remember little about it other than a party which he had taken Vinia to before they were married. A Christmas party. Luisa, Thaddeus's daughter, had been there and her husband, George. Joe remembered how very beautiful she was and the affair that they had had, so when he was ushered into the sitting room and saw the portrait of her above the fireplace he could not help staring.

'Remember her, do you?' Thaddeus said heavily. He hadn't got up but Joe knew it was not bad manners on his part, he didn't get up because he couldn't and Joe remembered how much he had liked Thaddeus, how much help Thaddeus had given him before Joe and Luisa had the affair and everything was ruined.

'How are you, Mr Morgan?'

'You didn't used to stand upon ceremony, Joe. Come and sit down, I want to talk to you. How are you, how's your wife?'

'She's fine, thank you.'

'She's a grand woman.'

'Yes.' Joe found that he didn't want Thaddeus to be nice to him now when it was too late. They had scarcely spoken in twenty years and Thaddeus had done everything he could to stop Joe's business progress. Where was the point in Thaddeus being kind to him?

'I've had the police here, they seemed to think I had something to do with Niall McLaughlan's being hurt and I didn't. I've never done such a low-down thing to anybody in my life and I'm hardly likely to start now. I didn't want Niall to think so either. I was angry, you see, but that was about the will. Ian Souter might have done it, I don't know. I don't know where he is or that he had sufficient reason to do such a thing. He didn't like Niall, which was hardly surprising, because Niall got rid of him and made him feel stupid. Whether it was sufficient for him to do such an awful thing I don't know. Did Niall say anything?'

'He told the police about Ian Souter and that he said he was acting on your behalf and he didn't know the other men. What's this about the will?'

Thaddeus looked carefully at him.

'You don't know, do you?' he said. 'I didn't think you did. My wife, Alice, left Niall some jewellery in her will.'

'Why would she do that?'

'She liked him,' Thaddeus said and smiled, but Joe didn't think he liked the look behind the smile. 'It was for his wife when he married.'

'I didn't know he was so well acquainted with your wife.'

There was a long pause before Thaddeus said, 'She thought he was her grandson.' There was a little pause before Thaddeus said, 'Luisa's child.'

Joe couldn't think, he didn't understand for seconds afterwards and nothing was in his consciousness but the beating of his own heart.

'Niall is a . . . he's an adventurer. I think that's the polite word for it,' Thaddeus said. 'He has no . . . no ideals, he's like rubber, he bounces back, always the same shape and without being affected by things. I thought he was trying to . . . trying to ingratiate himself with us.'

'But he bought the steelworks from you and tried to run it,' Joe said.

'Yes, I know.'

'He paid you, didn't he?' Somehow this tack was easier than any of the alternatives which were just beginning to gnaw at the edges of Joe's shocked mind.

'He paid me well. I was suspicious.'

'Did he say that he was . . . that he was your grandson?'

'No. I had the rector to see me earlier. I think I was influenced by what he said at the time but he told me, now that it's too late, that Niall went secretly to Luisa's grave when he thought he was unobserved. It was only after that that he and Alice . . .'

Joe gazed up at the portrait of Luisa above the fireplace. He couldn't decide whether Niall looked like her and then he caught sight of his reflection in the mirror on the other wall and knew who Niall looked like. But for the eyes, it was so like him. Joe felt sick.

'I tried to stop her from seeing him. I told him he wasn't welcome here,' Thaddeus said. 'The thing is, you see, that all these years the only thing that kept me sane was the idea that George had looked after him. I made enquiries from time to time and I knew that George had sold everything and gone to live in Edinburgh and I thought . . . I don't know. I lost track of him. It didn't seem important. George would hardly let us see him and, although he was the only grandchild we had, I didn't feel that we were entitled to anything. I also . . .' Thaddeus looked ashamed. 'I also thought that, if we'd made contact when he was a child, you would somehow try to take him away . . . having none of your own. I thought so, but it seems to me now that Niall's life has been . . . Alice said that George had died when Niall was very young but she didn't seem to know much after that, he didn't tell her and I feel so guilty, so responsible.'

'Does he know about me?'

Thaddeus looked at him and nodded.

'That's why I asked you here. I think he must or he will very soon find out, because people will remember what happened. So I thought I should see you.'

'That was very considerate,' Joe said.

It was midday by the time Joe reached Newcastle and a short time afterwards he was directed, by a man who looked curiously at him, towards Black's. He had never been to a brothel in his life.

He knocked on the door but there was no response and as far as he could see all the windows were thickly curtained. It was not until he banged loudly for the second time that he heard bolts being drawn back and then the door inched open and a woman peered at him from inside.

'What do you want?' she said.

'I've come to see Niall McLaughlan.'

'He don't see people at this hour. There's nobody here . . .'

'Please,' Joe said. 'I'm his . . . I'm his father.'

She opened the door more widely and Joe peered into the gloom. He smelled stale tobacco and empty whisky bottles. The lights in the hall illuminated dark red velvet curtains.

'There's nobody up yet,' the woman complained, wet cloth in hand. 'And I've hardly got started.'

'It's very important that I see him.'

'All right. You go upstairs, not the first flight, the second. Up there and right along to the end. They might be up and about by now. Mind you, don't cause no trouble, because Carl will be here in a minute.'

With this explanation she disappeared back along the hall. Joe followed her instructions, trod up the stairs on thick carpets. It was silent up there and all the doors were closed. It was dark too, he had to move slowly. There were no city sounds and tiny slivers of light tried to make their way past the curtains from what must have been a big garden or yard in the middle of the building. The stairs had wrought-iron banisters and you could look through them and see the hall below. Not that you could see much.

The smell of cigarette smoke and drink was thick in the air, as well as something else. Joe wasn't quite sure what. Drugs? Sex? He didn't know. And there was the odour of well-used beds, the early morning smell of bodies not yet awake or washed. Up another flight, which no doubt in older times had been where the servants were housed, and here a little light fell through not-quite-closed curtains and the carpet gave out, not as though somebody had run out of money but as if the illusion of sex on offer had ceased. The floorboards were bare, varnished, and the walls were white. The doors were all closed.

Joe walked along the hall to the very end and not knowing what else to do he opened the nearest door. Inside was a very big room. It must indeed take up most of the top storey. Other doors led off it.

It was light. There were curtains but they were pulled well back and the early afternoon sunshine fell across the room in great swathes. The windows were huge, they took up most of the walls on two sides and even opened out as doors on to a balcony and there was a view of rooftops, chimneys, sky, with pigeons strutting about. The floor was again polished boards and there was not much furniture. Against the far wall was the biggest bed Joe had ever seen. Around it were strewn bottles, glasses, ashtrays and a variety of partly eaten food on plates. There were also clothes discarded as though two people, eager for one another, had stripped them off as their bodies met.

The bed itself was completely white and in it lay Niall and the most beautiful woman Joe had ever seen. Her hair was so blonde it was almost white and it was long, it must go way past her waist. It was a tangled mess as though he had run his fingers through it a dozen times and it partly hid her perfectly formed naked body.

They looked like children sleeping on an island. It made Joe think of fairy tales, turned in towards one another, she very close with her face at his shoulder and he with one arm across her as though in protection, their naked shoulders only just visible above the bedclothes. They looked vaguely incestuous, so fair, so apparently alike. On the round table at Niall's side lay a knife within reach, as though even in his dreams he felt he was not safe.

Joe didn't know what to do. He felt as though he shouldn't be there. Should he go back outside and knock? Should he say Niall's name? The matter was resolved for him, as, without moving an inch or even opening his eyes, Niall said in a low voice, 'One more step and you're dead meat.'

Joe tried to speak, to identify himself, but he couldn't. He stood still. Niall opened his eyes, turned slightly, sat up. He was unshaven, his hair was a tangled mess, bruises from his recent beating like shadows on his face. He looked narrowly at Joe and reached for a cigarette, lit it, sat back against the pillows.

'Who let you in?' he said.

'The . . . the woman downstairs. The cleaner.'

The beautiful girl beside Niall moved slightly, put one creamy arm out of bed to where a discarded robe, thin, silky, dark-blue, lay on the floor. With practised ease she drew it in beside her and put it around her body and then, without a word or a look, she slid from the bed and then from the room. Her hair was indeed longer than her waist, she was small, slender, but her figure was womanly, Joe thought. Her eyes were almost black they were so dark, the lashes around them thick, smoky, like velvet, her face oval, her mouth . . . men would have given years of their lives to touch that mouth.

She went out and closed the door.

'So, what do you want?' Niall said.

Joe couldn't remember.

'Nothing,' he said.

'You come all the way to Newcastle and invade my privacy for nothing?' Niall said.

'I wanted to see you.'

Niall didn't help him. He sat and smoked the cigarette and sunlight fell all over the bed, lighting up the blue smoke that came from it and showing up the bruises on his body, some of which had begun to fade into his creamy skin. To Joe it was like looking at himself all those years ago except for the eyes. He thought Niall had the coldest, bluest eyes that he had ever seen.

'Is that Bridget Black?'

'She's my wife.'

Joe stared. Niall laughed. He pushed the cigarette down hard into the ashtray.

'You didn't think I bedded women I wasn't married to? Dear, dear,' he said.

Joe could hardly breathe somehow.

'I went to . . .' How long had Niall been here, how many years had he lived such a life and before that . . . ? 'I went to see Thaddeus Morgan. He'd had the police there. He didn't send Ian Souter . . .'

'You mean he says he didn't.'

'He says he didn't,' Joe muttered. 'He says Souter hated you for throwing him out and because he couldn't get another job and . . . He says that you think that you're his grandson.'

'He says I claim to be his grandson,' Niall corrected him. 'Actually I don't claim anything.'

'He said that too, that you had had dozens of opportunities to tell him and you didn't. He said that you befriended his wife.'

'Is that what he calls it?' Niall said. 'And so, you came all the way to Newcastle to find the truth. You ventured into a whore-house and into a whore's bedroom to discover whether I was in fact your son. Do you think I look like you?'

'Well, yes . . .'

'Do you think I look like Luisa McAndrew?'

'I think you look very like her.'

'Thaddeus couldn't see it. I could be anybody. You had no right to come here.'

Joe stood in the silence, like a child in the corner.

'What did you hope to gain?' Niall said. 'You're not going to tell me you're sorry, are you? Because if you do I think I might just break your neck.'

Joe's throat ached.

'Have you come here to claim something?' Niall said. 'Go on then, do it. Tell me who you are. Tell me why you gave up your child. Tell me what you were doing all those years that was so very important. Justify yourself to me. You can do it, you self-righteous bastard. You're so good, so respected. People look up to you.'

The room was like a merry-go-round to Joe after that. All the way here he had told himself that it was not true, that Niall was not his child, that there had been some mistake, that Niall would give him coffee and laugh and everything would be all right. His child was in Scotland, he was by now the head of a great enterprise, living in luxury, as George McAndrew's son. Having had no rights to him, Joe had left it, comforted himself, when he was lonely for his son, that things were better as they were.

'Niall . . .'

'Don't call me by my given name. Don't you ever call me by it.'

It was true then or Niall would not be this angry. His son had lived in ways which Joe knew nothing of nor had wanted to, had grown up in a world where women sold themselves and men . . . what did men do?

'I don't want to know how sorry you are, because I'm going to make you sorry. I'm going to show you what it's like when people abandon you. I'm going to abandon you, Joe. Watch me.'

There was a polite knock on the door and through the mist in his eyes Joe could see the biggest man he had ever come across, who opened the door slightly.

'Miss Black said you might need help, sir.'

'Thank you, Carl. Could you show Mr Forster out?'

Fourteen

It was mid-evening when Niall went to Aulay Redpath's house. He made himself go. It was the last place he wanted to be and he knew that he was not welcome there. The whole place looked so welcoming, the cream light spilling from the windows, breaking up the dark foggy night. As soon as the door was opened Niall wanted to go inside. He always did. Aulay's house with its garish furnishings had been precious to him once and still somehow held promise of better things. The smell of good cooking rushed him like a tide and in the hall behind him some bright yellow flowers stood in a huge vase as though Fiona had decided not to let the gloomy weather invade her house. There was a big fire burning and a dog lying asleep in front of it. The maid who opened the door recognized him but did not say anything other than that she would enquire. She kept him standing in the cold for a considerable time and then came back to tell him that Mr and Mrs Redpath were not at home.

'Like hell they aren't,' Niall said and moved past her.

She protested, and then he was into the hall with its big sweeping staircase, where he had been so many times, and Aulay was striding angrily towards him and saying, 'What do you think you're doing?'

'I want to talk to you.'

Aulay was thinner, Niall thought, and it didn't suit him. He was the kind of man who should have had a comfortable middle age. It had been denied him. There were new lines on his face, his red hair was sparse and there were threads of white in it.

'How dare you come here?'

'Five minutes, Aulay, just five minutes. I've got a business proposition for you and it's to your advantage.'

'You piece of shit!' Aulay said when the maid had gone back into the recesses of the house.

As Niall's gaze followed her he saw a shadowy figure emerge from another room and then she became substantial and it was Caitlin.

It changed his day, it meant everything, even just a glimpse would have been enough and he got more than that, because, unable to believe what she was seeing, she ventured nearer, so that Niall was able to feast his eyes. She was thinner too and she didn't look beautiful any more, because he had put her through hell, but he thought she was more precious than anything on earth. He had not realized before that her eyes were just like Joe's, what a coincidence. Her gaze was harsh on him but he didn't care, it was enough to know that she was alive, that she was there, that she was just across the town from him and every time he slept she was only a few streets away. He hadn't thought of it like that before, how near she was to him, almost breathing the same air, seeing the same sunrise, walking the same streets. They might bump into one another. She wore such a beautiful dress, it was so pretty, it was green and short and . . . She even said his name, she said it with distaste but his name had met her lips, there was the connection. He could not stop looking at her. There was no reason why he should, because any moment now Aulay would tell her to go back, would have him thrown outside, so he should hang on to that time, to those few seconds, so that in the night she would be imprinted upon his memory and he would have her there in the darkness.

Aulay didn't tell her to go back and he didn't have Niall thrown out, he just opened the nearest door and then they were inside and she was not there. Niall went on looking at the door, half convinced it would open and then Aulay said, 'You have ruined everything.'

Niall was surprised, he did not expect openness from a man who must despise him.

'Oh, surely not,' he said.

'Yes, you have.' Aulay stared sadly at the night. The curtains were not drawn against the window, the draughts and the dark had not been shut out. How was that? Had they no maid to see to it or did they not care?

It was the last, beyond the last thing that Niall expected him to say and it was sufficient to fell any decent man. Not him of course.

'You married your whore,' Aulay said.

'She was never that. I think it must have been a word that men devised to suit their evil purposes, don't you think, that women should hold such disfavour? She never sold herself.'

Aulay laughed.

'Everyone sells themselves, don't you know? Caitlin is my only child and she will never marry now, you ruined her. It was a . . . a hard equalizer, Niall, for what I did to you.'

'It was never meant to be that. I always cared very much for all of you. Look, Aulay, I want you to have the Morgan steelworks. I can't go on running it while you're trying to stop me and I wouldn't have the men put out of work. If you would only say that you might keep it open, I would give it to you.'

'Give it to me?' Aulay stared at him. 'Why would you do that? The fight isn't over yet.'

'It's over. You can have the works but there is a condition. I want you not to buy your coal from Joe Forster. I want everything that he owns.'

Aulay didn't say anything and Niall could almost see his brain working, trying to decide why Niall should stop mid-battle, why he should turn on the man he had liked and respected, why he should give up at this point.

'He's on his last legs now,' Aulay said.

'Yes, I know.'

'You want him bankrupt?'

'I want him on the street.'

'Literally on the street?'

'Very much so. If you promise to do this for me I will have the papers drawn up and you can have the steelworks.'

'I didn't take you for a vindictive man.'

'You took me for everything else. Why not?'

Aulay hesitated.

'Please, Aulay, take it.'

'What will you do?' Aulay's voice was soft.

Niall couldn't believe now that he had ever wanted the steelworks, that it had mattered. Nothing mattered any more. 'Will you take it, if I sort the legal things?'

'I would be a fool not to.'

'Good. Well then, that was my five minutes. I'll have the papers sent to you,' Niall said and he left.

It was a wonderful night. The fog had lifted as the evening progressed. There was a star for every person, a moon you could have sat upon, it was still and cold and made you not want to die ever. When he got back she was waiting for him, his wife. She had made dinner, she wondered where he had been and why he was not on time. Had he said what time he would be back? He didn't think so. The dinner was good and so was the wine and she was there, looking after him. He wished he could have told her what he had said to Aulay Redpath, because it was true. She had never given herself to men for money, though she had paid other women to do so. She sat on his knee and kissed his face and she said, 'Where have you been?'

'Jesmond. I went to see Aulay Redpath. I've given him the Morgan foundry.'

Bridget put down the cup and saucer on to the tray. She liked the trappings of respectability, he thought, she had always aspired to them, at least in some ways, but she did not want to be respectable and poor. Nobody wanted to be respectable and poor but then not many people were prepared to live as she did in order to have money.

'I don't understand,' she said.

'It's obvious, surely. It hasn't made money, it's losing more every day and if the men are to have a chance of work then somebody must run it who has money and influence. He tried to stop me and he won.'

'But Niall, you can't,' she said.

'Why not?'

'Because . . .' She stopped there and regarded the tea tray with dislike. 'Because I wanted to give this up and go and live in the country and be . . . and be Mrs Niall McLaughlan.'

It made him want to laugh, as if that was anything at all other than illusion. Bridget had lived all her life without illusion. What would she want with it now?

'I want us to be . . . a family.'

'We are a family, Bridget, we've always been one.'

'Yes but . . . a proper family with . . . with a garden and days off at weekends and . . . a real day, so that we go to bed at night and . . . so that I don't have to do any more of this.'

'Brid, look, I will find something else.'

'But you don't have any money.'

'I can start again. I'm not exactly in my dotage.'

'I'm tired of all that,' she said.

'We could buy somewhere small in the country and—'

'I don't want anywhere small! I never wanted you to be – to be anything unimportant. You have a great many talents and a lot of ability and . . . I want to be there. How could you give away a business like that which is worth a great deal of money?'

Niall was irritated.

'It wasn't,' he said.

'It must have been. Surely you wouldn't let Aulay just have it. That's ridiculous. The site alone must be worth money. You must know that. And the buildings and the machinery and the goodwill . .'

'There is no goodwill left. Aulay stole it.'

'I don't believe that Aulay Redpath is so much cleverer than you are,' she said, getting up. 'Tell me why you did it.'

Niall hesitated.

'I'm your wife. I have the right to know why you just supposedly gave away something you cared for so very much. No, don't deny it, you did. And I don't believe that you have turned into the kind of do-gooder who cares so much about the men's wellbeing that you would sacrifice all your interests and everything you've worked for for such a reason.'

Niall had never had secrets from Bridget.

'I found out that Joe Forster is my father and I want revenge.'

Her reaction did not disappoint him. One of the things he

loved best about Bridget was that she understood everything about him.

'So that was why he came to see you,' she said. 'You didn't tell me.'

'Aulay will take everything from him if I give up the foundry.'

'I see,' Bridget said.

She didn't ask a single question and Niall knew then why he loved her. Bridget accepted him and everything about him and her acceptance and understanding always made him feel warm and that was the way that family were supposed to make you feel, he thought.

'Did you have a father?' he said to her.

'No. I had a lot of uncles. I think one of them was my father,' she said. 'But they would move in and then a while later they would move back out again and we were always moving around anyway, my mother was the moonlight-flit expert. We never paid, we always ran, and then she died. How could he have given you up?'

This was exactly the question Niall had asked himself over and over, so many times that he thought he was tired of it, except that when Bridget said it she made it sound as though he was the best person in the world and that nobody in their right minds would have done so.

'I'm sorry about the foundry,' he said.

'Who cares?' Bridget said. 'It was just that . . .'

'It was just that what?'

She shook her head.

'No, go on, tell me.'

'It was just that I would have liked a nice house and some peace.'

He thought it was a strange request and most unlike her. She had always been proud of the fact that she made her own money and had her independence. Perhaps he had been wrong and there was some reason which he had not worked out why she wanted to be married. Perhaps it had nothing to do with Caitlin Redpath.

Fifteen

When Joe got home that afternoon he was so tired he could hardly get out of the car. He tried to smile because he didn't know how to tell Vinia what had happened. For once she was early so he had no time to compose himself. She came anxiously to him across the front of the house.

'Joe, whatever's the matter?' she said.

He couldn't tell her. He couldn't move. All he could see was the hard look in Niall's eyes and he knew that it was not entirely because he had come to hate Joe, it had always been there. The circumstances of his life had made it so, whatever they were.

'You're frightening me,' his wife said.

'Vinny . . .'

She put her arms around him and walked him into the house.

'It can't be so very bad,' she said.

'It is.'

'Tell me.'

'I don't know how to.'

'Come and sit down. Here.' She sat him on a chair in the living room, kneeled down, got hold of his hands. 'Whatever it is, we'll manage.'

He couldn't look at her but there seemed nowhere else to look and anyway it was cowardly so he made himself do it. She was the most important thing in his life and had been since the day he married her all those years ago and he knew how badly she had wanted to have a child.

'It's Niall,' he said.

'You've found him?'

'He went back to Newcastle, to Bridget Black.'

'That dreadful woman. Why ever did he do that?'

'They're married.'

'Oh dear.' Vinia sighed and sat back slightly. 'I hoped he would marry Caitlin. How did you find out?'

'I went to see him.' It was his home, Niall's home was a place where men went to satisfy their grosser desires.

'You went there? What on earth was it like?'

Strange. It had been strange, Niall and Bridget like a small oasis of purity, somehow, in a rubbish dump, except that their eyes gave them away, for people so young, they were all-seeing, all-knowing, the eyes of experienced people. As though the darkness they had faced was too dark and the world should never come close again. He didn't answer and then she asked the question he most dreaded.

'Why did you go there?'

Joe couldn't focus.

'Because I discovered that Niall is . . . is . . .'

Is possibly my son? Is probably my son? It wouldn't do.

'My son.'

There was a great big gap between him saying the words and his wife having any reaction. It seemed to Joe that it took minutes, maybe hours, before the puzzled look in her eyes held tears.

'He's the child I had with Luisa,' Joe said.

'How do you . . . How do you know?' she said.

'Because he's so very angry with me,' Joe said, trying to smile and not managing it.

'Dear God,' Vinia said and got up.

They had not discussed children for years but he knew the amount of feeling that was there for himself, how much more must it be for her and how hurt would she be now to discover that he had a son who had nothing to do with her.

'What is he doing here?' she said, which had been his first reaction.

'I don't know.'

'But . . . but he . . . he's lived in Newcastle for years. Where is George? What happened?'

'I don't know. He won't tell me anything. He hates me.' Joe could hardly get the words out. 'What was I thinking about all those years?'

'You were thinking you weren't entitled to upset his life.'

'Upset it? I think he's been on his own for years and years and I think he blames me. Why shouldn't he? I do.'

Vinia got down and touched his shoulder in reassurance but somehow that made it worse. Joe wanted to sob like a child. He said, 'I abandoned him and now he says he's going to abandon me,' and put both hands over his face.

Amelia Mackenzie and Mr Wilson had followed Niall into the room, being not quite dead somehow, and he became Mr Wilson in bed with Bridget, bad teeth and greasy hair and thick, hairy hands, disgusting, loathsome, evil. Only in the grey dawn when he awoke the next morning did they disappear. He pulled on some clothes and went down to the kitchen and lit the stove. He sat there for a long time until the kettle boiled and when it did he made some tea. It was quiet.

By noon no one had stirred so he bathed and dressed and walked to the Crown and sat in the bar with a whisky and soda, smoking and deliberately not thinking about anything. A figure appeared at his side at about two o'clock. It was Jonty.

'I've got a couple of hours free. You want to play billiards?'

Niall was so grateful that he let Jonty win twice. He thought he could have stayed there for the rest of his life with half his mind on the game and the other on what a bloody mess he had made of his life. He liked the sound of the coloured balls as they chinked, fell dully into pockets, cannoned off cushions. He had the feeling that Jonty had more important things to do but he didn't mention them or let them get in the way of the game. Maybe it was just because he was winning, Niall thought, demolishing him so neatly that Jonty grinned.

'You could have let me win three in a row,' he said.

Rain pattered against the windows but nobody disturbed them. Jonty didn't ask stupid questions, in fact Niall couldn't remember the last time they had had a conversation that wasn't about football or billiards. This room was Jonty's indulgence, it was not for the public, it was at the back of the huge building which made up the Crown. There were prints on the walls, mostly of racehorses, and there were big cut-glass decanters containing whisky, brandy and port, and there was a soda siphon and thick stout glasses.

All through the afternoon they played while the rain fell steadily beyond the window and from time to time Jonty topped up the glasses with whisky and there were no sounds beyond the big door which cut off the billiard room from the rest of the hotel. Niall wanted to stay there for the rest of his life, slightly drunk, safe and warm, and watch Jonty, jacket off, trying to decide how to play an impossible shot which Niall had created.

The following day Niall went to see the solicitor to sort out signing papers for the business to be legally made over to Aulay. He felt better for a few days when he had done something about this and then he was bored. He wished that he had the right to go and see Aulay, to talk over what they had done, to make progress, to be somehow involved, but he was not.

On the Friday of that week Niall had slept all morning and was inclined to go to the Crown and see if Jonty had time for another game of billiards. It was a wet day, thick fog. Wasn't one supposed to dispel the other? He could hardly see to the far side of the street. It was mid-afternoon, quiet, just the odd passing car and horse-and-cart, women going about their shopping.

On the opposite corner stood a slight grey figure in the rain. Niall could not have mistaken her in a thousand years. It was Caitlin. He crossed the road towards her. She didn't move. She was standing in front of the shop on the corner, the kind of shop which sold leather goods, handbags, wallets, trinkets, musical boxes, the kind of whimsical goods which only well-off people bought. The rain was dripping off her hat. Her face was wet. Her clothes were dark with rain and Niall had a terrible desire to get hold of her, to hail a cab and run away with her.

'Cat,' he said. 'What are you doing?'

She barely acknowledged him.

'Nothing,' she said.

'Are you waiting for someone? You'll get your death, standing there. Why don't you come up to the Crown and I'll buy you some tea?' Just as though everything was normal.

She didn't say anything. They fell into step and the rain went on falling as though it had nothing better to do. He wanted to say vaguely paternal things to her, like what was she doing out in such weather, didn't she own an umbrella, anything so that they would be closer, but he couldn't. His stupid heart sang over her presence, he enjoyed each moment. He loved the pavement she stepped on, he envied the rain that fell on her and the clothes that touched her skin. He resented each person they passed. He hated every day he had not seen her. He wanted to go on walking with her in the cold rain for miles. The fog was so bad you couldn't see to the end of the road or the tops of the buildings. And he was happy. He didn't recognize the feeling at first.

They reached the Crown. Jonty was not expecting him but you wouldn't have known it. When Niall knocked and walked into the office he responded as though he had known all along that Niall would bring a woman who was not his wife to the hotel. After all, Caitlin had been there before. He had a private sitting room behind his office and he ushered them in there, saying that he would send for some tea.

Caitlin stood before the fire and Niall looked around him and thought he had never liked a room more. It was big, private, the curtains half closed against the day. It overlooked an empty yard. There was a big squashy sofa and a thick rug in front of the fire, several armchairs in a semicircle and books and a small table. He watched Caitlin strip off her wet gloves, unpin and remove her hat, put both down and hold out her hands to the blaze. Her hair had curled into little tendrils, making her, if it were possible, more beautiful than ever. Tiny drips clung to the curls like dew.

'Where were you going?' she said.

'Here. I sometimes play billiards with Jonty. He has a couple of hours off mid-afternoon.'

'You have nothing else to do of course.' She had turned around and was looking at him. Her eyes were very cool. 'You gave my father the steelworks.'

'It wasn't worth anything to anybody else. I couldn't have sold it. I thought it was worth a try just on the off chance that he would keep it open.'

'I don't understand why you did that. I thought you cared about it, were prepared to fight for it.'

She was right. He cared very much about the steelworks, he missed the warm smells, he missed going in to see the processes start up early in the day. He missed the frosty mornings and the men stamping their booted feet against the cold and the chill blast before the dawn broke beyond the village, turning the grey stone light and the river to silver. He missed the men playing football and shouting and laughing at midday. He missed his office with the little black fire surround and Angus and Mrs Elmott, his secretary, and the office staff and each man who worked there. He missed watching them go about their tasks with quiet competence. He missed all those who had gone to Aulay's for better pay and the general day-to-day of being there and of having Caitlin in the office next door and all this was the least of what he missed. There was his freedom and, however much he told himself that it didn't matter, being married was so very different from anything else he had experienced in his life. It was like being suffocated. But most of all he missed Caitlin. He missed her in the night and in his arms and the smell of the perfume that she favoured and her laughter and the knowledge that she cared for him without reserve and the taste and feel of her and the wonderful presence of being inside the circle of her love.

'Why did you give it up?' she said again.

She came to him. He had not realized that he had gone as far away as he could across the room in some vain attempt to avoid her questions.

'I didn't want it any more.'

'I don't believe you. Something happened.'

The tea arrived with little shortbread biscuits that smelled warm and creamy and sweet as though they had just been made. The waitress poured out the tea, offered cake, put a cup and saucer into his hands. Niall didn't want tea, his body clamoured for whisky. Whisky in the middle of the afternoon, he thought, I'm getting as bad as George. Since he'd known that George McAndrew was not his real father, he wondered why George had wanted him. It was not as though he had some business to be carried on, George had sold all that before they moved to Edinburgh. George had not seemed to want him very much, if he had, Niall would surely not have been banished to the nursery and then sent away to school. Alison had been to blame for that, or rather that George had fallen in love with her and thereafter ruined himself over it. Niall understood such things a little better, turning and regarding the woman who was sitting by the fire, drinking her tea.

'What were you doing there?' he said.

'Waiting for you,' she said, as though it were a matter of course.

'But you didn't know I was coming out.'

'I'd been there for hours.' She spoke so quietly that he could hardly hear her. He got down beside her. She turned her face away. 'I have no pride left, you see,' she said. 'No shame. I run after married men.' She moved away as best she could, considering that she was sitting in an armchair with a cup and saucer in her hands. 'The last time I did this you were there to rescue me. I miss you, so very much. All I want to know is why you married Bridget. I would like it to be the truth. After that I will go away and leave you alone.'

'What makes you think I want that?'

He took the cup and saucer from her hands and then he turned her hands over and kissed her fingers and the palms of her hands and her wrists.

'Believe that I love you, because it's true,' Niall said.

'I wish that you would just tell me why you felt you had to marry her. Is she having your child?'

Niall laughed.

'No,' he said.

'Why is that funny?'

He didn't answer her even though he knew without looking into her face that she was watching him closely. All he managed was, 'It isn't.'

Caitlin was still for several moments and then she said, 'I don't think we have anything more to say to each other, do you? You made your choice. I should have accepted it instead of encouraging you to behave badly again. I have to go.' She got up.

Niall thought about Nora. He could go to Nora and drown in her and she wouldn't ask him for anything, she wouldn't wonder why he didn't love her. He could pretend she was Cat and she wouldn't care. He tried to concentrate on this, because Caitlin was getting up and he might never see her again except across a street.

'Are you going to tell me why you married her?'

Niall couldn't find any words.

She left.

When she was gone he couldn't move. He hoped to God Jonty wouldn't come in. All he had to do was to get up and go.

Nora wouldn't mind that it was early, that she hadn't seen him in months, that he was useless and faithless and stupid. And then Caitlin came back into the room.

'My gloves,' she said.

Niall was sitting on the rug back against the sofa with his knees drawn up and his head in his hands by then. He couldn't get out of the way or pretend nothing was the matter. She stopped and then she came over.

'Niall?'

'Leave me alone. I'm fine.'

And then she did the very worst thing she could have done. She got down beside him and got hold of him and Niall thought that, yes, this was where he wanted to be, here, safe in her arms. It was the only safe place left, perhaps it had always been, so normal, so ordinary, the way things were meant to be. All he really wanted for the rest of his life was to have this woman to come home to and it was not going to happen, because God had left men to sort these things out by themselves and stupid bastards like Joe Forster had made a mess of it. And he had not the right to make another mess here.

'Please, just go,' he said.

He would go back to his wife. It was not really so bad. He did love her and she was kind to him and he could hold the ghosts at bay with perpetual policing of his mind. He could hold off the past for Bridget most of the time. It was all there was. He had no future with Caitlin.

She went. After she had gone Niall even remembered how to breathe properly and then how to get up and to present a bright face to Jonty and suggest billiards the following day as he went out.

*

When Niall got home there was a letter waiting for him in a long white envelope. There was tea on the tray by the fire and Bridget was behaving as she thought a wife should, discussing dinner and asking how Jonty was. Niall had always rated lying among his accomplishments and managed to tell her all about the game of billiards he had not played and who had been at the hotel that she might have known before he opened the letter.

It was from Mr Rayburn. Thaddeus Morgan had died, the funeral was to be the following day and Mr Rayburn would very much like to see him. Could Mr McLaughlan make an appointment?

Niall's appetite for dinner went. It was nothing to do with him that Thaddeus Morgan had died. Thaddeus wouldn't have given him the time of day and if he had relented and said that Niall could have Alice's pearl necklace, well, Thaddeus knew where he could stick that.

His wife perused the letter when Niall had retreated to an armchair and silence.

'You must go to the funeral,' she said, 'and I will write and tell Mr Rayburn that you will see him one day next week. Monday?'

'I am not going to any funeral,' Niall said.

And then he tried to imagine Thaddeus dying. If he was about to relent even a little, surely he would have asked Niall there to say goodbye to him? Had he died by himself? Had the maid found him apparently asleep in his chair or had he been in bed and had a hard death with the doctor there, struggling for his last breaths?

'You have to,' Bridget said.

'Why?'

'Because it's the right thing to do.'

'I could have been there,' he said and then thought, *They'll put that on my grave.*

She persuaded him, she even offered to go with him to the funeral and she wrote the letter to Mr Rayburn. Niall couldn't rest. For the first time he felt hatred for this place which had kept Bridget and himself for so long and he hated the evenings most of all, the time when respectable people sat around the fire and then went to bed, when this place came alive, more so as the evening progressed. He didn't have to have anything to do with it. Bridget had bought the house next door when it came up for sale, so that there was a lot more room, and she had made the entire top storey private for them with a sitting room and kitchen and bathroom, back stairs and a separate entrance, so that he never had to have anything to do with what went on below, but the very atmosphere of it all pervaded the entire building and sometimes the noise intruded from below and even though Bridget said that she no longer took an active part it was a rare night that she did not have to go down there for some reason, however trivial, and that broke the peace.

He wondered what it was like to die and have no one to mourn you. He wouldn't have gone to the funeral except that she made him go, talked all the way there, held on to his arm as they walked up the path towards the church.

The first thing that Niall noticed was how few people were there, and they were all in the front pews, at either side of the coffin. He could see Joe's fair head and Vinia beside him, so dark, and Dryden next to her and then several people whom he did not recognize and then the servants. They were no more than two dozen people in all. He wouldn't go to the front. They slid into a pew near the back and left before the service was over and Niall could not concentrate, could not sing a hymn or remember a prayer. All he could think was that Thaddeus would be buried beside Alice and Luisa and that they were his family and only one of them had he known at all well. Alice's image rose before him like she was real, smiling at him. It stopped him wanting to rush to the front of the church and batter Joe Forster over the head with something heavy.

He did not look at Joe's house when he passed it on the way back and he did not glance towards the Black Prince pit either, he just kept his eyes on the road and thought it was something else he would never have to do again.

The following week, having received a letter from Mr Rayburn saying that he would be happy to see Mr McLaughlan on the Monday morning, he drove back to Frosterley. All the way there he thought of how he would get Bridget out of that house and away from the business, how she shouldn't have to go on working and worrying about the place. He parked the car outside Mr Rayburn's office and could not help thinking of the last time he had been here and how unfruitful that had been.

Mr Rayburn greeted him cheerfully after telling him how sorry he was to hear of Mr Morgan's death, sat him down and then said, 'Barring two small bequests to people who had looked after him, Mr Morgan has left you his entire estate.'

It had been many years since Niall had wanted to faint but he thought it was as well he was sitting down. Everything changed, was not quite as it had been, shifting before his eyes. In leaving him everything Thaddeus had finally acknowledged who he was. It made Niall want to weep. He didn't want Thaddeus's money, all he had wanted from the old man was recognition. If Thaddeus had spared him even half an hour, if he had sat him down and offered him tea, it would have been enough. It was like a form of mockery that he had not been able to make friends with his grandfather.

After that Niall didn't hear much of what Mr Rayburn said. He was sure he even seemed rude, staring into space for minutes at a time, trying to nod and comprehend.

'And he has left it to you in the name that you took for yours, so this time there should be no problem,' Mr Rayburn said, smiling. 'It won't take long to sort out. Mr Morgan was very thorough and so am I.'

His own name. It had never been his own, just the name of a woman who had been kind to him when he was so small that if she sat him on the kitchen stool his feet didn't reach the floor. And yet it was his name. Mr Rayburn was right, he had chosen it. It was who he was and, by that, in a very small way, he acknowledged Peggy McLaughlan's influence wherever she might be. Every time he thought of her it was a happy memory, the sight of apple pie coming golden from the oven, a roast of beef so big that it would hardly fit into the oven tin, surrounded by potatoes, parsnips and carrots. The kitchen with its shining pans, warm stove and Peggy's melodious voice ever lifted in the middle of 'The Skye Boat Song'. It made him homesick just thinking about her. He loved best the sweet lilt of Edinburgh accents. Every time he heard it it lifted his heart. He wanted its squares and its streets, its wet weather and its wonderful buildings and the childhood that he had had there which he had tried so hard to hold on to.

It was not the childhood he should have had. When he drove Bridget out to look at the house which Thaddeus had left him, he stood back as she exclaimed happily over its golden stone, long wide steps and tall windows. He imagined himself as a small boy, playing in the garden, being there for Sunday tea with his parents, how proud Alice and Thaddeus would have been.

Bridget was delighted at his new-found wealth. It was exactly what she wanted. She had not been able to contain her excitement. She wanted a place in society so that other women did not cross the street to avoid her, so that she was not at the very bottom of the social ladder. She was thrilled. She would be happy to leave the brothel forever.

'I'm Mrs Niall McLaughlan now, I shan't need to be anybody else.'

Niall thought it was strange that at least part of his dream had come true. He would be able to come home to a woman, even if it wasn't the right woman. He didn't see Caitlin now. Sometimes he strained his eyes in the Newcastle streets for sight of her but he felt guilty and tried not to think about her. Bridget needed him and she needed him not to care about another woman.

Sixteen

Joe had always been friendly with his bank manager. Tod Starmer knew that Joe had tried all his life to keep the pit going, that he had been careful and put his money back into the business. When Joe had been obliged to mortgage everything, Tod had been against it but what else could he do? That summer Tod called Joe into the office, asked kindly after Vinia, asked him to sit down.

'I know what you're going to say, Tod.'

'Do you?' Tod sat back in his chair, his clear eyes disillusioned. 'You know what's happened? Redpath has crucified you.'

'It was just business,' Joe said.

'No, it wasn't. You know as well as I do that McLaughlan gave the Morgan steelworks to him.'

'He has closed it?'

'Friday.'

'I don't think Niall intended that,' Joe said.

'You're in the shite, Joe.'

It made Joe want to smile. How many bank managers would say that to you?

'There are two ways from here, either you let yourself go into bankruptcy or you sell the pit as a going concern.'

'Who the hell would want to buy it?' Joe asked and then

knew by Tod's expression. 'Oh, don't tell me. Redpath wants the pit.'

'He's offered to buy your house and the pit.'

'No,' Joe said.

'He's made a good offer. As your bank manager and your friend I would advise you to take it.'

'Wonderful,' Joe said, sitting back and gazing around Tod's bare office. It was the barest office Joe had ever seen, like it was uninhabited. 'So I have to go back to my wife and say that we've lost the pit and her business and the house. He'll shut the pit and then there'll be nothing left. How will I tell the men? What's going to happen to them?'

'Can you talk to Niall? He seems to have Redpath's ear.'

Stupidly, strangely, Joe felt a pang of jealousy and realized that he resented, even hated, Aulay Redpath's relationship with his son. He understood why Niall had gone to Aulay. Aulay had no son and had helped him right from the beginning when Niall had no one. Joe had never wished to be another man but he did now. He wanted to be the man who was so respected by Niall. He wished evil on Aulay, he wished . . . He stopped wishing it, it wasn't a healthy thing to do and it wasn't fair to Aulay either. Why should he care about that, but he did, he cared because of Niall. He was glad that Niall had had somebody to go to, he just wanted it to be him. He had spent hours and hours lately thinking over how things could have been and all the years of Niall's childhood when they had not seen one another.

'You're aware of the situation,' he said. 'Niall hates me.'

'He has a great deal of influence,' Tod said.

'He wants me out.' Joe suddenly felt very tired, as though nothing was worth fighting over. The things he really wanted could not be brought back no matter what battle he joined in. 'He wants me out of my house and away from my pit and . . .'

'You'd be wise to sell,' Tod said.

He knew Tod was being kind, that he was trying his best to be positive, but Joe couldn't.

'That house on the fell is my home. I don't know how to leave it.'

'You have to,' Tod said. 'You have no choice.'

Niall knew that he had come up in the world when Aulay invited him to a party. He wouldn't have gone, he wouldn't even have told Bridget about it but the thick, white envelope came addressed to them both and she gave a little scream of joy over the breakfast table. It was Aulay and Fiona's thirtieth wedding anniversary.

'They've invited us to their house!' Bridget declared and Niall did not say, *I've been to lots of parties there*, because he didn't want to spoil it for her.

He had never taken her to a party like that. She had never been anywhere, so even though he was extremely reluctant to go, all he said was, 'I think this calls for a new dress.'

It was odd. The balance of power had changed. They were married. They had gone to the country to live and were rich, but he had most of the money, so he could say things like that to her, whereas not long before she had been earning money for him. She didn't mind. Her shining eyes told him that she didn't care about such things any more. Now she could go to parties with the cream of Newcastle society because she was his wife and he was somebody.

She got up from the dining table and came around and kissed

him and then she sat down on his knee and put her arms around his neck.

'Will everybody be there?'

'Everybody,' Niall said.

'And will you introduce me to them?'

'Certainly,' he said. He had no idea how society would react but presumably they were shallow enough to accept anybody who had money and the very fact that he had been invited there by Newcastle's most powerful man meant they had to accept him, and his wife. 'Would you like to dance?'

He got up with her in his arms and swept her off her feet, she was so light it wasn't difficult and she giggled like a child. He had never seen her so happy. She was like somebody reborn, hardly ever swearing any more, not bad-tempered, not demanding in any way.

'I do love you so very much,' she said when he put her down. 'And I love being here with you.'

'I'm so glad,' Niall said.

It was a perfect September evening when they went to the anniversary party. He thought that she was pale and he knew she was nervous. These people knew what she had been. It seemed to Niall that everybody was aware he had inherited a fortune and a country house, because from the moment they entered the front door they were accepted, welcomed.

Fiona kissed Bridget. Niall tried not to look too eagerly for Caitlin. Fiona went away with Bridget. Aulay bore Niall off to the study.

'Got a present for you,' he said.

The evening shadows were gathering in the garden beyond the

windows. He wanted to ask about Caitlin but was obliged to be patient. Aulay closed the door and then with a flourish he took some papers from the desk and held them out to Niall.

'What are they?'

'Something you really want. Call it an exchange for the steel-works.'

'You closed the steelworks. You promised me you wouldn't.'

'No, I didn't,' Aulay said. 'You asked me to keep the foundry open and you knew all along that I couldn't, not if my own place was to be profitable. Here, take them. They're the deeds to Joe Forster's house, the papers to his pit. His family owned it right from the beginning. Of course the great irony is that it isn't changing hands, not really.'

'It depends how you look at things,' Niall said, trying not to be fascinated with horror by the so-innocent-looking documents upon the desk. 'And you closed the pit?'

'I did, yes. That was what you wanted.'

Niall took the papers. He had not been to Deerness Law. He avoided it, had not gone over the fell, past the pit and Joe's house to come here. He had gone a long way round. He knew that Joe had left and the pit was closed. He was living just three miles away and only half a mile from Aulay's successful steelworks. The Morgan steelworks which Thaddeus had worked so hard for would have locked gates. He tried not to go past it. He kept out of the village. He had no reason to go there. He had nothing to do with the people. He and Bridget shopped in Durham or Bishop Auckland and the people who helped in his house and garden were not local, he had made sure of that.

Halfway through the evening Niall went outside into the garden to smoke a cigar but really because he wanted to be by himself. He wandered away from the house to where there were apple and plum trees and it was quiet. He had not been there long when Caitlin said his name and he turned and she was behind him.

She was wearing the most beautiful dress Niall thought he had ever seen, it was lace in the palest of green and had silver running through it. It was full length, almost backless from what he could see, and had a train.

'You look wonderful,' he said.

'Why thank you. Bridget is stunning.'

'Yes.' She was always the loveliest woman in the room and she was wearing black patterned silk, the dress held by tiny straps across her shoulders so that every man at the party would want to push those straps aside. Tantalizing.

'Would you like to go back inside and dance?' he asked.

She laughed.

'We can't dance together. I can barely dance with old men, their wives worry. I wouldn't have come downstairs at all but my mother insisted. People don't talk to me more than they have to, because of my father. I am that worst of things, an unmarriageable daughter.'

'What do you do?' Niall said.

'Do? I don't do anything. Sometimes I go shopping with my mother but it's very embarrassing for her. Other women have daughters who are married with children and she has me. What do you do?'

Niall didn't answer that. She laughed then too. He wished she wouldn't. There was a brittle quality about it as though it was the only thing preventing tears.

'Perhaps you've done enough,' she said. 'You've ruined me, you've beggared Joe and Vinia and you sit there in your fine country house in idleness while people starve on the streets three miles away.'

'They are not starving,' Niall said.

'Aren't they? When was the last time you went to Deerness Law? The men have no work. What do you think they're going to do when the winter comes? And what for? Because your father let you down. You miserable bastard, Niall.'

'Oh, do be quiet,' Niall said, throwing the cigar on to the ground and putting his foot on it.

'Why? I bet you five pounds you didn't come through there on your way here. I'll bet you went all the way round by Durham . . .'

He got hold of her. She made a little noise of resentment and then Niall brought his mouth down on hers and she sighed and her whole body yielded instantly, not as though she wanted to, just as though she couldn't help it.

Niall had been wondering for the last few minutes what his fingertips would feel like against her bare back. He didn't have to wonder any more and when he had had his fill of that his hands found the fastenings on her dress so that he could reach the rest of her and that was when she objected.

'I'm sorry,' Niall said, letting go of her. 'I didn't mean to grab you. It's just that you look so lonely. The dress . . .'

'I wore it for you. I hate Bridget so much. She is so beautiful . . .'

'There's no need for you to hate her . . .'

'She has you.'

'Not really,' he said.

'How much more really can she have you? She's your wife. You spend your days with her.'

He didn't answer.

It was almost dark now, the sun had set splendidly in red long since and dusk was gone. He did not miss the summer. Another summer spent in idleness and he might come to hate it.

'Why do you dislike Joe so much?' she said.

'He gave me up.'

Caitlin, like a ghost in the half light, seemed to consider this for a moment.

'He was very young. Isn't it something young men do? Do you remember Christmas night?'

He would never forget, would have given almost anything to have that again. It was his perfect memory and he kept it in his mind like a sacred object.

'I could have been pregnant,' she said.

'If you had been, I wouldn't have abandoned you.'

'But you did,' she said.

'That's not the same thing, Cat.'

'Can you afford shoes for the children of Deerness Law now that you've forced Joe to shut the pit?'

'You are very brave.'

'Am I? I knew one of us was,' she said.

'I love you, Cat. I love you more than anything in the whole world.'

Face to face, almost nose to nose she said, 'Do you know, I believe you.'

'No, you don't. You think I'm a bastard.'

'No, I believe you and I believe you're a bastard. Now are you going to let me go back inside before somebody realizes what we're doing?'

'I want to see you.'

'How can you do that?'

'Please. At the Crown. Will Wednesday do, mid-afternoon? Please, Cat, say yes.'

'Yes,' she said and he let her go.

Seventeen

The house that Joe and Vinia moved to in Oaks Row in Deerness Law was by most people's standards a good house. It was the middle of the terrace. It had a yard out the back and beyond that was the railway line and beyond that a field which you could see from the upstairs rooms. It had three good bedrooms and a kitchen that you went down steps to and a dining room which looked out across the yard and a sitting room which looked out across the street at the other houses. Joe hated it. He felt as though he couldn't move. He longed for the fell and for his house. He couldn't breathe and he had nothing to do.

He felt as though he had nothing in his life. He had no money. He needed to find a job. When he went out he was faced with the men he had been obliged to put out of work and that autumn as the weather steadily grew worse there was no coal to heat the houses – coal was one of the things pitmen got free – and little money for food. When that time came Joe did everything he could to support the village. He persuaded the various ministers to open the churches so that each day the people had hot food.

Joe was glad to have something to do – he blamed himself for Niall and Aulay closing down the pit – so he went to Sweethope and did the same and he approached everybody he knew who had money or influence and talked the local doctors, solicitors and shopkeepers into giving so that the children should not be hungry. And when there was nothing else to be gained he went to Aulay Redpath's steelworks and asked them for a job. He knew the manager, Bill Ellison.

'I'd be glad to have you,' Bill said. 'I'm not as young as I used to be. It would be good to have somebody reliable running the office.'

'You did what?' his wife said, eyes large when he told her.

'I had to do something. It is the only place I could think of. Bill took me on, in the office. Redpath will never know. He hardly ever goes there.'

Vinia left the vegetables she was preparing for dinner and came the tiny distance across the small dark kitchen towards where he stood by the window and she hugged him.

'I'm so proud of you,' she said.

Caitlin had had a long argument with herself about that afternoon. Before had been different, unplanned, spontaneous and therefore somehow not serious, but meeting him in a hotel was a commitment. She had forgiven herself twice. She would have no excuse for doing so again. If she started an affair with him where would it end? On the other hand she was bored, lonely and wanted him with a hunger that was worse now than before they had touched. She had never been in love like this, not even Rob had mattered to her in the way that Niall did. She was angry with him, for getting married, for being married, for thinking he could have her when he was married, for knowing that he could have her when he was married. How could she want him when he quite obviously loved another woman more? She wasn't going to go to the hotel that afternoon but she found herself dressing carefully, thinking up excuses for her absence, especially if she was going to be late back, getting a tram, walking, reaching the street opposite, and then she had stopped, within sight of the hotel, and was afraid. What if she did get pregnant? She had let her parents down so often but it would most likely be the only way she could have a child and that had become important.

She considered going back home but the very dullness of it put her off, so after a full hour of watching people she went across the road to the hotel and Jonty was looking out for her and very discreetly gave her a key with a number on. Somehow that made her more angry. How could Niall do this, how could he make her feel so cheap? It was sordid, it wasn't fair. He would have her and then he would go back to his wife and damned well sleep with her.

By the time she walked into the room she was furious with them both and ready to argue with him over just about anything. Who did he think he was? But somehow she couldn't do it. The relief on his face when he saw her stopped her.

'I thought you'd changed your mind and weren't coming,' he said, and he came to her. 'I've missed you so much and I do love you.'

'I'm not sure I want to do this,' she said.

'It doesn't matter,' he said, rather wildly. 'I don't care. Just stay and have some tea. I'll order some fresh.'

He did and then he stood away from her across the room as though he thought she was going to run away if he touched her. Caitlin couldn't help going to him and putting her arms around his neck. He buried his face in her hair.

When it was late, too late for reasonable explanations of where she had been, he slept heavily in her arms and she had no intention of waking him. She was not quite sure what was going on but whatever it was she had made things better and he was happy to sleep there. When he finally stirred in the darkness he said, 'God, what time is it?'

'I don't know. Do you have to get back?'

'No, I'm staying the night, but you have to.'

'I don't care,' Caitlin said. 'I don't think my parents care much any more either. I think my father at least has a very good idea how I feel about you and what is going on.'

'He'll cut me into little pieces.'

'I think if he had been going to he would have done it long since,' Caitlin said.

'I could buy you a nice house,' he said, half joking.

'You might have to if they throw me out.'

'Get dressed and I'll drive you home,' he said, sliding out of bed and finding his clothes.

It was very late indeed when Niall put Caitlin down at her door, and the lights were still on in her house.

'I should come in with you. He's obviously waited up. He'll go mad.'

'That would make it worse.' She made as if to get out.

'When can I see you?'

Caitlin stopped opening the door and kissed him.

'Any time you like,' she said.

'Tomorrow?'

'Be reasonable.'

'I don't want to be reasonable. I want to see you every day.'

'Next Wednesday.'

'That's too long.'

'Tuesday then, at three in the same place.'

She went inside as quietly as she could but, even so, her father, whose hearing was a lot better than it ought to have been, came through into the hall.

'And how is Niall?' he said.

Caitlin spent several seconds wondering whether it was worth a lie but he went on looking at her, so in the end she said, 'He's fine.'

'I know you're unhappy, Caitlin, but do you think this is the answer?'

'He doesn't make me happy,' Caitlin said, smiling a little. 'Whatever made you think that?'

'I do blame him,' Aulay said. 'If it hadn't been for Niall's influence you would have been married by now, so what have you gained?'

'I love him,' Caitlin said.

Her father looked down.

'What if there's a child?'

'I thought you were desperate for grandchildren?'

Aulay sighed.

'I fought hard for respectability. Niall McLaughlan seems determined to take it from me. Our friends must spend hours gossiping about you. You must love him very much to carry on like this when he's married to someone else.'

'I do.' She was fighting the tears.

'I told you. He has no principles, no guidelines to his life. I don't think he cares for anyone. You're deluding yourself.'

'No.' The tears were beginning to run down her face. 'I believe in order to show love you have to have been shown it. Niall has no concept of love and he's so very lonely.'

'Not as lonely as you will be if you have his child,' her father said.

'He'll look after me.'

'This is not the way, Cat.'

'What else is there for me?' she said, and when he didn't answer she ran up the stairs and escaped into her bedroom.

Eighteen

Aulay Redpath sent Niall a letter that October, saying that he would be at the Redpath steelworks the following week and would like to see Niall on the Monday morning at eleven. Niall had a feeling that it was about Caitlin and he almost didn't go but his curiosity defeated him so he went. He was going to walk but the coward in him was not prepared to face the men who had been his workmen as they stood about on the street corners, so he drove, not looking anywhere but straight in front. It took five minutes.

He did not look across the river at the Morgan steelworks but he thought about it as he pulled into the yard, how guilty he felt that he had as good as given it to Aulay and that it was closed. It was good to see the big iron gates pushed back and the men going about their tasks. It was sandy in the yard and the moment he got out of the car all the old smells and sounds came back and he realized how unhappy he was at home, where Bridget was fussing with new curtains and making plans for a party at Christmas. He opened the outer door and went into the big office and there the first person he saw was Joe. Joe saw him too because he was getting up at the time with a piece of paper in his hand. He stopped, looked down, and Niall strode through the office, looking nowhere but in front of him. Niall pulled open the door to Aulay's office.

'What the hell is Joe Forster doing here?' he said.

Aulay didn't seem surprised. Had he been waiting for the outburst and was now prepared to enjoy it?

'What are you going to do, hound the poor bastard into his grave?'

Niall slammed the door. It had not occurred to him until that moment that Caitlin looked exactly like her father. They even sounded alike, their eyes warming when amused, and Aulay was no more willing to accept Niall's definitions of things than she was. He had the uncomfortable impression that Aulay was fully aware that two afternoons a week Niall bedded his daughter at the Crown.

'You really know how to hold a grudge,' Aulay said.

'I don't think it's any of your goddamned businesss.'

'And it isn't any of your business who I choose to employ, though I have to say it was Bill Ellison who took him on. Ellison manages the place these days.'

'Get rid of Forster,' Niall said.

'Don't tell me what I'm going and not going to do. I'm the master here,' Aulay said.

Niall strode across to the nearest chair, flung himself into it and sat there, saying nothing, while Aulay rearranged papers on his desk.

'I know you don't want to hear this but essentially Joe is one of the nicest people you're ever going to meet—'

'I thought you didn't like him.'

'I don't and do you know why? Because he's a better man than I am. He organized food and clothing for the out-of-work families—'

'Oh yes,' Niall said. 'He'll go straight to heaven.'

Aulay was looking very carefully at him.

'He made a mistake,' Aulay said.

'Is that what you call it?'

'That's exactly what I call it. What do you call it?' Niall didn't answer. 'Why don't you just go ahead and slit his throat, then you'll be happy?'

'It would be too quick,' Niall said.

'Well, you've taken the house that he loved and the pit that was his family's livelihood for three generations. He's living in a little terraced house with a job well below his considerable capabilities, he's hurt and humiliated. Isn't that enough?'

'I don't know. Maybe. We'll see. What did you get me here for?'

'I want you to reopen the Black Prince.'

'What?' He had all Niall's attention.

'The coal from there is the best and I need it and other people need it. I've had a lot of complaints from people because I was instrumental in shutting the place. Nobody operates as well as Joe did, you're going to have to face that, they got what they wanted, at the right price and on time, and having talked them out of it I'm now having to face a barrage of discontented customers.'

'There's no way I'm going to open it,' Niall said.

'Tell me, Niall, what are you going to do with the rest of your life?'

'It's nothing to do with you, and you can't win that way.'

'The pit is just sitting there, there's a lot of coal to come out and Joe's house is empty.'

'It's not his house, it belongs to me and so does the pit.'

'You could open it and run it.'

'I don't know anything about mining.'

'Dryden Cameron does.'

'He isn't there any more.'

'He's at Esh Bank at the Louisa but I daresay you could get him back if you tried.'

'You're being funny,' Niall said.

'He's a good pitman, one of the best, and he's not manager there. You could offer him manager.'

'I'm not going to go and see Dryden Cameron. He scares the shit out of me.'

Aulay laughed.

'Come on, Niall. Open the pit. You're not doing anything. Your life must be about as interesting as Sunday afternoons. You don't have to deal with Joe, you don't even have to see him.'

Niall couldn't resist, in the end. He wanted to because of how much he hated Joe but he couldn't because it was far too interesting to turn down.

'Dryden wouldn't do it,' he said.

'You don't know until you ask him.'

Aulay, Niall thought later, when he was driving across the fell towards Esh, could talk anybody into anything. It was a bright day in the valley as the car went down into the sunshine. The pigeon crees and allotments at the bottom stood out in the sunshine and the washing was hanging in all the back lanes, it was the busiest day of the week for the womenfolk.

He halted the car at the pit head and walked into the office and there, after enquiring, he found Dryden, talking to another man. When he saw Niall he stopped for a second and then went on talking, just as though nobody was there, so Niall was obliged to say, 'Can I have a word with you?'

Dryden stopped again, turned his dark gaze on Niall and

then gave some papers to the other man, who went out of the room.

'Do you mind if I shut the door?' Niall said.

'Please yourself.'

Niall did and then looked at him and knew he had been honest with Aulay. Dryden was the only man he knew who really frightened him. He had no idea why. Dryden had no money, no influence, no possessions, no family. He had no life beyond his work, and Niall had taken his house and his pit away from him. The thing was, Niall knew very well, that men who had nothing were very dangerous because they had nothing to lose. Dryden Cameron had lost everything in his life, his wife, his child. He gave off an aura of complete objectivity, as though he had no self left.

'I'm . . . I'm thinking about reopening the Black Prince. I wondered if you would be prepared to manage it for me.'

'Who, me?' Dryden said, as though he had never heard of the place.

'Yes.'

There was a long wait after that and Niall was thinking that Dryden wasn't going to answer him at all.

'Why?'

'Because it has the best coal in the area.'

'Why me?' Dryden said.

'Because you know it.'

'This is for Redpath, right?'

'Yes.'

'I have a job.'

'You're not the manager though, are you?'

Dryden let a little smile almost break across his lips.

'No, but on the other hand I don't have to work with a nasty little shite like you.'

Niall held on to his temper.

'It would mean work for the pitmen in the village,' he said.

Dryden hesitated.

'Don't you want the pit to reopen?' Niall said.

'There are other men you could ask.'

'I don't want to ask them. I want you to do it.'

Dryden didn't say anything even though Niall waited and waited.

'You could have full control.'

'And the house?' Dryden said.

'What house?'

'Joe's house.'

'I suppose, yes.'

Nineteen

Niall had suspected that Bridget would be pleased with the plans Aulay had made. Her idea of him being somebody did not include his sitting around the house all day. She liked him going off to work and in his honest moments Niall liked it too. He was pleased to see the pitmen trooping back into work the first day that the pit was open and going home dirty and tired. In a rare moment of tact he gave Dryden Joe's office, was there before him and when Dryden turned up said only, 'This is mine, that's yours next door,' but he was sure the compliment was not wasted though Dryden merely nodded. Dryden had also very reluctantly moved into Joe's house. Having said that he wanted it he seemed to have changed his mind.

'It's far too big,' he objected.

Niall wasn't sure whether Dryden would move in so he went there the first evening after they started work. Dryden answered the front door and seemed taken aback that it was him.

'I just wondered if everything was all right,' Niall said.

Dryden invited him in. It had not occurred to Niall that Joe and Vinia might be there but he should have known, because even in the hall there was a woman's touch, flowers and the smell of polish, the old scarred furniture lovingly looked after.

Dryden ushered him into the sitting room and there they were, unpacking boxes before a great big fire.

'I didn't mean to intrude,' Niall said.

'How could you possibly be intruding?' Vinia said, getting up, her eyes like needles on him. 'Would you like some tea?'

'No, no, thank you.'

'How is your wife?'

'She's fine.'

Vinia left the room. They were both glad of it, he thought.

'I've got some Scotch somewhere,' Dryden said.

'No, no, really, I didn't . . .'

He could no longer avoid Joe's eyes. The light was almost gone from them. Joe looked tired, as though everything was an effort. Beyond the windows there was a full moon and the sky was clear above the fell and Niall realized for the first time what it was like to be put out of the place you loved more than anything in the world. Joe had been born in this house and so had his father. His grandfather had built it, it was morally his, and Niall could see how tactful Dryden was being, like a caretaker even though the house belonged to Niall now. The chain had been broken. Niall had not been born there, nor grown up on the fell, nor sat around the fire.

Amongst the bare trees in the garden two owls were hooting to one another. Joe glanced at the window.

'They're still there,' he said, going across to look.

Niall tried to excuse himself and leave but Vinia came back with the tea on a tray, so he had to drink tea and eat ginger cake and reply suitably to her polite enquiries about his house, how she remembered it, and she got him to tell her what the garden was like, at least what he could remember.

'Bridget's the expert,' he said. 'She really likes living in the country.'

Niall had trouble getting the ginger cake down. It stuck in his throat and required two cups of tea and then he left. Vinia saw him to the door. She didn't tell him what she thought of him only because she was obliged to be civil because he controlled everything, Niall knew, but then she did not have to walk him to his car.

'New car?' she said. 'Nice.' And then she looked at him and said, 'Joe and your mother were very much in love.'

'Did I want to know that?' Niall said, surprised and eager to silence her.

Vinia ignored the interruption.

'She came to my shop in the village, crying, and begged him to run away with her. They couldn't have stayed here, you see. She was a married woman and it would have been a terrible disgrace and he couldn't leave because there was nobody to look after things here, so she stayed with George. It seemed the right thing to do. Joe didn't want to get in the way. He thought it would be better for you to be brought up as George's son. He thought about you every day. He didn't imagine that your life was difficult.'

Niall regarded the moon for a few moments and Vinia said, 'Try not to hate him so much, Niall.'

'I have to go,' Niall said.

When Niall got home Bridget was in the kitchen, making Christmas puddings. She had decided from the beginning that the only people she would have in the house were cleaners and people to see to the fires and help generally. She did the cooking herself and everybody went home at tea time. Now her face was red and shiny with effort and the smell was glorious. It made Niall happy, the heady fumes of alcohol, raisins and whatever else went into it.

'Oh Brid, that's wonderful,' he said, kissing her on one sticky cheek.

'I hope they will be. I haven't done this before. You don't think I've left it too late, do you? The dinner is almost ready.'

Niall could smell that too, beef, vegetables, all in one pot, he guessed, and about to fall apart, ready for the plates. They ate in the kitchen. He sat at the table with a glass of wine and told her about his day while she put the dinner on the table, and it was exactly as he had thought it might be. Bridget sat down opposite and she spooned the beef out of the pot while he told her about his visit to Dryden's house and how Joe and Vinia had been there and what Vinia had said.

'They don't know about the home and what happened?' Bridget said.

'I don't tell people.'

'No, neither do I, but because they don't know they think you're . . . I don't know . . . going too far?'

'I don't want anybody to know.'

Bridget wasn't eating her dinner. That meant she had something on her mind.

'Niall, do you think we could have a baby?'

Niall choked on a mouthful of hot carrot.

'What?' he said.

'I know.' Bridget fingered the tablecloth. 'But this is almost perfect. A child would complete it. I don't see why we couldn't have a child, do you?'

That finished him off, he couldn't eat a thing.

'But we've never . . . I mean, you've never . . .'

'I would like to try. Things are about as different as they could be and I do love you very much.'

Steam rose from the full plate in front of Niall and he thought back to Mr Wilson. Sometimes things were never over, never finished. Mr Wilson had ruined Bridget's life. He didn't think that a night of attempted passion, or several nights of it, would mend anything and it might put her off him because she would thereafter link the two. There was also Caitlin to be considered. What a strange situation that would be.

'You don't think it's a good idea?' she said.

'It has to be a good idea, I mean . . . it is . . . it's just . . . I don't think you'd ever trust me again,' Niall said.

'But I do trust you completely,' she said. 'I always have done.'

'If you had we wouldn't be having this discussion and I don't think I could stand having you loathe me.'

'We could have a normal relationship.'

'This could never be a normal relationship,' he said, and he got up and walked out.

He went into the drawing room and closed the door, he thought Bridget might let it lie for a little while but she didn't. When she came in he said without turning from the fire, 'We have a lot of good things. Why not just leave it like that?'

'You sleep with other women. You could sleep with me.'

'You once told me you were the only woman I slept with.'

'That was before Caitlin Redpath.'

Niall heard the words as though through an echo.

'You go to bed with her in the afternoons,' Bridget said. 'I know you do. You have that look on you when you come home. I've seen that look a million times.'

'It is not like that,' he said.

'You're in love with her. It isn't like when you went to Nora. You are, aren't you? You could fall in love with me. I want you for mine,' she said. 'You belong to me. You've always belonged to me and you always will. I had no life before I met you and you are the only person I have ever loved. I'm your wife. I will go to bed with you and you will not see her any more. Promise me.'

Niall shook his head.

'Promise me.'

'You're going to spoil everything we have,' he said. 'I don't understand why you want to change things now after all this time.'

'I want a child. Surely with your experience you would want the child to have two loving parents.'

'It's not going to work,' he said.

'How do you know?'

'Because you can't stand a man near you.' He was almost shouting and she stood near the door, looking uncertain, and he hated himself for that. He didn't want to be there, he wanted to be at the Crown with Caitlin and for it to be the afternoon. He couldn't understand what had happened here, how swiftly everything had gone wrong. It had been an awful day one way and another. He was ready to go to sleep and forget about it and hope that in the morning it would all have gone away.

'I sleep with you every night.'

'That's not the same thing! You would feel . . . invaded and dirty and lost and you would think that I was Mr Wilson.'

'I would never think that!'

'How do you know? Has anybody touched you since then?'

'You have.'

'Brid, it's like sleeping with a nun,' he said and she came over and tried to hit him but she was crying so much that she couldn't focus.

'I can make you want me,' she said, sobbing.

'Oh no, you can't. I've slept naked beside you for years. I know every breath you take in the night, I know exactly what your body looks like and how your eyes change when you're hurt or angry. I know everything about you. There's nothing you can surprise me with.'

'You are so horrible,' she said.

'I am, yes. I've killed people. I've stolen and lied and had nice people put out of their houses so that I could make money. I've slept with women I cared nothing about. The one thing I haven't done is to go to bed with a woman who didn't want me and I have no intention of starting now.'

'I do want you.'

'No, you don't, you're just jealous because somebody else has me. Well, you had plenty of time, Bridget. You had years and years when you could have made me yours and you didn't. You're too late.'

Bridget stared at him.

'Are you going to leave me?' she said.

'Do you want me to?'

Bridget went on looking at him uncertainly and then she fled.

Niall called himself every name he could think of when she had gone. He knew that she couldn't survive without him. Hadn't she just said that he was the only person she had ever loved? He went upstairs when he could trust his temper and there she was on the bed, sobbing into the pillows. He pulled her into his arms and held her there.

'I'm sorry,' she said. 'I didn't mean to say any of that. I don't care about Caitlin, I don't care about anybody.'

'Hey.' Niall pushed back the wet strands of hair. 'I love you. I love you more than anything in the whole world.' It only occurred to him when he had said it that it was exactly the same thing he had said to Caitlin not very long since.

It felt wrong from the beginning. All his senses shrieked. For years he had wanted her and never touched her except in affection. He was used to Caitlin. It felt as though he was betraying her and it was ridiculous really because Caitlin had always assumed he was having sex with both of them. It made him smile. How little she knew him, how little she knew about the important things of his life other than herself. She was all he had ever wanted and she was prepared to put up with the man that she thought he was for the sake of a few hours a week in a hotel bedroom.

I get more and more like Joe, Niall thought. Hotel bedrooms. Dear God. He had visions of running away with Caitlin to Edinburgh but he couldn't.

Bridget was not like a whore nor like a wife and she was nothing like Caitlin. To him in some ways she was still a young girl being raped by a middle-aged man. He didn't think he was going to get past that here. The fairy tale was about to turn into a horror story.

He had thought he was used to how beautiful she was and they had lain in one another's arms thousands of times and very often she wore nothing, but this wasn't like that. For the first time in her life Bridget was encouraging him to make love to her, for the first time in her life she was encouraging a man to make love to her.

It still wasn't anything like Caitlin but nor thankfully was it like Nora or Gypsy. He wanted the lines blurred for sanity's sake but not too far. If he didn't get this right, if he was careless or assumed anything he might turn into Mr Wilson. He kept waiting for her to cry or to push him away or to turn away or that he would know she was back in the home with the sunlight shut out and Mr Wilson was doing indescribably awful things to her. The trouble with sex was, if you were going to do it, it was very difficult to be anything other than the person doing it and since it was essentially the same why should he not turn into Mr Wilson?

'Are you sure about this, Brid?' he said.

'Positive.'

'I'm still not Mr Wilson?'

'How in God's frigging name could you be Mr Wilson?' She sounded so normal, so much her sweet, foul-mouthed self.

'Because . . .'

Bridget raised her gaze to the ceiling.

'I don't think I can do this,' Niall said.

'You wanted to for years.'

'I know but . . .'

The truth was that the bedroom had lost its fire, its warmth, the oak furniture, and was fast turning into the bedroom at the home that stank of Mr Wilson's cigarettes and dirty clothes and Niall's memory gave him Mr Wilson's eyes burning with pleasure and Rozzer coughing, grey-faced as Mr Wilson beat him and Bridget's hopeless crying in that cold dank bedroom.

He pushed himself away from her and escaped into the pillows, breathing very heavily and trying to remember where he was. Bridget put a hand into his hair gently at first and then she yanked and Niall shouted and turned over. She brought her mouth down on his, slid her hands down his body, became someone else, somebody bold, not his wife who made dinners in the big kitchen and not the victim of a nasty man's fantasy, but who she really was, the Bridget Black who had survived, who had looked after him, who had had ambition for him, who was entirely his equal. She was not a whore and she was not Caitlin and he was not afraid to touch her, not in fear of hurting her any more.

Their bodies matched. His only bad feeling was regret because she had not given herself to him when he was eighteen or twenty, when he adored her. He had filled that space with Caitlin, had given away his love to another woman. He didn't think it was something that could be retrieved, certainly not like this. Bridget had kept it from him as though she was afraid to lose control both of him and herself. She was doing it now, of course, losing control. He had never seen her do it before and he understood why. She had been afraid that, if she did, Mr Wilson would go on controlling her forever. But he was not Mr Wilson and she didn't think he was. It was strange though. Having waited all those years to have her, there was something mechanical about the whole thing. Other women had taught him what to do and he knew also that women assumed men were fully intent on what they were doing, so that the ceiling could have dropped, but it wasn't like that, it was like a shadow of something that could have been, all the joy was gone from it. She did this now because she was afraid of losing him. In some ways she could never lose him but this was not one of them and only her inexperience would have led her to think so. Nothing could do away with the afternoons spent in Caitlin's arms. He was glad of that. He had the feeling that he would be left with the memories.

Niall did not have to explain himself to her these days, because he went to work and she would not know where he was in the afternoons, at least he hoped not. Niall left that Wednesday at two and put his head around Dryden's door. He said nothing but, 'I'm going out. I'll be a while.'

Dryden nodded. He was not the man to ask questions. Niall didn't want to go. He couldn't not go but he would have given a great deal to have closed his office door and sat over the fire, doing some dull paperwork which suddenly held attraction. It was as though his stolen time had brimmed over into reality and everything was changed in the cold daylight.

It rained all the way to Newcastle. The streets were shiny. The lights were on in the hotel and looked welcoming. It was a typical autumn day, never more than half light. The tea was brought upstairs. He drank it gratefully. She was late. That made it worse. He wondered whether he looked any different. He went over and observed his reflection in the mirror and thought, is this a man who only just started laying his wife? What's the difference? He couldn't discern any but he thought Caitlin might. It was stupid to think that he had become the man she had thought he was all along. He went on looking and suddenly saw Joe and he understood how men ended up like this, how they made a mess of things. The trouble was that you didn't know you were in the mire until it was too late and it called for huge sacrifices.

He heard the door and turned around and there she was. It was one of the hardest moments of his life. He wanted to tell her how much he loved her but he couldn't because it had become a great, fat lie. He had said the same thing to both women like the unbelievably crass bastard that they both thought him. He was about to become that person, going from one woman's bed to another like an ignorant fool who values nothing.

She came in, smiling, taking off her wet coat. The rain was like gems on the hair which had escaped from her hat and she was laughing now and demanding tea and kissing him and her lips were cold. She liked him better now that he was working, he thought, now that she thought he had done the right thing and opened up the pit again. She drank her tea and then he found her looking closely at him.

'You're very quiet.'

Quiet? Conversation had become a battleground, he had to remember where he was, who he was with, what he said, where he had said he would be, and the timing was crucial to everything. How very complicated it had all become. Bridget expected him to give up Caitlin, so the whole thing was instantly a lie. He didn't know how to give her up. It was like asking him to stop breathing. Bridget was now providing everything a man should need.

'Are things going wrong at work?' Was something off in her manner too or was he just too sensitive?

'No.' He and Dryden worked well together, much better than he had thought they would. A lot of this was because Dryden knew exactly what he was doing. The other important factor was that he did as Dryden told him. Not that Dryden ever made it sound like an order. He didn't. He often prefaced it with 'do you think you could' or 'do you think we might', very tactful stuff, and Niall, knowing little about mining, was not given to questioning him in his decisions, asking only the kind of questions which resulted in relevant information. Dryden caught on very fast and after the first days Niall didn't need to ask questions, Dryden would volunteer what he wanted to know before he asked. He only wished he could enquire whether this was like the way Dryden and Joe had always worked, they seemed to slip into it so comfortably.

Niall liked being there and he liked to have an older man there who knew what he was talking about to such an extent that it was almost a game. He knew that Dryden would not have thanked him for being likened to Aulay Redpath but they were very similar in some ways.

Niall tried to make normal conversation to Caitlin while the light died beyond the windows but neither of them was comfortable. He wanted to go to bed with her but he didn't. It was like being given two superb bottles of malt whisky and told you had to drink it all at once, but she would start to think there was something going on if he didn't take her to bed, so he did.

The wickedness helped. That was why men had mistresses and she was really that now. She was his bit on the side for the first time, even though she thought she'd always been one. It hurt him to think of how that felt, that she would go on giving herself to him when he was obviously the kind of person who regarded other people's feelings as less important than his own bodily pleasures. He tried to think how she had felt when he had told her that he was getting married. This was how she had thought it was. No exclusivity, no single regard, no real partnership. Why could you never get what you wanted? This had become something he shouldn't do in a completely different way. That was very heady. He was lying and cheating and deceiving like never before and he had not intended any of it. Perhaps people never did. He thought he was getting away with it until she looked across the pillows at him as the afternoon turned into evening and said, 'You've hardly spoken a single word to me since you got here. Is there something the matter? Are you tired of me?'

'No, of course not.' He kissed her.

'It isn't much though, is it, this?'

She was right, it wasn't much. It wasn't much for being the most important thing in her life, the only thing which stopped her existence from being dull. She should have had a house and a husband and children and some kind of future. And it wasn't as though it could go anywhere in any way. Outside of this hotel they were not a couple. They could not be. And where was the progress to be made when all you could do was drink tea and go to bed?

'I think maybe we shouldn't do this any more,' she said and she got out of bed and began putting on her clothes.

And then he realized. She had come here with the intention of telling him it was over. What very fine instincts she had. And the moment she said it he realized that he couldn't give her up.

'Oh, Cat, no.' He got out of bed and went to her.

'You expect to have everything,' she said, looking fondly at him.

'No, I don't.'

'Yes, you do.' She touched his cheek with her fingers. 'You're going home to Bridget now. I think of you there with her, sleeping in her arms and kissing her goodbye when you go to work and . . . and she has everything, she has your house and she makes dinners for you and . . . I miss you so much in the early evening. Isn't that strange? Most of all in the early evening.'

Was it the hardest time for everybody, Niall thought. The night was bad too but the early evening when people went home to one another had always haunted him. Seven o'clock, when the day was giving itself up, when the red sky came down to meet the land, when in winter there had already been darkness for three hours and it was beginning to seem interminable, as though the silence would go on forever. He could imagine Cat's loneliness when her father came home to her mother, and all those hundreds of thousands of women who had no one, whose hopes had been left in a ditch in France, endured the silence and thought back to the dancing and the music and evenings and their youth.

'I don't think I can do this any more, Niall,' she said. 'If I can't have a man I can come first with, I think I would rather do without.'

He couldn't ask her not to leave him, because the way that she looked at him he didn't deserve her, he wasn't entitled, and it was true. Nobody should go on like this. He had a full life, he had everything any man could want, money, work, a beautiful wife, a lovely home. She wasn't crying, she was looking clearly at him and when he didn't say anything more she began dressing so that there was nothing left for Niall but to do the same. He panicked. What if he never saw her again? What if he never was allowed to touch her again? He couldn't say the treacherous words to her and nothing else seemed suitable or would have any influence.

'I never meant it to be like this,' he said.

'I'm sure you didn't,' she said. 'I'm sure men never do. It's just unfortunate that they are . . .'

What? Selfish? Self-centred? The kind of pathetic person who might cry? Not worth the candle? As sexually desirable as a slug? Incompetent? Stupid? Too tired to make sex any good? What?

'What?' he said.

'Married,' she said.

Married. Well, he had no quarrel with that, he was certainly married, wedded, bedded and about to go home. Condemned without appeal, left with barely a word. But she had words. Women always did. She couldn't just leave him feeling cut in half, she made a sort of stew out of him before she left, just in case he might have any illusions about himself, so that he would remember it. She should never have gone to bed with him, since he had made it clear in the first place that she was not much better than a toy, somebody to play with in the afternoons. She never wanted to see him again, she never wanted to touch him again.

She thought he was all the things her father had said he was. He just hoped she wasn't going to list them all but she didn't, so that was good. And also she thought he had behaved very badly over Joe.

'I did what?' Niall said, managing to look at her.

'You could have forgiven him.'

'I don't know how to.'

And then it occurred to Niall that he was clinging to his hatred of Joe because he was afraid that Joe didn't really want him. If he let go there might be nothing. He wanted so desperately for Joe to accept him and he was afraid.

'Go away, please,' was all he could think of to say to Caitlin.

She picked up her coat and her bag and her gloves and all the other ridiculous paraphernalia that women couldn't move from the house without and then she ran.

He couldn't go home somehow. He couldn't go back to Bridget in such a state. He felt that what he had said and done was written all over his face. He went to the pit. The lights were on in Dryden's office and the pit was always alive because the shifts came and went around the clock. Dryden's office door was closed and Niall didn't like to go in but he knocked lightly and opened it and then enquired, 'Got no home to go to?'

'Got nobody to go to,' Dryden said.

The other side of the same problem, Niall thought. He liked that Dryden said things like that. He didn't care what people thought about him, he didn't bother to hide his feelings in front of Niall. He did to other people. Niall couldn't understand that. He went inside and closed the door. The fire would have gone out long since in his office. It would be cold. He stood beside the fire.

'Have you ever thought about getting married again?' he said.

'Once was enough,' Dryden said.

'Didn't you like her, then?'

'It wasn't her, it was me. I wasn't happy unless I was laying half the bloody county. Is that what you're doing?'

Niall tried not to falter under Dryden's cynical gaze.

'I just . . . I'm not . . . I don't seem to be able to get things right.'

'They should put that on every man's grave,' Dryden said.

'Do you think? I think I distort it, you know.'

'Why?'

'Well . . .' Niall was gazing into the flames. 'I was . . .'

'Badly treated?' Dryden said.

Niall thought that was particularly acute. He shut his eyes against the fire but Amelia Mackenzie's fat white face floated into view. The rest of her followed and she was placing her wet mouth on him and her sausage-cold fingers.

Niall thought of Dryden by himself in the house on the fell.

'Is your house lonely?'

'It's always been like that. I think the bloody place has a curse on it. Joe was lonely there for a long time.'

'Was he?'

'For years and years. His mother died when he was very small and his father was a drunk. And his father was lonely there too, that's why he drank so much, so it has its reputation to keep up, you see.'

'I didn't know that.'

'Why should you? I suppose I should go, otherwise it'll be time to come back,' Dryden said.

Niall went home. His wife was in the kitchen but she looked up and the first thing she said was, 'You went to her.'

It must be written on him. He'd thought it wasn't.

'Did you finish it?'

'She did.'

'Really?' Bridget scanned his face as though looking for untruths and then she went back to finishing the cooking.

Twenty

Caitlin was not crying when she got home. Dry-eyed and determined she stood in the quiet darkness of the hall and looked up into the gloom. The smell of dinner lingered. Duck and onions, she thought. Her parents would be sitting over the fire, unless they had gone out to dinner with friends, she rather hoped they had, and then she could go to bed and not face them, or her father could have decided to do some more work and would be in the library, her mother reading or sewing alone. Had she been a boy she would have been involved in his work. Had she married . . . There was no point in thinking what might have been. As she stood there her father came into the hall, she thought his steps were slow though he must know who it was. He looked gravely at her and she thought that her parents had always been sorry that they had not had more children. Perhaps they had recently been glad they didn't have more than one, all the trouble she had caused.

'Are you all right, Caitlin?' he said.

'I think . . . I think I may go away for a little while.'

'That's a good idea. You and your mother could go to Italy—'

'No, I mean to live.'

'I see. Come into the library and talk to me about it.'

She shook her head, afraid that she could not get words past her lips. He touched her shoulder and guided her in.

'I don't mean to interfere,' he said, 'but if you're in trouble . . .'

'No.'

She could remember wanting to come in here. She could remember wishing she could go to work with him. Always he brushed her off. It was silly to think about it but the happiest time of her life had been when she had lived in the shabby hotel with Niall and gone to work with him each day. She had enjoyed her days at the foundry.

'You're not . . .' Her father started his sentence and stopped. 'You're not having his child?'

The ultimate sin and, oh, how she had wished it. She had thought in these past weeks while Niall was bedding her with enthusiasm that surely, surely she must be pregnant, but there was no sign of it, she bled regularly almost to the day. Her parents would be relieved, she was only sorrowful that her life should be so empty.

'Has Niall done something to make you leave?'

He had done something, he had pushed her into the margins of his existence and she couldn't bear it any longer.

'I can't have any life here,' she said. 'I want to start up somewhere fresh. I'll get a job . . .'

She stopped there as the door opened, admitting her white-faced mother.

'Is there trouble?' she said.

'No, no.' Aulay went to her, closed the door, put a reassuring arm around her shoulders. 'Caitlin wants to leave.'

She was her mother's life. If she left, her mother would have nothing to do and nobody to do it with during the days, while her father worked. Her mother had many acquaintances but was not good at making friends and since she had provided scandal the people her mother had been close to had dwindled away.

Why was it that women should have to endure such frustration and loneliness while men were fulfilled through work? All her mother had was her company. The house ran smoothly and Aulay was gone at least ten hours a day.

'Leave? To go where?'

'I thought I might find a job of some kind.'

Her mother's eyes filled with tears and her father said, 'Do you know, when Rob Shannon came and asked me if he could marry you I almost told him he couldn't. I thought he wasn't good enough for you because his father was a solicitor and Rob was going into law. Isn't that funny? Things could have been so different. Where were you thinking of going?'

'Edinburgh.'

'Why Edinburgh?'

'I don't know. I just thought . . . nobody knows me there and perhaps I could find something I want to do.'

'It's so far away,' her mother said.

'No, it isn't,' Aulay said. 'No distance at all. I tell you what, Caitlin, we'll all go and we'll find you a really nice house and we'll be able to come and visit. How would that be?'

'That would be very nice,' Caitlin said. 'But I don't want to be a financial burden. I think I've been that for long enough.'

He left Fiona and came to Caitlin.

'Cat,' he said. 'I'll buy you the prettiest house in Edinburgh.'

He didn't say, *It'll get you away from that bastard*, but she knew exactly what he meant.

Niall had to stop himself from going to her. He told himself over and over again that she didn't want him, that there was nothing worse than somebody who had been rejected wishing that they still mattered and making a bloody embarrassing nuisance of themselves.

It was Christmas and every Christmas, he thought, would always now be for him the time of Caitlin and the fur coat and the walk on the cold fell and her laughter, the time when he and Joe had still been friends and the old house was festive and they had spent the day together and then Christmas night in Caitlin's arms.

This Christmas was very busy. Niall had had Vinia to the office, encouraged, he rather suspected, by Dryden. She was, he thought, looking at her, very unhappy. This time last year she had had a successful business, one of the biggest houses in the area and a husband who owned a pit.

'I hope you'll . . . forgive the intrusion,' she said.

Niall, on his feet, guilty.

'Please,' he said. 'Do sit down.'

'No, thank you. I won't. Dryden said I should say this to you myself. We always had a party for the pitmen and their families and . . . considering the year that we've all had . . . it's a tradition. I know you don't care about things like that but . . . I used to organize it. Maybe your wife would . . .'

Bridget was very caught up with the idea of decorating the house and having a party for the professional people of the district but he didn't think she would be interested in the workmen.

'Couldn't you do it?' Niall said.

'It's not my place.'

'But you could. You know what to do, and I'll pay for it, whatever you think. Presents?'

'Just small ones for the children.' She had gone pale now.

'Are you all right?' Niall said.

'Yes, I just . . . I didn't want to come here.'

Niall almost smiled. It reminded him of the first time they had met. They had quarrelled then and she, frank as ever, had persuaded him not to leave because she had made cake for him.

'Sit down a moment.'

'No, I have to get back.' To the grim little house in the dark narrow street? What did she do there? She looked levelly at him. 'I'm teaching millinery in the church hall this afternoon and I've been making clothes for a bring-and-buy stall to raise money for a Christmas party at the chapel. You want me to go ahead and organize it then?'

'Yes, please.'

He saw her to the door and there she turned.

'Can I offer something else?'

'Certainly.'

'If you're going to give extra to the men at Christmas – I know you did that at the foundry – could you do it in foodstuffs, otherwise some of them will go rolling home and others will never get there.'

'I will,' Niall said.

Twenty-One

Niall could not help but notice Joe's absence from the party which they held in the big room of the mechanics institute. Dryden and Vinia were both there and so were all the miners and their families and there was music and lots of good food and everybody got a present, not just the children. There was beer. Vinia and Niall had argued about this. As he had come to expect, they argued about everything and, because it had been a long day and was early evening by the time the argument began, it was more heated than usual. She said that the men could go to the pubs for beer, they didn't need it at the pit Christmas party and it had always been that way and he said this was not the chapel Christmas party and she would do well to remember that.

'They aren't children,' he said. 'They work bloody hard all year and they deserve to be treated as adults.'

'Don't you swear at me,' she said. 'They'll get enough beer over Christmas. We shouldn't be encouraging them. You asked me to organize this and now you're interfering.'

'You came to me.'

'I thought you might like to know how a proper pit owner goes on!' she said and then realized she had gone too far and put her hand over her mouth, but she obviously couldn't help adding, 'I did it for the men and their families, not for you.'

So there was beer but Vinia had nothing to say to him. Bridget had refused to go. He would have liked the support of having her there, especially since she and Vinia had never met and it would have been nice if Bridget could have thanked Vinia for all the work she had done towards the party but Bridget didn't seem to understand how he felt about it.

'She should think herself lucky you speak to her,' she said.

It wasn't like that, he found that the more he saw of Vinia and the more that they argued the more fond he was of her. He wanted to thank her but it was difficult and he couldn't give her anything, not when he and Joe never spoke. When the party was over and he did try to thank her she brushed him aside.

'I told you, it wasn't for you.'

'But you'll let me thank you.'

'I don't want your thanks,' Vinia said and she went into the back where the stove was burning and making a peculiar smell with the half-dried outdoor clothes. She collected her coat.

'Shall I walk you back?'

'Dryden will do that.' As she was about to walk out she stopped and said, 'If you had anything good about you at all, which I doubt, you would come and see your father on Christmas Day.'

'Don't call him my father.'

'It's what he is, and I might as well tell you now you're exactly like him.'

'I'm nothing like him,' Niall declared.

'Niall, you're the very spit of him,' she said and then she left.

The trouble was that he felt warmed, comforted, and it was not a nice feeling while he was still stirring up his bitterness against Joe. He didn't want to feel that. Joe was to blame. Somebody had to be.

*

On Christmas Eve there was the party at the house and Bridget wore a white dress and managed to look better than any other woman in the room but all he could think about was Caitlin and wonder where she was that evening and what she was doing. The local people had gathered and Bridget was happy. Musicians had been hired, there was dancing and Niall was sure that the old house had not seen such merriment in many years. Everybody they had asked came, some out of curiosity, some so they would have something to talk about, some women to admire one another's dresses, some for the food and the champagne and others, he thought, merely because they could not afford to offend the richest man in the area. After all, he was sure they said to one another, look what he had done to Joe Forster.

It was three o'clock when he and Bridget finally went to bed and she said to him, 'Got an early Christmas present for you.'

'What's that?' Niall said, turning towards her in the darkness.

'I think I'm pregnant.'

'Already?'

'I've missed twice and I feel different.'

'That's wonderful,' Niall said, kissing her and taking her into his arms.

'Isn't it?' she said. 'It means we don't have to do this any more,' and she pushed him away.

Niall went on looking down at her.

'When did I turn into Mr Wilson?' he said.

'You were never Mr Wilson, and I do love you very much but I only did this for a child. I can't go on being whoever the person is that you want. It isn't me, I know that.'

'I didn't realize it was so awful.'

'It wasn't, at least as far as I can judge. I just don't like it, you knew I didn't. You can always go to whores. You know plenty.'

'You're my wife.'

She looked patiently at him.

'Wives do this because they don't have any choice. They do it so that they can have children. It isn't meant to be entertainment. When it is, men pay for it. You can afford to pay for it.'

'I don't want to pay for it.'

She tried to get up. Niall stopped her. He held her there and as the seconds passed he realized by the faint degree of fear that edged into her eyes that she would always be caught in the horror of what Mr Wilson had done. She had pretended. She had hidden from him. She knew how to do such things and she knew everything there was to know about sex. When he released her she got up and went into the bedroom next door and left him. Merry Christmas, Niall thought.

Joe and Vinia went to Dryden's house for Christmas. By then Joe had learned to think of it as Dryden's house, though he didn't think Dryden had. He knew that Dryden must have asked for the house, he didn't think Niall would have given it to him, or offered, it must have been part of the deal to get Dryden back to the Prince. Niall had been right, Dryden was the best man in the area for the job, perhaps the best man there was, and he deserved the house. Joe couldn't think of it as his any longer, Niall had somehow come between him and it. Niall had not lived there when he should have and therefore it was no longer what it was meant to be. How odd to think that people imagined they would go on and on. It had been a happy house since he and Vinia had been married. It would have been happier still with a child in it. His child had had a splendid party at the Morgan house, so he had heard, all the district invited except him, of course, because he was nobody any more. Not that that had mattered, but he would have given a great deal to see his son that day. You never knew how long you had and even though everything had gone wrong there might still be time ahead of them. They should share it but he couldn't go to Niall, he knew that he would be turned away from the door. He and Thaddeus between them had made a good job of Niall, with George's help of course. George was easier to blame. He wished he could unload all the guilt on to George. It seemed fitting somehow. And Thaddeus, firstly for not recognizing Niall and then for not allowing him into their lives, but Joe had not recognized Niall himself. You would think you would, when it was blood. Why didn't you? Niall looked so much like him.

Vinia came to him.

'What are you thinking about?'

'Last year.'

'Ah.'

'Last year I had everything. I didn't know it of course but I had.'

'Whereas this year you have a wife and a son and a good friend and a job and—'

'Yes, I know. I'm ungrateful. I wish I could go to him.'

'That would be fruitless and whatever would you say to that dreadful little trollop he's married to?'

'Vinia!' Joe said, laughing.

'Well. When you think he could have married Caitlin. She's so sensible and . . .'

'I don't think she's that sensible,' Dryden said as he came into the room. 'He's been seeing her.'

Vinia turned around.

'That doesn't necessarily mean that they were having an affair.'

Dryden looked sceptically at her.

'He could have married her. He could,' Vinia insisted. 'If he wanted her why did he marry Bridget Black?'

'Have you actually seen her?' Joe said.

'No, I haven't.'

'Caitlin is very pretty. Bridget Black is the kind of woman men kill for.'

'So then. Do men marry Bridget Black and have affairs?'

'No,' Joe said.

Dryden said nothing but when Vinia went into the kitchen to see to the meal Joe said, 'You know, don't you?'

'He did,' Dryden said.

'But why?'

'I have no idea.'

'And now?'

'Now . . . he doesn't go to Newcastle in the afternoons. He stays in his office, goes home late and comes to work early. It bothers me.'

'He's not happy?'

'No.'

'I wish there was something I could do.'

'There isn't,' Dryden said.

It snowed in Scotland. Fiona and Aulay took Caitlin to the Highlands. The scenery there was enough to make you weep, it was so beautiful. The little grey churches and the houses so neat and like fairytale castles and Loch Rannoch silver and the air so bitter that it hurt your face when you ventured outside. There was snow on the beach at St Andrews and a huge rolling tide. They fed the ducks and swans in the harbour and walked back through the churchyard of the cathedral to their hotel and then Edinburgh for Hogmanay and all the time Caitlin wished to be in Durham where she had no doubt Niall was sleeping with his wife and going to parties and not thinking about her. She wore the fur coat he had given her and tried to remember how she had felt on Christmas morning when she had sat on the bed and opened the big oblong box, so excited. She had been so sure that he loved her.

There was a house for sale in Charlotte Square and her father, seeing she liked it, was determined to buy it for her though she protested that it was too much money. It was a lovely house, the kind of thing that families were meant to have, with big high wide rooms and ornamented ceilings. She tortured herself by thinking of being there with Niall, married to him with children and having the day-to-day life which some people took for granted and she never would, she promised God, if she ever got that far. It seemed unlikely.

Her father bought the house for her and then they went home and she was left in the cold silence, smiling and nodding at people as she went by and wondering how she had ever become this lonely. She had no friends, finding the sort of work she wanted was difficult to get and day after day there was nothing but sleet and wind and wondering whether to venture out and having no acquaintance and going to the shops for something to do and coming home as the evening closed in and wishing she had not left her parents. But there was no going back. She could not.

The house seemed so big with nobody in it and she was reluctant to leave the fire and go to bed, even though there was a fire in the bedroom which was seen to by Christine, who looked after the house for her. She and Christine began sitting over the kitchen fire in the evenings. There was nothing else to do somehow and she learned that being lonely was nothing to do with other people, it was you. No matter how many friends she might have the loneliness was like a broken line between herself and Niall. There was a space around her where he should have been and she could not go on to other people. She had done that before, tried to go on past Rob and reached Arthur and then hoped again and put up with Simon but none of it had been the kind of thing she had felt for Niall. It was almost unseemly somehow, that she could care for anyone so very much. It was leaving your happiness in somebody else's hands and that was such a dangerous thing to do because you could never be sure that they cared for you. He had shown how much he had cared for her and it was not very much in the end.

She got a job eventually. She went to night classes for typing and accounts and she found work in the office of a big shop but it was not what she wanted. She didn't enjoy it and she knew that it was not the job, there was nothing wrong with the work, it was because Niall was not there. The foundry had been the foundry and Niall. If the shop had had Niall there working in the office next door it would have felt like paradise. As it was, she made herself work hard because it was all she had.

Twenty-Two

Niall was convinced that he and Bridget would sleep together again soon but they didn't. She moved all her personal belongings into the room next door and stayed there. She told him that she didn't want to risk the baby until she was sure but, in any case, her interest in sex had ceased. They would go back to where they had been before she decided she wanted a child. Niall protested but it didn't make any difference. He couldn't force her to go to bed with him and he soon discovered that when somebody had made it plain they found you repulsive it didn't exactly encourage you to make love to them. That winter Niall spent a lot of time at work.

One night in February, longing for Jonty's company and having nobody about except Dryden, Niall knocked on the door of Dryden's office mid-evening and said, 'I don't suppose you'd go out for a drink with a nasty little shite like me, would you?'

Dryden put down his pen, laughed and said, 'I might.'

They went across the road to the Royal and the first person they encountered was Paddy Harper.

'What are you doing up here, Paddy?'

'I have friends,' Paddy said.

'Can I buy you a drink?'

'You can.'

Niall wasn't used to beer. The men here drank pints and pints of it. He bought Paddy a drink but Paddy tactfully went back to his friends and left them sitting over the fire.

'Do you have any friends?' he asked Dryden.

'No, just Joe, and he drinks very little because of his father so . . . we don't go out. I discovered a long time ago that if you're friendly with the pit owner then you can't be friends with anybody else and I'd rather have Joe.'

'You only took the pit house because of them, didn't you?' Niall said. 'You could have your old house back if you like.'

'There's somebody in it,' Dryden pointed out. 'Besides . . .'

'Besides, what?'

'I'm getting to like it, the whole thing, you know, having the running of the pit almost to myself and the house is . . . it's new ground in that respect.'

'You don't mind working with me then?'

'No, not so long as you do as you're told.'

Niall laughed.

'Do you want another drink?' he said.

When Niall came back from the bar Dryden accepted his beer and said, 'So, how's the missus?'

'Expecting.'

'Ah.'

'You like children?'

'No.' Dryden shifted on his chair. 'I can't say as I do. I brought up Tommy on my own, nine years, and then . . . Now I just go to work and on Sundays Vinia and Joe come over and she makes the dinner and that's it. Are you pleased about the bairn?'

'I don't know.'

'Look at it this way,' Dryden said. 'You can't make a much worse job of it than either your father or your grandfather.'

'I'd like it to be a girl. People don't fight so much. Do you think George would have taken me if I'd been a girl?'

'Probably not but then I didn't like him and I could be wrong. What happened to him?'

Afterwards Niall blamed it on the beer but at the time it seemed the most natural thing in the world to sit over the fire in the little old pub and tell Dryden about George. He had never told anyone else about the big house in Edinburgh and how George had married Alison and thereafter lost his money and how they had left because the creditors were banging on the door and had walked all the way to Newcastle and then how George had killed himself. He wasn't even sorry he had said it, because Dryden said, 'Jesus, that's hard. What a thing to do to a bairn,' and Niall realized that he had wanted somebody to know, somebody to sympathize, somebody he respected.

He remembered himself sufficiently to say, 'You won't tell Joe,' and Dryden promised that he wouldn't but Niall also realized that Dryden wouldn't tell Joe because it would hurt him, that his child had suffered so much, that George had not looked after Niall, that he had not been there, that his role of father had been, as Dryden so rightly said, not the best thing Joe ever did in his life. When he was lying in bed that night, alone – she still wouldn't sleep with him – he thought back to the things Dryden had said and stored them in his mind for comfort. He was not afraid of Dryden any more.

That spring Bridget grew big. Niall had no experience of pregnant women but she didn't seem to enjoy it at all. She was very sick for three months and some days did not get out of bed and then she began to put on weight and took to looking at herself in the mirror and bemoaning the loss of her figure. She did not want him near her, not that that was anything new. He had thought they might at least sleep together but she wanted to be by herself. She lost interest in the house and he had thought when the weather got better that she would at least want to be in the garden but she didn't. She huddled over the fire and would not go anywhere even though they were invited to all manner of events in the neighbourhood after their successful Christmas party. He thought that this was what she had wanted, to be accepted, to be part of things here, to be able to lord it over the local people because she had a bigger house and a richer husband than anyone else, but she didn't. She dismissed the maids for trifling offences and Jim the gardener left in a huff when he inadvertently chopped down the wrong bushes and she complained, so Niall kept coming home to a grubby cold house with no dinner.

Niall tried to talk to her but she lay in bed all day with a book and wouldn't discuss it so he hired people from Sweethope to come in and clean and cook and to take their orders from him, and then he came home one day in May to find his wife contrite.

'I'm sorry,' she said. 'I feel much better. I'm not sick and I've got lots of energy. I've been to see Jim and he's going to come back and do the garden and I've made a roast lamb dinner.'

Niall was relieved.

They ate together in the kitchen for the first time in weeks. She was even prepared to accept invitations to go to dinner with a local landowner and his wife, something they had not done before. It was for Saturday night and Niall was happy to see his wife in a pretty dress, rather proud of her bulging though somewhat concealed front and he thought the change would do her good, but he could see as soon as they got there that she was not enjoying herself and he understood why. The wives of these men had not had the awful experiences which had been a part of her life. He sometimes felt like that himself. He thought one of the reasons he liked Dryden so much was because Dryden's life had been so difficult. He knew from gossip about Dryden's childhood that he had been given away by his mother, lived with religious fanatics, been outcast from the village. These people had been cushioned, they had education, parenting, love, and the women had been looked after, cherished even, they were so glossy, so cared-for, like delicate plants. He did not blame her for having nothing to say to them. They bored him. The talk was trivial and he hated the formality of it, the numerous servants, the glitter of silver at dinner, the way the men were left alone to their port. They talked of hunting and shooting, things which Niall knew nothing about. He was below his company, he thought wryly, he would much rather have been sitting in the pub with Dryden. He could not help thinking either that if Joe had been there it would have been all right because Joe was comfortable in any kind of company and would have bridged the gap between these men and himself. He was too hard, too lonely and too young to be at home here. It also occurred to him that he could have taken Caitlin there and she would have enjoyed it. He imagined driving back with her and laughing about the other guests but she would have made such things a part of her life if it had been required of her as his wife, instead of which Bridget complained all the way home about how stupid they were, stamped upstairs and slammed the bedroom door.

Niall went after her, only to find that she turned around on him as he knocked and then walked into her room. She looked accusingly at him.

'You should never have taken me there.'

'You said you wanted to go.'

'I didn't realize it was going to be stultifyingly boring!' Bridget declared, flinging her coat across the bed. 'I hate country people, I hate their ways and their silly little lives. They don't know anything. And fancy being marched from the room before the port arrives. I like port. They knit. Can you believe it, those women actually knit. They sew. They . . . talk about nothing but their blessed children and their husbands . . . God, I've never seen such fat awful middle-aged men, pompous old gits.'

She sat down on the bed.

'We don't have to go again,' Niall said.

'I thought I was going to like the country. Nothing happens here. Just the seasons – and I'm beginning to look like a whale.'

'No, you aren't. You look wonderful, you always do.'

'You think I'm going to go to bed with you, don't you?'

'I gave up thinking you were going to go to bed with me four months ago, I just thought you might have bothered to be polite for my sake.'

'Now that I'm your wife? I'm having your child, what more do you want?'

Niall was too tired and irritated not to point out to her that the child had been her idea.

'I can't think why,' she said. 'If I had known what it was going to be like going to bed with you I would never have bothered.'

'That was your idea too.'

'I had to do something. I didn't want you running off with Caitlin Redpath.'

'I wasn't running off with anybody,' Niall said.

She didn't argue with him any more. They got undressed, they went to bed. Half an hour later when she had decided he was asleep she got up and went into his bedroom.

*

It was not that Joe hated the foundry, he didn't. He liked being there, the atmosphere was good. There was plenty of work, Bill Ellison was a good manager and treated Joe like the underman-ager, though officially he was not. Bill was older than Joe and said that he liked having somebody there with experience. They worked well together. Joe didn't expect to be given anything else. Aulay Redpath had been right. Now that there was only one steelworks, it thrived, but when Joe came past the entrance to the other one he itched to do something about it. He even thought that, had he wanted to, Aulay Redpath could have opened the other works, because he had been clever enough to bring in so much work that it was beginning to spill over. Joe was frustrated. He could have done Bill Ellison's job easily. It upset him too that he had cost Vinia her business. She didn't say anything but he knew how hard she had worked to have the shops and, after him, it had been her whole life. Now all she had was the awful little house where they lived and her work at the chapel which she threw herself into, but that winter she began working from their house, making hats and dresses for other people. It didn't pay well, the local people could not afford much, but she liked doing it and it was all money. Every penny was important. Most of that Joe gave away. There were people around them who were not well off. It was not so bad now that the pit was underway, things had picked up considerably. If only Mr Redpath would open the Morgan steelworks things would be so much better. Joe could not resist, one day that spring, choosing his time carefully when Mr Redpath came to the foundry on one of his infrequent visits to say, 'Do you think I might have a word, Mr Redpath?'

Joe couldn't like Aulay Redpath, because he was so jealous of him with regard to Niall, but as a man he found it difficult to dislike him. Aulay managed to combine intelligence, ability and a sense of lightness which Joe knew was a rare combination. The men who worked for him didn't like him because he ignored them and he didn't know much about the making of steel but he employed men who did and the standard of the place had improved. Aulay ushered Joe into Bill Ellison's office. Luckily Mr Ellison was not in it, he was in the works, Joe had watched him go.

'I just wondered if you had given any thought to opening up the Morgan foundry,' Joe said.

Aulay looked long at him and then suddenly he smiled.

'Do you know, I think I was waiting for you to say that? You never give up, do you?'

'It would make good business sense, surely.'

'Go on,' Aulay dared him. 'Tell me you'll manage it for me. There isn't enough work, Forster.'

'But there's getting to be too much for here, isn't there?'

'I'll grant you that,' Aulay said.

'Even if you opened it part-time, stored things there . . .'

'It would take more capital than it's worth. I do understand that your interest is almost entirely altruistic—'

'No, it isn't,' Joe said. 'I want something for mine!'

It was not what he had intended to say. He did not wish to bring into Aulay Redpath's eyes the kind of cruel, knowing look that he was aware Aulay was capable of, but in fact Aulay just looked rather ashamed and said, 'Ah, but I can't do that.'

'You own it,' Joe declared.

'I don't. That . . . bastard you call your son has me wound up legally.'

'He owns it?' Joe stared. 'But I thought . . .'

'Neat, isn't it?' Aulay said. 'When he gave it to me, as he called it, there were conditions. He wanted me to keep it open. In the event I couldn't, and he knew that, but I'm not allowed to employ you there even to sweep the floors.'

'There's a solution to that,' Joe said.

'And what is it?'

'You could make me manager here and give it to Mr Ellison.'

He expected Aulay to say, sarcastically, *I'm sure Mr Ellison would be delighted*, except that he didn't, because they both knew that Bill Ellison had not been well of late and might be glad of something less to manage.

'You think I want to make an enemy of Niall?' Aulay said.

'I'm good,' Joe said.

Aulay laughed.

'Sometimes he reminds me of you. Let me think about it.'

'For how long?' Joe asked.

'I'm here for the rest of the day.'

Joe went back to his desk. He tried to work. The figures danced before his eyes. He wanted this place, he wanted it so much, he wanted back respectability and, more than that, he wanted to go home to his wife and tell her that he was a man of substance again. All around him the work went on in the office and Joe heard every door opening and everybody going in and out and every conversation starting up and ending and he heard Mr Ellison and Aulay going into the little office together. They were closeted there for a long time and by then it was after half-past five and the rest of the staff had gone home. Not long afterwards Mr Ellison came in and he said, 'Mr Redpath would like to see you, Joe,' and disappeared along the corridor.

Joe tried to breathe normally but he was uncertain and shaking by the time he reached the manager's office. He tried to imagine himself there and then not to, in case his idea had not worked and he would have to go home just the same as usual. He closed the door. Aulay Redpath stood behind the desk and he was smiling.

'You can have the manager's job here,' he said.

It had been a long time since Joe had gone so happily back to his wife. When he got in, the little house had never looked so welcoming. A bright fire burned in the kitchen grate and it was obvious by the smell that she had been baking bread that day. Joe clattered up the yard, letting the gate slam as he did so, up the steps at the back door and into the house and then he grabbed her, she gave a little squeal of shock and when she turned around he kissed her and he said,

'I've been made manager of the Redpath foundry!' They were the sweetest words in the world, he thought.

'You've what?'

'We get a big stone house and I get paid well and I get my own office and you, my sweetheart, get to be married to the manager. What do you think about that?'

She told him he was wonderful. She told him he was just entirely the best thing in the history of the world. She kissed him all over his face and he saw in her eyes an expression he hadn't seen in a long time. It was pride.

'How did you do it?' she said and he told her and she kissed him again, and Joe determined that as soon as they had any money at all they would rent a shop for her.

On the Monday of the following week Dryden was in at the pit office before Niall and when Niall arrived Dryden put his head around the door of the office and said, 'I'd like to talk to you.'

'Now?'

'Yes.'

'Well, come in. Is it important? Has something happened?'

Dryden looked at him, frowning.

'I just want to tell you this because I know it and I don't want you hearing it from anybody else. Joe has been made manager of the steelworks.'

Niall couldn't take it in.

'He's what?'

'Mr Redpath made him manager. Mr Ellison is going to run the Morgan works.'

Niall tried to breathe and not to shout. 'Did Joe tell you this himself?'

'Yesterday. He gets a nice house and . . . He does have a lot of talent and it's a shame not to use talent.'

Nobody said anything. The fire in Niall's office had just got away nicely and was crackling in the background with huge energy.

'Are you going to hate him for the rest of your life?' Dryden said.

'I suppose so, yes.'

'You're going to spoil your life over it, Niall.'

'There's nothing left to spoil,' Niall said.

'You've got to stop blaming him.'

'Why?'

'Because that's what people do when they become adults. He's your father but he's also a lot of other things . . .'

'I know exactly what he is,' Niall said.

'No, you don't. There are a lot of important things about him that you don't know. He could have left this place but he didn't, he kept the pit on while his father drank himself to death, and Joe was younger then than you are now. He's risked his life half a dozen times down this pit, he's rescued other folk, he's helped a lot of people . . .'

'I don't want to hear it!' Niall said.

'Why not? It's part of who he is. He's a person and you would do well to remember that. You could show him a little respect if nothing more.'

'He doesn't deserve my respect!'

'He's earned it, over and over. You're never going to be as good a man as he is. You're too bloody selfish.'

There was silence. What Niall wanted to do was go for Dryden and knock him off his feet. He should be able to do it, Dryden was a lot older than him, but he wasn't sure whether he could and the more he thought about it the less he wanted to.

'Well go on then,' Dryden urged him. 'You never know till you try. Frightened?'

'I'm not afraid of anybody.'

'No, I know. Look, I'm sorry, all right?'

'Fine,' Niall said.

Dryden turned towards the door and then changed his mind.

'You aren't going to go down there and slit Joe's throat?'

'I haven't slit anybody's throat in years.'

'I'm so relieved to hear that,' Dryden said. 'I'm going underground. Do you want to come with me?'

'No.'

'It was actually a rhetorical question.'

'One of those? Right then,' Niall said.

He couldn't think. They went down into the depths of the pit. He was usually very aware of how afraid he was. He did his best not to let Dryden know that he was afraid of small dark places, because he could not explain that his fear came from being thrown down cellar steps on to the cold dank floor and left there for days at a time. Sometimes going down the pit made him sweat and sometimes it made the sweat cold, but he never refused, because he thought he would get used to it and to a certain extent he had. The darkness down there was so thick you could raise your hand in front of your face and see nothing. The cellar had been very like that because there were no windows in it, the only light came from a sliver under the door. He could remember watching that thin line of light as it left the cold winter day. Sometimes he had thought it would not come back.

Dryden, knowing nothing of this, seemed to understand that he was afraid. He never let Niall go down there without him and he would talk so that his thick Durham voice sounded warm and syrupy in the darkness. So much so that in Niall's dreams about the cellar, and he had them often now for some reason, Dryden's voice was there and it had stopped them from being nightmares. His voice was beginning to replace Mr Wilson and Mrs Mackenzie and Niall's fear. He didn't often listen to what Dryden said, he didn't think Dryden intended him to, it was just the rhythm of the words rather than their meaning that was important. If Dryden had anything important to say he said it when they got back, or more often he said it to the men as they went. It was just as well he didn't need Niall to be intelligent down there, he couldn't do it. With a father and a grandfather who had been both mine owners and miners, Niall had to admit that he was too afraid here to be of much use.

The calm voice of reason went on and on at his side all the time but this morning Niall didn't notice what was going on and he was not afraid. He was so angry with Aulay for giving Joe the kind of work he loved so much and he was planning that at the first opportunity he would drive to Newcastle and tell Aulay exactly what he thought about him and he would not let Dryden distract him with talk of who was doing what where underground. He was not interested, he didn't care. All he wanted was to go to wherever Joe happened to be and pull his head off.

'Are you listening to me, Niall?' Dryden demanded as the cage stopped at the bottom of the shaft.

'Yes.'

'No, you bloody aren't,' Dryden said. 'Pay attention. You might learn something.'

'Yes, sir,' Niall said heavily.

Dryden turned to him.

'Forget Joe. Forget what happened. We're down here now. We have more important things to think about. Come on.'

Dryden went down there every day. He called it an inspection. He spoke to everybody, he noticed everything. Niall congratulated himself on having gained Dryden for the manager's job, he was so good at it. Niall knew so little of pits, yet he thought, like somebody who had spent a great deal of time in the darkness, he had good instincts for it, and suddenly, when they were at the far end of the pit, so far they could go no further and were about to turn and come back, it suddenly felt quite different, as though somebody had opened a hatch or the door at the top of the cellar steps. The air felt lighter, the darkness was not quite so dark. He didn't understand it and Dryden sensed nothing or he would have said so. He grabbed hold of Dryden's arm, said his name and then there was a rumbling noise and the world caved in. As it happened, almost in slow motion, he knew which side it was coming from. He still had his hand on Dryden's arm, so it could not have been happening as slowly as it seemed. All he had to do was shove in the opposite direction and Dryden was not expecting it so it was easy to move him. It was not quite so easy to follow him. Somehow the slowness and the fastness of the whole thing got in one another's way and the sound of the falling rock filled his entire hearing and it was as though it held him in its embrace and after that, when the noise stopped and the dust settled, there was silence.

Dryden was not there, where had he gone? There was not the sound of his voice. Dryden, he thought in amusement, had a voice that was like treacle pudding, all warm and soft and comforting. Where was it? Dryden should have been there. The darkness was too dark without him, difficult to move in, like wading in the North Sea. And then he realized that Dryden was not there because he was back down the cellar. All his nightmares were coming true. He had not thought he would have to go back there. How could it be happening now? He did not remember being put there, he did not remember what had happened. He could not bring to mind Mrs Mackenzie's voice or Mr Wilson's hurting grip on his arm and yet his arm hurt. Other parts of him hurt too, in fact, everything hurt, so they must have thrown him down the steps. He thought he could feel the stone slabs beneath him and the rats scuttling about in the corners and he could smell the damp and the peculiar rat smell which was a mixture of shit and sugar somehow. Horrible.

He did not know how long he had been down there but he wanted to panic because there was no light at all under the door and he could not remember that there had been and no matter how long he lay there and looked at it the light did not come back. It was so dark that there were no shadows. It had never been so dark before. He had always been afraid but he had never been as afraid as this. It seemed to him that they were not going to come back, that he was not important enough for them even to consider he might be alive.

The pain was so bad that he didn't know where it was coming from, it was coming from everywhere. Everything hurt.

When he awoke he was in Mrs Mackenzie's room and she was holding out a glass of water towards him. She didn't give him the water, she kept saying that she would and he kept holding out his hand for it but she didn't. Mr Wilson was there and they had hold of him and they were dragging him along the dark corridor and he was fighting with them and crying and begging them not to and Mr Wilson opened the door which led into the cellar and in spite of the way that he struggled and fought they had got him to the top step and then it was just a question of disentangling themselves from him and shoving him and they did. He was clinging on to them and then their clothes and then thin air and then he was falling, he was falling all the way down and the cold air rushed past, and the walls, and then he hit the floor and after that there was nothing.

Joe was so pleased with his new office. The sun shone in there all day. Aulay Redpath and Bill Ellison were showing him around the steelworks as though he had never been in a pattern shop before, as though he had just arrived and the other men in the office did not resent him, they were pleased for him, they were glad that he had been promoted, they had never, he thought, been happy to have him there as almost one of them. He should not have been there and, now that he was the manager, they seemed pleased. Two days of instruction and then Aulay Redpath did not come back and Bill stayed there for the rest of the week while they went over what they needed to go over.

He was glad, he said, to give it up, go part-time, he was getting tired, he had only stepped into the gap because the previous manager had left suddenly, he had never wanted it. He was getting too old. He wanted to be in his garden and playing golf and going to football matches. Did Joe know that there was to be a new golf course nearby? Joe was a stranger to golf but so pleased about everything that he nodded and smiled at what Mr Ellison told him. He and Bill went to the other works and that week he helped Bill because he knew that works, he knew how it had been when he and Niall had run it for that short time, and it was, he thought, as Niall would have wanted it to be.

Aulay Redpath was prepared to spend time and money putting things right. Aulay was at the Morgan steelworks – he still called it that, perhaps it was easier not to call it anything new – and he took on every man he could find a job for and there was work and Joe was so glad. He could at last admire Aulay Redpath. He was succeeding where other men failed because he was prepared to go wherever he needed to to find work and you had to give it to him, Joe thought, Aulay was so confident that people believed he could do anything. Joe was ready to believe that Aulay could do anything.

'Niall told me there wasn't room for two foundries in this place, but I'm going to prove him wrong,' Aulay told Joe. 'Bill doesn't know it yet but I'm going to have this place up and running full-time if I have to go halfway across Europe for the work.'

Joe didn't like to say to him that if he had thought that two years ago they could have saved a lot of grief, but Aulay wasn't the kind of man who dwelt in the past. He was energetic with regard to the present and the future, so Joe would have to be glad of that and not try to resent Aulay's part in his downfall.

Joe liked best the day that Aulay left him alone in his new domain. He was what his wife would have called as happy as a pig in muck. He loved it. He didn't love it as much as he loved the Prince but he was heading in that direction and he didn't mind quite as much as he had done that Dryden had his pit and his house, because that was the next best thing to having it himself and Dryden gave him good reports of Niall, things that made Joe pleased, that Niall was not the sort of man who thought that, because he had suddenly obtained a business, he knew all about it. Niall had done the right thing by getting Dryden there and Dryden said he was just like Joe in that he soaked up information, took notice of what he was told and was happy to be there.

Joe was glad too and he had been glad to tell Vinia, via Dryden, that Niall's wife was expecting a baby. Joe wasn't sure whether another generation of his family was a good thing but he was pleased for himself. Having a grandchild, even if he couldn't see it, must be a wonderful thing and maybe in time Niall would relent, soften, and they would be friends. It was Joe's dearest wish.

He and Vinia had moved into the manager's house. It was not quite as big as Stanley House, which was their home, but it was a big square solid stone house which stood alone and had gardens and he was grateful to move from Deerness Law, where he did not have his pit or his house, to Sweethope, where he was the manager of the works. Vinia loved the house. She had not yet suggested to him that she might go back to work but he had the feeling that all she needed was the security of a house and a job on his part and she would like to start again with her business. She was not the kind of woman who sat about at home making cakes and dusting furniture and calling her neighbours, she had always enjoyed what she did. He had no doubt that they could find a shop. He would talk to her about it tonight when he got home.

That first morning he walked out of his house and it was a lovely early summer morning, he was happy with everything. He went early to the works and walked around and greeted the men and then he sat in his office and watched the sun glinting upon the buildings. He had not been there long, enjoying himself, when he looked up and found Jack Fanshawe, one of the deputies from the Prince, standing in the doorway, looking gravely at him. Joe's heart did a nasty swoop. He knew what that meant.

'Mr Forster? There's been an accident at the pit. Mr Cameron has been hurt and . . . Mr McLaughlan is still down there and . . .'

Joe already was up off his chair.

'Is Niall hurt? Is Dryden hurt? What happened?'

'It was a roof fall. Mr Cameron has hurt his leg but the doctor thinks he'll be all right. We managed to get him to the surface but . . .'

'But what?'

Jack looked straight at him.

'The men are down there, digging. It might go back a long way. Mr McLaughlan can't be far in but . . .'

'It was a bad fall?' Joe guessed.

'Yes.'

That was the trouble, Joe thought, with starting the day off well. It was like God looked down and thought, by gum, Joe Forster's having a happy day. We can't have that. If you started off and everything looked black, things got better, but waking up to sunshine, a beautiful wife, a lovely house and new manager's job, you didn't stand a cat in hell's chance of getting through the next twelve hours without bloody disaster.

Joe tried not to think as he was driven out of the dale. The sunlight was pretty and golden on the fields, even the grey stone surrounding them was light. The lambs were skipping about and from the top of Redgate Bank when you glanced back the whole dale was set out before you for your delight and it was so damned beautiful. Even the steelworks looked nice from there and he could see Niall's house, just the top of it down the lane, where no doubt his wife, big with his child, was starting out her day. He would go to the pit and assess the damage and then he would go back and tell her . . . Tell her what? That Niall had died under a fall of stone, that God had seen fit to take his only son away from him. Why should he not? He had taken Dryden's son and Dryden had been a good parent. He had not been any kind of a parent other than the worst kind and in his heart Joe knew that the worst thing a person could be was a bad parent. If you couldn't do that right then it didn't much matter what else you did.

He tried to look out of the window so that Jack Fanshawe would not see his expression. If Niall was dead then there was nothing, then his wife and his new job and his house and his future would all be forfeit. Men went on living after their children died but they only did it because it was required of them by God. It seemed to Joe that very often people were not required to move anywhere or die to go to hell. God brought it to them, just in case they had some idea that death was a sweet and dreamless sleep. Have it now, was God's idea. Have it now, learn all there is to know. All those years when he had thought he did not have a child, that Niall must have died. To meet him, to have this dreadful fight and then to lose him . . .

They had climbed the banks out of the dale and were going across the top of the country, a thousand feet above sea level, where the air was clear. The sky was clear too that day, the farms across the top were awash with spring flowers and in the distance he could see the quarry, a big gash in the side of the hill. Down another bank and up the other side and past the entrance to the quarry and then the entrance to the slag works and then up the bank right to the very top in Deerness Law itself, past the lane end of the row where he had so recently lived and then out of the village again, past Prince Row and there it was, the pit that he loved so much. He would never love it any more if Niall were dead, and all that the family had ever had or ever been would mean nothing if Niall had died in the depths of the Prince. Joe had loved it so much and for so long. His love for Niall and the pit were the same thing really, they both had his heart.

The car stopped, Joe got out, throwing back a word of thanks to Jack Fanshawe he ran into the pit office and there was Dryden, grey-faced, obviously hurt, but sitting on a chair, waiting for him.

'What the hell are you doing?' Joe said. 'You should be in hospital.'

'I'm not going any place.'

'What happened?'

'The roof fell in. He didn't want to go down, he was so angry with you, and I made him. I . . .'

'Is it a big fall?'

'I don't know.'

'You've got rescuers down there?'

'Of course I have. He's not that far back. It isn't going to take that long but, Joe . . .'

'I know, I know. I'm going down.'

'It doesn't look good. It might go again. What if it happens when you're down?'

'Let me get Jack to take you—'

'I'm not going any place,' Dryden said again.

'Please yourself,' Joe said and left him there.

*

Once underground Joe's heart did that horrible sweeping thing again, which left him feeling sick. He had no idea how far back the fall was, that was hardly relevant if Niall were beneath it. Nobody could live under that. If, however, he had been thrown clear of it then it did matter how far back it went, because he could be badly hurt and he could die before he was rescued or, if things were bad enough, he could die from lack of food and water before they reached him. Joe did not know a miner who did not dread being buried alive. It was something you tried not to think about.

The creaking timbers did nothing to reassure him. Joe just wished he could have ordered the men back to the surface but he needed them there, moving away the stone. Any moment could be the end. At any time they could find a hand or a foot, some bloody part of his dead son.

Having refused to go to hospital, Dryden tried to sit still. His leg couldn't be broken, he thought, it would hurt more than it did. The doctor didn't seem to think it was broken and it did actually hurt like merry hell but he knew that the pain of broken limbs could be unbearable. He had broken his arm once and his collar bone and . . . His thoughts were interrupted as Vinia burst into the room. She stopped when she saw him and started to cry.

'I thought you were dead,' she declared.

'Don't be silly,' Dryden said softly.

'Tam Proud's husband came . . . He came back and said you'd been hurt under a roof fall.'

'I'm fine,' Dryden said. 'It's Niall.'

'Niall?' She stared into his face. 'Niall's hurt?'

'He's caught, at least I think he is, in the fall.'

'But . . .'

'Joe's down there.'

Her eyes held horror.

'Oh my God!' she said. 'If . . . if Niall dies Joe will never . . .
He will never . . .'

Dryden knew exactly what she meant even though she didn't
say it. When your child died there was so little left for you to be
concerned about. And she knew also how dangerous it was to
try to rescue a man trapped like that, that a roof having fallen
in could bring more after it, so easily.

'Look, there is something that has to be done.'

If he could distract her it would help. She sat back.

'What?' she said.

'Niall's wife.'

'Oh no.'

'Vinny, if he's dead and she hasn't been told, it'll be worse.'

'If he's dead how could it be worse? She's pregnant. Oh God.
I've never met her.'

'Somebody has to go and tell her and I'm not in any shape
and I don't think she has any friends.'

'I don't want to. I've heard such stories about her, how awful
she is and . . .'

'I'll get Jack to drive you.'

'No.'

'You have to,' Dryden said.

Vinia had been to the Morgan house once a very long time
ago when she first went there to a party when Joe had been in
love with Luisa. She even remembered the dress she had worn,
how very silly. The gardens were so neat, everything in place,

and the house itself looked perfect. There was nobody about but there was obviously a gardener somewhere near, because a wheelbarrow stood to one side of the drive near the house and was full of weeds. She got out of the car, Jack said he would wait and Vinia trod slowly up the steps to the front door. She stood there, waiting in the sunshine, wondering what on earth she was going to say to a woman she didn't know.

The door opened. The maid was dressed in black and white, perfectly neat and composed.

'I'm Mrs Forster. I would like to see Mrs McLaughlan, please.'

The maid showed her into the hall. Vinia tried to rehearse the words that she would use and then, all too quickly, was shown through double doors and into the drawing room. She remembered that. She remembered the picture of Luisa Morgan over the fireplace. As she walked in, Niall's wife got up from the sofa. She was very pregnant. She was also by far the most beautiful woman Vinia had ever seen. She thought about Caitlin and felt sorry. Who in the whole world could compete with this? She was so blonde, her hair was almost white, and her blue eyes were so dark and so thickly lashed and her skin was cream and her cheeks were perfectly pink and her mouth was full and . . .

'I don't think we've met before,' she said, smiling just a little.

'I'm afraid . . .' Vinia said and then began again. 'I'm sorry to bring you bad news but there has been an accident at the pit and your husband is hurt.'

'Niall's hurt?' Her eyes, if it were possible, went even darker. 'What happened?'

'The roof fell in.'

Vinia gave her time to comprehend but she feared that Niall's wife knew nothing about pits. Perhaps it was just as well.

'Is he in hospital?'

'No. No. My husband . . . They haven't got him out yet.'

'So you don't know how badly hurt he is?'

'Not yet. Joe is . . . Joe is down there and they are . . . They will get him out but it may take time.'

'How much time?'

'I don't know.'

Bridget frowned. It was instead of crying, Vinia thought.

'Can I go there?'

'Yes, of course. I have a car outside.'

Bridget hesitated. Vinia wasn't sure why, but then Bridget looked into her eyes and said, 'He isn't dead, is he?'

'I don't know. I don't think anybody knows.'

Bridget stood for a little while longer and then she said, 'I'll get a coat.'

Vinia waited in the hall until Bridget came back down the stairs. She was some time and Vinia knew that she had had to compose herself. This wasn't good for the baby, Vinia thought, but what else could they do?

It was almost three hours before they broke through, made a small way in. Joe shouted because he had begun to hope. Niall had not been found dead, he was not beneath that awful pile of stone but if he was conscious he would hear them and as they shouted and whistled and yelled his name he would respond. Joe made them listen from time to time but there was no sound. They had a lot more stone to clear away before the hole was big enough for Joe to squeeze himself through and be handed a lamp, because he could see nothing. Cut and bruised he crawled along the sharp edges which everything seemed to have and then the lamplight showed him the scene and there was Niall, further along, clear of most of the stone. Joe's heart did a big leap.

'Niall?'

Nothing happened. Joe moved nearer, brought the lamp as close as he could and checked for his breath, his pulse. It was there.

'Niall?'

He checked as a great big stone dropped just behind him. When he was fairly sure another would not follow he took the water bottle which was on him and put it to Niall's lips. Niall made a small cry of protest. Joe waited.

'Niall, it's me, Joe.'

Niall opened his eyes, looked up at him and then said, 'What are you doing here?'

'Where are you hurt?'

'I don't know. They were here.'

'Who were?'

Niall looked uncertainly at him. And then the roof came in. Joe shielded him but most of it didn't reach them. He waited until the noise ceased, the dust settled and he didn't think any more was going to come down, at least for a while, and then he moved so that he could try to assess the extent of the damage. He had no idea how much had come down at the other side. He couldn't help worrying that the rescuers were hurt. If it was a big fall they might well be, and if it was a big fall it would take a long time to do anything about it but at least they had light and some water.

'You all right?' he enquired.

Niall didn't answer him. Joe gave him another drink of water and then he said, 'Are you hurt?'

'No.'

Joe took Niall into his arms and it had been the right thing to do. Niall burrowed his face against Joe's chest.

'I thought I was going to die down the cellar.'

'You're not going to die, not down any cellar and certainly not down your own pit,' Joe said.

He gathered Niall closer and heard a little sigh of contentment.

'I thought I was back there,' Niall said.

'You aren't back anywhere and if those bastards at the other side get themselves sorted we'll be out of here in no time. Don't worry. Everything's going to be fine.'

'Are you certain?'

'I'm positive.'

Niall went to sleep. Joe was glad it was only sleep, Niall was heavy in his arms but his breathing was so regular and Joe loved to hear it. He was propped up against a big lump of stone. What a stupid circumstance to discover that you were the happiest you had ever been in your life, with your child in your arms behind a roof fall at the bottom of a Durham pit. Life was very strange.

They tried to find Bridget a comfortable chair but there weren't any. Dryden couldn't take his eyes off her. He hadn't thought there were women like that in existence. He tried to remember his manners and not stare but she was exquisite. He could quite see why Niall would not give her up and why he had given up Caitlin Redpath, pretty as Caitlin was. She was several months gone, he thought, beautifully rounded with Niall's child, her eyes almost black with concern. She sat, drinking tea, and they waited for news, then she said, 'I hate this place. I didn't think it would be like this. Do you think he's going to be all right?'

It was the third time she had asked him. Dryden said again

that he was sure Niall would be fine. Nothing happened and the waiting was hard. Dryden had visions of the roof falling in and both Joe and Niall being dead and then what would happen? The idea of never sitting down with Joe again over a glass of wine and talking about the work problems wasn't something Dryden thought he could manage. As for Niall . . . if Niall died he would feel guilt and responsibility and he was so tired of all that. He wanted never to feel any responsibility for anybody ever again. Life had taught him to stay back, to build walls around himself. Sometimes now, in fact almost every night when he got back to the house on the fell, he liked the silence. He would not have told Joe for worlds, because he had asked for the house for Joe and Vinia's sake but he actually was having a love affair with the house on the moors. He wanted it for his own now and for nobody in the world to come between the sound of wind across the fell at night, when he was safely tucked in his warm bed, and himself. It was the childhood he had never had and he was providing it for himself now. He had the feeling Niall had the same problem, trying to create something out of the mess other people had made. It was one of the reasons he liked Niall.

He thought of his house when he could think of nothing else that was positive. He thought of going inside and closing the door and being there all by himself in the quietness with nobody to take up space or interrupt. It was no longer Joe and Vinia's house. It was his. He thought that no matter what further horrors the day might bring, and life had so far demonstrated almost every horror that there was to him, he would still go back at the end of the day and shut out the world. The night would fall over the fell, the moon would rise, the sun would come up in the morning and it was all you could be sure of.

As he sat there, one of the rescuers, Hen Shaw, came into the office.

'We got Mr Forster through but there's been another fall,' he said.

'Can you hear anything?' Dryden said.

'No.'

'I'm going down.'

'Dryden, you can't,' Vinia said. 'You're hurt. If you go . . .' Her voice trailed off because of the way that he was looking at her and when there was silence he said, 'You take Mrs McLaughlan to my house.'

'I'm staying here,' Bridget said.

'No, you're not,' Dryden said. 'If this turns out to be a long job, we don't want other problems as well. I don't want Niall blaming me for you having that bairn early. When there's news I'll let you know.'

'I do love a masterful man,' Bridget said.

Dryden went to her.

'Please,' he said. 'As soon as I know owt I'll send somebody. If Niall thought I had you holed up in this place on a hard chair he'd skin me.'

'I hadn't realized I had turned into a shrinking violet,' Bridget said.

'It's just along the road. It couldn't be much nearer and you'll be more comfortable there. Vinia will make you some tea.'

'All right, all right,' Bridget said and she went out.

'You can't go down there, Dryden, things are bad enough,' Vinia said.

'Just keep that woman away from here.'

'You're trying to get rid of us. You think he's dead.'

'I don't think anything of the kind. Please, Vinny, for Joe's sake, do as I ask.'

Vinia followed Bridget outside and Jack Fanshawe drove them to the house which had been hers. She looked wearily at it. She unlocked the door and went inside. Bridget glanced around her. Vinia went into the kitchen, opened up the fire, filled the kettle and put it on to boil.

'This was your house, wasn't it?' Bridget followed her in.

'It was, yes.'

'Do you miss it?'

'Not any more. The foundry manager's house is fine. I don't miss the pit, I can tell you. Give me a safer job for my husband any day.' And then she realized how crass that sounded and looked at Bridget. 'I didn't mean . . .'

Bridget sighed and sat down.

'We should go in the other room, it's more comfortable in there.'

'I'm having a baby, I'm not ill,' Bridget said. 'It was a mistake.'

Vinia couldn't believe what she was hearing.

'But you're married.'

'That was another of my ridiculous ideas. I thought marriage would be . . . What did I think it would be? It's funny now. I can't remember. No, I can. I thought it would be a way of getting rid of Caitlin Redpath.'

'And was it?'

'No. He had an affair with her.'

'You've only been married five minutes,' Vinia said. 'And I wouldn't have thought Caitlin Redpath any competition for you.'

'I did see her off in the end. That's what this was.' She indicated her bump. 'And what about your husband?'

'Joe? He's wonderful.'

Bridget looked respectfully at her.

'Is he really?'

'Really. I couldn't imagine living without him.'

'Niall looks exactly like him. I got such a shock the first time I saw your husband. He came to see us in Newcastle. Niall was so angry. Do you hate him for what he did?'

Vinia was not about to say that she hated a man who could be buried alive down a pit and then she realized that the truth of the matter was that she didn't hate him at all, in fact she was very fond of him, not simply because he was Joe's son but because she couldn't help it. She hated what he had done but in her finer moments she thought she understood partly why he had done it. If they got out of this she wanted to do better, to have Niall and Bridget as part of the family. She would talk to Niall and to Joe and make things better. Things were already getting better, she thought, what with Joe's new job and status and house.

'Has this happened before?' Bridget had to repeat the question, Vinia hadn't been listening.

'My first husband, Tom, died down there,' she said before she thought better of it. 'Mind you, in those days Joe's father had had the say over things for a long time before Joe took over, and Mr Forster never spent any money making things better. It's much better now. Accidents do still happen of course but not often.'

'You think they'll get out, then?'

'You have to think that.'

'I don't know how you stand this life,' Bridget said.

Vinia did not like to point out to her that she was the one who was the pitman's wife. She hoped there would be word soon, not just because she was anxious for Joe and Niall, but because she didn't think she and Bridget were going to get on together very well if they were left alone for long. She also thought as the time crept by that the longer it took the worse it would be. She put the sitting-room fire on and could not help thinking back to what things had been like during the past couple of years before Niall caused problems for them. The war had been dreadful because Tommy had died, but after the war there was peace not just in the land but particularly for them. It had been hard for Dryden but she and Joe had spent a lot of time with him. He had practically lived at their house for a couple of years after Tommy died, but once that time was over he went back to his own house and the work went on and in a way they had all three of them hidden in their work. They hadn't been able to hide in it since Niall's arrival. He had upset everything. She hoped to God he wasn't dead. She thought it would finish everything off, not just Joe's clumsy and belated attempt at parenting but anything that they had left at all. She didn't think any of them could stand another blow.

Bridget fell asleep on the sofa in front of the fire and then Vinia heard the door and flew through the hall. It was Dryden. He was limping badly. She took him into the kitchen, softly closed the door.

'Anything?'

'No.'

'They can't be that far back. I thought you said . . .' She turned away. 'I don't know how to live without Joe.'

'Don't worry,' he said. 'It'll be all right, I promise.'

'Don't promise,' Vinia said, moving away and sniffing.

'Hey, look, it'll be fine. It takes more than a roof slip to kill Joe.'

'What about Niall?'

'I don't know. They couldn't hear him and . . . Is she asleep?'

'Yes.'

'Best thing,' Dryden said. 'Try not to worry.'

'We can't lose him. We lost Tommy and . . . I didn't think we would get through that. Niall's all there is left. If he dies Joe will never get past it.'

'I never got past Tommy.'

'I know you didn't. It starts to feel as though it's all for nothing. You shouldn't be going down there. You look awful and that leg . . .'

'I'll call back later,' he said and went.

When he had gone she stood there in the silence of the kitchen and cried and it was not just for Joe and Niall, it was for Tommy too and for Dryden and for the children she and Joe had not had. Then she heard a noise and Bridget was standing in the doorway.

'Has something happened?' she said.

'No. Would you like some more tea?'

'Might as well,' Bridget said. 'There's nothing else to do.'

Joe had fallen asleep, woke up and tried to ease his cramped position. The lamp had gone out, the water was finished and Niall was either sleeping or was hurt somehow and was unconscious. He didn't know which. Joe hadn't been much on prayer lately but he offered something up hopefully because he could not believe that the child who had been given him was going to be taken away. He didn't like to waken Niall but he was afraid. If Niall had been banged on the head the last thing he should do was sleep, but then Joe didn't know if he had been hurt anywhere. Would he have said so? He thought probably not, because Joe's knowledge wouldn't help, just worry him, and Niall, Joe thought, was given to practicalities in an almost brutal way. He had had to be.

Joe had no idea of the time. When there was no night and day you lost track of everything. He had to move, his body was seizing up. He eased Niall away from him, only to find that as he did so Niall awoke. He was so relieved.

'How do you feel?' he said.

'Hungry.'

'That's good. Anything else?'

'Is there any water left?'

'No. Are you hurt anywhere?'

'No.'

'Sure?'

'Joe . . .'

His name was so sweet upon his son's lips. Joe moved about as little as possible. He didn't want to upset Niall in any way. He listened carefully but there was no sound. Surely it wasn't going to take much longer for them to break through.

'Do you know,' Niall said, 'I'm scared of small dark places.'

Joe laughed.

'You're in the right profession then,' he said.

'I wasn't going to come down here at all this morning. Dryden made me do it.'

'He's a shit,' Joe said.

'I like him.'

'I'll like him too when he gets us out of here.'

'Do you think he will?'

'Of course. It isn't a bad fall.'

'It could be though, couldn't it? We don't know what happened at the other side. The whole damned thing could have come in. Other people could have been hurt. It could be blocked. How long do people last without water?'

'I don't know. I was hoping it was something I wasn't going

to have to put to the test,' Joe said. 'It doesn't matter, you can't judge time when you're down here. It's only been a few hours as far as I can guess.'

'I don't want to die here, even with you.'

'What do you want to do?'

'I want to go home to my wife.'

Joe sighed.

'She's a bonny one,' he said.

'Men have always wanted her.' Niall's voice didn't sound very steady.

'And there she is, having your bairn.'

'That's right.'

'Have you known her a long time?'

He heard Niall hesitate. He didn't want Niall to feel obliged to lie to him but there was nothing to do except talk.

'Yes,' he said.

Joe didn't enquire any further and as the quietness lengthened he said, 'I'm sorry I wasn't there.'

'I'm sorry you weren't there too.'

After that there was a long silence. Joe didn't know what to say. Everything he thought of turned into a subject he didn't think Niall would want to discuss and he was beginning to get a bad feeling about all this. If Niall was right, if the fall had been particularly bad at the far side, they might never get out. It wasn't much of a way to die but then he didn't think any way was. Men had not been made to welcome death but to fight to exist for as long as they could draw breath. To have it taken away so cruelly was devastating. Perhaps God thought it fitting that he should be there when his son died. Joe closed his eyes against the thought even though it wasn't any blacker that way. He lay back against the stone again and then he thought he heard something. Niall had heard it too, because he moved almost soundlessly, listening. Joe heard it again and he started to laugh.

'That's that bugger, Dryden Cameron. I'll give him bloody pit, leaving my son down here.'

It took time but the sounds grew and the whistling, and then the noise became Dryden shouting and then finally they broke through and after that there was the beam of a lamp and eventually Dryden handed food and water to Joe, who stretched the few yards in to reach them. Jam sandwiches and water. It was raspberry jam. Joe was pleased about that. When Dryden finally emerged, at least the front of him, Joe said, 'You took your bloody time.'

'I was busy,' Dryden said. 'At least I got it right. Howay out of here, I'm not happy with this roof.'

'He's not happy,' Joe grumbled.

Daylight had broken. The spring sunshine poured into the living room in a most unsubtle way and Vinia awoke to find Bridget crying.

'What if he died?'

Vinia always found the daylight hardest. It was strange, you would think night was the most difficult time, because the darkness fell and you had got all the way through the day and you were tired, but for some reason the mornings always made her want to weep and she did not blame Bridget for giving way now. She had done so well, been so strong.

'I don't want to do this. He's the only person I love, the only person I've ever loved. It wasn't part of the bargain that he should risk his life in stupid ways.'

'Pitmen do that every day.'

'He's not a pitman. He's . . .'

'I think you'll find it's in the blood,' Vinia said.

'What do you mean?'

'I mean that it's quite possible his ancestors have been mining here since the fourteen hundreds. It's what they do.'

'I don't want to do it,' Bridget said.

They went into the kitchen and Vinia made herself busy with the fire and the kettle even though she thought she would never want a cup of tea again and then she thought she heard the front door. She ran through and there was Joe. She didn't see anybody else, she flung herself at him. He smelled of the pit, coaly and dusty and he was covered in it, his fair hair was lost to black and his green eyes peered out of a dark face. Vinia gazed at him and then she saw Niall and she left Joe and got hold of him and kissed him and she said, 'Your wife's in the kitchen.'

Niall went through into the kitchen. Bridget was standing by the fire but she heard him and turned around. She didn't come to him, she just stood, her eyes filling with tears, so he went to her and enfolded her in his arms.

'This was all I wanted,' he said.

Twenty-Three

'I have to go back to the pit.'

'What, now?'

They were sitting in the kitchen drinking tea. Joe had taken Dryden to hospital even though Dryden was protesting that he was fine and Vinia had gone with them because she didn't want to let Joe out of her sight, in case he did some other awful thing.

'The roof fall has to be cleared and there are a lot of other things to do. I'll get Jack Fanshawe to take you home.'

'I don't want Jack Fanshawe to take me home,' Bridget said. 'I want you.'

'It's all right now.'

'Other people can do all those things.'

'The pit belongs to me.'

'Oh my God.' Bridget said, slamming her teacup in the saucer so that he was surprised it didn't break. 'Wherever did men get to be so important?'

'It isn't importance, it's just—'

'Very well then,' Bridget said, getting up. 'And while you're about it you can tell Jack that he's to wait and when I have my things packed he's to take me to the station. I've had enough of this. I'm going back to Newcastle. I miss it. I miss the house and the girls and the life. I don't want to stay here.'

'Wait a minute. What are you talking about?' Niall said, getting up too.

'It was a dreadful night,' she said.

'Yes, but . . . it's not likely to happen again.'

'It does happen though, doesn't it? Do you think I want to spend the rest of my life wondering whether you're going to be coming in for dinner or at all?'

'Forget Jack. I'll take you home.'

'Don't bother,' she said and swept out of the room. Niall went after her.

'Bridget, you're having a baby soon.'

'Why do I wish I wasn't?' Bridget said. 'It was the stupidest idea of my whole life, that and marrying you.'

'Brid, don't.' He caught her by the arm as she would have left the house. 'You're upset, angry. I understand that. We're all tired. Let's just go home. We'll talk about it later.'

'I've said all I have to say. Things have got worse and worse and this was the worst.'

'But everything's fine.'

'Everything's not fine, Niall,' she said.

They drove home in silence. Once there Bridget went up the stairs, calling for her maid. Niall went after her.

'You can't do this,' he said. 'What about the baby?'

'Women have babies all the time. I do believe you care more for the baby than you do for me.'

'I don't care more for anybody in this world than I care for you.' And as the maid came to the door he said, 'We're busy. Come back.'

'No. Theresa, come in. Tell Jim I want my suitcases and my trunk down from the attic and . . .'

He wanted to shout at the maid to go away but he thought

that in some ways she was right in what she had said. He was not in his right mind when he came out of that pit. He didn't know what he was saying or doing. He should have gone home with her straight away, but something of duty called to him and told him that he couldn't because neither Dryden nor Joe was at the pit and somebody had to be. The men were upset at what had happened. But shouldn't his wife's needs come before those of the pit and the pitmen? The trouble was that somewhere in his head he thought that Caitlin was standing in the kitchen waiting for him. To have gone through something like that where he might have died and not have her there was a nasty surprise and there was a part of him which had known that for some time now Bridget had considered leaving. He didn't think she would, he thought they would go on and on with this sham of a marriage but there would be a child and for that he could sacrifice anything. It was true that the child was very important to him but that was because he thought of it as part of her. It was also because he had sworn to himself that it would have two parents and everything that he could give it, his attention, his love, his time, his money. He did not believe she could walk out and take his child with her in that sense.

'I'll do anything,' he said.

'Then come back to Newcastle with me.'

'Back to the house? I thought you didn't want to live like that any more.'

'Compared to the way we are living now, it was wonderful,' she said.

'It wasn't. It isn't the way families live. We're going to be an ordinary family.'

'I don't want to be ordinary,' Bridget said with a touch of humour against herself. 'You should know that by now. I don't want to be your wife and some howling infant's mother. I don't like it. I don't like you very much any more.'

'You don't like me?'

'No. Sorry.'

'It's because we started going to bed together,' Niall said. 'I knew it wouldn't work.'

Bridget raised her eyes to the ceiling.

'Oh, I'm sure you're perfectly adequate in the bedroom. I wouldn't like to cast aspersions. I know that men worry about things like that . . .'

'You're killing me here,' he said flatly.

Bridget laughed and then she said, 'I do love you very much but I would rather not be married to you. You're going to turn into the kind of man that Dryden Cameron is, telling women what to do. Oh dear. It's fun at first but it's tedious playing the wife after a while and nodding your head in all the right places.'

'I don't think this describes me.'

'I wonder how long it will take women to discover that marriage is to benefit men.'

'I thought it was to benefit both if there were children.'

'You lack imagination,' she said. 'The truth is, I really don't want your child.'

Niall looked at her. He wanted to go over and kiss her and beg her not to leave him and to promise her the world but he couldn't breathe.

'It isn't even born,' he said.

'I tell you what. When it is I will send it back to you.'

It was, Niall thought, the worst thing that anybody had ever said to him.

'You don't love me, Niall.' The tears shone with white brilliance in her eyes. 'The day you met Caitlin Redpath you stopped loving me.'

'That's not true, I always loved you.'

She tossed her head.

'You never cared about things that didn't matter before then. After that you cared who you went to bed with.'

'It should matter, surely.'

'No,' she said. 'No, it shouldn't. When people really love one another, barriers cease. There's no night and no day, no man and no woman. You aren't capable of that kind of love any more. You – you fell to earth when you met her and what a tawdry thing it turned out to be. I loved you purely. I should have known, and last night . . . I realized that if you came out of this I was going to leave you. I don't want to be anybody's wife. There's something ugly about the whole notion. I don't want to be your property.'

'You're not.'

'That's the way wives are regarded. It's not for me. Mothers are people who put themselves second or third or even further back. I don't want that level of responsibility. All my life I would be dogged by another person's needs. I don't think I would like that. You can have a divorce. I don't mind taking the blame. I'm sure I've led the kind of life which should make it easy for you to obtain, and then you can marry some pathetic woman who will put up with you and your disgusting needs.'

'Children need both their parents.'

'We survived.'

'That's all we did. Survive. Look at us. We wouldn't have made such a bloody mess of things—'

'You don't know that.'

'Please, Brid, think about it again. It'll be different when the baby's born . . .'

'I'm sorry. I don't think I can stand any more of this, not after yesterday. You say children need both parents and then you risk your life so that people can have fires in their houses. How stupid is that?'

'I'll make things better.'

'You can't. If the child is a boy I'll send him to you.'

'What?'

'I wouldn't want a daughter of mine anywhere near a man.'

'But . . .'

'You can tell him I died. That's what they do, they tell you your mother died.'

'Mine did.'

'You were lucky. I slept in the same bed as my mother and her men. All I remember is how much I hated her and how they liked the little blonde girl. Nobody will touch my little blonde girl. Now, I'm going to call the maid, unless you have some other objection, and she can pack my bags and by this afternoon I'll be out of your way.'

The doctor had been right, Dryden's leg was not broken. He had already pointed out to Joe that it could not possibly be, or he would not have been able to crawl through a hole and rescue them. Joe forebore to point out that he'd been there. Dryden, however, had gone very white, because they'd pulled him about so much at the hospital and the doctor was not very happy and said that he could have permanently damaged that leg, though he thought that with rest and care it would probably be all right. Dryden just wanted to go home. Joe did too. He was exhausted. He did, however, think he should call in at the pit. Niall had insisted he would sort things out but Joe knew from previous experience that accidents took their toll on your mind as well as your body. He drove Dryden home and then he took Vinia to their new home and then he went back to the pit. He didn't want to go, he couldn't stand much more, but neither did he want Niall to think that he must cope with anything alone.

He pulled the car up outside the pit. Things were not normal there, they could not be. Niall was not in the office, nobody had seen him. Joe went underground to see how things were progressing and there were enough men who knew what they were doing. He smiled and gave brief instructions but it wasn't really necessary, most of them were old hands and had been there for years. Niall was not there either.

It was early evening by now, the end of a beautiful day, the sun was sinking slowly beyond the horizon as Joe drove his car into what he still thought of as Thaddeus Morgan's drive. He parked the car and walked up the steps and banged on the door and a little maid in a uniform answered it and ushered him inside. She left him in the hall but came back a minute or so later and then showed him into the drawing room.

Joe half expected to see Thaddeus Morgan sitting in a chair by the fire. Nobody was sitting anywhere, Niall was on his feet, though he was so grey-faced Joe wondered whether he wouldn't have been better seated. Niall greeted him with, 'I should have been at the pit, I know.'

'It's of no matter. The men can manage very well.'

'Yes, but they shouldn't have to, not after something like that.'

Joe remembered something he thought his wife had told him a long time ago.

'You can't take care of everything,' he said. Niall's wife was nowhere to be seen. 'Bridget's upset, eh?'

'You could say that.'

'It's not surprising. Waiting is the hardest part.'

'She's left me,' Niall said.

Joe thought he was making some kind of unfunny joke.

'Left you?'

'Yes. She's gone back to Newcastle. She wasn't happy, it isn't just this, I don't think she's ever been happy, at least not since I . . . since I . . .'

He didn't go on. Joe wanted him to, waited, wished that Niall trusted him enough to tell him anything that mattered, but he obviously didn't. Joe didn't know what to say. Niall looked at him.

'That was what my mother did, she left you?'

Had she? She had left him several times in several different ways, he thought, and always for the same reason.

'It wasn't like this,' Joe said.

'What happened?'

'I . . . I asked her to leave George and come to me and she wouldn't.'

'Why not?'

'Because he was rich and powerful. He was important. I didn't feel that I could desert the pit and the men and a woman leaving her husband and living with another man was frowned upon but . . .'

'But you wanted her?'

'Yes. I was very much in love with her. She was exciting, fun and . . . very beautiful.' Joe didn't say, he didn't think it was fair when he had no way of knowing but looking back now he didn't think it would have worked well. He thought Luisa would have been bored with the life they would have led and that he had married the right woman. Niall had not been so lucky.

'Are you going after her?' Joe asked.

'No.'

Joe watched his face for a few seconds and then he said, 'Forgive me if this is wrong but . . . are you sure you want her?'

'Of course I want her!' Niall came back at him so fast that Joe knew he had touched a sore spot. 'She's having my child. I'm not you, I can't just . . . I can't . . . I'm sorry, I didn't mean to say that.'

'No, I understand. The thing is that I was very much in love with Luisa but we would have made a very bad marriage.'

'You don't know that.'

'I think I do.'

'And your happiness was more important than your child?'

'I thought I was doing the right thing.'

'By letting a man you despised take your son?'

'Didn't he love you?' Joe said.

Niall didn't reply.

Niall had not considered until that moment that he might love Joe. He didn't think he could ever love Joe and would never stop hating him even when Joe was long dead for what had happened, but it suddenly seemed to him that Joe had rescued him, not just from the depths of the pit but from the cellar. The moment Joe took Niall into his arms in the darkness everything changed. He was fighting it even now. He didn't want to forgive Joe for what had happened but he could no longer deny that Joe's presence and his voice were beginning to close out every negative thing in his life. When a man put his life in danger for you it altered everything and Niall was beginning to comprehend how dangerous it was to go down there like that when there had been a roof fall. They could both have been killed so easily and Joe would be aware of that, he had been a pitman all his life.

So when Joe asked him whether George had loved him Niall's first reaction was that whatever he said it must not hurt Joe any further. Part of him was angry at the decision but there was an overwhelming feeling that Joe had stood enough, that he must not put him through any more as far as he could help. He went on looking at Joe until Joe said, 'He didn't look after you?'

Niall wanted to unburden himself, to say all the awful things about George which hurt, but he thought of the house in Edinburgh, the holidays when they had gone fishing and stayed in wonderful hotels.

'He looked after me, yes. I think he loved me.'

'But? He died?'

'Yes, he died.' Niall was grateful at that moment for the night sitting in the Royal, when he had told Dryden how they had left Edinburgh and how George had died and he was even more grateful for the fact that Dryden had not told Joe. He had the feeling that, if Joe knew, he would be crippled by the knowledge of what had happened, and it could be made better in other ways now, not by going over that ground for no better reason than unburdening himself to his father. He didn't think he had the right to do that.

'And then what?'

Niall smiled brilliantly at him.

'And then I looked after myself,' he said.

Twenty-Four

Caitlin's parents had wanted her to come home for Easter and she had wanted to. She had wanted to come back so badly that she made herself stay in Edinburgh through the spring and early summer. The reason was entirely Niall. She did not think she could go on in the silence. She felt as though he had died. If she could have had a letter from him, even a word, it would have helped. She sat by the fire at night and wondered why on earth she had let him go. He had been married, yes, he had belonged to somebody else, but even to see him occasionally would have been enough. This was like purgatory. She wanted him so badly she sat and wept in the evenings until she realized how foolish it was. She had brisk reports from her father, that Niall appeared to be happy, that he had opened the pit, that his wife was having a baby. He had everything. He did not want her. She had to try to go forward with her life.

The trouble was that she was bored without him. She tried to think back to what her life had been like before Niall and could not. It did not seem that anything mattered, that anything could have mattered before him or without him. She thought back to the afternoons at the Crown and almost lived in the memories.

She couldn't concentrate on her work so gained little from it except money. She did not want to make new friends because everybody was not Niall and though she made herself busy day after day the loneliness without him was insupportable. Her parents urged her to go back even for a few days but she determined to stay where she was, because going back to Newcastle seemed only to make things worse. But she longed to go home and the more she put off going the worse it grew and the more her mother's letters and father's terse notes did not ask her to go the more she felt as though she should.

She dreamed about the house in Jesmond where she had lived all her life. She dreamed about walking in the front door. She dreamed the fell beyond Joe's house and the winter day and Niall smiling at her and in the end she packed her bags and took the train home.

It was a bright morning and the train ride had never looked so beautiful, the sea and sky were bright blue, the little villages white and clean, and when she reached Berwick she became very excited at the idea of not being far away. Strange how it had seemed so far when it was only a train ride, a couple of hours. It had felt like another world.

Her mother was there to meet her at the station, apologizing because her father was at Sweethope, there had been a problem at the pit and everybody was involved. There had been an accident. Niall had been there. He was not hurt, her mother assured her, everything was fine. Caitlin questioned her but learned nothing. Apparently he was well, and Joe Forster too, and the mine manager had been slightly hurt but everything was over now and she did not understand what her father was doing up there when he should have been meeting her at the railway station. Such a fuss.

'And?' Caitlin prompted her when her mother stared from the car window as they were driven home.

'What?'

'There is something else?'

'No.'

She knew her mother too well not to know when she was holding something back. Fiona, however, had nothing to say and asked her about Edinburgh and her job and her friends and all the exciting things she was doing in the evenings. Caitlin regaled her with fascinating stories of reading circles, drama groups, and lectures which she did not listen to. Her mother said how much she liked Edinburgh and what a pretty house hers was and how she was glad that she had made a life for herself there.

They reached home but it was not at all as she had imagined it. Her mother fussed and helped with the unpacking and Caitlin bore it and then she heard the door in the early evening and ran down the stairs, into her father's arms, and kissed him.

'I should have been at the station,' he said. 'I'm sorry.'

'Is Niall all right? Is he? Was my mother lying to me?'

Her father walked her into the drawing room and closed the doors before he said, 'Niall is fine.'

'Is he really? You wouldn't tell me—'

'He's fine.'

He sat her down, as she had known he would, and told her exactly what had happened and she was horrified. She wanted to run out of the house and be transported to the Durham fells and into his arms but she knew that she couldn't. Her father too, she felt, was holding something back.

'Niall was hurt and you don't want to tell me.'

'No. I wouldn't lie to you. It was touch and go for a while, especially when the roof fell in for the second time, but it wasn't a bad fall and they got them out and there's nothing to worry about.'

'But there is something wrong?'

Aulay still didn't look at her but eventually he said, 'I didn't want you to know, but since you have come home, you should be told . . . His wife has left him.'

Caitlin could not help the small degree of lift that struck her heart.

'She's left him?'

'I always said he had a nasty streak. Niall has no moral code, he just does whatever he decides he'll do, and you know that he is violent.'

'Are you saying that he hurt her?'

'No, I'm not saying that. Nobody suggested such a thing but . . .'

Caitlin remembered vividly the night when she had gone to him at the Crown and he was sitting on a stool in the bar and he had said, 'I'm not safe, Cat.'

She knew he wasn't and stupidly that was part of the attraction but it had never occurred to her that he could hurt a woman.

'What other reason could a very pregnant woman have for walking out?' her father said. 'I think Niall has become less and less happy . . .'

'She could have had a dozen reasons for walking out.'

'Like what?'

'I don't know.'

'They're rich. They have a wonderful house and he wasn't exactly keeping her short of money. She had everything. Why should she leave, and when she had his child in her, unless there was a very good reason?'

Caitlin thought back to being with him.

'He would never ever hurt a woman,' she said.

'I hope you're right,' her father said.

*

The baby had come early and Niall had had a note from Gypsy to tell him that he was to go to Newcastle and see Bridget. He was worried. She had been very big when she had left him. He wondered whether the worry about the accident and then the added pressure of deciding to leave him had brought it on. Gypsy put no detail in the letter at all, it was a mere instruction, so he drove there. He didn't want to go, he didn't want to think that she had preferred such a life to anything he could give her, and he hated how when he got there in early afternoon Gypsy was wearing a silk robe to open the door and yawned into his face.

Niall had almost forgotten what it was like, the sounds, the smells, the quietness of midday in that place. What had she been doing, wanting to come back here? Had it really been so awful being married to him? It must have been, he decided, as Gypsy led the way into the kitchen.

'Is Bridget all right?' he said, looking about him and not seeing her.

'She's fine. She's still asleep. Shall I make you some tea?'

He didn't want to ask about the baby. It shouldn't matter whether it was a boy or a girl, and he had thought it didn't matter, but it did because he knew that if it was a girl she would not give it up. She would bring it up here and he had no right to ask her to do otherwise. If it was a boy then he was not sure what she would do. Perhaps she would let him have it but he had an idea that once a woman had a baby, no matter what its sex or the circumstances, then to give it up even for a good reason must be the most difficult thing on earth.

He accepted the offer of tea because it was something to do and waited patiently. He did not want to do anything wrong, say anything out of place. Gypsy handed him a tray and two cups of tea.

'I'm sure she's awake, or at least she should be, if you want to go up,' she offered.

Niall made his way slowly up the stairs, trying not to remember what living here had been like. He couldn't understand what there was here that he could not give her. It had not changed and by the time he reached the top storey and opened the door into their bedroom it was like he had never been away.

It was white, cool, the afternoon sunshine spilled through the gap in the curtains and Bridget lay in bed looking so beautiful that he thought he had forgotten the effect she had on men. In a cot of some kind, all white and lace, there lay a child. He put down the tray on the bedside table and sat down carefully on the edge of the bed.

'Brid?'

Bridget opened her eyes, smiled.

'Hello,' she said. 'I was dreaming about you.'

'I hope it was something nice. I brought you some tea.'

'Thank you.'

She sat up. Niall tried not to look at her because she was naked but she leaned over and put on some garment or other in pale yellow. She took the tea from him.

'Have you seen the baby?'

'Not yet.'

'It's a girl. I called her Bethany. I hope you don't mind.'

She was so polite, as though they had never touched, as though it was nothing to do with him.

'I asked you here because I was sure that you wouldn't try to take her.'

'Take her?'

'You do want her?'

'She's my child. Why should I not want her?'

Niall got up and went over to the cot. The child was perfect, fair, had dark eyelashes like crescents, a lovely mouth, flushed cheeks.

'You can pick her up if you want, though I have just got her to sleep. I want her to stay here with me.'

He said all the right things because it was obvious that Bridget did not trust him on this matter. He couldn't think what reason he had given her.

'You're her mother,' he said. 'She needs you more than anybody.'

That was the point, he thought. If his mother had been alive then he would have gone back to Scotland with her and it would have been different, it would have been better. The more he looked at the child the more he was disinclined to leave. The house in the country, which he had thought mattered, and the pit and the foundry and Joe and Vinia and the life he had made there suddenly seemed so unimportant. He could do better than his father had done. He left the cot and came back to the bed.

'Brid, look . . .'

'No,' she said.

'How do you know what I'm going to say?'

'Because I know you.' Bridget smiled. 'You can't come back here. We can't be a normal family, nothing is normal here. That's awful but it's true. You didn't like it—'

'I could like being anywhere if we could be together . . .'

'You're just saying that because of the baby. You grew to hate it here. You dislike this life as much as I dislike yours. And anyway . . .'

'And anyway?'

'I don't want you. For the first time in my life I don't want you. I think I can live without you. I would like to try. I don't . . .'

I can't . . .' Bridget put down the tea untouched. 'I hate saying these things to you because I love you so much but I don't want a man near me. You're so . . . Considering everything, you're really just like every man. You stared at me when you came in . . .'

'I'm supposed to help that?'

'No, but I don't want you looking at me like that. I don't mind the customers doing it because they can't touch but you . . . I love you and so I put up with you . . .'

'You didn't put up with me,' he said. 'That's the point.'

'I always put up with you, Niall.'

Niall got up.

'Well, thanks very much.' He moved away. Bridget got out of bed, fastening the robe around her, and she came to him, into the middle of the room by the fireplace. There was no fire burning, the room was warm in the afternoon sunshine.

'You can come and see her as often as you like. I'm not trying to take her away from you.'

'Oh, stop being so civilized,' he said.

Bridget kissed him.

'I miss you,' she said.

Niall pulled away.

'I'm not going there, Bridget.'

'Where?' Her dark eyes were so innocent.

'Into the land where people never grow up. You'll make a wonderful companion for her, at least until she's an adult. Then what will you do?'

'I shall be old then.'

'You'll never be old,' he said.

The baby was not inclined to wake up and Bridget looked tired so he did not like to suggest that he might hold her, because once she was awake she might keep Bridget awake for hours and that did not seem fair, but he found that he did not want to leave. He wanted to beg her to take him back under any circumstances, any way. He wanted to say that he would give everything up and go back to the life they had had, that he didn't care. In the late afternoon, therefore, he found himself getting back into the car and driving over the fell.

He couldn't face going home and he didn't want the pit. He drove down to Sweethope and the lights were on in the foundry manager's house, though he doubted Joe would be home yet and when he banged on the front door Vinia opened it. She looked surprised. Joe had made noises about how he should visit them but he didn't think they really wanted him there, which he understood, especially Vinia. Niall couldn't think what to say to her. He managed, 'I just . . .' and then, 'I just . . .' and then he couldn't imagine what he was trying to say.

She drew him into the hall and then into the sitting room. It was a cool evening by then and the fire was lit. It was a nice house, big hall, big rooms, solid, sturdy, just the right kind of thing for a man to come home to. Was he never to have that?

'I was going to invite you to Sunday dinner,' Vinia said, 'but Joe wouldn't let me. He said he thought we were . . . crowding you. I didn't see it like that but . . . How is Bridget?'

All the things he wanted to say wouldn't come out. He wanted to sit down like a little boy who had bloodied his knees and cry his eyes out. She asked him to sit down but he couldn't. He couldn't do anything except stand in the middle of the room and admire the high polish on the furniture.

'Joe should be home shortly.'

He thought she was going to suggest tea. If she did he would leave. She went over and got hold of a decanter and poured a great big measure of whisky into a glass and then she came back and gave it to him. She guided him into a chair by the fire, it was a big leather armchair, very comfortable, with velvet cushions, and she sat him down and then she said, 'Drink it,' and she got down as he had seen her do with Joe and also he thought with Dryden and she put her arms on his knees and smiled and looked into his eyes. 'Go on, drink it,' she said.

He did. It burned pleasantly all the way down to his stomach.

'Thanks,' he said. 'I went to see Bridget. She's had a little girl. We've . . . had a little girl.'

'Joe will be so pleased.'

He stayed. He told her about the baby and she asked all the right questions and then Joe came in. They had some kind of beef stew for supper, it was very good, and then he tried to leave but she wouldn't let him. She brought him coffee and brandy and they talked to him. They sat around the fire and when it was late and he tried again to leave she directed him into possibly the neatest cleanest bedroom in the whole world. Clothes were laid out for the next day and there was hot water and the bed was turned down. He peeled off his clothes and got into it and it was wonderful. He hadn't realized he was so very tired. It smelled of soap and felt so soft. He closed his eyes and then he thought that it was the first time there had been anybody else belonging to him to lock the doors and put out the lights and see that the fire was banked down. If something went wrong it was nothing to do with him. It was Joe's house. His worries floated to the back of his mind and disappeared and he was so glad to let go of them.

When he awoke all he wanted was to run away to Caitlin. He couldn't think of anything else, he couldn't do anything else.

He wanted to see her, he wanted to pour out the problems, he wanted to be in her arms. He lay in bed thinking about it. It was very early, the sun had not risen, the dawn was grey, but there grew in his mind a conviction that he must see her. He did not know where she was, only that she had left. He had not liked to ask Aulay, since he felt responsible for her going, but he thought that if he drove into Newcastle before Aulay left for work and asked and managed to make it sound sufficiently important, then Aulay would give him her address and, however far, he would go and see her.

He washed and dressed and left a note thanking Vinia and Joe and then he drove. It was just after seven by the time he reached Aulay Redpath's house. The streets there were deserted. It reminded him of that day so long ago when he had watched the people emerging from their houses and going to work and going out to take their children to school and going shopping and the maids and the postman and the world revolving around families.

He banged hard on the door and after a little while a maid answered it. She looked amazed to see him there. He asked for Aulay.

'Mr Redpath is still abed, sir. I'm sorry, I—'

'I have to see him before he goes to work. I'll wait.' He brushed past her and she directed him into the library, where it still smelled of Aulay's cigars from the night before and the dead fire. She pushed back the blue-and-green curtains. Light flooded from the garden, throwing unwelcome emphasis on to the dirty grate, the unemptied ashtrays, the cushions which had not been straightened. She went out. Niall stood by the window, since there was nothing else to do, and regarded Aulay's almost military-type garden, all neat bushes and tidy paths and yellow and red spring flowers.

'What the devil do you mean by this?' said a harsh voice behind him and Niall turned to face Aulay. He almost smiled. Aulay looked immaculate. How did he manage that so early in the day? Was he going to work already?

'I know this is an imposition . . .'

'An imposition? Niall, this is bloody ridiculous. I haven't even breakfasted yet. What the hell do you want?'

'I want to get in touch with Caitlin.'

'No,' Aulay said. 'Not in a million years. You have done enough damage to my family. Leave her alone. She's built a new life for herself. You are not and never could be part of it. Have a little pity, for God's sake. You're nothing to her. Give her a chance to lead a decent life without you.'

'Aulay, I must see her.'

'No, you must not. Now leave. I have a lot to do today.'

'Please. I just want to talk to her . . .'

'I've seen the way you talk. You took my daughter to the Crown Hotel and bloody well . . . No, Niall, I won't stand it. Leave before I throw you out. I will not let you spoil her life. Don't you think she's been through enough, much of which you put her through?'

'No, I didn't.'

'You married another woman. You married your whore and then you bedded my daughter. Deny it, go on.'

Niall couldn't.

'Your wife is pregnant,' Aulay said.

'No, she isn't. We have a child, a little girl.'

'How marvellous for you. I hope she causes you a good many sleepless nights when she's twenty-five. You cannot imagine what it's like when some bastard comes along and destroys everything you wanted for your child. I hope it happens to you. As for the rest, I hope you rot in hell. I heard your wife left you. Do you think I would let you anywhere close to my daughter after that? Leave us alone, Niall.'

Even as he spoke, Niall saw a flurry of white and when he looked up there she was. Niall couldn't believe it, he thought it was some kind of illusion. Her hair was plaited. It made her look about fifteen and the long white whatever it was was so pretty. She stood there framed in the doorway like a painting. Niall let go of his breath in a sigh.

'Oh,' he said. 'I didn't know you were here.'

'I've just come home. I'm here for a few days and then I go back to Edinburgh.'

'You live in Edinburgh?'

'Yes, I do.'

'How lovely,' Niall said.

'Caitlin . . .' her father said.

'I think I can handle this,' she said. 'Go and have your breakfast.'

'But . . .'

'No, really, I'll be fine. Things have changed. Trust me.'

She kissed him on the cheek, smiled, and Aulay went out. Niall remembered what her mouth was like.

'What are you doing here?' she said.

'Nothing, I wanted to write to you, contact you.'

'I see,' she said.

Niall was amazed. He didn't see.

'What do you mean?'

'Your wife has left you and since I was always second best, I get promoted. Is that it?'

'Promoted?'

'Isn't that what they call it? Isn't that why you wanted to see me?'

He didn't know why he wanted to see her. He could hardly tell her that he had woken up that morning and she had been his first thought.

'I didn't know you were here.'

'You were going to travel to Edinburgh?'

'Anywhere.'

'How very flattering,' she said.

Niall began to live this in slow motion. It had been wrong. His mind took him back to the early morning and his impulsive decision. Impulsive decisions were always wrong. How many times had he told himself that? She was so lovely that he didn't mind what she said, he could go on watching her standing there for all the rest of his life, for however long or short that might be. She wasn't going to give him a chance, he could see by the mean look in her eyes. He didn't blame her for that, he had treated her so badly.

'How's Bridget?' she said.

'Fine. We have a little girl.'

'How very nice for you. Niall, look. You made your decision. You put Bridget first. My father says that you treated her badly and that was why she left you, but I said it couldn't have been, that you would never be violent towards a woman. Isn't that so?'

Niall brought back to himself the images of Amelia Mackenzie, her fat arms and legs flailing as he suffocated the life out of her.

'Well, isn't it?' Caitlin prompted him.

'She was bored,' he said.

'What?'

'I bored her,' he said. 'I was . . . demanding and stupid and she didn't like what I did.'

'How do you mean, she didn't like what you did?'

'Mining,' he said, running for safety.

'I heard about the accident. My father told me.'

'Everything was all right,' he said. 'Everything was fine. I should go. I was wrong. I . . . I don't know why I thought that I should see you and . . . I don't remember why now. And you look . . . you look so well. You look so . . . so well.'

'I have a pretty house in Edinburgh.'

'Whereabouts?'

'Just above Princes Street.'

'I used to live there,' he said. 'Just above, just beyond Charlotte Square.'

'Really?' she said.

'Yes. We had a nice house there and my father had lots of parties.'

'Edinburgh is so beautiful,' she said.

Oh, it had been. It had been the very best ever in the whole world. Edinburgh was like nowhere else for being homely and magnificent all at once, with its shops and tea shops and houses and childhood. It tore away at him for what it had been and he wished that Edinburgh had kept him, had wrapped him around with its cold grey streets and kept him like a mother. He hoped that his last sound on earth would be the voice of some Edinburgh matron, all cool and correct and neat and vital, like Jean. Where was Jean? Where was his childhood? Where had it all gone?

'I think that you had better go now,' she said.

'Yes,' he said and smiled. There was nothing else to do and manners decreed it. George would have been pleased with him, smiling and pretending that things were all right. 'I'm glad that you're happy. I'm sorry that I got in the way. You don't have to see me out. I know where the door is.'

He got as far as the door and then she was there and she said those awful words. She said, 'Just tell me why you married her and not me.'

He tried to smile it off, he tried to get away. He tried to think up excuses. He thought of the day beyond the windows and his child across the city and how he knew that Joe had done his best because your best was never enough. He knew that now.

'I married her because I owed her. We were children together and she couldn't marry anybody else.'

'Why not?'

The day was bright beyond the house. He could go into it. He did not have to explain himself here. Even if he did what would it gain him? He gazed at the door.

'I couldn't marry anybody else either,' he said.

'Why not?'

'Because.'

'Because what?'

Caitlin's eyes were focused fully on him and he told himself as he had told himself a thousand times before that he could not tell her, that he could never tell anybody, because people were not meant to hear such things, because people were not meant to go through such things.

'You married her when you loved me. Didn't you?' she said. Her eyes were so clear. How had she known that?

'Yes.'

'Why?'

He didn't answer her.

'Was it some strange kind of perversion?' She smiled at him.

'Perversion? Is that what you think I'm like?'

'I don't know. That's why I'm asking you. You use violence.'

'I do? Yes, I do, don't I? God. I think I had better go.'

'No. I want to hear you say it. I want to hear you say that

you married Bridget Black because some awful part of you was pleased with it.'

'Some awful part of me . . .' Niall got that far. It seemed so easy. All he had to do was say it. It didn't mean anything. It was just words and after that there would be fresh air and the morning and he could go back to Deerness Law and never ever come out of it again, never think about anything or anybody. She would go back to Edinburgh and he would be pleased. He wouldn't have to see her or talk to her and he would go work every day and return home like Dryden did. It was fine. It would be as much as he could bear. He was violent. He was not fit for company. He had known that he was not. He had known even as Amelia Mackenzie's struggles ceased, as Mr Wilson lay still in the blood under his hands. He would go home and it would hide him forever and ever. He would have Joe and Vinia and Dryden and everything would be all right because they didn't know. They would never know. Nobody would ever know.

'You can't even say it, can you?' she said.

He didn't remember what it was he was meant to be saying.

'I do love you so very much.'

'No,' she said. 'You aren't capable of loving anybody. I'm going back to Edinburgh tomorrow and I never want to see you again.'

That was fine by him. He smiled brilliantly at her, just as he had done with Joe. You didn't have to tell people things, it only hurt them. She and Edinburgh would always now be bound up together for him and that would be nice. He could imagine her in the streets there.

'You married her,' Caitlin said.

'I did, yes.'

'Why?'

'We were in a children's home together.' That wasn't so hard to say.

'A home? In Newcastle?'

'Yes. A home.' Who on earth had thought up the title? It was not a home, it was not even a house. It was a nightmare, a terror, a vile existence.

'Were you there a long time?'

'Oh, yes, years and years. We broke out together and then we . . . we . . .'

'What?'

'We got the house and the girls and . . . made money.'

'How old were you then?'

'I was fourteen.'

'Fourteen? You broke out of a home and got a business together when you were fourteen?'

'I suppose, yes. Bridget was older. She was . . . I suppose she was almost sixteen.'

'Why didn't you stay?'

Niall knew it was a bad idea not to have left before now. She was sticking knives into him with her questions.

'We couldn't.'

'Why not?'

'They ran out of blancmange.'

She smiled. She moved away from the door. Had she been standing in front of it? He didn't think so. And he could go now. She would go back to Edinburgh and he could go home. He wanted to go home so very badly, to the house where his grandmother and his grandfather had lived and where he had been born and his mother had died. It was his and he could have it and he could have his father and his work and everything would be fine.

'You aren't going to tell me about it, are you?' Her eyes were so clear, so challenging.

'There's nothing to tell.'

'I think there is.'

She had always, he thought, had such very good instincts.

'We wanted to get out. The people who ran it were . . . the kind of people who like children too much.'

'How can you like a child too much?'

'They did. They liked hurting them.'

Her expression changed as she understood and he wished he had not said it. People didn't want to hear things like that.

'Mr Wilson . . .' Rozzer's face came into his mind. 'And Mrs Mackenzie.'

Just saying their names out loud seemed to bring them back. He was afraid of that.

'The people who ran it?'

'Yes.'

Suddenly, very short of breath, he hauled open the outside door and escaped into the sunshine. The day had awoken, it was warm and bright. He could have the day. He could drive back over the moors, Dryden would be waiting at the pit, complaining probably about his leg, and for the first time he had a family to go home to. Vinia and Joe had accepted him, were glad to have him. He shouldn't have walked out that morning, but they would understand. That's what families did. He could go home. He reached the car and would have got into it and left except that Caitlin had followed him outside. She looked lovely. She looked like a wife seeing her husband away to work. She looked as though she had just got out of a warm bed.

'When are you going back to Edinburgh?'

'At the weekend. I thought there was something here for me but I was wrong. It was just my dreams.'

Niall looked across the drive to the lawns and beyond to where all the summer flowers were coming into bloom.

'I killed for her,' he said. Wasn't that the expression men used? That she was the kind of woman a man would kill for? Bridget Black had been the kind of woman that even a fourteen-year-old boy would kill for. 'I killed Mr Wilson because he was forcing her. I stabbed him. The blood was everywhere. It bonded us together, you see. And ever after that she hated men and I was all caught up in how she hated them and what she owed me. We got married because she thought she was losing me to you. I'm always fourteen to her, always fourteen and saving her.'

'You stabbed him?'

Niall had almost forgotten Caitlin was there and glanced at her. She didn't look shocked or surprised, which was strange, because he thought she should.

'Lots of times, it took quite a bit of doing but I had learned to use a knife. Thinking about it now, I really killed him with the first blow, because I slit his throat. The rest was just panic and . . . revenge. He'd hurt us both such a lot, and other children too.'

'Did nobody find out?'

'I made it look as though somebody had broken in and, even though we disappeared, nobody seemed to think about it. I don't think anybody cared.'

Caitlin didn't say anything. She put an arm around him and then her face in against his neck, so that he could feel her hair, little wisps of it lifting against his skin in the morning breeze.

'We'd been there for years and years and it was . . .' It was a nightmare and it never quite went away though of late, with Joe and Dryden and Vinia, it had receded to the point of some-thing pale, as though he was uncertain it had happened. Since he and Joe had been caught underground together, somehow the present seemed much more important than the past.

He moved away.

'I shouldn't have told you. It wasn't fair. I have to get back.'

'Niall . . .'

'No. I really have to go.' He went, very quickly, and before she could say anything more.

He drove but he didn't notice the fell, just that for the first time he had told somebody else what had happened and he was panicked, thinking that the consequences would be huge. She would go back to Edinburgh and never speak to him again. He was so glad to reach the pit, even more glad to get into his office, where the sunlight fell unforgivingly on the old furniture which had probably been Joe's father's or even his grandfather's, it was in such bad condition and so dusty.

Dryden appeared in the doorway.

'You all right?' he said. 'I had Vinia here fussing.'

'I'm fine.'

'She's like a mother hen,' Dryden said and went back to his office.

The idea of Vinia going there to see if he was all right made Niall smile. He worked. Work was easy in comparison to everything else. They stopped at midday and Dryden shared out his sandwiches. He had got into the habit of bringing twice as many as he could eat, because of Niall never bringing any.

They had just finished eating when he heard a woman's light footsteps in the corridor. Vinia, no doubt, back again, wondering how he was. A slight commotion, some conversation in the main office and then Caitlin, wearing a little grey outfit with a neat matching hat.

'May I come in?' she said through the open door.

'I'll go back to work,' Dryden said, getting to his feet, and he went.

She came in and closed the door and then she came over to where Niall had got up and she kissed him. It wasn't the kind of kiss that any man in his right mind would try to get away from, he thought, but he had to because her words were coming back to him. *You use violence.* He had been avoiding his thoughts all the way back, finally deciding that it didn't matter, he didn't have to tell her any more because, nice and safely, she had gone back to Edinburgh. He would never have to tell her. He would never have to tell anybody. He drew back. She looked at him.

'I don't want to go back to Edinburgh,' she said. 'I understand now and I won't try to keep you from seeing Bridget and the baby. I want you. I want us to be married and . . .'

She stopped because somebody shouted at her.

'No!'

'You don't want to hurt Bridget?'

He tried not to shout.

'Bridget wants a divorce,' he said.

'But you wouldn't want to marry me anyway?'

He didn't answer her.

'Have I got this wrong?' she said.

'No.'

'But?'

'I thought you were going back to Edinburgh.'

'Niall, I have my father's Rolls Royce outside with my suitcases. Now, if you want I can take the next train to Edinburgh. Just tell me it's what you want.'

Niall hesitated.

'It isn't what I want,' he said.

'Tell me you want me to stay here, Niall, or I'm going and this time I won't be coming back. Tell me.'

She deserved better than the boy who had slept with a middle-aged woman and then killed her. Every woman deserved more than that. There must be hundreds of men in Edinburgh who would love Caitlin. That was why he had married Bridget, because they were alike, because they were almost the same person, because Bridget knew who he was. But she didn't want him. She wanted the boy who had rescued her. The truth was that he did not want to be that person any longer.

Caitlin obviously thought she had waited long enough. She turned around as if to go and he stopped her. He got in front of her and leaned back against the door and then, not looking at her, he said, 'Cat, I don't want you to leave and I do want to marry you, I've always wanted to be with you but I don't think . . .' He was never going to be able to say it.

'You don't think what?'

'I slept with the woman at the home.'

There was silence.

'I went to bed with her.' For half a glass of water. Had he said that? The silence went on for so long that he could hear somebody typing in the outer office and other noises from beyond, Dryden calling somebody's name in the corridor. 'They used to . . .' He stopped again because Caitlin drew in her breath sharply and he thought that she was about to exclaim that she couldn't listen to any more, that he must let her out, that she had to get away from such filth and from him, but she didn't, and when he ventured a glance her eyes were full of tears and she said, 'But you were a child.'

'No, I wasn't.' He had not felt like a child, not after George died and they put him in the home. 'I was . . . a problem. They used to lock me up and then she used to . . . she used to make me . . . the point is that I killed her. I'm not safe. I suffocated her with a pillow. I lay on it until she died.' There was a long silence during which he didn't look at Caitlin. He would have given a great deal to get out of the office but somehow he couldn't move.

Then Caitlin had him in her arms. He thought he must be imagining it but he wasn't, and as he stood there in the office which he had come to care for so much, with the woman that he loved trying to protect him, the stone of the responsibility for the deaths of two people fell away for the first time ever.

'Why didn't you tell me before?' She was stroking his hair. It was wonderful.

'I thought you would hate me.'

She drew back slightly and looked into his eyes and she was smiling and she said, 'You are an imbecile.'

'I am?'

'You are. I won't let anybody hurt you ever again in the whole of your life. I swear it to you. I love you.'

'Are you sure?'

'Quite sure. Oh, Niall, Niall.' She started kissing him again with his name all mixed up amongst it so that he wasn't quite sure which was his name and which were the kisses and he didn't care, it didn't matter. What he wanted now was to make lame excuses to Dryden so that they could get away, drive back to the house and spend the rest of the day in bed, and the rest of the week and the rest of his life and somewhere in the far distant future he wanted to take her to have Sunday dinner with Joe and Vinia at the foundry manager's house, to introduce her formally to his father as the woman he wanted to be with and, when the legalities were sorted out, would marry.

There was a soft knocking on the door. They moved away, disentangled themselves, and Niall opened it to reveal Vinia, an anxious look on her face.

'I was worried about you,' she said. 'Caitlin. How are you?' Her face wreathed itself in smiles. 'Are you staying?'

'Yes.'

'Then you must come to dinner on Sunday. We're having lamb and new potatoes and garden mint.'

Garden mint with the rain all fresh upon it, the smell of it filling the kitchen, and potatoes small and round and glossy with butter, and every vegetable that Vinia could get her hands on and trifle and coffee and if it was warm enough they would sit in the garden.

He thought about Bridget and the child. They would always hold his heart. In another life, in another time, he and Bridget would meet as adults, young, somewhere in a ballroom, and he would cross the room to her and the young men surrounding her would fall away and she would have a look in her eyes such as she had never had, undamaged and in love. He had the awful feeling that he never would be the man that Caitlin wanted, that there would always be a part of him that was afraid of the cold darkness, the part that Amelia Mackenzie and Mr Wilson had destroyed. Sometimes in the night Mrs Mackenzie's fat fingers were all over his body just as Mr Wilson was always there with Bridget. In a few days he would go back to Newcastle and see Bridget and the baby. He would not let his child grow up without knowing him. He would not let Bridget turn her into the kind of woman who hated men. She would know her father and with a bit of luck she would grow to love him. No matter what happened, he swore, he would do better than Joe had done, better than Joe's father. It would not be an endless chain of failed parenting. In the meanwhile he had Caitlin. He put an arm around her, just to make sure that she was there, as she and Vinia chatted and then, in the middle of the afternoon, with a nod to Dryden, who merely grinned and said nothing, he led Caitlin out into the bright sunlight and the huge presence of her father's silver Rolls Royce. She was being practical.

'We could go and leave my father's car at the foundry,' she said, 'and then drive on to your house in your car.'

It was a very good idea, he thought. No doubt Aulay would be along to collect it later and no doubt he would have a lot of things to say about the situation. He wouldn't be pleased with it, he was never pleased with anything, Niall thought, smiling as he got into his car and followed her into the village and down the bank which led to the dale.

The Quarryman's Wife

Elizabeth Gill

When hope is lost, can she rebuild her home?

After her daughter Arabella passes away, leaving a poor,
motherless child in her wake, Nell Almond doesn't think
her life can get any worse. But then tragedy strikes
a second time and she finds herself widowed,
with her husband's quarry to manage.

But it's baby Frederick, her grandson, who troubles her
most. Being cared for by one of the local families, he lives
in hand me-down clothes in a cramped and unrefined home.
Nell desperately wants him to return to his rightful place,
as heir to the quarry, but should she put all her hopes
in one child?

**From the bestselling author of *Miss Appleby's Academy*
and *Nobody's Child* comes the next book in the
beloved Weardale Sagas, continuing the story
begun in *The Guardian Angel*.**

Quercus

The Coal Miner's Wife

Elizabeth Gill

Torn between love and duty . . .

When Vinia walked down the aisle she knew it was a marriage
of practicality: as the owner of the local pit, Joe could provide
her with a life of status. But her heart lies with another . . .

With gypsy blood in his veins and an intense passion
in his soul, Dryden has always held a torch for Vinia.
And with the death of his wife, he vows to make good
on the lost years when they were apart.

**Will Vinia find a new chance of happiness or be
forever destined to a loveless marriage?**

Quercus